SLAYING A BREXIT DRAGON

Edith Friel

Edith Friel was born in Suffolk, where she has lived for much of her life. Edith describes herself as 'an avid political observer'. It was as a teenager, during the turbulent, volatile events of the Thatcher years, that her attention was gripped by the ideological drama being played out on the political stage. She has watched a series of actors take to and exit the stage – *'The people cast their votes, trusting and hoping that the new drama to be played out will have a better ending than the last.'*
'Slaying a Brexit Dragon' follows Edith's characters as they negotiate their way through the Great Brexit Debate engaging the nation.

This paperback edition first published in Great Britain 2024 by Porgymouse.

Copyright @ Edith Friel 2024.

A CIP catalogue record for this book can be obtained from the British Library.

Paperback Fiction ISBN: 978-1-3999-9231-2.

All parts of this publication are reserved. No part may be reproduced, stored or transmitted in any form or by any means without the prior permission of the publisher nor circulated in any cover other than that in which it is published.

Apart from the known, named and recognisable people from the political stage featured in this book, all other characters and events are purely the invention of the author.

Contents

1	Sally and Jack	11
2	Jack	23
3	'J'	37
4	A Day of Destiny	50
5	Sally	64
6	Lucinda	78
7	Christian	91
8	Julian	103
9	Jack	113
10	Sally	128
11	Sir Richard Goffe	141
12	Julian	159
13	Jack	173
14	Lucinda	189
15	Die Drachentoter	199
16	Jack	215
17	Julian	231
18	Lucinda	246
19	Sally	256
20	Jack	269
21	Buckshot Hall	282
22	Slaying a Dragon	292
23	Sally and Lucinda	305

Dramatis Personae

Jack Willet
A very angry, deserted husband.

Sally Willet
The deserting wife – a self-effacing beauty.

Myrtle
An altruistic eco-warrior. Sally's mentor.

Julian Tennant
Rich, 'a stunner', a screwed up, decorated war hero.

Lucinda Tennant
The long-suffering wife of the war hero.

Christian
A man from the shadows.

Supported by a cast of minor and not so minor characters.

Chapter 1

Sally and Jack

Being wound up, wound as tightly as a coiled spring, wasn't on this occasion such a bad thing. It had overridden - for a while, at least, long enough to get him settled in his seat - his fear of flying.

Jack had been ten when his father, Ron, explained the theory of flight. It was on an outbound flight to Portugal. Ron had taken a page from his newspaper, torn it into rectangles, and by blowing hard between two pieces, explained the movement of air above and below the aircraft that brought about what Ron termed, 'lift'. It was the engines driving the plane forward at speed that caused the air to flow as it did and kept the plane in the air.

'But what would happen if the engines stopped?' Jack had asked.

'Ah, now, that's most unlikely to happen.'

Jack hadn't been satisfied with his father's answer. Engines were always breaking down. The family Ford Sierra had often broken down; Ron had spent a good many hours with his head under its bonnet. The ten-year-old Jack was unconvinced. The passage of time, the benefit of adult logic, the safety supporting statistics, the chances of his plane going down standing at one in 5.4 million didn't lessen Jack's fear; someone's plane was going down.

It was with a sense of foreboding, suppressed fear that he climbed the steps of an aircraft and, with a sense of having avoided disaster, that he walked back down onto solid ground.

They were heading for a grey, drizzly London. The flight was on schedule, expected arrival time at Heathrow, 5:50 p.m. Jack fastened his seat belt, gripped the arm rests, closed his eyes and prepared for the trauma of take-off.

He didn't believe himself alone in his fear. An almost tangible wave of relief rippled through the cabin, a collective release of breath, an acknowledgement of danger averted as the ground receded and the cabin became enveloped in a shielding blanket of cloud. In this happy state of dislocation, lights glowing, books opened, laptops and phones switched on, they winged their way towards their destination.

His wife, Sally, sat in the middle seat. She was showing photos to a woman occupying the window seat. Sal talked to everyone. She had hit lucky on this occasion; the Australian, heading to the UK on a work visa, was as anxious to talk as was Sal. They had hardly parked themselves on their seats before an exchange of life histories had commenced. Sal was now relating to her new friend the event that had been the highlight of her holiday - the event that had ruined his. He rested his head against the seat back; he was tired, physically tired; tired of listening to Sal banging on. He thought of reclining his seat, but space was tight and thought better of it.

Sal's voice droned on. Snatches of conversation broke through Jack's fitful sleep.

'That's Rima, the poor little love. When I think of what she's been through!' - Sal's voice.

'Little cutie!'- Australian's voice.

'There isn't much left of Homs now; that's where they come from, you know,' - Sal's voice droning on and on.

It had started well! Three days in Athens, nice hotel, good food, great sights. Nicely relaxed, they had set off on a tour of the Greek islands. It was on Lesbos that events took a disastrous turn. They had been in the habit of spending their mornings visiting traditional villages or wondering on horseback through fabulous pine forests. After lunch, they would head for the beach. It was on the fourth afternoon of their stay, as they had made their way down the zigzagging steps that led from the hotel grounds to the private beach, that the chaotic scene had unfolded before them.

'God!' said Sal.

Two guys, Jack recognized as waiters from the hotel, had pounded past them down the steps.

'What's happened?' Jack had shouted after them.

'Boat people!' had been shouted back.

He needn't have asked. Two black, inflatable boats had been dragged from the water. The beach had been crowded with people.

'Where have they all come from? They can't all have come in those two small boats,' said Sal.

'Looks like they have!'

'No, there looks to be at least a hundred people down there.'

'Well, however they came, the beach is out of use. Come on, Sal, let's get back, we'll have to do something else with our afternoon.'

Sal had sat down on the steps, her eyes glued to the scene below them. 'Look, there are young children with them, some of the women are carrying babies!'

'Yeh, I can see that. Come on, Sal.'

She hadn't been listening, 'Poor things! Those little bundles they're carrying. Is that all they have with them?'

'I'm going back, Sal. Are you coming?'

'What did you say?'

'I said I'm going back. Are you coming? There won't be any sunbathing on that beach today!'

'No,' she fixed him with an uncomprehending look. 'No, I want to see what's happening. We might be able to help.'

'For God's sake, what the hell can we do? Come on.'

'No!'

That had been the end of Jack's 2014 holiday, the beginning of what he liked to call Sal's journey to 'Planet Myrtle.'

Jack had sat on the terrace for half an hour, but there had been no sign of Sal. He had brought down a book, ordered a drink, skimmed and flicked through pages and wondered what she was up to. He had been determined to steer clear of it all.

'What's going on down there, Alex?' Jack had asked the waiter who had brought his second ouzo.

'Not good, more come in boats. More and more come. Every bloody day, boats come.'

'Difficult for you people!'

'Bloody right, it difficult. What we to do with them? Many Greeks hungry! How we to feed all Syria, give them house?'

'Too right, Alex. Do all the local people think the same?'

'Most think this! Some bloody do-gooders, they very sorry, say we must help people. We all sorry for people, but how we to help? We a poor people now. Bad government and EU make us poor country. We nothing to give anymore!'

'Yeh, Alex, it's a disgrace.'

Late in the afternoon, small groups had been led up the steps and across the hotel grounds towards the road. They were accompanied by Greeks wearing official looking tabards. Alex had told Jack that they were being taken to the reception centre. Those in tabards were employed by the local council.

'Reception house now many houses. Not real houses, come on lorries,' Alex had explained.

He had been standing with two other waiters and a female receptionist, glowering at the passing groups. Two minibuses had arrived and were employed in a shuttle service to transport the boat people away from the hotel: presumably to the multi-house reception centre.

'What your wife doin?' Alex said.

A woman carrying a baby and leading a toddler by the hand had been crossing the grounds; following her had been Sal, holding the hands of two small children. Behind Sal came a hippy-type woman carrying a baby. Jack hadn't been able to take his eyes off Sal as she stood with the group waiting for the buses, her arm about the shoulders of the woman carrying the baby. As the woman began to cry, Sal cupped her face in her hands and kissed her forehead.

Hell, what was she doing!

A great many hugs and kisses from Sal and the hippy woman had accompanied the woman and her children onto the bus. After minutes of animated conversation, the hippy hugged Sal and walked off down the hill towards the town.

'God, I'm exhausted,' Sal had said, flinging herself down opposite Jack. 'I need a drink.'

Jack had signaled to Alex. Sal had looked to him to be emotionally overwrought rather than exhausted, her colour high, her eyes wild.

'What the hell were you doing?'

'Oh, Jack, you have no idea what those people have been through - crammed into those boats, freezing cold, terrified they were going to drown with their children. There isn't much anyone can do except try to make them feel safe. Let them know that there are people who care.'

'Very commendable, Sal, but what you can do to guarantee their safety, I don't know! Best to keep out of it. The locals won't thank you for interfering.'

'Oh, yes, Myrtle has been telling me about the attitude of the locals! How they can turn their backs on people in such need; people fleeing for their lives from a war zone, people who have lost loved ones - I just don't know! You might think differently if you were struggling to feed and house your own family.'

'It's mean-spirited! Anyway, I'm determined to do my bit. I'm meeting Myrtle tomorrow. We're going to the reception centre to see Jamila and the children. They do what they can at the centre, but they don't have enough in the line of clothing. Myrtle and I are going shopping; we are going to buy some clothes for Jamila, little Rima and Ahsan. All they have is what they stand up in.'

'You are joking, of course. We're on holiday. What am I supposed to do while you act the good Samaritan with this woman, Myrtle? Who the hell is Myrtle anyway?'

'Myrtle is an example to us all. She has taken extended, unpaid leave from her job back home. She is funding herself to be here in order to offer some comfort to these unfortunate people.'

'Well, bully for her, but we are supposed to be on holiday. How long are you likely to be employed in your humanitarian work? Can we make any plans?'

'I have no idea. Perhaps you would like to come with me? In the grand scheme of things, just how important is our holiday? It's an indulgence at the end of the day.'

'Bollocks to that! It's downright patronising and presumptuous of you to imagine you can come here and understand what's going on. The people here are good people, but they're poor and overwhelmed by what's happening. You've been here for a couple of days; you understand nothing. You need to mind your own business.'

Jack had been called a selfish bastard and left to amuse himself. Sal would leave after breakfast and return late in the evening. She had spent her days visiting an apartment where Myrtle and other hippy types hung out, shopping for essentials for Jamila and her children, or visiting those detained by the Greeks. When she did spend time at the hotel, she had been full of it all, boring everyone with her stories.

There had been a couple of bad scenes in the hotel room. He had let her know exactly how he felt. He knew how to handle Sal. But on this occasion, his methods had proved singularly ineffective. He had been astounded by her determination!

'Not joining Sal?' Allan had said. Sally and Jack had got quite friendly with Allan and his partner, Sophie. They had been on a couple of trips together.

'No, not my thing at all. I wish Sal would keep out of it!'

'I know what you mean! The locals are pretty pissed off with it. You can see their point; there are boats arriving along the coast every day. Where exactly are they coming from? Do you know?'

'They all claim to be Syrians. They're coming from Turkey; Lesbos is quite close to the Turkish coast.'

'Yeh, of course! Look, mate, feel free to join up with Sophie and me. We're off to Molivos this afternoon. Come along if you're on your lonesome.'

'Thanks, Allan, it's good of you to offer, but I think I'll take a bit of a stroll around the town. I haven't seen much of it yet.'

'OK, well, the offer stands. If you change your mind, tag along. *Bloody embarrassing!*

He had spent the last week of the holiday skulking about, trying to avoid people and getting rat-arsed on Greek plonk in a backstreet bar in the old town.

**

They had just got off the coach and were making their way across the tarmac towards the airport building.

'Will you please button it. It's wearing and very embarrassing.'

'What! Just because you don't have an ounce of humanity, it doesn't mean that other people don't care.'

Sal's voice was intentionally loud in criticism of the woman with whom she had argued on the coach. Fellow passengers turned away and hurried on past, as Sal attempted to make eye contact and gain support for her forcefully expressed opinions. It was the criticism of the Greeks that had incensed their fellow passenger.

'I'm fed up listening to your ill-informed crap. You haven't shut up since we left the resort. Have you visited the centres in Athens where the Greeks are trying to feed and find shelter for their own starving and homeless? No, of course you haven't! You have seen some boat people come ashore on a Greek beach and because the local people are not jumping for joy at the thought of feeding yet more mouths, you damn the Greek nation. How dare you! Nobody is helping the Greeks. The islands are full of people like your friend, flinging their arms about the boat people, not giving a damn about the locals. Think about it!' said the irate woman as she dragged her shoulder bag and jacket from the overhead locker.

**

Sal inclined towards flash in the pan, hair brained ideas and schemes. Nothing on a par with the holiday episode, but Jack was sure that once back home, she would soon tire of the latest obsession. How wrong he had been!

Myrtle returned home in late October; her extended leave ended. She returned to her social work in Southwark. She shared a flat in the borough with her partner and fellow social worker, Art. Myrtle and Art, Jack learned, were professional protestors, well known for their exploits in protesting motorway construction and tree felling. So much of their time was spent lying before bulldozers or being dragged out of tarpaulin-covered tree perches that Jack imagined them on almost permanent, so-called, 'extended leave'.

Sal hung on Myrtle's every word, believed all the left-wing propaganda spewed out in the Peckham flat. Jack was accustomed to Sal hanging on his words; he was at a loss to know how to deal with her mutinous behaviour. They no longer went out together; Sal didn't have time for the mundanities of life as she went about her unpaid social work with Myrtle. Endless hours were spent manning food banks or collecting donations from supermarkets. Myrtle had a long, ever-growing list of those in need of her help. There were those requiring assistance in dealing with the immigration authority, those who needed help in contesting Home Office decisions, those who were about to be evicted from their homes. There was a lot of this type of work about, if you knew how to find it, and Myrtle certainly knew how to find it. Sal's recruitment into Myrtle's humanitarian venture left Jack feeling impotent, excluded, angry.

Home life was turning into one endless round of rows. It was with an enormous effort that Jack was maintaining self-control. But a voice was sounding loudly, warning him to keep his hands under control. He knew Myrtle's type; it wouldn't take much to have her crying physical abuse. He had to content himself with a good old shout that shut Sal up for the moment but had no lasting effect.

Gone were the days when Sal enjoyed cooking, when they sat down together in the evening to a home-cooked meal. If Jack objected to the ready meals Sal popped into the microwave, he was encouraged to learn how to cook. The flat was going to pot. The quick tidy-up, the flicking of a duster, the cursory mop of the kitchen floor, carried out by Sal on Saturday morning, just didn't cut the mustard. Jack had to fish out the washing machine instructions and learn how to wash his clothes. He could now manage a washed and reasonably ironed shirt.

When the arguments got overheated, Sal took herself off to the spare room. He wondered if he would be within his rights to put a stop to that! But how to do it? That was the question! Getting a bit physical – a bit of a push or shake - had been enough in the past to stop Sal in her tracks! But the ever-present specter of Myrtle loomed large in Jack's mind.

They had arrived in an old camper van, liberally decorated with environmental stickers and painted slogans. Art's greeting was a high-five and 'Hey man'. Sal had spent hours in the kitchen, and expended much love and care in the production of the tasteless bean and tofu feast they were obliged to consume. All was washed down with vegan sodas; Myrtle favoured elderflower, while Art downed a raspberry kombucha. Abandoning the vegan beer provided by Sal, Jack headed for the kitchen and grabbed a bottle of red.

'Anyone joining me,' he offered.

Art rudely grabbed the bottle and read the back label. 'You can't drink that, man. It's full of crap,' he announced.

'Let me be the judge of the wine,' said Jack, grabbing the bottle.

'Please don't drink it, Jack,' said Myrtle. 'Creatures have been abused and died to produce that wine. I'd much rather you didn't drink it.'

'And which creatures might that be, Myrtle?' Jack asked.

'It's to do with the filtering process. Blood and marrow from murdered animals; fibres from crabs and shellfish. It's too horrible to think of!'

'Well, Myrtle, you'll have to look the other way. This wine tastes great when consumed with the other parts of animals I regularly eat.'

Myrtle stared at Jack, speechless, unable to find the words to turn him from his evil intent.

'Look away, Myrtle; I'm about to pour it into this glass,' said Jack provocatively.

Myrtle continued to stare. Jack found it quite unnerving. She was a straggly kind of woman, thin, with sharp features. Her straight, mousey-coloured hair, draping to either side of a narrow, long nosed face, seemed to somehow merge with her ankle length, floaty dress to give the impression of a seamless, flowing, shapeless drape. Although there was no visible evidence of dirt, she somehow didn't look very clean. Jack thought it had something to do with the colours she wore - earth colours, muddy browns and greens. Art was positively scruffy. He sported an unkempt beard, pony-tailed, shoulder length, reddish hair, dusty looking black jeans and a grey hoodie. In contrast to Myrtle's thinness, he was a big bloke, broad-faced. Both wore ankle-high, black docks.

Jack endured a thoroughly unpleasant afternoon. He felt patronised and mutinous. His views on a number of topics had been excused on the grounds of 'his unfortunate Tory upbringing'. Art declared the Tory Party in sharp decline, its membership made up of what their own leader termed 'swivel-eyed loonies'. A socialist revolution was imminent, bringing with it a thorough and extensive programme of re-education.

'That's what the Chinese do!' said Jack.

Myrtle and Art fixed their eyes on him. After quite a pause, Art said, 'Do what? You've lost me man!'

'Re-educate; they specialise in it! They have huge detention camps dedicated to the process.'

'Yeh, man, exactly. Re-education, that's what's needed!'

After they left, Sal and Jack had a massive row.

'Never, ever, bring them here again,' Jack had said.

'Oh, really! Well, I think I'm at liberty to bring whoever I like to my own home.'

'Yes, you are, you're quite right; just don't expect me to be here.'

'I wouldn't want to subject my friends to your rudeness ever again. I'm sure they wouldn't come if they were asked. You were rude and insulting. You made no effort to put them at their ease.'

'Put them at their ease! What are you talking about? Me, rude and insulting! It would be difficult to match their rudeness. They are thoroughly objectionable people, Sal. They talk a lot of anti-establishment rhetoric, are absolutely convinced of their own propaganda, and won't even listen to any other point of view. What's wrong with you, Sal? Why can't you see what these people are about?'

'Because I think they're right. They don't just talk; they live by their beliefs. It was gross, Jack; imagine drinking that wine in front of Myrtle; it really upset her.'

Chapter 2

Jack

One tradition that wasn't abandoned was Sunday lunch at Jack's parents' home in Windsor; Sal liked to keep up a pretence that all was well in Richmond.

The previous Sunday had seen his dad, Ron, in a downcast mood. Labour and Conservatives were running neck and neck in the polls for the upcoming general election.

'There's every possibility of a Labour victory,' said Ron, a lifetime Conservative.

'Great! I'm voting for Ed Miliband'. Jack's sister Julia never missed an opportunity to be contentious, to attempt to goad her father.

'And why would you do that? You know zilch about Labour Party policy,' said Jack.

'Really! That's all you know. I've been reading loads about it. I really like what they have to say.'

'Well, do enlighten us, Julia! I hadn't realised that Miliband's policies were particularly advantageous to people living your lifestyle,' said Ron.

'Spoken like a true, pompous-arsed Tory, Dad,' blazed Julia. 'Money, that's all you people care about.'

'Well, my dear, I will take you seriously when you transfer Poppy and Sam to the local primary school.'

'And you, Mum, who will you be voting for?'

'Oh, leave me out of it, dear. I have voted Conservative all my adult life; I don't propose changing at my age.'

'Have you any idea what the Conservatives stand for, or do you just take Dad's word for it?'

'Leave your mother alone. I'm sure she has far more knowledge of what she's voting for than you have.'

Julia brought out the very worst in her father.

'I'm sure it won't come as a surprise to any of you to learn that I will be voting for Ed,' said Sal, attempting to take the heat out of the conversation.

'Well, Sal, I expect you know what you are voting for. But the last Labour government left us in quite a pickle. They do like to spend money we don't have. Yes, indeed, they do!' said Ron.

Julia, in high dudgeon, turned on the unfortunate child, Sam. 'Stop it! How many times have you been told? You're too old to eat with your fingers.'

'Oh dear, it's my fault,' said Jack's mother, Margaret, jumping up. 'I forgot to lay the little knives and forks. Poor child, I'll go and get them.'

'I'll go,' said Sal, starting for the kitchen.

'Anyone for UKIP?' piped up Julia's husband, Graham.

**

Jack hadn't slept. He had meant to stay up for a couple of hours and catch the beginning of the election coverage, but the results as they came in were not what had been expected, not what the polls had been predicting. Sal had stuck it out until 1:15 before being overcome by tiredness and forced to reluctantly take to her bed. In truth, Sal was quite bored by all the political speak. By six-thirty, it was all over.

**

The result of the 2015 election was a surprise Conservative victory. Ed Miliband had suffered a heavy defeat - 232 seats to David Cameron's 331. Labour had been wiped out in

Scotland; the SNP had taken 56, mostly Labour seats. Bloody Marvellous. That's Saint Ed finished!

**

Myrtle and Art's socialist revolution wasn't coming just yet! Jack rang his dad, had a shower, ate breakfast and went happily to work.

The result caused huge distress in the Peckham household. Sal was in mourning. Jack thought that David Cameron looked as shocked as everyone else at the result. The pollsters were on the back foot, having made a total hash of their predictions.

Ron was in high good humour at Sunday lunch. 'Well, David Cameron's pigeons have well and truly come home to roost. Thought he would lose or find himself back in coalition with the Libs, that was his game. Never imagined he would have to give us the referendum he promised. Funny old game, politics - never can tell what's around the corner. Yes, it's gone pear shaped for David. A European vote is on the way!'

'What do you mean? What are you talking about?' said Julia.

'An EU referendum, my dear, that's what David promised us.'

'What happens in a referendum?'

'We all go out and vote. We will be given a choice of staying in the EU or leaving.'

'What if people vote to leave?'

'Then that will be it. We will sally off on our own and leave the lot of them behind.'

'You mean we won't be the same as France, Italy or Spain?'

'Exactly!'

'God, that would be dreadful.'

'On the contrary, I think it would be rather wonderful,' said Ron. 'Unfortunately, I think it unlikely to happen. My money would be on a remain result.'

**

25

Things had become a little calmer on the home front. Myrtle and Art were in the north, organising anti-austerity demos and rallies. In Myrtle's absence, Sal was relieved of all but her food-bank duties, leaving her more time to attend to home matters. Sal, it appeared, was not yet considered quite experienced enough to handle the more demanding work.

Sal had made a particularly enjoyable evening meal. Jack had made a big effort and helped clear the table and load up the dishwasher. They had sat down to watch The Big Bang Theory.

'Well done, isn't it, Sal?' said Jack.

'Yes, really well done.' Jack knew that she wasn't paying much attention. She had her food bank accounts out, her attention focused on stocks of tins, toiletries, disposable nappies and bread. Bread was a constant worry. Sal's greatest fear was that the basic, essential commodity should run out in any of the three food banks she helped stock. A picture of concentration, brows knitted, she flicked between a number of account books stacked next to her on the sofa. It was stiflingly hot for June; every window in the flat was open. Sal was wearing shorts and a low-cut top. Her shoulder length, blonde hair, pulled back and wound into a knot at the back of her head showed off her long neck. Her tanned legs were stretched out on the footstool. Sal was very beautiful. Even after four years of marriage, Jack was still in awe of her beauty.

He had just flicked onto the BBC in time to catch the news. 'It's the candidates for the Labour leadership election. They've been announced.'

'Oh, turn it up,' said Sal, abandoning her accounts and giving her full attention to the TV. 'Andy Burnham, Evette Cooper, Liz Kendall. None are a patch on Ed. Poor Ed, I can't understand what happened! Jeremy Corbyn! I've never heard of him. Have you, Jack?'

'Can't say I have, Sal. A surprise candidate, apparently. Left wing.'

'Oh, interesting!'

Jeremy Corbyn's inclusion in the Labour Party leadership election brought Myrtle and Art rushing back to London. Sal was filled in on Jeremy's CV.

'Did you know, Jack, that Jeremy holds the record of being the most rebellious MP in parliament? He has defied the Labour whip 428 times. Think of that!'

'Is that good?'

'Well, it shows he has a mind of his own!'

'I don't quite see it. Hardly seems worth while staying in the party!'

'I suppose he wants to bring about change from within.'

'Yeh, perhaps. Doesn't seem to have had much success, though.'

'This is his time, Jack. If he gets elected everything will change.'

Jack didn't argue anymore. He just let Sal rabbit on and repeat all the left-wing speak she heard in Peckham. He doubted that she had much idea what defying the Labour whip and other parroted jargon meant. She had paid £3 to join the party as an associate member. It meant that she could take part in the leadership election and vote for Jeremy Corbyn. Myrtle and Art had also taken advantage of the offer. It looked as though every extreme left-winger in the country was joining up. What existing members, paying the full membership fee thought about it, Jack couldn't begin to imagine!

Myrtle had again picked up the cudgels on behalf of the oppressed and needy. Sal was back in harness as her trusted lieutenant. When work allowed, they went along to meetings and rallies to cheer Jeremy Corbyn to the rafters. No distance was too great for them to travel in support of their hero. Sal had even taken a day off work to go to Liverpool.

The flat was more neglected than ever. Jack was now very lucky to get the microwaved meal he had once so despised. More often than not, he got a message similar to the one that had just popped up on his phone: 'Eat at The Green Duck or pick up something that doesn't need cooking at M&S,' Sal, advised. He wasn't surprised to learn that she was going to Islington with Myrtle, Art and other lefties to attend Jeremy Corbyn's last rally. Sal was acting like a deranged groupie. Jack found it toe-curlingly embarrassing, it made him very angry. But some instinct told him to keep his anger under control; he was no longer sure how Sal would react. His power over his wife wasn't what it was. A now familiar warning voice urged caution!

Saturday 12th September 2015 turned out to be a day to be remembered. Sal had stayed over with Myrtle. The nation's future, possibly the future of the world, hung in the balance; it was the day the Labour leadership result was to be announced. 'The Comrades' felt the need to be together at such a pivotal moment.

Jack was slobbing around in flip-flops and dressing gown. He had fried bacon and sausage and heated half a tin of beans. He popped four slices of bread in the toaster and made a mug of coffee. He was surprised at how proficient he had become in providing his own meals. The microwave was invaluable, as was the oven for the cooking of pies and chips. He had got quite good with eggs - boiled, scrambled or poached. Toast was child's play! Much of the mystique had gone out of the process. Roast dinners, casseroles and complicated meals from scratch could be left to his mother and Sal. He had no intention of stealing their thunder - no intention at all.

He paused; a forkful of sausage suspended between plate and mouth as the startling news wended its way across the airways. It really had happened.

**

The old protestor, the defier of political party whips, Jeremy Corbyn, had been elected leader of the Labour Party, the leader of Her Majesty's Loyal Opposition. It was a landslide victory, sixty percent of the vote. Started as a two hundred to one outsider. Nice one Jez!

**

There was a new chant, 'Jez we can!' His first engagement, it was reported, was attendance at a 'Refugees Welcome' rally.

Sal and the comrades were ecstatic. Art had declared it the beginning of the rebirth of the nation. To celebrate the pending rebirth, this renewal of hope, Myrtle, Art and Sal announced their intention to take the good news to the Calais refugee camp, otherwise known as 'The Jungle'. They were going to inform the residents of Jeremy's election, to tell them of the bright, shining utopia he was about to create and into which they would all be welcomed.

It's the second coming. Does the guy know he's the new Messiah?

**

'You can't be serious about this, Sal. Have you any idea of the conditions in that place, the types that are shacked up there?'

'What do you mean by types?'

'I mean the type of people, mainly young men, that are in the camp.'

'Refugees, fleeing from oppression, you mean.'

'No, I don't. They are mainly economic migrants. There's quite a lot of violence; lorry drivers are being attacked.'

'That's rubbish; there are women and children there. They want to come here where they'll be safe. It's disgraceful that we won't allow them in!'

'For God's sake Sal, use your head, you're an intelligent woman. Most have no right whatsoever to be here, no right to asylum.'

'You are just so wrong. They are desperate people trying to reach safety.'

'Sal, they are safe in France, a civilised, European country. Why don't they claim asylum there?'

'I think they have a right to choose where they live!'

'Not so desperate then, just picky!'

'I'm going, Jack, no matter what you think or say. I know how biased you are against these people; I saw it when we were in Greece.'

It's a bloody, hair-brained scheme. For God's sake, give it up and keep away from those half-wits, Myrtle and Art; they have the brains of fleas. What do they think will happen if we open the doors to the Calais camp? Don't they realise that the whole of Africa and a good part of Asia are queuing up behind them! Come to think of it, it's probably what they are hoping for!'

'How dare you, how dare you speak about Myrtle and Art like that! How would you like to hear your friends spoken of in that way?'

'I take care to choose my friends with more care!'

'You're an arrogant, insensitive, Tory bastard!' she shouted as she jumped to her feet, the colour drained from her face, her eyes blazing.

She packed a bag, called a cab and slammed the front door very hard as she went out. Gone to Peckham, he presumed. Jack was left angry and frustrated.

Bloody Myrtle!

Jack returned home the following evening to find Sal's

wardrobe empty, the bedroom floor cleared of the various items of clothing, shoes and bags that normally lived there. The surface of her dressing table was daubed with spilled cosmetics and littered with balls of cotton wool and paper tissues the detritus of the potions, lotions, makeup and the myriad of perfumes and nail polishes carried away by Sal. Everywhere he looked, there were orange stickers. A note on the kitchen table told him that the stickers identified Sal's belongings and that a removal van would arrive between seven and nine the following evening to remove all stickered items.

The bed had a note pinned to the headboard identifying it as a wedding present from her parents; it too had an orange sticker attached. The sofa and TV were sticker free, as was the coffee table. On the coffee table, with 'Jack', scrawled in heavy black marker across its 'Happy Birthday' wrapping paper, was a parcel containing their wedding album, wedding video and Sal's wedding and engagement rings. A message written inside a 'Congratulations' card featuring a bottle of champagne with two bubbling glasses instructed Jack to keep the contents as a cautionary tale of two people who had absolutely nothing in common, having imagined themselves compatible. Despite the message, Jack had to smile; the irony of her choice of wrapping paper and card, he knew, would have eluded Sal, who would have used what was to hand.

Jack was stunned! He began walking aimlessly about the flat. Sal's wardrobe doors hung open; he stood mesmerised by the empty hanging rails. The little orange circles seemed to echo Sal's disdainful, accusing voice. He felt suddenly very hungry. He found eggs and cheese in the fridge and set about making a cheese omelet. Jack could make cheese omelettes; even Sal said his omelettes were good.

He broke two eggs into a bowl and began whisking with a fork. He watched, fascinated, as watery drops plopped into the whisked eggs to the accompaniment of a strange noise that started as a whimper but quickly turned to a strange, high-pitched wail. He became aware of the wetness on his face, streaming, hot wetness. Recognising the noise as his own, he clamped his hands over his mouth to try to stifle the noise. His body shook as the wailing turned to laughter - loud, out of control laughter. What was wrong with him? His wife had left him and he was laughing like some raucous fairground automaton. He sat on the sofa, head in his hands, attempting to quiet the racket, to conquer the hysteria, the panic that threatened his ability to breathe.

The van arrived at 7:15 p.m. the following evening. Jack watched as most of the furniture in the flat was carried out. 'Where's it all going?' he asked as the bed was maneuvered through the hallway.

'Not supposed to say, mate,' answered a shaven-headed guy, his arms tattooed from his wrist to a line halfway up his muscular upper arms, his hands with a firm hold on the bed - their bed, the bed he had shared with Sal for four years.

Jack pulled out his wallet. 'Ten quid?'

'Yeh, mate. A storage facility in Tottenham,' was the answer as the guy grabbed the tenner and shoved it in his back pocket. 'Oh, and this needs signing, mate. Just put your moniker there.'

'What is it?'

'Just to say we haven't taken anything we shouldn't have. Don't want to find ourselves in the middle of a dispute over the dog!'

'We haven't got a dog!'

'No, mate, just a figure of speech, like. Tricky business, breakups.'

Jack was given 'his copy', dated 29th March 2016, a material reminder of the day Sal left with most of the furniture.

'Thanks', I'll frame it!'

'You do that, mate.'

The bedroom looked weird - all lopsided, the wardrobes and chests of drawers clinging to the walls around the huge, vacated space where the bed had been. Most of the kitchen equipment and the dining table and chairs remained, but the living room looked bare. The second bedroom, that Sal had used as a workroom, was empty. There had been a nice, leather bed settee along one wall, used as their spare bed. Jack remembered paying his fair share when it had been bought; he remembered paying his fair share for much of what she had taken; he didn't care.

He remembered Sal, arms outstretched, whirling in the centre of that room. 'It's perfect, Jack, we've got to have it. There's so much light! This room will be perfect for our workspace.' Jack had laughed as he watched her; blonde hair fanning out about her shoulders, her check, summer dress swirling about her long, tanned legs. Jack had known that she meant her workspace. The one bed, pokey hole they had occupied for the previous six months had been overrun with the work she brought home. Sal was a visual merchandiser; she dressed shop windows, upmarket shop windows. She was talented, in demand, and earned more than he did. They had bought the flat and moved in a week before their wedding.

They had been happy together until bloody Myrtle had come on the scene. OK, they had their differences, but they laughed them off. Sal had been a bit of a leftie, but he had talked her round. Sal got on well with his family and he with hers. They went up to Newcastle, her home city, three or four times a year. Her family were great people. Robbed of his wife by half witted, do gooders, that was what it amounted to!

He kept calling and texting, but Sal was on permanent voice mail. He went out and bought a few cans and a takeaway. He sat on the sofa and ate his meal in the denuded, echoey room. He turned on the TV to catch the news. Jeremy Corbyn was at some meeting in Islington. Jack half expected to see Sal and Myrtle in attendance, but it was the usual bevy of black and brown women that surrounded the hero. He collected the pillows and duvet Sal had left folded on the bedroom floor and slept on the sofa.

On his way home the following evening, he drove to the clearance outlet and bought himself a bed. He ordered the leather headboard that Sal wouldn't let him have – she said leather headboards were chavvy! There was still no answer to his messages. He was sure she was with Myrtle, but where was Myrtle? He wracked his brains for clues as to where in Peckham Myrtle lived. He had hardly listened when Sal talked about the goings on there. He wished now that he had paid more attention; he had *absolutely no idea where to find his wife.*

He regretted what he had said about Myrtle and Art. Every word had been true, but Sal had taken it very badly. He should have kept his mouth shut. He parked the car at the flat and walked to The Duck; he couldn't face another evening rattling about in an unfurnished flat. He said nothing to the friends about Sal's defection.

The following Sunday, he broke the news to the family. He had considered saying Sal wasn't well but thought better of it. What excuse would he make the following week? Better to get it over with.

'Isn't Sal coming?' said his mother, looking behind him, through the open doorway.

'No, Mum, Sal won't be coming again; she's left me.'

Margaret took a step back and stared uncomprehendingly. 'What on earth do you mean?'

'Just that, Mum, she's left me!'

'Oh, darling, what on earth has happened?'

'A long story, Mum.' *Don't cry. For God's sake, don't cry.* He had steeled himself for the occasion. He mustn't cry like some daft kid!

'Darling, I am so sorry, so very, very sorry,' said Margaret, putting her arms about her son.

He knew it. He knew it would be his mother's comforting that would be his undoing. Tears had sprung to his eyes.

'What's going on? What are you saying about Sal?' said Julia, poking her head around the kitchen door.

'She's left me.'

'Left you! My God, what have you been up to. Playing around no doubt!'

Margaret got quite angry; for once, assertive. 'Go back into the kitchen, Julia. You know nothing about it. I asked you to put the water jugs on the table, go and do it.'

He wasn't blind to the anxious looks exchanged between his parents. Ron pretended an interest in the financial implications of Sal's desertion, the dividing up of the spoils! Jack said nothing about Sal's furniture grab. His mother, overly cheerful, was talking too fast, her eyes fixed on the joint of beef being expertly sliced by Ron and forked onto the plates being passed up the table. His news had upset them; he hated himself for it. They had supported him, believed in him, given their unconditional love, and what had he given in return? He couldn't even hold his marriage together!

He looked around the familiar room. The half-moon shaped fireplace, original to the 1930s house, its fire back blackened with the fires lit on high days and holidays, Ladro figurines, brought back from a holiday in Spain, sitting on a Georgian side table, a silver tea service in company with a crush of family photographs occupying the top of the sideboard, his mother insisted on calling a chiffonier - Jack had never quite seen the difference! The delicate legged dining table with eight matching chairs, the wine cooler and the silver tea service were all part of the valuable antique trove inherited from his maternal grandmother - all old inhabitants of the room. The carpet was new, the business of the walls toned down, but the room was otherwise unchanged from the room he remembered from childhood.

The peacock blue velvet curtains were conflict-hardened survivors of many battles and skirmishes. They had been hung in 1992, when swags, long tails, tassels and deep fringing were all the thing. Julia had declared war on them at the turn of the century. She had pronounced them tasteless and outdated items, that, together with the rest of her mother's clutter, should be consigned to the bin. Margaret had advised Julia to take a good look at her own soulless, clinical home, which in her opinion wasn't a home at all.

A scene materialising before him was startling in its clarity. He was back in the 1980s. It was Christmas morning. A Lego set lay open on the table, its plastic compartments filled with blue, black, grey and white bricks. Jack thought it most likely The King's Mountain Fortress or The Black Knight's Castle. He had loved his Lego, always had the latest set on his Christmas list. The boy sitting at the dining room table with his father leaning over his shoulder, helping him understand the instructions, was so real that Jack felt he could reach out and touch him.

The room was bright with strings of Christmas cards. Sprigs of holly and ivy topped the paintings. Looking into the hall, he could see the tree, tinsel decked, lights reflecting in coloured baubles, torn paper and unopened presents at its base. Good memories! It had been a happy home, a loving home. He could lay no blame at his parents' door for the setbacks life had thrown in his path.

'Trouble at the mill, I hear, old boy. Dear, dear!' Graham's voice cut across his thoughts.

Chapter 3

'J'

20th February 2016. David Cameron addresses the British electorate from Downing Street.

'Three years ago, I committed to the British people that I would renegotiate our position in the European Union and hold an in-out referendum. Now I am delivering on that commitment. You will decide. And whatever your decision, I will do my best to deliver it. On Monday I will commence the process set out under our Referendum Act. And I will go to Parliament and propose that the British people decide our future in Europe through an in-out referendum on Thursday 23rd of June. The choice is in your hands. But my recommendation is clear. I believe that we will be safer, stronger and better off by remaining in a reformed European Union.'

Boris Johnson called Cameron's deal 'The best of a bad job.'

**

The government sent out a leaflet to every household in the country warning of the dangers of leaving the EU. Jack had expected that the government publication would present both sides of the argument. What he read were dire warnings of years of uncertainty, of economic disruption, reduced investment, lost jobs. He learned that members of the government, with few exceptions, were campaigning to remain, as was the Labour Party. Jack was a bit surprised about old Jeremy's stand; he had understood the Messiah to be an EU sceptic. He tore up the leaflet and threw it in the bin.

Nine million of taxpayer's money spent on blatant canvassing. Bloody disgraceful!

Ron wasn't at all surprised by the government publication. 'I've heard it all before, my boy. Same old tactics they used in '75 when we joined the Common Market, frightening the nation into delivering the required vote. Be prepared for a deluge of dire warnings from the establishment. What's the bloke talking about? A reformed European Union! Wishful thinking! What has he come back with after months of talks with the intransigent outfit? A handful of crumbs, Jack, that's what he's got. But what he has given us is a date with destiny, my boy.'

Jack had to admit that he wasn't completely clued up on the EU. He had always been against it; he had picked up enough from his dad to convince him of the undemocratic, bureaucratic nature of the outfit. Their numerous councils and commissions made his head spin! Still, he needed to get to grips with it all. The official 'Leave' campaign was to be headed up by Boris Johnson and Michael Gove. Nigel Farage was running a parallel campaign.

Whoever said the Brits had no interest in politics needed, Jack thought, to be a fly on the wall in his place of work. Some amazingly heated arguments had broken out between Leavers and Remainers, shattering the peace of the normally quiet and tranquil office.

'Now, now, lads, let's not get overheated, let's show some respect for the opinions of others,' Jock would say, real name, James McNeill, the office manager.

Jock took his responsibilities as father of the office very seriously. There wasn't a file, a chart or an account that Jock couldn't immediately lay his hands on. There wasn't a senior or junior in the company who didn't respect Jock. At sixty-two, he had 'seen it all and done it all', as he himself was fond of saying.

Jack was the senior engineer in his division. Occupying the office with Jack were three other engineers: Simon, Ned and Rob and Caitlin, newly qualified and working towards accreditation. Jack had joined the company in 2010, straight from university. He was now an experienced engineer, promoted to Project Manager three years previously. He knew that he should be looking outside the company for promotion, but he was happy and very comfortable where he was. He pushed the matter of promotion to the back of his mind; he had no wish to work in some sixth-floor office in a glass box.

Carter and Curlow, Structural Engineers, were, in the words of the CEO, Arthur Curlow, 'A small, family-owned and run company, underpinned by traditional values and competence.' The company has been founded in 1926 by Arthur's grandfather, Fredrick Curlow and his partner Peter Carter. They had set up offices in Gordon House on the Victoria Embankment, in a building abandoned by the Colonial Office after WW1. They occupied the premises to the present day, as did its original Victorian fixtures and fittings. The oak panelling, the polished mahogany, the floor and wall tiling, the stained-glass, lending gravitas to the traditional values trumpeted by Arthur Curlow.

Jack's spirits rose when he pushed open the brass embellished, double mahogany doors and stepped into the checkered entrance hall. The general himself stood to his left, a life-size, bronzed, high-booted figure, slim in his figure-hugging uniform, his left hand resting on the hilt of his sword. His features finely drawn, the hero gazed above the heads of those who looked, his eyes fixed on some far distant, visionary land. Beneath his feet, engraved into a high plinth, were his battle honours: Sevastopol, Kinburn, Taiping,

Cixi, Changzhou. Jack wondered what the proud patriot would have made of the idea of rule from Brussels!

The walls were hung with oversized canvases in age-dulled gilt frames. Occupying some six square metres of wall space, Gordon was pictured at the top of a flight of steps wearing a gold braided, blue uniform and red fez. Swarming up the steps towards him, spears waving, were the Mahdi's soldiers. A brass plaque at the base of the painting, read 'General Charles George Gordon's Last Stand at Khartoum'. Grouped within an arched recess on the far wall, beneath a banner proclaiming 'The Ever Victorious Army' were reminders of the man the Victorians had named 'Chinese Gordon'. He was pictured astride a camel, lost in a sea of desert, and in Chinese dress, being presented with an Imperial yellow jacket by the Qing Emperor.

Shunning the lift, Jack climbed the wide marble staircase that led to the first-floor offices. He ran his hand along the polished rail and fingered the deeply carved fruit and foliage decorating the huge structure. Mythical gilt-bronze birds stood sentinel on the newel posts, their wings supporting metre-high, yellow, pineapple-shaped globes. At the turn of the stairs, the half landing was illuminated by a triptych of stained glass. Framed within Gothic mullions were images of empire: India, a riot of every colour and hue of the spectrum; Africa, in earthy reds and browns and Egypt, in blues and greens. The light striking through the coloured glass fell as a multi-coloured rug across the marble, just as it had done, day after day, for almost one hundred and fifty years. Jack thought of all those who had walked where he walked, whose feet had crossed the patchwork of light and had looked up at the spectacular sight, at the dazzling jigsaw of colour.

The office was at the front of the building, with views over the Embankment Gardens and the river. Daylight entered through a triangular-shaped oriel set into one corner, and a huge, arched central widow where David Livingstone looked towards the great cascade of Victoria Falls. Throughout Gordon House were images in stone, wood, glass and brass, all extolling the deeds and character of Empire builders. It wasn't everyone who shared Jack's appreciation of Gordon House. There had been those who had passed through the office - the history debunkers, the decriers and haters of empire who had been fulsome in their criticism. One temp had gone so far as to say that the place should be blown up or burned to the ground.

Philistines!

Jack and his colleagues sat at old mahogany desks. Concealed beneath their huge flat tops were deep, pull-out chart drawers and capacious filing cabinets. Incongruous, digital equipment now sat on the polished surfaces. They worked surrounded by oak panelling and carved bookcases. Leather-bound sets, the reference material of past engineers, lined the bookshelves. The books, decorative but obsolete, were annually, at the instigation of the CEO, taken down, hoovered, dusted and replaced by contract cleaners. The boards beneath their feet were wide, patinated by the footfall of time, and towards the end of the working day, washed purple and blue by the light shining through the Livingstone window.

Jack loved old places, had a deep admiration for the craftsmen of the past, hated the neglect and lack of appreciation of their legacy. When they were young, their parents had taken Jack and his sister to visit lots of old and historical places; Jack had soaked it up, but Julia had been bored. Julia liked to say that she had never been on a proper holiday as a child.

On the top floor of the building, off a narrow passageway, a door opened onto a steep stairway leading to an octagonal turret. Jack often went up there during his lunch hour. The turret's surprisingly large floor space was empty, but for one very old, well sat in, brown leather armchair. The chair stood in front of a window, which gave a view of The Embankment. There were windows to the eight sides of the structure, giving a three-hundred-and-sixty-degree view of surrounding rooftops and roads. But the view that engaged Jack was the one that had engaged the previous occupant of the chair - the view of Bazalgette's great feat of engineering, The Thames Embankment. Sitting in the chair, he ate his lunch and pictured the army of Victorian workers who excavated the great underground tunnels built to carry the railway and the city's waste.

Viewed from the high eyrie, the limes and London plane trees of the Embankment Gardens were foreshortened, made squat. The grime laden windows looked directly onto Waterloo Bridge and the National Theatre on the South Bank. To his left, he could see HMS Wellington moored alongside Temple Pier and in the distance, the iconic OXO Tower, Blackfriars Bridge and the Millennium Bridge. To his right were Cleopatra's Needle, Victoria Embankment Gardens and a long view of The London Eye and Big Ben.

He looked down from his silent perch at the thronged walkway, at the dwarfed figures crossing Waterloo Bridge and at the river traffic. He imagined the riverbank as it had been in years gone by; pictured Tudor boats making their way along the muddy, marshy bank towards the tower, a steady drumbeat timing the strokes of the oarsmen.

Jack was certain that nobody other than himself came to the turret. The floor and windowsills were heavy with years of London grime, the chair harboured decades of dust. He was fascinated by the chair, pondered who had put it there and when. Could it have been Fredrick Curlow or his partner, Peter Carter? Jack liked to imagine some long-dead Colonial office mandarin having his minions drag the chair up the narrow stairs so that he could sit and watch Sir Joseph Bazalgette directing his engineering work. The turret was a place apart, a silent, secluded world, a refuge on the days when the banter grated and Jack wanted only his own company.

When not in The Duck, he spent his evenings honing up on the EU. He had got to grips with the TROICA, which he learned encompassed the European Commission, European Central Bank and the International Monetary Fund. He had experienced firsthand the work of this unholy alliance in Greece!

Bastards!

Janis Varoufakis, the former Greek Finance Minister had much to say on the subject. Speaking before the Greek referendum on the rescue package offered to the Greeks in 2015, Mr. Varoufakis compared the country's creditors to terrorists. He spoke as his country faced shortages of food and drugs, and the banks had barely enough money to last the weekend. The Prime Minister, Alexis Tsipras, urged his people not to give in to blackmail, ultimatums and terror tactics as they faced threats of being thrown out of the Eurozone. Over 61 percent of the Greeks polled said 'No' to Europe's offer, but the creditors weren't to be defeated.

After resigning and being re-elected, Alexis Tsipras was forced to accept the bail-out conditions - 'The Memorandum of Understanding' - that's what the creditors liked to call it - the EU were good with words. What their fancy-worded agreement amounted to was raised taxation, lowering of public sector pay, job cuts and privatisation of Greek ports. It appeared to Jack to be a recurring theme; similar measures had been imposed on the Irish. When the Irish banks were bailed out to the tune of 64 billion, it was the Irish people who were required to pay the price: increased austerity, public sector pay cuts and tax rises. It made Jack's blood boil!

Come on, Boris, get us out of this shit outfit!

It was 5:45 p.m. on a Wednesday evening. Due to a delay on the tube, Jack had been forced to make the slow journey by bus. The 64 was making its sluggish way through the London rush hour traffic when suddenly, they were there, right by the window, walking along the pavement holding hands, keeping pace with the slow moving traffic.

For several seconds, they were almost within touching distance! He watched Sal's skipping step as she kept pace with the long strides of the man by her side. He was tall, well over six foot, much taller than Sal, who was a good five-foot-ten. The lights changed, the bus put on speed and began pulling away. He craned his neck for a last view of his wife's face as she smiled up at the man by her side. She was wearing the navy trench coat she had found in the Burberry sale, bought for what she said was a giveaway price! It was, he thought, an example of Sal's illogical thinking. She could shed tears for those forced to use food banks to feed themselves and their children while yet indulging her passion for expensively tagged clothes - a bewildering amalgam of contradictions, that was Sal!

He had suspected that she was seeing someone else. Most of her social media postings centred on her activities with Myrtle, the usual thing; lots of moralising clap trap. But the appearance of someone referred to as 'J' had aroused his curiosity. A photograph showing her at the centre of a group, glasses raised in a toast, a blonde man at her left, had in recent days popped up on her Facebook page. The caption read, 'Having fun on the Thames'. The blonde guy in the photograph and the guy walking with her were one and the same. Jack was certain of it.

Suspicion and imaginings were one thing; seeing her with another man was something else. His chest tightened; his heart settled into a tumultuous throbbing. Shock was superseded by a debilitating panic. He had convinced himself that she would come to her senses, would get fed up filling food bank shelves, consoling the needy, being Myrtle's little helper. He had been convinced that, despite everything that had happened, she loved him, needed him. Sal loving someone else, being with another man was intolerable. For the first time, he was forced to face the possibility that Sal wasn't coming back. He was gripped by a deep dread. His breath came in shallow bursts. He put his head down, tried to take deep breaths.

As the bus pulled to a stop, he jumped from his seat and rushed off onto the pavement. He remembered flattening himself against a shop window, feeling the cooling surface on his back and the palms of his hands, of trudging along pavements, crossing roads within inches of passing traffic, horns blaring. It was 9:50 p.m. when he climbed the stairs to the flat. He had no recollection of how he had got there. He had a raging thirst. He stood at the kitchen sink and drank glass after glass of water.

He sat down on the sofa, turned on the TV and watched the soundless images that flickered across the screen. He had been brought slap bang face to face with reality. What the hell was he going to do? She was his wife; no way was he letting her go. Find out where she was, that was the first thing. He had imagined her living with Myrtle but realised that he may well have been deceiving himself.

The following evening, he parked the car at the flat and headed straight for The Duck. Sal had been friends with Mark Atkin's wife, Clare. He wondered if she had kept in touch with Sal; maybe she knew what was going on. He hit lucky; Mark was in on his own. Keeping the conversation casual, pretending to knowledge he didn't have, he got the information he was after.

'Yeh, Bloomsbury, a flat in Tavistock Place, Artley House. I remember thinking that Sal had gone up in the world.' Mark had seen the address on a birthday card Clare had sent.

After work the following evening, he jumped on the tube and headed for Bloomsbury. It was only a couple of minutes' walk from Russell Square station to Tavistock Place. Artley House was a smallish Victorian block; probably no more than twenty flats. A porte-cochère spanned the front of the building, and wide glass doors gave a view into a central lobby. He walked quickly past, crossed the street and took cover behind a bus stop. He watched a chauffeur-driven car pull up in front of the building. The driver got out and helped an elderly man up the steps and through the glass doors before returning and driving the car away. He thought his best bet was a coffee shop a bit further up the street. He went in, got a coffee and found a seat from where he could watch the flats.

He didn't know why he was waiting or what he expected, and was about to leave when Sal came walking down the street with the same guy. He felt as though his stomach had been suddenly gripped by clutching, tearing hands. He couldn't move, couldn't take his eyes from the smiling, happy couple as they approached the building, walked up the steps and disappeared from sight behind the swinging glass doors. The coffee cup rattled as he put it down on the saucer, his hands were shaking, his forehead wet with sweat. He saw a light come on in a first-floor window and caught a brief glimpse of Sal as she raised a hand to pull down a blind. On weakened legs and damp with sweat, he had made his way back to the station, determined to keep away from Bloomsbury. Unfortunately, such resolutions are easily set aside.

The following evening, he found himself sitting in the coffee shop in Tavistock Place, waiting for their return. They arrived at around 7:00 p.m. It was the beginning of a new pattern to Jack's week - the start of his evening visits to Tavistock Place. They were usually back by 7:30; sometimes it was a bit later; sometimes they didn't appear and he had to give it up. He knew that he shouldn't be there, knew it to be a form of self-immolation, but it was a punishment that paradoxically satisfied a deep psychological need.

**

The polls were tightening. A nailed-on Remain victory was no longer certain. David Cameron was on the news, looking worried. In rolled-up shirt sleeves, he was filmed jumping into the fray like a prize fighter. Jack had watched Boris, Andrea Leadsom and Gisela Stuart take on three Remain backing harpies in a TV debate. Boris was doing a sterling job travelling about the country in the battle bus. In Gisburn, he had auctioned a cow at the cattle market. Described her as a 'beautiful milker, a beautiful cow'.
Great stuff. Michael Gove very convincing on sovereignty.

**

An after-work drink with Rob and Simon had proved informative. David Sumner had been in. Jack had been at university with David; they hadn't met for months, so had a bit of catching up to do. He was surprised to find that David knew about his split with Sal. It turned out that he had met Sal the week before at a firm's do. She had been with a guy called Julian Tennant; family dripping in money, founders and major shareholders in Porteus Mining. Tennant was a senior partner in the company, operated out of their London office. It explained the Bloomsbury address.

Should, no doubt, be grateful that she didn't leave me for a down and out!

The following afternoon, inventing a doctor's appointment, Jack left work at 4:00 to make his way to the Porteus offices on Kingsway, Holborn. He knew the area; it was pretty built up; commercial. It was where David Sumner worked. He wondered who else working in the area might recognise him. He needed to be careful. From Victoria Embankment, he took the route along Milford Lane, on to The Strand, across Aldwych.

The offices were just beyond Kemble Street. The building was a solid stone edifice, built to accommodate Victorian commerce. The Porteus offices were marked by a discreet brass plaque fixed to the right of double-doors and reached via a wide flight of steps leading directly from the pavement. Opposite the building was a small department store and tearooms.

It was 4:45 when Jack entered the department store. Keeping an eye on the window, he had a leisurely wonder around the men's department before heading for the next door tea shop. He bought himself a white tea and a Danish and settled himself at a table some distance from the window, from where he had a good view of the steps. It was a punt; he had no real expectation of seeing the guy, so was taken by surprise when, at 5:30, the doors swung open and Julian Tennant came tripping down the steps and headed off in the direction of the Strand. Jack was sure it was him; the blonde hair was unmistakable. He couldn't believe his luck!

He was moving at quite a pace. The offices were turning out, the pavements were crowded. Jack had to make a dash from the tea shop in order to keep him in sight. He was walking towards the river. He crossed Aldwych and the Strand and continued onto Waterloo Bridge. The bridge walkway was busy; following was easy. Reaching the South Bank, Tennant made for Waterloo Station. Sal was waiting for him. She was sheltering beside a newsstand, out of the path of the rushing tide of bodies. Tennant walked quickly up to her, threw an arm about her shoulders and guided her into the station. He didn't follow them. It wasn't a station that he was familiar with; he didn't know the layout. It was too risky.

It had taken him forty-five minutes to get from Gordon House to Kingsway. If Tennant was in the habit of leaving at 5.30, he would have to leave work early to catch him. That could be a problem. But what did it matter? He knew where they were going.

He felt a sudden surge of self-loathing and disgust. He scorned the voyeurism that had driven him to follow Tennant through the streets of West London, despised the man who prowled about Tavistock Place, torturing himself with visions of what was taking place behind the blinds of a first-floor window, who eavesdropped into Sal's life through her social media accounts. Sal hadn't thought to block him from her numerous sites – Facebook, Twitter, LinkedIn, WhatsApp, Snapchat. Sal was never offline. Too busy talking to remember to keep him out.

He jumped on the tube at Aldwych and made his way home. Before getting off the train, he had got his thinking back in order. He had a tendency to self-pity; it raised its head when he least expected it. When in that frame of mind, he became possessed of a fatalistic mindset that required an acceptance of Sal's betrayal and the loss of his wife. It was a weakness of mind that had to be stamped out.

Chapter 4

A Day of Destiny

It was 23rd June 2016. Jack went straight from work to the polling station, cast his vote to leave the EU and drove to his parents' place. He was going to sit up with his father to watch the results come in.

There had been a heated discussion in the office. Ned had kicked it off.

'All this bloody whinging you're doing, Jack, about the treatment of the Greeks; what about the shit imposed by our own government on the country? What about our banks! I don't give a shit about the Greeks. They fiddled their way into the Euro, brought it all on themselves,' said Ned.

'As usual, you're missing the point,' said Jack. 'I agree that the banks have got away with murder; some CEO's should be in jail, but it's about sovereignty. We're talking about dictates from rich, northern European countries. There were Greek professionals - teachers, lecturers, social workers, thrown out of work, eating out of rubbish bins. How the hell can you condone that?'

'Yeh, the elite wouldn't condone debt relief. The German public wouldn't wear it. That's the same Germans who are quids in through their membership of the euro,' said Simon.

'How the hell are they supposed to have fiddled their way in? How did they manage that?' Ned asked.

'Cooked the budget figures for the years before they joined,' said Jack.

'Bollocks!'

'Look it up!'

'He's right,' said Simon. 'The Greeks fiddled the books, and the EU looked the other way.'

'Why would they 'look the other way,' as you put it?'

'Because it's what they do. They're capable of looking in any direction that suits their purpose. Look up the CEP report on the gainers and losers in the Eurozone,' said Simon.

'Who the hell are the CEP?' Ned, heckles rising, was sensing further undermining of his defence of his beloved EU. Simon always got the better of the argument.

'The Centre for European Policy. Note, European policy, not EU policy. The Germans do very nicely out of the Eurozone at the expense of other leading nations.'

'All bollocks. Nigel Farage and Boris Johnson bollocks,' Ned was red in the face; well wound up.

'Read the reports before you comment; that way, you might know what you were talking about. Get your brain in gear, Ned. Try thinking it out for yourself,' countered Simon. 'Stop listening to the garbage David Cameron churns out.'

'Give us one good reason for voting remain,' said Jack.

'Fuck off' said Ned, just as Jock walked through the door.

'Ach, laddies, will you give it a rest. Thank the good Lord the bloody thing's nearly over. For God's sake Ned, go and stick your head under a tap; you look about to self-ignite!'

'Fuck you,' said Ned, jumping up and heading for the door.

**

Jack found his father in a philosophical mood.

'Well, my boy, they've given it a good shot. Whichever way it goes, it was a good campaign. In the lap of the gods now!'

Margaret had left cling film-covered sandwiches and a delicious looking chocolate cake in the kitchen and had taken herself off to bed. Ron had topped up the grog tray and stocked the fridge with cans. The polls were tight but tipping to Remain.

After the 10 o'clock news, David Dimbleby appeared on screen, surrounded by the trappings of an election studio. Laura Kuenssberg sat to one side; her eyes fixed on her laptop. The pundits were predicting a Remain victory, the bookies offering 3/1 in favour. Nigel and Boris looked downcast. David Dimbleby was relaying the latest poll findings: YouGov 52% Remain, Ipsos Mori 54% Remain. All attention was on the North East, the coverage shifting between the commentators at the Newcastle and the Sunderland counts. Both areas were considered key barometers of the likely national result.

Just after 11:08 p.m., the Newcastle result came in: Leave 49.3, Remain 50.7.

'My goodness, that wasn't what the doctor ordered,' said Ron, sitting forward in his chair.

'How significant is it?'

'Very! Quite a convincing Remain vote was expected there.'

David Dimbleby and Laura Kuenssberg exchanged confused looks. The coverage shifted to Sunderland: Leave 61.3, Remain 38.7. Consternation in the studio!

'Hold on to your seat, boy. I think we just might be in for one hell of a night!' said Ron, pouring himself a double whisky.

**.

Red for Remain, blue for Leave. Disbelief turned to elation as they watched the BBC map turn blue. Hartlepool 70% Leave, Basildon 68%, Middlesbrough 65%. When Sheffield voted Leave, Nigel said it was 'amazing stuff'. At 2:15 a.m. Arron Banks, the founder of the Leave EU Campaign, declared victory. At 3:45 a.m. Nigel announced the reclaiming of the country and Jack and Ron tucked into Margaret's buffet. David Barnby, the Remain agent, said he had been against the referendum all along.

**

'Hard luck, too late now, matey. Bloody sore loser!' shouted Ron, waving his ham sandwich at the TV screen.

Peter Mandelson called it 'the worst day in post war British history.'

Tosser!

'Who is she?' asked Ron, looking at the woman on screen fighting back tears.

'Natasha Whitmill, Cameron's election agent.'

The celebratory racket woke Margaret. She came downstairs and peered, sleepy-eyed, into the sitting room. 'Is the result in?'

'It is, my dear,' said Ron, jumping up, pulling her into the room, lifting her from her feet and twirling her around. 'A wonderful result!'

'Stop it, Ron, put me down. Remember your back!' said Margaret.

**

David Cameron resigned. Threw a bit of a hissy fit. Didn't get the result he was expecting. Stood outside Downing Street and told the nation that he was off. The tune he whistled as he walked back into number 10, caught on an ITV microphone, said to be the theme from the West Wing. The media reporting no preparation for a leave result.
Bloody disgraceful. Not fit to govern.

**

It was a crazy day in Jack's office. Those who had voted Remain were shell shocked; couldn't believe they had lost. Ned had called all leave voters half-wits; said they had no idea what they had voted for.

'Well, that's rich coming from you, Ned. You who couldn't put up one convincing argument for remaining,' said Jack.

'Fucking half-wits,' said Ned.

Rob jumped up, pulled Ned to his feet and delivered one hell of a punch to his jaw. 'That's my family you're talking about, you arrogant shit.'

Ned stumbled backwards, falling across Caitlin's desk, blood spurting from his nose.

'God!' shirked Caitlin, jumping from her chair and pinning herself against the wall.

'You're all fucking lunatics!' said Ned, rushing towards the door.

It was unfortunate for him that Austin Peters, one of the partners, chose that moment to fling open the door, administering a further blow to Ned's rapidly swelling face. A huge cheer went up!

'What's going on here? What's all this about?' said Austin, as Ned pushed past him, hands to his face, attempting to staunch the blood.

'Bit of a Brexit disagreement, Austin!' said Simon.

'Get the mess cleared up,' said Austin, looking at the trail of blood left in Ned's wake.

'The Tea Room' was a long, panelled room on the second floor of Gordon House. It was the domain of Flossie Parks. Flossie was a plump redhead in her early forties. She had taken over the running of the establishment from her mother, who had been named Marge. It was a role held by a female member of the Park's family from the conception of the firm in the 1920s. The family took immense pride in their long association with Gordon House. Flossie liked to regale all who would listen with the likes and dislikes of the early directors of Curlow and Carter, as told to her by her grandmother.

'Now, Mr. Peter, Mr. Peter Curlow, that is, he liked sardines on toast. Come in once a week after the Wednesday board meeting, regular as clockwork, he was. "Nobody can make sardines on toast like you can, Flo. And that's a fact." Mr. Peter would say. My nan was Florence, like me. Thick, wholemeal slices with plenty of butter and the sardines in oil - always in oil - that's what he liked. Couldn't abide them in tomato sauce.'

From a partitioned-off kitchen at the end of the room, from a cupboard packed with tins, from a big freezer and an even bigger fridge, Flossie, assisted by her cousin, Dawn, did her best to cater for all tastes, providing for those who liked 'a sit down' and those who liked 'a takeaway'. 'The Tea Room', was, in reality, an old-fashioned canteen, free of charge to employees.

'I do not believe this!' said Simon, putting aside his toasted cheese and tomato sandwich and giving a phone article his full attention.

'What's that?' asked Jack.

'Some guy has got a petition going. Signed, it appears, by thousands. They want London to declare independence and go it alone. I quote, "60% of the capital voted Remain, which shows how radically different London is." They are calling for Sadiq Khan to become President of an independent London. He is quoted as saying that London should have a voice at the negotiating table.'

'What! As I remember it, there were a few Remain voting cities. What about Newcastle and Manchester, are they to have a voice at the table. And what about the Leave cities, are they to be invited? Sounds like a recipe for a bloody big shouting match to me,' said Jack.

'Just listen to this. Comments, I presume, from signatories to the petition. "One feels, morally, culturally and historically closer to Paris, Brussels and Rome than to Sunderland." Who the hell are these people? And this, "We need to break free, rid ourselves of this dead weight."'

'Arrogant bastards!' said Jack. 'They've got it in for Sunderland. It was the result that set alarm bells ringing, the first indication that the nailed on Remain victory was in doubt.'

'I don't know why I'm asking,' said Simon. 'We know damn well who they are; big money, vested interests hiding behind a cloak of screaming, deluded liberals luvvies.'

'Yeh, and don't they know how to make themselves heard. That lot in Parliament Square are bloody annoying.' Jack had been shocked by the anger and vitriol directed against Leave voters. The city appeared to have been overtaken by mass hysteria. The whole of London appeared to be rising up against the democratic decision of the people.

Westminster was awash with blue, gold starred flags and anti-Brexit banners. Guys with megaphones, draped in the beloved flag, broadcast their ire, drowning out the voices of those being interviewed by the media on Parliament Green. Painted faced families huddled together to ward off the threatening contagion, bemoaned the loss of their children's future.

Scapegoats were hunted down. Jeremy Corbyn was cornered at the Pride of London rally by LGBT Labour Party members calling for his resignation. He was accused of failing to get the Remain vote out in Wales, the North and Midlands, of running a 'lukewarm campaign'. 'It's all your fault, Jeremy,' they shouted. Dissatisfaction with Jeremy's leadership had spread from the Labour backbenches to the shadow cabinet. Looked like poor old Jez was hitting trouble.

It seemed to Jack that the whole focus of attention was on the

Remain protest. The leave voice was being drowned out by the loud pandemonium set up by the opposing camp. Night after night, the TV coverage was of the EU flag wavers about Westminster. There was the occasional glimpse of a Union Jack before the cameras moved swiftly on.

What the hell's going on!

His walk home from the station took him past the Lady Mabel. It was a big, Victorian pub that wrapped itself around a corner. It was the type of place that had big screens, showed a lot of sport. A union flag was permanently flown from an old flagpole on the first floor. A couple of guys with flags draped about their shoulders were sitting at the tables on the forecourt. Propped beside them were placards that read 'Leave Means Leave' and 'Believe in Britain'.

Interesting!

A chalk board outside the door announced the day's special as battered cod and chips or steak pie and chips with a choice of dessert. The battered cod looked good for a tenner. He went in, got himself a lager and gave his order. Jack was halfway through his battered cod when they started to drift in. The two guys from outside, together with half a dozen others, came first. They ordered drinks at the bar and came to sit in corner seats not far from his table. Half an hour later, Jack had found himself in the middle of a large crowd of likeminded Brexit voters, determined to make their voices heard and presence felt, at the 'March for Europe' rally the following day.

Fan – bloody -tastic!

Jack was up at seven, Saturday lie in abandoned! He got to the station at 8:35 to find the platform alive with pro-Brexit placards and awash in a sea of red, white and blue.

'Haven't you got a flag, boy? You need a flag. Fortunately, I have come prepared for just such eventualities. I will give you one of mine. Here, get this about your shoulders,' he said, pulling out and unfurling a flag from a spacious pocket on the inside of his jacket. 'You don't want to be going about the business half-dressed.'

The speaker was a very dapper, very small, elderly man dressed in a well-cut suit of Union Jack cloth.

He walked away down the platform, picking his way through the crowd, no doubt on the lookout for the similarly underdressed.

The old guy was right, the flag was transformational; it gave a sense of belonging; of being one with the disparate crowd. It was a silent declaration of identity. It could be twirled, draped, or raised over the head and flown parachute style.

A tall guy with an upper-class voice was glued to a mobile, giving updates on events as they were developing in the city. The whole thing was being organised on social media.

Bodies, placards, two drums and five cute, fluffy grey dogs on red, white and blue leads with their own banner that read 'Schnoodles for Brexit' crammed onto the 9.05. A woman, in charge of an unruly, flapping banner, took out a mouth organ to add musical breaks to a not-unimpressive rendering of 'The Village Green Preservation Society'. The whole thing, Jack thought, had something of the air of an oddly assorted Sunday school outing. Jack approved. He was getting into the swing of the thing. To the vintage Kink's lyrics, asking for the Lord's protection of all things quintessentially English, they rattled away from the leafy suburbia, towards the choked metropolis.

Things got sticky at Park Lane, where they joined up with other Brexit-supporting groups and edged their way into the march.

'Piss off!' said a hairy individual wrapped in an EU flag.

'Now, now,' said the woman with the unruly flag. 'This is an approved rally, so the roads are free to all, so piss off yourself,' this said as the huge flag was hoisted up on poles and unfurled.

The flag stretched the width of the road and had the effect of causing a huge space to open up, the blue flag wavers shrinking in alarm from the sight of their national flag inscribed with the slogan 'Traitors to the Tower'. To the beat of the drums, they marched on, the flag becoming a rallying point for other pro-Brexit groups who swelled their numbers. By the time they reached Parliament Square, they had become a sizable, irritating force and the focus of vitriolic abuse. Jack was enjoying it immensely!

In Parliament Square, they stood firm, defended their ground against attempted infiltration and crowd surging, waved their flags, sounded loud drum rolls and did their best to upset the speakers who took to the platform. They became the focus of a disproportionately large police presence. A French flavoured bun fight had broken out on their right flank. The boys in blue were in attendance, attempting to lay claim to the baguettes being bashed about heads. The 'Schnoodles for Brexit' barked their disapproval and helped themselves to the crusty French breakfast that was landing in tasty chunks at their feet.

An impassioned Bob Geldof urged people to take to the streets, and Jarvis Cocker made the informative announcement that geographically, the UK was in Europe. It was when Owen Jones claimed the platform that things took a nasty turn. It was the sight of a Union Jack rising in flames into the air that saw a flurry of activity and arrests.

'Move back, don't provoke them,' shouted a guy with a placard showing a dummy sucking, tantrum throwing baby.

It was an elated, happy group that boarded the 10.15 from Central.

'Are we all here?' asked the organiser with the mobile.

'No, mate, Charlie got snatched. Always gets himself banged up. He'll be out in the morning.'

**

Jack had stood in at the last minute as Simon's best man. Mike, Simon's best friend and appointed best man, had come off his motorbike the week before the wedding and suffered a broken leg and arm and concussion. He was under observation in hospital. A wedding was the last event Jack felt like attending, but he couldn't refuse Simon.

He had put on a brave face and stood before the alter, supporting his friend and colleague. He had been fine until the music rang out announcing the arrival of the bride - Pachelbel's canon - the same music that had been played at his own wedding. He turned with Simon to greet the bride, but it was a smiling Sal that walked towards him; hair piled about her head, silver flowers twisted through corn-coloured folds, her shoulders shrouded in lace, her dress floating and rippling about her body - tulle - he remembered Sal saying the fabric was tulle. Amanda had reached the alter. Simon had stood transfixed, looking adoringly at his wife to be.

Poor, besotted sod. I hope things turn out better for him than they have for me.

Following Amanda, in what Jack had secretly considered to be very poor taste, were a troop of eight bridesmaids, all done up in deep red and gold. A dark-haired girl, to the fore of the group, fussed with Amanda's dress - a puffy, wide affair - one eye on the huge train, the other on him.

Jack had managed the speech, partly from the notes Simon had got from Mike and partly from his own memories of amusing incidents from work. The speech over, he had relaxed into the red wine. The dark-haired bridesmaid, introduced as Olivia, had been a permanent fixture at his elbow, regaling his rapidly befuddling mind with endless inane chatter.

Returning from the toilet, making his way on unsteady legs along the hotel corridor, a door to his right had been flung open.

He had been grabbed by the arm and pulled into a bedroom. Jack likened it to a tarantula attack; Olivia's hands had been everywhere. Bright red, pouty lips had covered his mouth while one hand rummaged about his crotch, attempting to pull down his zip.

'What the hell! Jesus, what are you doing?' Jack had gasped, grabbing his tormentor by the arms and pushing her violently away from him. Olivia had lost her footing and fallen sprawled across the bed.

'What's wrong with you? Bloody hell, what's your problem?' she had hissed; dark eyes blazing; hair tumbled about her face. 'Gay, is that it? God, I'd never have suspected it. Hard to tell sometimes.' Her face had registering utter disgust.

He had stumbled from the room, rubbed frantically at his lips, wiped the bright red streaks from his hands on the sleeves of his jacket. Her smell clung to him. He had rushed down the stairs and out through the doors. Flinging himself down on a bench, he had taken deep breaths. What the hell had Sal done to him. The girl wasn't that bad; most would say she was attractive. But she had made Jack want to throw up. He had noticed a taxi parked up on the forecourt, made his way across, and spoke to the driver, 'Are you booked, mate?'

'I thought I was, but I've waited long enough. Hop in.'

Once home, he got straight into the shower, turned the temperature up, and scrubbed himself lobster red.

**

Theresa May, a Remainer, elected to lead the Conservative Party and drive through Brexit. Something not quite right there!

**

It was an unusually quiet lunch at the Willett's. Julia, Graham and the kids were away for the weekend. His father had spoken to him about Sal.

'Painful subject, old boy, I appreciate that, but what's the situation? Any chance of a reconciliation?'

'No, Dad, there isn't. It's not what I want; I'd have her back tomorrow!'

'Still in love with the girl?'

'It's no good. I must fall out of love with her. She's moved on, she's with someone else.'

'Ah, so that's the state of play! Who is he? Do you know him?'

'I don't know him, but I know who he is. He's called Julian Tennant, upper-class, wealthy, Porteus Mining, you may have heard of it, a family-owned firm. He works in the London office. He's ex-army; decorated, I hear.'

'Sorry about that, old boy! Better that the breakup comes early in a marriage, that's what I say. Gets very sticky a few years in when there are children involved. To be perfectly frank, your mother and I are worried about you. Your mother's convinced you are not eating. What does Sal want to do about the flat?'

'I've no idea, Dad. I haven't spoken to her since she left. She doesn't answer my calls or messages.'

'Well, well!'

'Yeh, there you go.'

'Look, why not move back here? We don't like the idea of you going home to an empty flat every evening. Your old room is waiting, and your mother's food is not to be sniffed at.'

'Thanks, Dad, I appreciate that. But it would be a bit embarrassing! Julia would have a field day.'

'A nine day's wonder! She would soon drop it. Besides, I don't think she feels herself on the firmest of ground at present; saying that Graham is having an affair. Bloody, silly girl, I don't believe a word of it. Don't think the fella has it in him. Swallow your pride, old boy. Get in touch with Sal, get her agreement to sell the flat or perhaps rent it. Move back in here. Make us very happy!

Chapter 5

Sally

Julian had messaged Sally several times in the week following their first meeting. His latest invitation was awaiting an answer. Sally turned to Myrtle.

'I've done it. 6:30 pm at the Hispaniola.'

'Good for you!'

'I don't know. It's cheating on Jack. Not my usual style.'

'Oh, for Heaven's sake, Sal, you're just too honourable for your own good! I thought you had made up your mind to leave him. What difference does it make?'

'I'm finding it hard to tell him. Several nights I made up my mind to do it. I just couldn't find the right words.'

'Find the words? How on earth can you be struggling for words with what you put up with? You need to tell the pompous, Tory prig exactly why you are calling it a day.'

'I haven't time to go and change. Do I look OK?'

'You look beautiful, as always.'

'I'll message Jack and say I'm with you.'

'Of course you are my darling. You're always with me.'

Sally left Myrtle shelf stacking and headed for the tube. She got off at Victoria and walked to the river. She could see the converted boat, which was now R.S. Hispaniola, in the distance. She felt hot and sticky; the underground always made her feel grubby. She wished she had found time to change. She could see some specks of dirt below the waistband of her white jeans, her top felt damp. She pulled a cardigan from her shoulder bag and threw it over her shoulders. She felt the need to cover up, to hide what Myrtle called 'her imagined, unworthy self.' She eyed the steps to her right; she felt an urge to turn, to run back to Myrtle, but knew that he had seen her. He was sitting at an outside table, legs outstretched, his eyes fixed on her.

**

She had met Julian a week earlier. The Eastaughffe Gallery had been exhibiting the work of a young Eritrean asylum seeker, Kitane Tikabo. They had got to know Kitane while Myrtle was helping him with his asylum application. Kitane spoke very little English; he talked in pictures. Myrtle had written his statement, informed by the pictures he had drawn. Sitting in Kitane's Redbridge bedsit, Myrtle had torn page after page from her note pad - Kitane had drawn the story of his journey from Eritrea and the brutality and horrors that had driven him from his homeland.

His Redbridge community had recognised a wonderful talent. They bought him cheap canvasses and acrylic paint. He gave them paintings for their walls and painted community banners and notices. They gave him food and clothes, and the luxuries he was unable to afford on his £40 weekly payment from the government. Kitane wasn't allowed to work; all payment was in kind.

Kitane had come to the attention of influential people on the council. Money had been raised to mount an exhibition of his work. The forward to the exhibition catalogue had been written by the council leader. She spoke of Kitane and his work as an example of the rich and diverse talent with which those who come to our shores seeking shelter and protection enrich our nation.

The walls of the gallery had hummed with the vibrant colours of the artist's homeland - the clear blues of the African skies, the red earth, the vibrant colours of his people - all with fear in their eyes. A loud belly laugh had rung out through the room.

'Oh, mi Lord, Kitane, wat yah done to mi curtains, boy?'

'What's that about?' said a voice at Sally's shoulder. 'Do you know?'

'Well, yes. I believe the canvas for the painting was made in the community centre. The fabric used was Mary's old rose patterned curtains.'

The painting attracting attention was huge, stunning! It depicted the occupants of an open-back truck travelling in darkness through a desert: men, women and children huddled together for warmth against the bone-numbing cold of the night. A man, a whip in his belt, anger etched on a face contorted with rage and violent intent, reached towards a screaming baby. The mother, her eyes terror-stricken, clutched the child to her breast. The baby, its face just visible amidst white wrappings, screamed, wide mouthed in anguish. Their fellow travellers were depicted as an amorphous mass, their faces ill-defined, spectral. At one corner of the work, crouching within the crowd, was a more defined figure, head covering pulled across his lower face, huge eyes fixed on the guard. It was Myrtle who had identified the watcher as Kitane.

'Very powerful, isn't it?'

'Yes, it is'. Sally had turned to face the man at her shoulder: Julian Arthur Tennant; Eton, 55th Oxfordshires, Military Cross. Julian was the epitome of the properly turned-out man: expensive navy suit, white shirt, blue tie with regimental gold pin, handmade oxblood lace-ups - tall, blonde, a head turner, a charmer, a totally fucked up war hero. He had been at the gallery representing Porteus Mining, one of a number of firms sponsoring the exhibition.

**

As Sally approached the table, Julian stood up and with one smooth movement, pulled out a chair, took Sal by the hand and guided her into her seat.

'You look wonderful, Sally!'

Sally was impressed. She disliked meaningless cheek pecking between relative strangers. Nicely judged, she thought.

Sally drank dry white wine and Julian had a couple of G&Ts before they moved on to Momo, where a table had been booked for 8:00 p.m. Julian was obviously well known at the restaurant; there was a lot of fussing as they were shown to one of the best tables. Sally was impressed. She had heard people at work talking about the restaurant; it was very popular, not easy to get a booking.

Julian was easy company, a good listener. Under his admiring gaze, Sally relaxed. She found herself opening up about her relationship with Jack, telling him of her decision to end the relationship.

'Well, Sally, we appear to be in the same unhappy position. Sadly, my marriage is also at an end. Like you and Jack, Lucy and I have grown apart. We don't see eye to eye on very much these days.'

'I'm sorry.'

'Yeh, sad when relationships come to an end. Distressing!'

'Do you have children, Julian?'

'Two, Cosima is nine, and Benedict seven. Lovely kids! Yourself?'

'No children. Cosima, that's an unusual name!'

'Is it? I've heard Lucy say that there are two others of the same name in her prep school!'

'Oh really! I haven't come across the name before! Do you see much of them?'

'Most weekends. I drive down on Friday evening, take Benedict to the cricket or rugby; father and son bonding time, you know.'

'And bonding with your daughter, of course?'

'Cos? Yeh, of course, gives her girlie time with her mother.

Shopping for pink and fluffy things - you know, the sort of things girls like to do.'

Oh, dear, what have we got here? Good job Myrtle isn't here to hear about the pink fluffiness!

'Your wife seems very laid back. Very accommodating. That kind of arrangement wouldn't work for Jack and me; it would be one constant row.'

'Try to keep it civilised for the kids, you know!'

'Yes, I imagine that becomes a top priority for parents. We don't have that problem. How long have you been living apart?'

'Became a way of life for us. Hardly at home when I was in the army. Since joining the firm, I need to be in London. Lucy prefers country life.'

'Which regiment were you in? My cousin is in the army!'

'The Flash.'

'I'm sorry?'

'There I go. Force of habit, using the old sobriquet. The 55th Oxfordshire.'

'Oh, I see!'

'You and Myrtle seem good friends?'

'Yes, very good friends.'

Julian neatly swung the conversation to Kitane, his paintings and her work with Myrtle. The gulf in class between them was becoming too apparent; Julian was attempting to steer back onto less contentious ground. He gave her his full attention as she talked of the hardship that drove people to food banks. He made appropriate sympathetic noises, but Sal doubted that he could even conceive of the existence of such people. She was cooling towards Julian. He was a nice guy, charming, but not for her. They had nothing in common and he was carrying a weight of baggage. Cosima, indeed! She was quite sure there were no Cosimas in her niece Alice's class in her state 'prep' school. Perhaps he sensed her unease as he reached across the table and took hold of her hands.

'You're a wonderful girl, Sally, I really want to see you again. What do you say? Shall we make another date?'

He really did know how to flatter! Under his steady gaze, her reservations slipped away, her inability to say 'no' overcoming her better judgment. She could hear Myrtle's voice - 'Sal, darling, you really need to practice using that one little word. It's a most useful little word, a word that can enable you to please yourself rather than others. People won't hold it against you; they will still like you. I promise!'

Jack was still up when she got home. He was sitting in the dark watching TV, feet up on the coffee table, nursing a can of lager. Several empty tins littering the table.

'You're late!'

'Yes, it is late. I'm going straight to bed.'

'Before you go, perhaps you would like to tell me where I can find a clean shirt for the morning?'

'I have no idea! You do your own shirts. Have you forgotten? My attempts don't meet with your high standards.'

'High standards! Jesus, Sal, all I want is a washed and ironed shirt!'

'Good night, Jack.' Sally closed the door and headed for the spare bedroom.

She turned the key in the lock and sat on the bed. He had been sitting up, spoiling for a fight; she wasn't about to give him the satisfaction. Minutes later, she could hear him bumping around in the bathroom, stumbling in the passageway. The doorknob turned, turned again, rattled.

'Sal, open the door. Open the door, Sal, I just want to talk. Please, Sal,' - wheedling, pathetic tone - vigorous rattling of the knob - 'Come on, Sal,' - fists hammering on the door, body slamming into the door - 'Open the door you bloody bitch, open

the fucking door!' - the door moving, hinges straining.
Please God, don't let the door give. He's completely lost it!

'Fuck you, Sal. Why don't you just fuck off to bloody Myrtle,' - several kicks to the door. Shuffling across the passageway, banging, and crashing about in the bedroom – silence.

Sally held her breath and listened. For the first time, rape came into her mind. He was seriously crazed! He had been on more than lager, no doubt a good few 'whisky chasers' as he called them. He had never really hurt her but had come close to it. Sal listened. No noise: he had crashed out on the bed.

Thank God. I have to end this.

He was still asleep when she left the following morning. She had crept about so as not to wake him; dressed in the clothes she had taken off the night before; washed in cold water; the boiler was noisy, it would kick in if she turned on the hot tap, skipped breakfast.

Julian messaged to say he had tickets for the opera for Friday night - Don Giovanni. What did she think? Sally messaged to say she hadn't seen it, but yes, she would like to go.

'Wonderful piece of tragic nonsense; you'll love it. J'

She shopped at Tesco and went straight home. She prepared Jack's favourite beef and pancetta lasagna, defrosted an M&S raspberry meringue, set a nice table, and put a couple of bottles of Chablis in the fridge.

Sally had a plan. She knew exactly how Jack would behave. There would be apologies for his behaviour the night before. There would be out of character offers of help with the meal, the clearing of the table, the stacking of the dishwasher; in short, he would make an absolute nuisance of himself.

After dinner she intended to tell him about the visit she planned to make, together with Myrtle and Art, to the Calais refugee camp. Tell him that they needed a little time out from one another, that the trip would be the ideal opportunity. She wouldn't make it sound too serious; he was to be eased gently into a permanent separation. Myrtle couldn't understand her reluctance to face Jack, to tell him their marriage was over, make a clean break. But then Myrtle didn't know about Jack's temper, or his flaring anger, of her awareness that he was on the edge of violence. She didn't know because Sally hadn't told her. Sally was too ashamed to confide in her friend. Too ashamed to admit to the weakness that had kept her tied to an overbearing, manipulative man.

Sally didn't get past the first hurdle. Jack blew his top when told about Calais.

'What the hell are you thinking! Why would you want to go to a stinking hole like that?' he said. Went on about violent economic migrants. Called Myrtle vacuous, brain dead! Sally was truly shocked - shocked by the language he used about desperate people, shocked at how he spoke of her friends. Shocked and very angry. It was anger that overcame her fear, anger that enabled her to pack an overnight bag and leave.

She gave the taxi driver Myrtle's Peckham address and sat back in her seat. She took off her wedding and engagement rings and dropped them into the zipper pouch of her bag. She held out her left hand; she felt so much better, free, excited.

That's the last he'll see of me!

Being perfectly honest with herself, she had to admit that Julian's reaction to the trip hadn't been encouraging. It wasn't so much what Julian said, it was what he didn't say that gave the clue.

'Do take care, Sal. Could be a bit rough over there. I don't know, of course, no firsthand experience. It looks a bit hair raising in media reports.'

The following morning, the messages started, hourly messages: 'Where are you, Sal?' - 'Ring me, Sal?' - 'For God's sake, answer' -

'Sorry, I was rude about Myrtle, it's just that I worry about you,' - on and on. She deleted all messages and put her phone on mute. She knew she should reply; tell him that she had made her decision, that their relationship was over. She needed to make him understand that it wasn't a spur of the moment decision, nothing to do with his latest rudeness about Myrtle, that it had been yet another instance of his failure to respect her friends, her opinions, her choices. She continued to delete his messages; she knew it was cowardly, but she couldn't face the arguments, the pleas.

She had given up trying to pinpoint when the relationship had started to unravel. Meeting Myrtle had been a turning point. Myrtle had given her confidence in her own opinions, given her self-belief, had enabled her to challenge Jack. She had reached the conclusion that the marriage had been blighted from the beginning.

She had met Jack shortly after moving to London to take up her present job. She had been flat sharing in Richmond. Sally and her flat-mate, Molly, often met up in the local pub after work. The Green Duck did a two for the price of one evening meal and was frequented by a young, lively crowd. It was in The Duck that they had met. She had admired his understated self-confidence. He had old fashioned manners; held doors open for women, jumped up and offered his seat. Manners that had gone out of fashion but admired by Sally.

He was no head-turner; medium height; only a little taller than Sally herself; medium build; regular features; beautiful eyes. His eyes were of the kind she had heard her gran describe as 'melting' - liquid, expressive, deep-lash fringed. His short, side parted, slicked-down hair should have looked old fashioned, stuffy, but on Jack, it was edgy, cool.

Soon they were seeing each other every day and spending most nights together. They were regular visitors at his parent's home in

Windsor, and she took him to Newcastle to meet her parents. Within six months, they were engaged and within twelve months, married. With a large deposit, a wedding present from his parents, they had bought a two-bed flat in Richmond. They liked the area, had friends there and property prices were just affordable. They had returned from a honeymoon in Bali and settled into married life.

Everything should have been perfect, for a while it was. They were both young, had agreed to put off having a family for a few years, get some savings together, get on a firm financial footing. It was little things that began to niggle with Sally. She began to think his hairstyle significant. Jack had the mindset and traits of her grandfather. The cleaning, shopping, cooking, the washing and ironing were, in his opinion, women's work. Getting him to wash up was as much as she was able to achieve. His mother was a lovely person but had archaic ideas about men and housework. His father had never washed a pot or wielded a duster in his life. Sal doubted that Ron knew what a hoover was.

Jack's sister, Julia, considered her mother a slave to her father and said so openly. Sally liked Julia; they had got on well together. She had her reservations about the way Julia spoke to her husband, Graham; she could be quite scathing! It wasn't good, but Sally kind of understood what drove Julia; it was impossible to get a reaction from the guy. Sally didn't like him. She had a feeling that behind his dead-pan expression, he was laughing at them all. She secretly thought him quite creepy.

Jack had strong opinions on most matters, politics in particular. Like his father, he was a member of the Conservative Party; he had been a Young Conservative. Sally had resisted his efforts to get her to join the party. Her parents, her whole family were Labour Party supporters. They wouldn't think of voting anything but Labour. He enjoyed nothing better than correcting Sally's political views.

Sally started to keep her opinions to herself. She read her book or magazine or searched the clothes or home categories on eBay, leaving him to shout at the TV. She interested herself in decorating the flat, buying the furnishings and furniture they could afford. She tried to be happy, but a niggling little voice, which she tried very hard to ignore, told her otherwise.

One morning, sitting on the tube, she thought, *God, he's trying to turn me into his mother.* The thought came out of nowhere, erupting from some hidden, suppressed place, bringing with it a barely controllable panic.

**

Myrtle was wonderful, made her comfortable in her spare room. She would have been quite happy for Sally to move in permanently, but Sally had no intention of taking advantage of her friend's good nature and booked appointments with a couple of letting agents. The day after leaving, she had taken a day off work and gone with Myrtle to the flat.

'OK, let's get your stuff out. He needs to understand it's final. I don't trust you to stick to your resolve. You're a soft touch, Sal! Does he have my address?'

'He knows you live in Peckham but has no idea of the address.'

'Good, it will be like searching for the proverbial needle!'

Myrtle drove her over to Richmond. They emptied Sally's wardrobe, packed up all her belongings and piled them into the van. Myrtle had thought to bring stickers to identify furniture belonging to Sally. Rummaging in a drawer, Sally found cards and wrapping paper. She wrapped up the wedding album, video and her rings and left them on the coffee table. Myrtle had googled storage facilities and contacted a company in Tottenham that seemed very reasonable. They would come the following evening to collect Sally's furniture. A card telling Jack of the arrangement and explaining her reasons for leaving was propped against the parcel.

Sally stood in the hallway and looked back through the open doors into the rooms she had shared with Jack for the past four years; Myrtle's orange stickers appeared to Sally as a myriad of tiny witnesses to their failed relationship, they gave the place the look of an auction room, a repository for abandoned and failed hopes and dreams.

The following Saturday, Sally went clothes shopping. She was finding her wardrobe of jeans, casual tops and work clothes totally inadequate for dinners at the Wolsely and the Goring or drinks at George's Bar, not to mention seats in the grand tier at the opera and dining in the opulent Crush Room.

Sally had entered a new world! Trawling the familiar, affordable, high-street stores, she thought, not for the first time, of Julian's wife. Where, she wondered, did Lucy shop? In places well out of her price range, she was sure. Lucinda! That was Lucy's real name. She didn't think that women named Lucinda shopped in Top Shop or River Island. She tried to get a mental picture of this wonderfully accommodating woman - a woman who was prepared to entertain her estranged husband every weekend. Was Lucy a blonde, like herself? She thought it likely; it was generally accepted that men went for the same type. Was she a glamorous or a fresh-air, wellies-type person? She preferred to live in the country, so possibly the latter! Julian was thirty-nine; was Lucy the same age?

She was in Zara, eying up a deep blue, narrow strapped sheath dress, when the voices drew her attention.

'Oh, Mummy, please. All my friends are wearing them!' The girl was about twelve or thirteen. She was holding up a garish, multi-coloured, tie-dyed top.

'Agatha, darling, it's disgusting, truly disgusting!'

Sally listened and watched while giving the blue dress added attention. The voices were female versions of Julian's. Mother and daughter were blonde haired; the girl's shoulder length hair was worn loose, the mother's upswept into a chignon. Without hearing the voices, she would have recognised them as upper class. What was it, she wondered, that marked them out? There was nothing unusual about their clothes; the girl wore brown jeans and a white top, the mother wore a floaty skirt and pale pink tea shirt. They were clothes she might wear herself. It was something about the way they wore the clothes - the way they carried themselves. Even the most scruffily dressed of their class were recognizable as such.

'It's dreadful quality. It will fall apart in no time.'

'It won't, Mummy. Rowena has worn hers loads and it's still OK.'

'Darling, don't say loads, say often or many times. Well, if you are determined to have it, you can pay for it out of your own account. I'm not encouraging you to buy tat.'

Sally watched them walk towards the check-out, the girl clutching her prize. It could so easily be Julian's wife, his daughter in a few years' time. Would his daughter have her own account? They might as well live on another planet!

Sally returned to Myrtle's pretty pleased with her purchases - something for every occasion. £580 well spent! She had a couple of stunning dresses, the blue sheath from Zara and a similar dress in red from Gap. With her corn blonde hair, she could wear any bright colour. And high heels! She couldn't remember when she had last bought high heels. Finding somewhere to live wasn't proving so easy. She had viewed a couple of places. She had been to see a one bed in Bexley and a large bedsit in Newham. The Bexley flat was tiny and the rent exorbitant, the Newham bedsit needed a thorough refurb. She knew that Julian was secretly pleased at her lack of success.

'I know it's a bit soon, but I do wish you would think about my place. I don't expect an answer right away. Do think about it, Sal.'

'Julian, I have just walked away from a failed marriage. I'm not ready, not in the right frame of mind to make such a commitment. I need far more time.'

'Of course you do. You take all the time you need. I'll be waiting!'

Chapter 6

Lucinda

Julian's dark blue, BMW was parked on the forecourt.

'Oh, look, Mummy, Daddy's home,' said Cosima, as they turned into the driveway.

'Yes, I can see that,' said Lucy.

'He's come to take me to rugby,' said Ben.

'No, he hasn't, stupid! He's come to hear about my audition. Hasn't he, Mummy?'

'That's quite enough, I'm sure Daddy's looking forward to seeing you both.'

Julian was in the kitchen, making coffee. Cosima flung her arms about her father's neck.

'Daddy, Daddy, I'm almost certain to get the part! I was the best. Bea was quite good, but she didn't project. Harriet was hopeless, really stiff. Mrs. Giles is bound to choose me.'

'That's wonderful, Cos! I have every confidence in my lovely daughter,' said Julian, laughing as he held Cosima's hand high above her head while she pirouetted on the spot.

'You've come to take me to rugby, haven't you, Daddy?' A pushing and shoving match started as Ben tried to push in between Cosima and his father.

'I'll be taking you to rugby, Ben. Get your kit together and both of you get changed.' Lucy directed a silencing look towards her husband.

'But I want Daddy to take me.'

'Daddy has a lot of work on this evening.'

'But Daddy, you promised!' wailed Ben.

'Don't argue. Go and get changed,' said Lucy.

'Sorry, old sport. Lots on this evening! Make sure I'm free next week. Defo, next week.'

When they were alone, Lucy turned to her husband, 'What the hell do you think you're up to? You're as high as a kite!'

'Oh, come on, Luce, that's a bit strong!'

'No, it isn't. You're not fit to drive. If you want to kill yourself, go ahead, but there's no way you are driving my child in that state!' Lucy picked up her bag, threw it over her shoulder and walked into the hall.

'Come on, Ben, get your skates on or you'll be late.' She sat waiting in the car, white knuckled hands gripping the steering wheel; furious. She no longer loved Julian! She didn't much care what he did in London, but what he did while at home affected the children. For several years, they had played out their travesty of a relationship, deceiving family and friends, attempting to convince themselves that it was done for the benefit of the children.

Afghanistan had robbed Lucy of her husband. What had been returned to her was a frighteningly life-like carapace that looked like Julian, sounded like Julian, but housed an altogether different man. It was Julian's tragedy that his physical body had lived on while his soul and spirit had died with his men in the remains of a concrete village in the sands of Helmand Province. At first, she had refused to acknowledge her loss. She had probed the carapace, determined to encourage the real Julian to emerge. In her anger, she had hammered and banged on the hard shell until, in the end, she understood that it was only a physical image that remained. The man that inhabited Julian's body refused to admit to being an imposter; instead, he drugged his senses and shunned the dark shadow that stood at his shoulder by day and terrorised his sleeping hours. Lucy was the only person who knew of Julian's death.

Not for the first time on a Friday evening, Lucy sat down to dinner with her children while their father lay crashed out on his bed. She was tired of lying to them, saying that Daddy was very tired, that Daddy had been working very hard in London. Tired of looking at the doubt in their eyes,

'Poor Daddy! I wish he didn't have to work so hard; it makes him very sad. But, Mummy, have you noticed that his eyes get very sore? I asked him about it. He said it's why he wears his sunglasses. Perhaps he needs to have an eye test. Hugo Williams went for a test when Mrs. Giles noticed that he couldn't see the board properly. He has glasses now. Hugo's eyes used to get sore; that's what made me think about Daddy!' This from her nine-year-old daughter. Cosima and Ben were no longer babies. Cosima was beginning to ask questions and notice things.

'Daddy hasn't got sore eyes. He looks cool. His glasses are mega. I'm going to get some,' said Ben.

'That's really stupid. It's not good to ignore sore eyes, is it, Mummy?'

'No, Cos, it isn't good, you're perfectly right.'

Lucy sat alone in the semi-darkness, a single lamp switched on at the far end of the sitting room, a bottle of wine on the table in front of her. The children were asleep, Julian was in his own bedroom. It had been a long time since Lucy and Julian had shared a bed. It was fear that had driven her from the marital bed - fear for her life. The trained killer in Julian had a habit of emerging in the hours of darkness.

Lucy let her mind wonder back over the years of their marriage - a marriage she knew she should end. She saw a young Lucinda Bowes, upper six, about to take her 'A' levels. She was spending the weekend at the home of her best friend, Clara Tennant. The girls were sitting together on a bench at the side of the tennis court. Out of breath, red in the face, she had looked up and seen him making his way down the steps towards them.

Clara raised her arm and waved, 'It's Julian!'

The garden swung about the house in deep terraces; the levels joined by wide flights of steps. The tennis court was on the lower level. Lucy watched him as he made his way down the steps towards them; tall, blonde haired, beautiful, just graduated from Sandhurst. It was the moment she had fallen in love with Julian. He was twenty-three; she seventeen, his baby sister's best friend. It was four years later, at Clara's wedding, that they got together, become a couple. They were married a year later.

Their first home had been a small flat in Oxford. Julian's regiment was based just outside the city. It was while they lived in Oxford that Cosima was born. Such happy times! Julian loved his little, blonde daughter; she was so like her father. The present house was bought just before Julian embarked on his last, ill-fated tour of Afghanistan in October 2009. Benedict was born while his father was on tour; he was three months old when Julian returned. The real Julian never saw his son; Benedict had never known his real father. With a young child to care for and a baby on the way, Lucy hadn't wanted to stay in Oxford with Julian away. Always the country girl at heart, she had wanted to return to her roots; to be near to her own and Julian's family.

They had learned of the house through Julian's parents. Old friends of theirs in the next village were about to put their house on the market. Ted, Julian's father, arranged for them to have a private viewing. The house was in a tiny hamlet of two other houses and a gentrified row of what had been labourer's cottages just outside Burford in Oxfordshire. It was an area Lucy knew well; her own family was a twenty-minute drive away.

The house, euphemistically called Sea Cottage, had six bedrooms and three bathrooms. Dating from the late seventeen hundreds, it had embraced the additions and changes of time to present a pleasing face to the world. It was crowned by a cloak of brown thatch that fringed windows set high in walls of mellow Cotswold brick. Roses crept over aged garden walls and copper beech hedging complemented peach-tinted walls.

Lucy had felt the old, worn flagstones beneath her feet, stood before the huge, stone fireplace, walked the passageways that linked the time-added rooms, looked out under deep overhanging eaves at the ancient fruit trees, the trickling stream that bordered the garden and had fallen deeply in love.

There had been a mad dash to finalise the purchase so that Julian could see Lucy into their new home before his tour began.

'Are you sure about this, Luce? It's a big change from our little flat. You will be on your own with Cosima and the baby on the way! We can go ahead and finalise things, but you don't have to move in until I get back.'

But Lucy had wanted to move in. She felt a deep need to be in the house, a need that she couldn't explain. Since the latest tour had been announced, she had felt a growing unease. It wasn't Julian's first tour, but this was a feeling she hadn't experienced before. Daphne, Julian's mother, had viewed his past tours with dread, a dread that she fought hard to hide from Lucy. But Lucy hadn't felt her fear, had believed that he would return to her unscathed. This time, it felt different. She tried to put the feeling down to her condition but couldn't quite banish the anxiety.

The whole family had pitched in to get her settled in their new home. The Palmers had arranged for their gardener to continue, and Hazel, who 'did' for Daphne, 'stretched herself' to manage three, two-hour sessions for Lucy. Her mother arranged for a company of interior designers from London to design and decorate a room for Cosima and a nursery for the baby. Lucy bought a bed for the spare room and their own bedroom furniture occupied one of the larger bedrooms to the front of the house. Otherwise, the house was sparsely furnished with the few pieces that had crowded the Oxford flat.

The people, in what the locals called the 'village', were welcoming and friendly without being intrusive. Lucy enrolled Cosima in a playgroup in Burford and took her there three mornings a week. She joined with a group of other mothers who went for coffee and sometimes lunched together when the sessions ended. Daphne and Ted were a ten-minute drive away; Lucy often visited in the afternoon, or Daphne came to her for afternoon tea.

But the times Lucy liked best were the evenings when she was alone with Cosima. She would sit at the little pine table that was far too small for the kitchen with Cosima in her highchair by her side. Cosima was a calm, thoughtful child. She had been an easy baby, sleeping through the night at just over four months. She had spent hours cooing and reaching up to the animals suspended from a mobile twirling above her cot. She rarely cried; even teething had proceeded without much anguish, the little white seeds popping seemingly effortlessly from her pink gums.

As the daylight faded, they became wrapped in the cosy glow of the light above the big, green Aga. Sitting in the half-light, eating her own meal, she watched Cosima's chubby little fingers moving over her plate, her full attention fixed on the little squares of fish fingers and sliced carrot as she tried to decide which piece to grasp. For pudding, she liked little mini-pot yoghurts that she had become most proficient at eating with her plastic spoon. The meal finished, Lucy would put the plates into the dishwasher, unbuckle Cosima from her highchair and carry her upstairs to her own bedroom. Two years old and quite tall, Cosima was in her first bed.

'Cosima, do that, Mummy,' she would say if Lucy offered too much help while she dressed or undressed. She tried to fold her clothes; managing to get them into a bundle and put them on her chair. Her shoes, she put side by side on the floor. Sometimes, struggling to get something over her head or taking off leggings, she would say, 'Mummy can help!' Her pyjamas on, she would go to her bookshelf and choose a book, more often than not, 'The Elephant and the Bad Baby'; she never tired of hearing about their naughty romp. The story finished, she would jump into bed, point to the characters on her duvet cover, and say, 'Daddy say dats Mr. Big Ears and dats Pwikly Fweddy,' before pulling the cover up to her chin and closing her eyes.

The duvet cover had a pattern of hares and hedgehogs. Julian had named them for Cosima. Her room had been decorated in shades of white, mauve and grey. Mr. Big Ears featured prominently; even her little chair was made in the form of a grey hare with huge ears. Cosima talked a lot about Mr. Big Ears and Prickly Freddy. Julian had made up a lot of stories to amuse his little daughter.

When Cosima was asleep, Lucy would wonder through the warren of upstairs passageways, going from room to room. In the very old rooms, she liked to run her hands over the unevenly plastered walls and bleached wooden supports. She looked down on the garden, cloaked in its mysterious darkness and felt the comforting arms of the house close about her.

When it was chilly, she would put a match to the kindling in the kitchen grate and watch the fire spring to life. She would seat herself in one of the big, Georgian armchairs that stood to either side of the hearth. The chairs had been Daphne's latest finds in an Oxford antiques centre. She would rest her head against the chair back, close her eyes and think of those, who, over the centuries, had sat by the ancient fireplace, had looked beyond the flames into the age blackened hearth and wondered if they also had felt the strong infinity with the old house that she felt. As the wind sighed in the chimney, she dozed in the flickering firelight and let the aged bricks tell their stories, and the centuries old whisperings lull her to sleep.

When the weather was warmer, she took the baby alarm and sat on the lower terrace. She watched the bats fly from under the eaves, their small black shapes tumbling through the darkening sky. She heard the owls calling; caught glimpses of their silvery shadows as they glided through the trees. She listened to the gentle gurgling and soothing splashing of the stream, put her hand on her swollen stomach and felt her baby move. She thought of Julian, of the happy times in Oxford, of the short time they had spent together in their new home before he left for Afghanistan. She didn't think of him in Afghanistan. She had a strange, superstitious feeling that she mustn't picture him in that place; to do so was to invite disaster, to make real the fears that she kept locked away, refused to confront.

Benedict had been ten days overdue. Everything had been arranged. Lucy's bag, together with a bag for Cosima, had been packed. Cosima was to be dropped off at her Auntie Clara's house. In Julian's absence, Daphne was to be Lucy's 'birthing partner'. Daphne found her title most amusing.

'I'm very touched and feel very honoured to be chosen, darling, but really, these modern terms are very silly. In my day, we would have spoken of being present at the birth.'

Despite being overdue, the pains that had woken her at 6:00 in the morning had come as a surprise to Lucy. She had called Daphne, who had arrived within minutes, dressed Cosima, made Lucy a drink, gathered up their bags and bundled both into the car. They had been on their way before Lucy had time to think. Benedict had been born at 2:48 in the afternoon. He weighed 7 lb, 2oz. He had a head of dark hair - Lucy's hair.

Cosima wasn't impressed with her brother. 'He too small, Mummy and he winkly like hippo. Mr. Hippo winkly like new baby. Hair not like Cosi,' and after a long pause and much consideration, 'It bwown.'

'Yes, darling, he has brown hair, and you have blonde hair. You both have beautiful hair,' Lucy had said.

'Baby hair not nice, Mummy. It bwown and it not smoov like Cosi. It howid, it wuf.' Cosima, it appeared, had expected a ready grown, blonde-haired sibling, made in her own image and likeness.

Julian had been over the moon; the grandparents delighted; Julian's father, thrilled. Benedict was his first grandson to bear the Tennant name. All partying and celebration were to be put on hold until Julian's return. But Benedict was nothing like Cosima had been as a baby. He was a poor feeder; Lucy's breasts had become sore and swollen forcing her to give up breast-feeding. The togetherness and peace of Lucy and Cosima's life together had been shattered by Benedict's demands and noise.

'Bendy always cwying, Mummy,' Cosima would complain, as she trotted after Lucy, tugging at her mother's jeans. She had pulled a doll from her toy cupboard - a doll she had never liked. The doll was an asexual creature with soft, padded, rubbery skin. It could swallow, wee and cry. Lucy had found Cosima in the sitting room; the doll, stripped bare, was lying face down on the sofa, being smacked very hard on its bottom. When asked what she was doing, Cosima had said, 'He a very bad baby, Mummy, he always cwying, he need bottom smacking.'

Lucy had been shocked; she hadn't thought that Cosima knew about smacking. She had never been smacked and she couldn't imagine she had seen another child being smacked. The implications of her daughter's behaviour had alarmed Lucy. Lucy's mother had stayed overnight and declared Benedict a handful. She had wanted to hire a nanny. Lucy had refused,

'I think it would be a poor show if I couldn't look after two young children. After all, I don't have to work for a living. It's not as though I have anything else to do.'

Daphne had been Lucy's rock. She came in the mornings and evenings and often stayed overnight. When Lucy had been up half the night with Benedict, Daphne would take over, allow her to catch up with her sleep, feed, wash and dress the children, and if need be, put them in their car seats and drive to Cosima's play group.

She felt the drops on her neck, put her hand to her face and felt the wetness; only then did she realise that she was crying.

**

Lucy had been changing Benedict's nappy. She had seen them from the nursery window. She had recognised the military registration as the car turned in at the gates and drove slowly on to the gravelled forecourt. She had stood transfixed as the doors opened and two uniformed figures got out. They had stood for a moment, put on their hats, exchanged a long look, stood shoulder to shoulder and walked towards the house. Lucy had known what it meant, she had expected them, wondered when they would come.

She had leant for support against the drawers of the changing unit, gripping the guard rail to stop herself sliding to the floor, every ounce of energy drained from her body. Finding that she had been holding her breath; she lifted her head and gulped in great mouthfuls of air. Picking up the half-dressed baby, she walked towards the nursery door. Her feet had felt strangely rubbery as she placed them on the boards. Propping herself against the passageway walls, leaning, half bent, across the stair rail, the baby pinned beneath one arm, she had made her way forward and flung open the front door. Standing before her had been a woman sergeant and a major whom she had thought she recognised. She had heard the major's voice, 'Mrs Tennant?' - saw the sergeant dash forward, felt Benedict grabbed, felt the strength of the majors arms around her, heard the sergeant's voice, 'In here, sir, bring her in here.'

She must have passed out. When she came to, she had been sitting on the sofa, the sergeant by her side with Benedict on her knee, Cosima standing on the sofa between them. The major had been sitting in front of her on a side chair he had pulled over. She had thought she was going to be sick.

'Head down, deep breaths,' the sergeant had said, gently easing Lucy's head down.

'It's all right, Mrs Tennant, it's not the worst news. Major Tennant is alive. He isn't critically injured. He's on his way to the UK. Mrs Tennant, do you understand what I'm telling you. It's Lucinda, isn't it. Do you understand Lucinda? I'm Major Morgan, I think you may remember me.'

Lucy had nodded. 'Yes, I understand. Lucy please, everyone calls me Lucy.'

'Yes, Lucy! Terrible shock, I know, having us arrive unannounced. Unfortunately, there's no other way of doing these things.'

Cosima had started to cry, alarmed at her mother's distress - her arms about Lucy's neck.

She remembered pulling Cosima onto her lap, hugging her daughter to her, saying, 'It's all right, darling, Mummy's better now.'

There had been the sound of tyres on the gravel, a car door closing, the doorbell ringing. The sergeant had got to her feet and gone into the hall.

'It's Major Tennant's father, sir,' said the sergeant, returning to the room.

Very little happened, went unnoticed, in sleepy Oxfordshire villages! The military car and personnel had been spotted driving through Burford, heading towards the house. Two and two had quickly been put together, and Ted, alerted to their presence, had got into his car and driven to stand by Lucy's side, preparing to hear the most devastating news that any father would ever hear! Ted would remain calm, do his duty. Lucy was filled with admiration for his stoicism and courage as he rushed into the room, the house phone in his hand.

'How are you, my dear? A dreadful shock for you. In my rush, I came without my mobile. Must ring Daffers; left her in a most dreadful state!'

After dinner, she had sat with Daphne beside the kitchen fire. They had sat in companionable silence, lost in their own thoughts, warmed by the flames that licked the logs to a glowing orange. Cosima had been asleep, and for once, Benedict had settled early. Daphne had arrived just after the military had left, advised stiff G&Ts and made lunch. After Ted had gone home, they had cried together and indulged in relived laughter.

Theirs wasn't the usual daughter-in-law, mother-in-law, relationship. Daphne had been a substitute mother to Lucy since she was twelve years old. Her father's work in construction had seen Lucy attending a number of prep schools in the Middle East. At twelve, she had been sent home to attend boarding school. She had been one of the girls who were obliged to spend their holidays in school. Daphne had confided years later that she thought it a most cruel way to treat a child. Lucy had been lucky; she had been taken under Daphne's wing and spent her holidays with her best friend Clara Tennant. Clara's home had become her home; it had been her base throughout university, her home before her marriage. Daphne had guided her through school, through her teens, had been the shoulder on which she cried when things went wrong, the first person to hear of her successes.

Her parents' contribution had been profuse thanks to Daphne, flying visits, a generous allowance and expensive presents for Daphne, Clara and herself. Lucy was married by the time her father retired and her parents moved to their present home.

A log had rolled forward, sending a shower of sparks up the chimney. Shards of burning wood and grey ash had tumbled from the grate onto the hearth. Lucy had reached for the fire tongues to deposit the burning pieces back into the fire. Watching Lucy as she swept the hearth of the fallen ash, Daphne had articulated the thought to the fore of both their minds, 'That's it, darling, it's over! They will never be able to send him to another war zone.'

The date had been 12th February 2010. A day seared in Lucy's memory.

**

Lucy picked up the empty wine bottle and glass, took them to the kitchen, turned off the lamp and went upstairs. She crept into Cosima's bedroom. It had become a nightly ritual to check on her nine-year-old daughter and seven-year-old son, to stand by their beds and listen to their breathing. She knew it to be ridiculous; it had become one of the many superstitious rituals that she had allowed to creep in and govern her life. Cosima lay on her back, her blonde hair fanned out on the pillow, her face serene, a slight smile playing about her lips. She knew exactly how Benedict would look. He would be on his side, knees pulled up as though he strove for a fetal position, his dark hair tufty, disordered, a slight puzzled frown on his face. She put an ear to Julian's door - just gentle snoring!

Chapter 7

Christian

Jack was late out of work. He had been held up by Austin Peters, who had asked for a file just as he was leaving. Jack had an arrangement with Jock. He made up a story about unusual congestion on the tube at the later time of travelling home. He was now starting at 8:30 and finishing at 5:00. The arrangement with Jock was only a partial success. He rarely got out in time to follow Tennant. But that evening, he had made a dash to get to Kingsway and got lucky. Just as he approached the Porteus building, Tennant had come running down the steps. He took his usual route across Aldwych, but instead of heading for Waterloo Bridge, he had turned left onto The Strand.

Jack found himself retracing the steps he had taken only minutes before. He followed Tennant down Milford Lane and into Temple Place. Sal was waiting for him outside Temple Station. She was wearing a new, dark blue denim dress. She looked gorgeous! It was Friday rush hour; a great crush of people were racing for trains; lots of cover! It was a station he knew; he risked it and followed them.

The crowd was fast-moving. He kept his eyes on Sal's blonde head as they made their way past the Circle line and on to the District. He stood well down the platform, edging towards them only when the train was pulling in. Getting into the next carriage, he jammed himself against the doors, keeping an eye on the platform. It was hard work! He was jostled as people got on and off, and had very nearly missed them, when, lost in the great mass of bodies, they left the train at Fulham Broadway. He spotted them at the last minute; just managed to jam the doors open and jump off.

Jack was discovering that following without being seen wasn't that easy, but he was getting the hang of it - tailing, that's what they called it in detective novels! Open areas were tricky, turning corners dicey, judging the following distance critical. Always keeping a look-out for suitable cover to dodge into was a good idea. He followed them out of the station and on to Fulham Road. Tennant seemed unusually animated, gesturing wildly. After a good ten-minute walk, they made a left turn and stopped a short way down a street of Victorian terraced houses. They stood at the edge of the pavement, looking up at a house with a 'For Sale' board in the front garden.

Jack dodged into a newsagent on the main road, from where he had a good view of the pair, who were sitting on the low wall in front of the house. He made a pretense of looking through magazines on the racks that were conveniently positioned near the window. Tennant kept checking his watch; they were obviously waiting for someone! They got to their feet as a black Merc drew into the kerb. A suited and booted guy jumped from the car; hand outstretched in greeting. Jack recognised an estate agent when he saw one! Watches were consulted, as the suit gestured in Jack's direction, indicating heavy traffic, no doubt, apologizing for his late arrival. Leading the way up the path, the agent unlocked the door and held it invitingly open.

Hell! They are buying a house together!

The guy behind the counter was beginning to look suspicious; there was only so long you could read through magazines without drawing attention. It was a good three quarters of an hour before the door opened and they reappeared. There was more chat and handshakes before the agent got into his car and drove off. Sal and Tennant came back down the street and walked away in the direction of the station. Jack bought a magazine, walked to the house, noted the number and the selling agent.

The following morning, he phoned and made an appointment to view the house at 12:30 and arranged with Jock to take an extended lunch hour. He was cautioned by the agent, who had introduced herself as Pam, that an offer above the asking price was confidently expected by the close of business that day. It was a fairly standard Victorian terrace; small garden to the front, bigger garden at the back, four and a bit beds, converted attic, two rooms knocked into one downstairs, an extended, well-fitted kitchen.

Nice place, but Jesus, 1.5 million!

The agent was doing her upbeat, enthusiastic chatter! Jack wasn't listening. They were standing in the 'master bedroom' - a large, first-floor room looking out on the back garden. He pictured Sal's things strewn about a king size bed, surely not their bed - the bed she had taken and stashed away in the storage unit in Tottenham, the bed they had shared for more than four years. For Christ's sake, surely, she wouldn't go that far! He suspected that she just might; it being a wedding present from her parents and all that. He felt sick; he had to get out of the place!

He was back at work by 2:00, but he couldn't concentrate. Images of Sal and Tennant in the house on Edgar Street plagued his mind. He pulled a sickie and was on his way home by 3:00. It wasn't much of a lie; he couldn't shake off a debilitating nausea. He didn't doubt that the offer expected by the agents was from Tennant. They were moving out of his flat, buying a house, setting up home together. Sal was serious about the guy; it was no casual affair.

Sal's not coming back. I've lost her. It's bloody Myrtle's fault - all that left-wing crap she's put into Sal's head. Probably introduced her to Tennant.

He wanted to shout, kick and punch everything in sight. He felt emasculated, cheated. It was all spiralling out of his control. He came out of the station and rushed along the pavement. He felt a desperate need to get home. He was running, head down, when he almost collided with a guy standing at the entrance to the flats. For a moment, before recognition dawned, he thought it was Julian Tennant - same height, same blonde hair, same look.

'Hey, mate, what's the rush?'

Jack stared; the images of two blonde men competing for recognition.

'It's me, mate! Don't you recognise your old buddy?'

'Christian?'

**

Jack had been halfway through his first term at Harriman Hall Comprehensive when Christian entered his life. They had met at the school gates. It was Christian's first day. He was tall, blonde, edgy, his uniform just legal, his bag slung carelessly across his shoulder. He moved with long, confident strides to face whatever obstacles the world threw in his path. Jack was in awe!

Christian's dad was in the army, serving abroad. His mum, fed up living as a lone parent in army accommodation, had moved in with his Nan. They became firm friends; Christian's confidence rubbed off on Jack, he learned how to deal with the bullies who had made his first weeks in the school miserable.

'You have to be strong, mate. You are either strong or weak, there isn't anything in between. Don't let anyone tell you otherwise,' was Christian's mantra.

Jack learnt how to use his fists, got very strong - strong enough to become a key player in a lucrative protection racket. Money, or cigarettes, was the price to be paid for the protection of Christian and Jack's fists. Mrs. Holt, Head of Pastoral Care, found out about the little earner and summoned parents to school. Jack found his Christmas present list slashed - no Nike Air Max trainers or prepaid Vodafone.

Jack and Christian were in top sets for all subjects. Clever boys, they didn't feel the need to pay much attention to schoolwork. By year eight they were regularly bunking off school. They spent their days playing on gaming machines, and sometimes, when his mother was out for the day, in Jack's house listening to music or watching TV. Their reports were bad, Jack's parents were worried!

In year eleven, when the money Jack could safely filch from his mother's purse or his father's pockets - Christian's mother and Nan kept a tight grip of their money - fell short of what was needed to fund their gaming habit, the pair turned to shoplifting. Ever vigilant, Mrs. Holt discovered the illicit trade in t-shirts, tights, makeup, jewellery - anything that could be put into pockets or hidden under jackets and coveted by year eleven and sixth form girls. Jack and Christian were named as the leaders of the trading gang. Mrs Holt, after much soul searching, mindful of the lasting stigma of criminal proceedings, had decided against notifying the police.

Jack's parents were shocked, mortified! It was at this time that they began to understand the damaging, destructive nature of the boy's relationship. They also found that help for clever boys with behavioural problems wasn't top of the council's list of priorities. Private help was secured for Jack, who spent his sixth form years in counselling.

Christian had wanted them to join the army together, but Jack had decided against it. He had gone to university, become interested in politics, given up his bad-boy behaviour. Christian took his four Grade A results and disappeared into the secretive world of the security services. The friends saw little of one another, drifted apart, their lives moving in different directions.

'Yeh, me, mate! What's wrong, you look as though you've seen a ghost?'

'Sorry, just a surprise to see you. Where have you sprung from?'

Christian wasn't about to tell Jack where he had come from, where he was going, what he was doing! Christian's was a secretive world, his life an enigma. Once recovered from the surprise of his unexpected appearance, Jack was glad to see him, welcomed his company, told him everything.

'Damn hard on you, mate, shouldn't have to put up with it. I've kept clear of serious entanglements with women; my work isn't conducive to the wife and family thing. You've got a problem, mate! In my line of work, we know how to deal with people who cross us!'

Christian picked up Sal and Jack's wedding photograph, 'Bloody lovely girl, Jack, if it were me, I'd kill the bastard.' Christian advised him to get rid of the Golf. 'From what you say that car has been seen too often about Bloomsbury. You don't know who's watching.'

He took the advice and put the car up for sale on eBay. He had been to the car supermarket and bought a three-year-old black Clio. A guy was coming to view the Golf the following Wednesday. He needed to sell it quickly; he couldn't afford to keep two cars. Money was getting tight. Since leaving, Sal hadn't paid a penny towards the upkeep of the flat. He kept trying to contact her, but she didn't reply.

He couldn't keep away from Tavistock Place. He felt safer in the Clio; Christian was right, you didn't want to be driving around in a silver car; black was best; black cars weren't noticed. On the nights they didn't come home by 7:30, he had to hang about, waiting for their later return. It was hard work finding a vacant spot to park up. He found himself constantly moving on, driving around Russell Square and Tavistock Square and slowly through Tavistock Place. There was a side street where he quite often found a place. He was parked there with his headphones in when a tapping on the window made him jump in his seat. He looked up to see an angry looking woman.

'Can I ask you why you are parked here? I've noticed you on several evenings. Are you waiting for someone? Parking is difficult enough around here without non-residents taking up parking spaces.'

'I'm waiting for the guy I carshare with. He's quite often late. I'm sorry if I'm causing a nuisance; we will have to come to some other arrangement,' he said, starting up the engine, pulling away at some speed, leaving the woman looking after him, startled by his sudden departure. His hands were shaking on the wheel; the woman had given him one hell of a scare.

I have to give this up!

He didn't give it up; he couldn't give it up! It was pointless and futile; he knew that. It had become a superstitious ritual; abandoning the ritual was tantamount to giving Sal up.

**

It had been a tiring day. They had been a man down in the office all week, Simon had been off with flu. He was driving back from a site meeting in Hillingdon, intending to drive home, when he found himself on the M4 driving into central London. Sal had him on a string, an elastic, bungee-like string; the harder he pulled on the string, the more violent was the snap back.

The lights were off in the window in Artley House, they weren't home yet. He had eaten a snatched sandwich for lunch; he was hungry. He drove over to the burger bar he had discovered off Russell Square. He bought a double burger and egg muffin with fries and a latte. He ate his meal in the car while parked on yellow lines. It was 8:00 p.m. when he drove back through Tavistock Place – still no lights. When they hadn't appeared by 9:30, he decided to give it up for the evening.

At 7:30 the following evening, the flat was still in darkness. Something told him that it was empty; it had a deserted look to it. Had they moved?! He drove straight over to Fulham, where he found the house on Edgar Street lit up like a Christmas tree. The curtains were open, he could see straight into the front room. He drove to the end of the street, turned right, looped around and crawled back past the house. Sal was standing in front of a bookcase, Tennant behind her, his arms about her waist. They appeared to be considering the book arrangement.

**

29th March 2017. Theresa May has triggered Article 50, the instrument that will take us out of the European Union. It's been voted through Parliament. We leave on 29th March 2019. She has made a major speech; the pundits are calling it the Lancaster House speech. It seems pretty well on the money; Brexit means Brexit' and 'No deal is better than a bad deal'. Still have my doubts about a Remainer in charge!

A day of significance for the country and of equal significance for Jack. It was on the same date in March the previous year that Sal had left.

**

Sunday lunch at his parents' place was eventful! Julia was making a great fuss about events in Parliament. Theresa May was public enemy number one.

'You have something to answer for, Jack. You do realise that you have robbed Poppy and Sam of their future?'

Julia considered that the only future for her children lay within the protective arms of the EU. She was looking particularly tarty, blingy, even for Julia! She had on a long-sleeved dress that featured a short, flared skirt. The dress was in a revolting shade of purple with brass buttons at the cuffs. The iridescent circles of her necklace were the size of drink mats. The heels of her reptilian looking shoes added a good four inches to her height. Julia wore her dark hair chopped straight below her ears and across her forehead; together with her red lips and black-lined eyes, it gave her the look of a somewhat aged and angular, Cleopatra.

Julia bought her clothes and took her style from the exclusive boutiques about Hanger Hill, referred to by Julia and 'her set' as 'The Village'. They were, in Jack's opinion, a set of coffee morning idlers. Julia was the least convincing socialist on the planet.

'What about your mother and me, Julia? Don't we get any credit for the catastrophe?' Ron enquired.

'I expected it of you, Dad! People of your age just don't seem to understand the modern world. As for Mum, well, I won't say anymore.'

'I think you need to stop there, my dear, before you dig yourself in any deeper,' said Ron.

'I think you will find others, apart from Theresa May and your family, responsible. A large majority in Parliament voted it through,' Graham chipped in.

'What's that supposed to mean? What does it matter who voted for it; it's a complete disaster!'

'Just saying, my dear!'

'Don't bother just saying!' was spat at her husband.

'Spoken like a true democrat, Julia! You would be very dangerous if you had a brain. For someone who wouldn't know which country your beloved Brussels is in, you have a hell of a lot to say. You and your coffee morning friends need to check your facts before preaching to the more informed,' said Jack.

'How dare you!' Julia was on her feet, her face grotesquely red against the purple of her dress, her eyes blazing as she faced Jack across the table.

'Thank you both; that's quite enough,' said Ron. 'Sit down, Julia. For heaven's sake, what do you expect with your provoking remarks? And in an attempt to turn the conversation. 'How is the new contract going, Graham?'

'In the office until all hours! I hope it's worth all the time he spends on it. One thing is for sure, the children and I don't see much of him!' cut in, Julia, who had a habit of speaking for her husband. Jack couldn't understand how he put up with it.

'All worth it in the end, no doubt. Keeps the wolf from the door!' was Ron's tongue-in-cheek remark.

There were no wolves gathering at Graham's door! He was the senior partner in a law firm, a firm inherited from his father. It was a profitable practice, specialising in corporate work. The new contract was a huge acquisition and development deal in the Docklands. Graham's business allowed them to live in at a two million property in Hanger Hill, Weybridge, drive top of the range cars, enjoy expensive foreign holidays and send their children to private schools.

Jack thought about the dark-haired woman he had seen Graham with the day following the referendum result. He had been on his way home in a taxi after a night out with the guys from work. Graham had been walking through Kensington with the woman by his side. It had been well after midnight. Maybe, he would up and leave his harridan of a sister.

Serve her right if he did, the overbearing bitch!

Jack found his mother in the kitchen, stacking the dishwasher, wiping tears from her eyes. 'What's wrong, Mum?' he asked, putting an arm around her shoulders.

'All this shouting and ill-feeling. The way she speaks to Graham. It's dreadful! Then she's on the phone to me, crying because he spends too much time at work. I'm not at all surprised that he doesn't want to go home. Then there's the cat!'

'The cat?'

'Haven't I told you, the Patels are threatening Whisky.'

'Threatening Whisky!'

'Yes, shouting across the fence because Whisky has been pooing in the vegetable patch.'

'What are they threatening to do?'

'It's Mr. Patel that does all the shouting; says he will turn the garden hose on him.'

'Don't worry, Mum, Whisky will dodge the hose!'

'Yes, dear, I know, but Mr. Patel is so aggressive. I can't cope with that kind of behaviour. We lived in peace for years with the Dysons. There was never any unpleasantness until these people arrived. People are so very rude to one another these days. Your father telling Mr. Patel to calm down and to stop making a fuss about nothing, hasn't helped! Oh, my goodness, what's happened?'

The kitchen door was thrown open. Ron, carrying Sam, came rushing through, followed by Poppy, sobbing loudly and a distraught Julia.

'God, he's unconscious!' Julia screeched.

'He isn't unconscious,' Ron reassured. 'He's just had a bit of a tumble.'

'Why are his eyes closed? He is unconscious! Call an ambulance, Graham. He's fallen from a height! My God, this is all I need. Darling, darling, open your eyes; yes, that's it, my darling, keep them open.'

'Julia, you are alarming the children. Please, please, calm down,' said Ron.

'Shush, my lovelies, the ambulance is on its way. Keep calm, that's the thing, keep calm!' persisted Julia.

It turned out that Sam had slipped from the fourth rung of the tree house ladder; this ascertained through Poppy's evidence and the calm questioning of the paramedics. Sam, who had a sprained ankle, was carried to the car and propped with his legs along the back seat. Poppy was squashed into a corner with instructions to keep absolutely still lest she nudge her brother's ankle. Graham got behind the wheel of the Range Rover, having said not one word throughout the drama and drove away to the accompaniment of Julia's strident voice.

**

Theresa May has called a snap General Election for the 8th June in order to increase her majority. Sounds like a good idea, Conservatives well ahead in the polls. Put a spoke in the wheel of the Remain brigade!

**

Chapter 8

Julian

'Evening, just moving off. No need for that,' said Julian, adopting his most authoritative tone while indicating the ticket device held by the warden.

The man looked up, regarded him for a couple of seconds before continuing to book the car.

'Come on now; I've been here less than two minutes.'

'You are parked on double yellow lines, sir.'

'Yes, yes, I can see that now. I was in a rush, I hadn't noticed. Put that away, there's a good chap!'

'I can't do that, sir. As you should know, parking on double yellow lines is a traffic offence.'

Julian could feel his temper rising. Fists clenched, eyes blazing, he moved towards the man. 'For fuck's sake, put the bloody thing away.'

'I'm doing my job, sir,' said the warden, backing off.

Julian wanted to grab him, rip the device from his hands, give him a good old slapping. The warden had retreated to the opposite pavement, he was summoning assistance. The police would be on the way. Temper raging, Julian jumped into the car, slammed the door shut and screeched away.

He knew that he was losing control, recognised his inability to manage his growing anger. The circumspect, civilised Julian Tennant - the pre-2009 Julian - watched in despair as this self-serving, angry imposter grew in strength and determination. He parked outside his flat, put his head in his hands and leaned forward onto the steering wheel. It was the second time in the space of a few days that he had come close to hitting out as his temper flared. Thinking through the run-in with the traffic warden, he knew himself to be in the wrong. The poor guy was, as he had tried to explain, doing his job. He had risked the yellow lines, needed to get to the cash machine, needed cash to get a fix. He sat up, picked up his phone and called Carl.

He had just driven up from the family home in Burford. It had been an uncomfortable weekend. His father had all but accused him of abusing his position in the company. Though retired, Ted still acted in a consultative role. He met up regularly with the older directors at his London club. Julian had been aware that on the previous Wednesday, his father had lunched with Hubert Monk. When asked to drop in on Ted on his way home, Julian had known what was coming.

'How are you, old boy?' was Ted's opening gambit.

'I'm fine, Dad. What's all this about?'

'Well, I might as well come straight to the point. Hubert has told me of a particularly unsavoury incident that took place in the office. It involved yourself and a junior member of staff. Let me say, Julian, that Hubert has raised the matter purely out of concern for you; the incident being so out of character. What on earth came over you, old boy? Sit down, let's have a drink and talk this over.'

'A bit of a spat, really. I must admit to having lost my temper. I'm surprised that Hubert has found it necessary to bother you with the matter! A bit of a storm in a teacup, really!'

'That's not the way Hubert tells it. He tells me that you attempted to blame a junior member of staff for your own mistake, questioned the man's ability in the most colourful language, and yes, lost your temper so badly that another member of staff was forced to intervene. Really, Julian, that just isn't you!'

'Well, you seem well briefed, Dad. Hubert hasn't spared the detail. It wasn't my finest hour, I admit that.'

'Certainly not! Never been the way in our outfit, you know that. Always took responsibility for our own decisions and actions; never pulled rank to cover our tracks. Not the done thing!'

'No, indeed, not the done thing!'

'Are you completely well, Julian? Sometimes I think you a bit edgy. I wonder if you gave yourself enough recovery time after Afghanistan?'

'I'm fine, Dad. Afghan's a long way back. It was a regrettable incident. I apologise for any embarrassment it's caused you. It won't happen again.'

Fucking Herbert Monk, fucking busybody, fucking tittle-tattling old woman! The sooner the gaggle of old fogies of his father's generation got out from under everyone's feet, the better. Bloody anachronisms in today's cutthroat business world with their codes of behaviour and outdated ethics.

Julian's suppressed anger didn't help when he got home. He had gone on to argue with Lucy and been irritable with the children. Lucy had little time for anything other than the children; all else was secondary to their needs. Julian considered them spoilt and liked to use what he perceived to be Lucy's mishandling of the children as an excuse for his own lack of feeling towards them. He wasn't jealous of them; he had no real feelings towards them.

In his more soul-searching moments, he had to admit that he didn't love his children. He had loved the two-year-old Cosima that he had left behind when he went to Afghanistan. He could still feel her little body; legs fastened around his waist, plump little arms flung about his neck. He could smell her, hear her giggles and baby voice. He couldn't relate to the big, eight-year-old, demanding, self-absorbed child that she had become. The intervening years were hazy; somewhere in that haze, Julian had lost the little girl he had loved.

Benedict had been five months old when Julian came out of rehabilitation and returned home. He was a crying baby. Lucy was up half the night trying to settle him. Julian had found the sound of his crying unbearable; it shattered his nerves. Lucy did her best, she took him down to the kitchen and closed the door, but still, he could hear his noise. He was a dark-haired scrap with a scowling little face. He seemed to be in a constant state of distress!

Lucy refused to engage a nanny. Her mother and his mother had tried to persuade her, but without success. Lucy said that by doing so, she would be announcing her inability to care for her own children. Benedict continued to cry, and Lucy continued to be exhausted. Julian had become adept at acting the part of the proud, supportive father. He was very convincing.

Julian stood at the window, looking into the street. His anger had receded; he felt drained, lethargic. He knew the pattern; soon he would descend into a deep depression, overwhelmed by guilt. Guilt that he couldn't make Lucy happy; guilt about the women he took to his bed; about his inability to love his own children; guilt at being alive. He watched the car pull into the kerb and went to answer the buzz of the intercom.

Carl wore an expensively tailored suit, handmade shoes and drove a new BMW. He wasn't most people's idea of a drug dealer! He didn't sell cheap; Julian knew he paid over the odds but didn't care. Carl's stuff was good, delivery was quick and reliable. Carl handed over a small package, Julian handed over a roll of cash.

In the kitchen, he opened a drawer, took out a tin box and sat down at the table. He spread a sheet of tinfoil, took the elastic band off the plastic bag and sniffed the white powder. He tipped out a small quantity, gathered it, cut it with an old bank card, rolled a bank note, put it to his nose and snorted the cocaine. Within minutes, he was on his feet, heading for the shower, energised, ready to go. He dressed carefully - navy chinos, a soft white button-down shirt and navy blazer. Combing back his blonde hair, he studied himself in the mirror – all good, a convincing image of the old Julian. He would walk down to The Bell and Whistle; Andy and Brad were sure to be in.

Andy was about Julian's age, traded on the Commodities Market. Like Julian, Andy spent his weekdays in London and his weekends with his family in the country. Brad was in his late twenties, flat-shared with Andy and worked the Bond Market. He had just broken up with his partner of two years. The men had become friends, part of a wider, looser group of acquaintances, all linked by their ability to fund a fast, bachelor-type lifestyle in the city. Julian, Andy and Brad drank and dined together, frequented night-clubs together, went to mid-week games at Arsenal together. They ran spread-betting accounts and bet against each other. They hunted down one night stands together.

On the occasions when Lucy came up to town, usually to attend a company function or for a shopping trip, she stayed with Margo Hadleigh. Margo's husband, Paul, was a rising star in the company. Margot and Lucy were old friends. Lucy liked to speak of Julian's flat as a typically pokey, ill-kept bachelor pad, offering none of the facilities required by a visiting lady. In reality, the flat was a roomy second-floor apartment in a Victorian block. Julian had a large, lofty-ceilinged sitting room, a high-spec kitchen and two bathrooms, all tastefully and expensively furnished. Its drawback, from Lucy's perspective, being its one spacious bedroom with its one super-king bed. The second bedroom had been converted into a library cum study in the 1960s by the uncle from whom Julian had inherited the apartment.

There were, Julian discovered, no shortage of women as anxious as himself to avoid commitment in personal relationships. A dinner at a top restaurant, decent wine and a night in his bed were their requirements. In the morning, they searched his fridge and kitchen cupboards, made coffee and ate a knocked together breakfast before going cheerfully on their way. What initially surprised him was the status of his 'one-nighters'. They were well-educated women in top jobs. They cared, not one jot, who had shared his bed the night before, nor did they care about his marital status. Marriage didn't seem to feature on their bucket list. Most would disappear off his radar, often for months on end, before popping up in an email or voice mail.

Julian kept two mobile phones - one for family, friends and work that accompanied him wherever he went, another never left London. It was on the London-based phone that he would hear from Chloe, Freya, Millie, Nancy - a long list of blonde-haired women. It wasn't that Julian preferred blonde women; rather that dark haired women reminded him of Lucy, of his betrayal of Lucy. But the 'one-nighters' had an advantage over Lucy, they did what she was unable to do; they banished his nightmares. None had woken to shouted commands, flailing arms, kicking legs, a sweat drenched body pinning them to the bed, choking hands about their throat.

The uncontrolled violence of his nightly return to the bombed-out concrete complex in the Afghan desert, had terrified Lucy. She had begged him to get help, to approach those who would enable him to confront the demons that drove his night terrors, that deprived him of rest, robbed him of feeling and empathy. He wanted to please Lucy, to make her happy. He wanted to be the man who boarded the plane to Afghanistan in 2009, not the man who had returned. But Julian didn't believe in shrinks; he didn't believe in their ability to wipe his memory clean of the images that haunted him, the abominations that would be with him until the day he died.

During his waking hours, he had taught himself strategies that kept the worst of the memories at bay, but sleep rendered him defenseless. When sleep came, when his guard was down, the Tornado appeared overhead, a silver streak in the cloudless blue sky. He heard the muffled boom as the missile found its target, felt the ground shake, saw the concrete compound from where the enemy was launching the attack rise into the air as a dense cloud of dust and debris. As the roar of the Tornado receded, an eerie silence filled the hot, quivering air. Dust and sand filled his mouth and clogged his throat. Grit tore at his eyes.

Next to him, his back resting against a low wall, was the machine gunner he had pushed aside to take charge of the gun. The man's dead, startled eyes were fixed on him. Apart from a trickle of blood from the side of his mouth, he was unmarked. Beside the gunner, a soldier lay motionless, face down, his helmeted head twisted at an unnatural angle, a pool of blood - oily, black - seeped from beneath his body into the sand. Lying on his back, between their forward and rear position was his sergeant.

His own left arm lay limp against his side, his legs were powerless, but somehow, he began to move his useless body towards Mike. Slowly, painfully, he hauled himself forward. Mike's lips were moving; He couldn't hear the words, but he knew he was speaking. He tried to answer, to shout reassuring words to his friend, but his dried-out throat and mouth smothered his words. Slowly, he inched himself forward; within touching distance he reached out to touch Mike's shoulder.

It wasn't speech that moved Mike's lips, but the involuntary twitching of facial nerves as life drained away. Julian looked at a body ripped apart from chest to groin, a cavity devoid of its vital organs. He watched as a huge convulsion gripped the body and lifted it from the ground, the skeletonised, bloodied hips arching upwards, the booted feet scrabbling for a footing in the sand, the head flung back, the mouth opening in one final, deprecating, soundless roar. Julian buried his face in the sand and screamed into the unforgiving earth. It was there that the paramedics had found him - unconscious, his right hand grasping his sergeant's arm.

Julian had no memory of the noise of the Apache as it circled overhead, of the Chinook that had taken him from the battlefield. No memory of the field medics who gave aid to the living and dignity to the dead. He had fleeting, muddled memories of his journey back to the UK. But the greater part of the journey by Globemaster to Birmingham and by ambulance to the Queen Elizabeth was a drug-induced blur. Short periods of wakefulness brought images of Mike's torn body and the medics running with yet another drug-filled syringe.

He woke, on what he was later told was his fourth day in the hospital. His bruised and lacerated hands rested on the smooth whiteness of the neatly folded-down sheet. Lucy sat by his bed, her pale, blemish-free hands resting on his. The room was clean, cool, ordered - anathema to the vivid, cruel and chaotic place in which he was still captive. He winced, turned his head from the light, which tortured his eyes. Lucy had gone to the window and adjusted the blinds.

'It's all right, darling. You have some slight abrasions to your eyes; they will soon heal.'

Lucy had been clean, whole and beautiful. She had no place in his blood-stained, barbarous world. She saw that his body, though broken, would mend; she rejoiced, she didn't know about his mind, how could she? The army medics understood; the doctors that came and sat by his bed understood.

He had stayed for six weeks in the Queen Elizabeth; learning to walk again on his pinned-together legs and waiting for his fractured arms to heal. His parents had come to visit. His mother had cried, hugged him, gave thanks that he would never again be sent to a war zone. Julian was unable to share her joy; his thoughts were for the women whose sons or husbands would never return, for the children who had lost their fathers.

Julian had led a patrol of twelve men, helicoptered to a position just outside a village in Helmand. They were searching for illegal arms caches. Within minutes of being dropped by the Chinook, they had come under machine gun fire and attack from rocket propelled grenades. Julian and two others had survived the attack. He had led nine men to their deaths. For this feat of leadership, they awarded him the Military Cross. He was wracked by a deep sense of guilt.

His father had spoken to him of practical matters; discussed him resigning his commission and joining the firm. Ted's generation didn't discuss the traumas encountered during military service; they left all such happenings on the battlefield, where they were thought to belong. Showing a brave front and a stiff upper lip were the qualities admired by his generation.

Lucy had waited until Julian was looking a little better before she brought Cosima and Benedict to the hospital. Cosima had been very excited. She had been told that Julian was in hospital getting better after having an accident. Lucy had told her about hospitals; told her that hospitals were places where people who didn't feel very well went to be made better. She had explained that they were very happy places in which babies were born; spoke of Cosima's own birth in a hospital.

She had told her that Daddy had very sore arms and legs, that Cosima must be very careful not to hurt Daddy. She could hug Daddy, but she must be very gentle. Lucy needn't have worried about Cosima being too boisterous; she had pinned herself to Lucy's side and fixed wide, suspicious eyes on her father. Urged to 'give Daddy a hug', she had hidden behind her mother, burying her head in Lucy's skirt.

When Julian became mobile, they would sit together in the little day room. As Lucy told of the children's little achievements, warmth and empathy had filled the soft, hazel eyes that circled her little family, attempting, through the force of her own love, to bond them together. He had seen the look of hurt in her eyes when he recoiled from holding Benedict and had hated himself for it. Cosima had sat by her mother's side, looking into her face and hanging on her every word. The tiny, dark-haired, Benedict, dressed in his body suit and blue, rabbit-decorated dungarees, was bounced and jiggled about on Lucy's knee. Benedict had needed to be kept in perpetual motion in order to silence the phenomenal noise his tiny lungs could produce.

The children had quickly become a further source of guilt for Julian. He had sat and listened to the mundane details of his son's swollen, erupting gums, to updates on Cosima's progress in her ballet class and her rapidly developing reading skills. He had made all the right noises; said all the things he knew Lucy wanted to hear. But he had found words hard to find when asked to admire the windy, wobbly-eyed smile his son directed on the world. Julian was discovering that his troubled, disturbed mind was incapable of reaching out to the limpet-like, needy creatures that attached themselves to the woman he loved. It was in the little day room that Julian had begun to hone the false persona of the proud, caring father.

Chapter 9

Jack

Jack had an established routine that only varied on a Sunday when he drove straight from Richmond to Fulham. On weekdays, he got home at 6:30, collected the car keys from the flat and headed for Edgar Street. Arriving at about 7:20, he would drive slowly down the street to check if they were home.

Florence Street ran parallel to Edgar Street, their backs separated by gardens and an entry. Jack had discovered that the curbside at the far end of Florence Street, beside the end house, was, for some reason, always vacant. He would drive around, double check his parking spot, drive to the little Waitrose on Fulham Palace Road, buy sandwiches, chocolate brownies, or perhaps a couple of packets of biscuits and four cans of Diet Coke - always four cans of Coke.

At 8:30, he would drive at a snail's pace down Edgar Street and force himself to turn his head to look into the brightly illuminated room where Sal sat with Tennant. Back in his parking space, he would lean back in his seat and take deep breaths to quell the rapid breathing that he recognised as a kind of hyperventilation. Equanimity restored; he would log into Sal's social media accounts. Sometimes he was tuned into a live conversation. It amused him that Sal had no idea that he was so close and listening in. Sometimes he slept for an hour. At 10:00, he locked the car and made his way to the entry that ran along the back of the terraced row.

It had been a Sunday evening; he had been late leaving Richmond. His parents had been upset; truer to say that his mother had been upset and his father upset because she was upset. Julia had been at her obnoxious best! It had been 9:50 when he had driven along Fulham Road and turned into Edgar Street. Tennant was sitting on the sofa, feet up on a footstool, surrounded by box files and papers. Being late, he drove straight round to Florence Street, parked up and headed for the back entry.

The houses being set back behind longish gardens made the entry dark. He paused to allow his eyes to adjust to the gloom before making his way forward. Straggly old privet hedges brushed his side, their hard, twiggy branches threatening his face. About twenty metres along the entry, quite close to number 34, a section of stone wall jutted out, providing a perfect, concealed watching place.

At 10:30, with unfailing regularity, Tennant came into the entry to smoke a couple of cigarettes. The first time Jack had explored the entry, he had almost bumped into him; he had made the excuse of having a piss and got out quick.

Tennant was a sitting, bloody duck!!

Three, sometimes four nights a week, for months, Jack had hung about in the entry. Crazy behaviour, psychotic, manic, schizoid - all words he had heard before.

'Jules, I'm going up. Don't forget to lock up properly!' - Sal's voice.

'Will do. Be up in ten,' - toffee-nosed voice.

A couple of minutes later, a light came on in the back bedroom. He listened to the sound of Tennant's feet as he walked up and down on the gravelly ground and the click of the latch as the gate was pulled closed behind him. Just a click, no bolt, no padlock.

Why hadn't he noticed that before?

He waited fifteen minutes, then walked up to the gate. He put his hand to the drop latch, pressed down, felt the bar lift, pushed and felt the gate open. He stood motionless, his hand on the cold metal, his mind racing. He should pull the gate towards him, let the latch drop, walk down the entry, get into the car and drive home. That was what any sane person would do. But Jack wasn't listening to the voice of sanity. He found himself edging through the opening, standing with his back against a high stone wall. He felt exposed, vulnerable. He had started edging back when Christian's voice sounded in his ear, 'That's the coward's way, mate, that bastard has stolen your wife. What are you going to do about it?'

So right! Christian was right, he was always right! He slid down into a crouching position. He could make out the outline of flower beds and tall shrubs marking the far boundary. A creeper clothed the back wall of the house, the light filtering through the bedroom curtains, turning its foliage to a spectral silver.

An inner voice advised caution, but it was little more than a whisper. He crouched low in the shadow of the wall and edged forward along the path that led up to the house. The voice of caution was becoming loud and fearful. Jack didn't want to hear it, wanted to silence the warning, admonitory words. He felt an overwhelming need to get close to the house, close to Sal. Reaching the wall of the house, he inched his way under a window and along onto a doorstep.

He sat on the step for some minutes. Voices were now thundering in his head. He put up his fists and pummeled his ears to drown out the insistent, conflicting chatter. It was now but the finest of threads that connected Jack to reality; that told him he must resist the urge to scream out his anger at the blonde-haired woman in the bedroom above his head, the woman who must be dragged from that bed, dragged down the stairs, down the entry and into the car that would take her back to the place where she belonged.

He woke at 5:50. He was on the back seat of the car, lying with his knees drawn up under his chin. It was the cold that woke him; he couldn't feel his feet, his left arm, pinned beneath him, was numb. Unwinding his stiff body, he sat up, opened the door and lifted his numb feet onto the pavement. It was a couple of minutes before he could stand and begin to restore some life to his defunct limbs. Feet stamping, arms thumping against his sides, he became aware of his mud encrusted trousers, his stained, torn shirt, his ripped jacket. He remembered sitting on the doorstep; after that - nothing, absolutely nothing. How had he got into such a state? He couldn't remember, couldn't remember a damn thing!

Jesus Christ, what had he done!

He had wanted to do serious harm. He had wanted to get into the house; he knew that. Had he got in? If he had, what had happened? He was covered in mud, not blood; that was significant!

A grey stillness hung over the houses. The rumbling, dull hum - the sound of the daytime city - was replaced by a strange, unnerving quietness, broken only by the rasping sound of a car engine starting and the putting of a moped making its way along the high street. The birds, taking advantage of their narrow slot, claimed the airways. He got into the car and sat behind the wheel. 'Till death do us part,' that's what she had said. Were they now separated by death? Her death at his hands! Was she lying dead in that back bedroom, beside her lover, in the bed that had been a wedding present from her parents?

The street was gradually coming to life. A mother with a baby in a pushchair was attempting to encourage a crying toddler to hold onto the pushchair and walk with her. Jack wondered what necessity compelled a woman to drag her children through the streets of Fulham at such an unsociable hour. He wanted to drive into Edgar Street, check on the house; he wasn't sure why, wasn't sure what he thought he might see! He resisted the temptation. The house would have to keep its secrets for the moment; he couldn't risk being seen on the street. It was gone 7:30 as he waited for a break in the traffic to pull out of Florence Street onto Fulham Road. To his right, a woman walked out from Edgar Street, walked a few metres up the road and joined a group standing at a pelican crossing waiting for the lights to change - a tall, blonde woman - it was Sal.

He drove home, had a hot shower, made a coffee and a slice of toast, left a voice message to say he wouldn't be in to work, then crashed out on the sofa.

**

The election's gone pear-shaped. All great until the manifesto was published. Theresa's plan for funding care for the elderly gone down like a lead balloon. Ended in a hung parliament - 13 seats lost. Northern Ireland, DUP stepping forward to prop her up. Paid them one billion plus God knows how many policy guarantees.
Dad's furious.

**

'I am beginning to think the woman very stupid. What did she imagine would be the result of a policy that directly disadvantaged the very people likely to support her? If she hadn't sounded the retreat, I couldn't have voted for her,' said Ron, adding a good splash of Pinot Noir to his already well filled glass.

'One thing it does prove, is that the country doesn't want to leave the EU,' said Julia.

'No, it doesn't,' said Ron.

'It means nothing of the kind, you foolish woman. You need to learn how to keep your mouth shut until you know what you are talking about,' said Graham Fairbrother.

It was as though a silent bomb had gone off. Recovering from the initial stunning blast, all heads swivelled from Graham to his wife. Julia sat motionless; she had gone very pale. Graham was helping himself to vegetables as though nothing had happened. The silence was broken by Poppy's giggles.

'Hush, stop that Poppy,' said Margaret.

'Daddy shouted at Mummy, he shouted at Mummy,' said Poppy, between increasingly hysterical fits of giggling. 'Daddy told Mummy to keep her mouth shut; that's what Mummy says to Daddy. Daddy doesn't say that. He shouted at Mummy, he shouted at mummy!' screamed Poppy.

Margaret grabbed Poppy and dashed her from the room. Julia jumped up and followed them.

'Pass your plate, Graham. The gravy is in danger of congealing,' said Ron, who had completely recovered his composure. 'Men only dinner. What a nice change. Sit up and enjoy the treat, Sam, you won't get many such opportunities. Indeed, you will not!'

'That's true, Sam, Grandad's quite right. Tuck in,' said Graham.

A semi-smile played across Graham's thin lips, registering a look of quiet satisfaction. He was a narrow-faced, thin, wiry man, his build giving the impression of a height he didn't really possess. Fine, light brown hair receded from a high forehead. Keen, intelligent hazel eyes sat beneath thick, mobile brows. Graham favoured tweedy-type sports jackets over dark, coloured shirts, usually worn with a woollen tie. He looked, Jack thought, more like an academic than a solicitor.

It was a good hour later that Margaret came in and took the remaining food to the kitchen for the ladies to dine, staff style.

Before leaving, Jack went to the kitchen to find his mother. Julia was sitting on her own at the table; eyes puffy, makeup smudged.

'Where's Mum?'

'Taken Poppy upstairs for a rest. She is very overwrought.'

'Mum or Poppy?'

'Poppy, of course! You think yourself so clever, don't you, Jack? Not clever enough, though, to hold onto Sal. Bloody men! All the same, always wanting to be in control.'

'Now, hold on there, Julia, I know that you have made it your business to make yourself as different to Mum as you possibly can, thinking her too subservient to Dad. But think of this, Mum is very happy with their relationship; they are very happy together and have been for over thirty years. Who are you to judge their relationship? Take care, sister, the worm might be about to turn!'

'What have you heard? What do you mean?' Julia jumped on his words, alarmed.

'Nothing, but it looks to me as though Graham has had enough. For what it's worth, I would advise a change of tack.'

In the sitting room, Ron and Graham sat in the fireside armchairs, the grog tray on a table between them.

'Having a couple of whiskies, Jack,' said Graham. 'Thought Julia could drive home for a change.'

'Good for you, mate.' Jack thought of the woman he had seen him with and wondered who she was. Graham was a strange cove. Happy to chat away about business, the golf club, holidays and such like, but when it came to personal matters, likes, dislikes, feelings, Graham had managed to throw up an impenetrable shield that said, 'don't go there'. Ron summed him up - 'not one of the boys.'

On Monday evening, Jack got a call from his mother. Julia was convinced that he knew about Graham's seeing another woman.

'Her imagination, Mum! She was goading me about Sal. I told her to watch her step, or she would be without a husband.'

Jack wasn't about to alarm his parents; his evidence wasn't exactly rock solid. There could be other reasons why Graham would be walking the streets of London with a woman in the early hours. Jack couldn't think of any, but that didn't mean a lot.

'What exactly is she saying?'

'That he's having an affair! She has no evidence, no idea who the woman is. He is away a lot, goes abroad to Zurich, Bonn and the like. She's very suspicious of it all, dear.'

'She's suspicious of everything he does. She suspects that he secretly voted to leave the EU!'

'I know, dear, she's very difficult. So, you know nothing?'

'No, Mum, but from what I see, he's getting to the end with her. She shows him up in public! You can't do that and not expect a reaction. What do you say to her?'

'I try to make light of it, dear. What else can I do? It was dreadful after you left on Sunday. She gave him an unmerciful tongue-lashing when she found that she had to drive home.'

'She's totally unreasonable! Why shouldn't he have a couple of after dinner drinks; she knocks back a good few glasses of wine?'

'It's the children I'm most worried about. You saw how Poppy was! She was still whimpering when she was bundled into the car. Sam is far too quiet; looking like a little, pale waif.'

'You are going to have to be up front with her, Mum. She's a tyrant! Could you live with her? I certainly couldn't! What's wrong with her? I just don't understand it.'

'Well, my darling, I would never say this to anyone else, not even your father, but I don't believe she loves him at all, and she certainly doesn't like him. She is such a strong character, she has found it far too easy to push him around. I think she has lost all respect for him!'

'Talk to her, mum.'

Later that evening, Jack sat thinking over the conversation with his mother. He thought of the mess of his own relationship. Was any of it his fault? He didn't think so. Sal, in her own way, had been just as unreasonable as Julia. He felt very tired. He shuffled himself into a comfortable position on the sofa and began drifting off to sleep. Jeremy Corbyn was doing something or other in Islington. Surrounded by his usual bevy of ladies, he was nodding his way across the soundless TV screen.

**

Jack's dentist was in on the high street. His appointment had been for 12:45. He was out by 1:30. He stood outside the surgery, indecisive, trying to make a decision. It hadn't been worthwhile going into work before his appointment, but he had planned to go in for the afternoon. He was ten minutes' walk from the flat, from the car, from a trip to Fulham. He was tempted. He turned and headed for the flat. He would ring work and claim a dental trauma that was taking him home.

The Fulham side streets were very quiet; he couldn't see a soul about. Parking up in his usual spot on Florence Street, he took a grey hoodie from the boot of the car and put it on, pulling the hood well forward; things were a bit more risky in broad daylight. He locked the car and headed for the entry.

It felt weird to be there during the day; it felt and looked very different. It was, Jack thought, a burglar's dream. Big, mature trees and high evergreen hedges bordered the gardens. He made his way to the back of the house and stood with his back against the opposite garden wall. With the trees in full leaf, the garden of number 34 was shielded from the houses opposite and those to its sides. The back wall of the house showed no evidence of an alarm system or of security cameras. He walked back down the entry and turned into Edgar Street. He kept his head down and his hood pulled well forward. Walking quickly up the path of number 34, he rang the doorbell. The sudden, shrill noise made him jump. He stood nervously listening; any noise or movement from behind the door and he would bolt. There was no movement; the house had an empty feel about it. He rang the bell again, a good, long ring - just to make sure.

Returning to the entry, he went straight to the back gate, pressed the latch, pushed the gate open, and walked swiftly up the path to the back of the house. To one side, there was an old outhouse, detached from the main building, a ginnel running between it and the house. Perfect cover! On the opposite side were double patio doors, to the centre the back door. Jack stood in the cover of the ginnel, in front of him was a small, single-glazed window. He tried to remember back to the day he had viewed the house, tried to remember the layout; he wasn't sure, but he thought it might be the window of a toilet.

It was an old window, probably original to the house. It was in bad nick. He reached out and touched the peeling paintwork, ran his hand along the sill; the wood was rough and brittle. He took his car keys from his pocket and pushed the ignition key into the base rail; without much pressure, it sliced into the old wood. He put his hand to the side of the frame and pushed. The whole window moved, a further push with both hands and he heard the wood splinter; he could feel it giving, splintering around the side catch. One final push, and the window swung open.

He stepped back, leaned against the outhouse wall - for a few seconds he hesitated, but the inner demon was soon back in control. It was easy work getting in - backside on the ledge, a squeeze, a swing of the legs, a jump over a sink and he was inside the house. His memory had served him well; he was standing in an old toilet. To his left was a toilet pan, its interior patterned in blue flowers. The cistern, held by cast iron brackets, hung high on the wall. A matching, blue patterned sink was under the window. There was a door to his right - cautiously, he opened it a few inches and peered into the hallway. The house seemed strangely still, as though aware of an unsanctioned presence, holding its breath, listening. Sunlight streamed in through a fanlight above the front door, dust mites danced in the hot air. The silence was punctuated by the ticking of a grandfather clock that stood to the left of the front door.

Small patches of grey rubber clung to the patterned floor tiles, remnants of the backing of a green carpet, ripped up and piled near the bottom of the stairs together with folded dust sheets and a steam wallpaper stripper. Surprising! Jack had imagined that the wealthy employed people to decorate their homes. Perhaps Julian Tennant fancied a spot of DIY! It wasn't something Sal had shown any interest in.

Crossing the hall, he pushed open the door leading into the front, bay windowed room. A grey, Victorian marble fireplace occupied one wall in company with an armchair upholstered to match a huge, deep blue velvet sofa. The sofa was most definitely bespoke; Jack hadn't seen anything like it in the sofa selling establishments he had toured with Sal. He had a quick look along the bookshelves. In addition to books he recognised as Sal's, there were hefty works on geology and quite a few novels; looked like the complete works of Graham Green. He didn't spend too much time exploring Julian Tennant's chosen reading matter, he was aware that the room was quite exposed; passersby would have a good view into the room.

What had originally been two rooms had been knocked into one. A fireplace, almost identical to the one in the sitting area, occupied the chimney breast of the rear room. Jack recognised the minimalist dining table and chairs that Sal had drooled over but had been way outside their price bracket. Laid out on the table was a set of architect's drawings together with correspondence from Hammersmith and Fulham Planning Authority, granting permission for a huge, contemporary, almost entirely glass extension to the rear of the property. Scattered about the table were costings and building quotes. There were two quotes for construction: one for £65K, the other for £72K, both less the cost of specialist glass. There was a costing for second fix items of £43K. The structural engineer seemed a bargain at £6K.

Jesus, creeping towards one and a half million. Not a word from Sal in eighteen months, not a fucking penny towards the mortgage — hard-faced bitch.

Upstairs, he found two rooms piled with boxes, a guest bedroom - the destination of their bed - a bathroom and a large room to the back of the house with a newly fitted ensuite boasting a copper bath - obviously their bedroom. Sal had always wanted a copper bath! The bed was a super-king with a plush, pale yellow headboard. The expensive-looking free-standing wardrobes and chests of drawers were light grey, the antique chairs upholstered in grey-patterned velvet.

Standing against the wall, between two white shuttered windows, was a dressing table, on the wall above it hung a huge rosewood mirror. The dressing table was stacked with cosmetics; creams, perfumes and jars holding brushes. Wipes and bits of discarded cotton wool littered the surface, a typical Sal mess! The room was untidy. A soiled linen basket overflowed, clothes were heaped on chairs, a wardrobe door stood open with a woman's dress slipping from a hanger, draping to the floor.

Lying on one side of the unmade bed was a woman's nightdress. Jack froze. He looked at the soft white cotton, at the lace edging to the neck and hem, the tiny, embroidered blue flowers covering the fabric. It was a nightdress he recognised; a nightdress Sal had worn lying next to him in the bed that now occupied the spare room. He bent down and picked it up. He carried it to a chair, sat on top of heaped clothes and buried his head in his wife's nightdress. It smelled of Sal, it took him spiralling back to the bedroom of the flat. Sal was lying beside him, he could feel her warmth, the softness of her body, hear her soft breathing.

The doorbell was ringing. For a moment, Jack had no awareness of where he was or what he was doing. His face was wet; he looked down at the damp cloth in his hands and was seized by panic. He rushed on to the landing and into a front bedroom. The bell was ringing again. He peered out through the side of the curtains. Myrtle was at the door. She was rattling the letterbox, looking up at the house. He didn't immediately recognise her; she was dressed for the August weather in navy pedal pushers and a white sleeveless top. Her hair was tied back and the docks had been replaced by sandals.

Jesus!

She walked down the path, looked up the road, took out her mobile, had a conversation, then sat down on the garden wall. She was waiting for someone, probably Sal. He was halfway down the stairs, desperate to get out, when his head clicked into gear. He was still carrying Sal's nightdress; it was all he was carrying. A break-in with nothing but a nightdress missing would look bloody suspicious! He raced back to their bedroom. He needed to grab something quick, something valuable. On top of a chest of drawers were silver backed brushes - his, Jack presumed!

What a bloody fop. Thought that kind of paraphernalia went out with the Edwardians!

He tipped out the contents of a plastic carrier bag and put the brushes into it. The top drawer was full of jeweller's boxes. A quick look in one revealed gold cuff links. He tumbled the boxes out of the drawer into the bag. His heart was racing. He dashed across the landing and into the front bedroom. Myrtle was still on the wall- he had a few more minutes! Racing back to the bedroom, his eye lighted on a lacquered jewellery box. He added the contents to the bag together with Sal's nightdress and headed for the stairs.

He got out the way he had got in.

His hands were shaking so violently that he struggled to open the car door. He threw the bag on the back seat and drove off. A loud blast of a horn told him that he had almost hit another car when pulling out onto Fulham Road. The guy in the car was making signs, shouting. He made an apologetic gesture and kept going. His heart was beating so wildly that his whole body seemed to be pulsating. What the hell had got into him? What had driven him to do something so stupid? If Sal had been on time, she would have been through the door and into the house with him in her bedroom. He was a bloody burglar, a criminal. It didn't take long for him to realise that he had left fingerprints all over the house. He pulled back from dumping the bag in a skip near Putney Bridge.

Don't do anything yet. Think. Get your head straight!

He had spent the following week waiting for the police to arrive. He was convinced that he had left incriminating evidence of his presence. He didn't know what the evidence might be, but didn't doubt its existence. There were the fingerprints he had left all over the house; he had never had his fingerprints taken, but he couldn't believe that they wouldn't somehow be the means of identifying him.

The strident buzzing of the intercom had set his heart racing. He pushed the answer button and waited.

'Are you there, Jack? What the hell are you doing?' It was Christian.

'Sorry, mate; I was doing. Come on up.'

'Are you OK? You look as white as a sheet,' said Christian, looking quizzically at his friend.

Jack trusted Christian. He blurted out the whole stupid episode of the break in.

'Wow, mate, I didn't think you had it in you. OK, let's think!

You sure there were no cameras?'

'Yeh, I'm sure, unless they were bloody well hidden!'

'That's unlikely!'

'The fingerprints will be of no help unless the police have them on their system. If they suspected you, that would be a different matter. Your prints will still be on lots of Sal's stuff, if they matched them, you'd be in the shit.'

'Jesus!'

'But why would they suspect you? Good job you had the nouse to take stuff. What did you take, by the way?'

Silver-backed brushes, belonging to the poncy git, cuff links and other stuff of his. The contents of Sal's jewellery box. A nightdress.'

'A nightdress? Not Sal's nightdress?'

'Yeh, Sal's.'

'Definitely not a good move, mate. Could point to a personal involvement. Have to hope they think the burglar a fetishist, or that they don't notice. Should have made it worth the risk, put something in the coffee jar while you were in there. Always plan ahead, mate. Planning is critical in my job, wouldn't last five minutes acting on harebrained, spur of the moment impulses. What's happened to the loot?'

'Dumped it in a bin on the Cally Road.'

'Should be OK!'

Jack had started to worry that his car might have been seen near the house. He imagined some neighbourhood watch type with nothing better to do than record the numbers of unrecognised cars, handing them to the police while they were making door to door enquiries. Christian thought this a huge joke.

'Don't make me laugh. The cops doing door-to-door to find Tennant's bits and bobs. That's for murder enquiries, not silver backed brushes.'

Chapter 10

Sally

Sally hadn't had so much fun, ever! She had gone out on the river in a boat hired by Julian and his friends. The idea had been to stop a flotilla of fishing boats, led by Nigel Farage, from sailing up the Thames to Westminster in support of Brexit. They wished to draw attention to what they claimed was the damage done to the UK fishing industry by the EU Fishery Policy. Julian had called it a Farage stunt.

The pro-remain flotilla of pleasure cruisers and inflatables had been led by Bob Geldof. Installed on Bob's boat had been huge loudspeakers blasting out the song 'The In Crowd'. Through loud hailers, Bob and his crew attempted to shout down and drown out the voices of the fishermen. From Tower Bridge up to the Houses of Parliament, a crazy game of chicken on water saw heavily laden boats sailing far too close to the fishing vessels, cutting across their bows while banners were provocatively waved and insults yelled. When water hoses were turned on opposition boats, the police came on to the water to try to keep order.

Julian and his friends had brought a crate of champagne on board. Striking through the water at high speed, the boat had been driven within feet of the bulky boats, while all on board raised their glasses of fizz to the Brexiteers. Sally had enjoyed it all immensely. The BBC had called it a spectacle. The press had called it 'The Battle of the Thames'. Nigel Farage had said it was a disgrace that multi-millionaires saw fit to show such contempt for the men and women of our proud fishing communities; communities that had been devastated by EU policy. Even the 'roasting' he got from his father hadn't spoiled Julian's enjoyment of the occasion. Ted had seen the footage on the news, seen the close-up of Julian's boat as it came alongside a trawler, thought the champagne stunt in extremely poor taste.

It was at the end of that week of exhilaration and high jinks that Sally moved in with Julian. It hadn't been an easy decision for Sally; it hadn't been a casual thing. They had talked about the move as a commitment on both sides. Julian spoke of it as a new beginning. Yet, Sally hesitated, she had discussed it with Myrtle. The more she saw of Julian, the less time she had to spend helping Myrtle. Julian was demanding more and more of her time. It wasn't that he said anything about the time she spent with Myrtle, but nevertheless, he made her feel guilty.

He looked so disappointed when an engagement with Myrtle meant they being unable to take advantage of the complimentary tickets he had acquired, or when the expensive takeaway from the latest trendy restaurant had to be cancelled, Julian would say, 'Sal, it isn't a problem, we'll do it another time. I just thought you would enjoy it,' or 'I thought it would be lovely to have a cosy night in together.' Sally felt torn; she hated letting either Myrtle or Julian down.

'Sal, you must focus on what's right for you. But there has to be give-and-take in a relationship. Make sure the giving isn't too one sided,' was Myrtle's advice.

'You think it is, don't you?'

'I'm not saying that. I'm not the one to advise you, because I don't compromise. I do exactly and only what I want to do. It's why I keep my relationship with Ed pretty casual.'

'God, I wish I was more like you, Myrtle, so in control!'

'That's rubbish, Sal, you just need to stop dithering and face up to situations. You still haven't had a face-to-face with Jack, which, in my opinion, has left him with hope of a reconciliation. You prefer to put up with his endless stream of messages rather than face him. You are going to have to toughen up, my darling. Only you know what's right for you.'

Sally had stopped dithering, taken the plunge and made her decision. But if her first night in Julian's bed had been an omen, it hadn't been a good one. She had woken in the early hours, her head on Julian's shoulder, a wet dribble making its way down the side of her face. Raising her hand, she felt the wet, sticky pool that had gathered above his collarbone. Half asleep and gripped by alarm, she had reached for the switch of her bedside lamp. It was blood; it covered Julian's mouth, his neck and chest. It had stained the pillows. On the sheets it had spread into a bright, amorphous stain.

Despite the light and Sally's alarmed voice, Julian slept on. In a state of growing agitation she shook him vigorously. Julian's eyes flew open. It seemed an age to Sally before he realised what had happened. In the intervening seconds, held in his vacant stare, Sal had looked into the opaque eyes of a dead man; she had recoiled, stifled a scream. The bloodied man staring from the stained bed linen wasn't Julian, the non-seeing eyes didn't belong to Julian.

'Oh, God, Sal, I'm sorry.' Julian sat up, grabbed a handful of sheet to wipe the blood from his mouth and viewed the soiled bed. 'How awful. Hell, Sal, some of it has got on you.'

'What's happened?' Sally asked, looking for the first time at her blood-stained nightdress, her bloodied hands, the blood streaking her hair.

Julian told Sally that the nosebleeds were infrequent, were the result of injuries he had sustained in Afghanistan.

Myrtle said, 'Cocaine! Must have been on it for some time.'

'Cocaine, I don't think so!' said an indignant Sally.

'Take my word for it, my darling, it's the result of snorting coke. Don't look so shocked; most working in the city are on it.'

Sally was shocked. She didn't know whether she should believe Myrtle or not. There had been so much discussion about the 'new beginning' that Sally had presumed the weekend trips to Oxfordshire would, at the very least, be far less frequent. She had been wrong. Julian said goodbye at breakfast on Friday morning and didn't return until late on Sunday evening. When he returned, it was as though he had never been away. He didn't like to be questioned about his weekends, so Sally gave up asking. His silence fired Sally's imagination. She began to question the real state of Julian's marriage. Did his wife know of their relationship? Did she know of his 'new beginning'? She began to obsess about the woman in whose home Julian spent his weekends, who was, according to Julian, his wife in name only. Sally suspected that there had been official company functions to which she hadn't been invited. Had Julian attended with his wife?

When she first moved in with Julian, into the flat, one of the first things Sally had noticed, was the absence of photographs of his family. Photographs didn't feature on the side tables, which were weighed down with art pottery, books and gaming boards, or on the walls amongst the plethora of paintings. It was a strangely fussy, over-furnished flat for a man. Sally had secretly rummaged through drawers and cupboards in search of the missing photographs but had found none. Probably removed out of consideration for her, Sally thought. But it only added to Sally's growing sense of exclusion from whole areas of his life.

But Julian, having thrown up a brick wall against any inquiries by Sally into his own family life, felt quite free to comment on and advise on her relationship with Jack. He was irritated by and resentful of the constant but unanswered calls from Jack. Sally was discovering a controlling, moody side to Julian. True to her nature, she tried to put these newly discovered negative aspects of his character to the back of her mind.

In Julian's absence, Sally spent most of her time with Myrtle, often staying at her place on Friday and Saturday nights. They had spent one particular Saturday collecting over-ordered and slow-selling chilled foods from local supermarkets to stock the newly installed chiller cabinets. The cabinets had been donated by Mr. Aboud, the owner of the Lebanese Deli on Denmark Hill.

'What do you know, girls! My walls are coming down! My customers want to look into my kitchen, want to see me making the khubz, cooking the kibbeh. Until now, I didn't know of their wish. For twenty-two years, they have been wishing to see my ovens, watch me chopping and mixing the fattoush.'

Mr Aboud had been persuaded by his son, Bilal, into a 'make-over'. Perfectly functional, if slightly bruised, equipment was to be removed to make way for shiny new replacements in keeping with their new, open plan setting.

'It's the new thing, girls. Open for all to view, with Faisal Aboud in the starring role. Oh, my!'

Mr. Aboud had the old freezer and chiller cabinets transported to the food bank, installed and checked out by an electrician. He had gone to some lengths to find insulated boxes for carrying food in Myrtle's van.

Myrtle and Sal had liked the look of a vegetarian lasagne, put £5 in the petty cash. They were eating their meal on trays while watching TV in Myrtle's place.

'What do you call this room Myrtle?' asked Sally, looking about her.

'This room? I don't quite know what you mean.'

'This room, the room we're sitting in. What do you call it?'

'A dump, I suppose.'

'No, it isn't. What do you call the room that you sit in, relax in, watch TV in, whatever?'

'Now you've got me thinking. We call it the front room. I'm

thinking that name originates in the rows of terraces built by Victorian and Edwardian speculators and rented to the working classes. Their front rooms became the pride of the lady of the house and were kept pristine for the reception and entertainment of visitors; front being synonymous with best. My mother would call it a drawing room, but then she would be referring to something a little different from this pokey hole. Why are you suddenly so interested in the naming of rooms?'

'Like your mother, Julian calls it the drawing room. Gets irritated when I call it the lounge. He says lounges are to be found in airports.'

'Pompous ass!'

'Your mother wouldn't agree!'

'Sal, my mother was born in 1940. When she was a child, the term would still have been in general use in upper and middle-class houses. There would still have been old ladies who at the end of a meal, had withdrawn from the dining room to allow the gentlemen to enjoy their port in peace and discuss important matters beyond the understanding of women. It's a ridiculously inaccurate affectation, clung to by people like Julian. Lounge is OK, people do lounge about in such rooms. You haven't started saying drawing room, have you?'

'No, I haven't'

'Good, don't you dare! But I bet you try to avoid naming the room at all.'

'You know me so well, Myrtle!'

'Indeed, I do, Sal, darling.'

Sal remembered the day she had first seen the Fulham house. Julian had asked her to meet him at Embankment. They had taken the District Line. It wasn't on the way home, but Julian wouldn't tell her where they were going. 'Patience, Sal. Wait and see!' he had said. The surprise had turned out to be the mid-terraced house in

Fulham.

'What do you think?'

'Very nice and no doubt very expensive,' Sally replied, looking at the white rendered, bay fronted house. The house had nothing to distinguish it from the other houses that occupied the area; row after row, street after street of them. What marked them out was the attached price tag.

'Would you like to live in it? Would you, Sal? If you like it, we'll buy it.'

'What!'

'It would be our first real home together. You'll like it, Sal. I know you will. Where the hell is the agent? Should be here by now'.

Julian had been impatient, quite wound up. Sally could see that it was a big thing for him. He had agreed a price, engaged surveyors and solicitors and within a month they had moved in.

'I bet there are old boards under these carpets. Can you imagine them sanded and varnished? They would look fabulous; change the whole look of the house!' Sally had remarked as they had followed the agent through the edge-to-edge carpeted rooms. Julian had been listening. The house that Sally moved into had stripped and repaired honey-coloured floorboards.

Julian left the furnishing of the house in Sally's hands. 'I'll leave it to you, Sal. I want it to be your choice; it's your home!' he would say when she sought his opinion on some major purchase. Sally had a wonderful time choosing and buying furniture and soft furnishings she never imagined herself being able to afford. Her first purchase was the Habitat dining table and chairs she had looked at so often. She found a sofa that was almost what she wanted, but the feet and arms weren't quite right and they didn't do it in the shade of velvet she had in mind.

'Get them to make it exactly as you want it,' Julian had advised.

'I don't think they will do that.'

'No, they probably won't. You need a bespoke maker. My mother had a sofa made a couple of years ago. I'll find out who she used.'

Sally phoned the company that Julian's mother had used. She directed them to the site where the 'not quite right' sofa could be found and explained the modifications she wanted. Within a week, she had received drawings of the exact sofa she had in mind, together with swatches of blue velvet. An attached sheet gave costings. Sally was horrified; it was a large sofa; she appreciated that; it was to be the central piece in the room. But fourteen-thousand and twelve pounds! A deposit of over four thousand was required. Julian when told of the cost hadn't batted an eyelid. The sofa that arrived four weeks later was magnificent.

It had been transported in a pristine, cream conveyance; van seemed somehow too common a word to use, out of keeping with the pomp of the arrival – the green signage announcing its makers as *'Clute and Frankles. Makers of seating to the discerning since 1876'*. It was lifted from the vehicle by three spotless, green-coated, white gloved handlers and escorted into its home by a liveried individual in green frock coat and top hat. As the sofa made its majestic way through the front door, the escorting gentleman stood to attention and doffed his top hat. Sally wasn't sure whether the hat was raised to her or to the sofa; on reflection, she decided it was in homage to the sofa.

Sally was left in no doubt as to the pedigree of her latest acquisition; she just hoped she was sufficiently discerning to fully appreciate its merits, a point she later made to Julian when he congratulated her on her choice. He had said the sofa was wonderful and pointed out that quality always came at a premium. Cost, no longer being the determining factor in what she bought, didn't sit easily with Sally. She tried not to think of the people who came into the food banks. She was careful to keep her mounting furnishing costs from Myrtle. She didn't mention the bills from Julian's Savile Row tailor that he left lying about or the cost of his bespoke footwear.

Sally wasn't sure whether her own family in Newcastle was working-class or middle-class. Her mother was a nurse and her father a local authority Housing Officer. Both had worked full-time to make a comfortable home in the pre-war semi they had bought soon after they were married. They weren't short of money, but she grew up understanding that money had to be earned, wasn't for squandering! Expensive purchases such as furniture or new carpets had to be saved for. Her mother put money aside for Christmas and holidays. Sally was given pocket money and was encouraged to save for what her parents called 'luxuries'. Sally and her brother had attended the local comprehensive. It was a good school and with the support and encouragement of their parents, both had achieved and gone on to university.

She was confused as to which class she herself now belonged. Jack's family, Sally thought of as middle class. His father was a retired accountant, a partner in a successful practice. His mother had never worked; she hadn't needed to and hadn't wanted to. Jack's family and her own family she thought of as representing the millions of ordinary families in the country. Julian's family was different; with Julian, she was stepping into unknown territory, unsure of the ground beneath her feet.

She was unsure of her status in the matter of the house. Julian called it her home and had said, 'If you like it, we'll buy it.' Not I, but we! The house was way out of Sally's price range, she was under no illusion about that, it was Julian's money that had bought it. But something niggled in her mind. In Sally's experience, couples bought houses in joint names. Her parents were joint owners of her family home, she was joint owner of the flat she had shared with Jack.

Julian went to his family home every weekend; divorce was never mentioned, their future status as a couple wasn't spoken of. It was an added confusion in Sally's life. She was beginning to feel like a kept woman!

It had taken Sally six months to tell her parents of the breakup of her marriage. Her parents liked Jack, got on well with him. She knew they would be upset and ask endless questions. She had put off the difficult conversation but had finally plucked up courage and gone home for the weekend. She had waited until after Sunday lunch to tell them, shortly before she needed to leave to catch her train.

'Left Jack!' her father had said, in a tone of utter disbelief.

'Left Jack!' echoed her mother.

There followed the inevitable questions - Why? When? Why wait so long to tell us?

'All those times I asked after Jack! All those times you told me everything was fine. You were lying to me. Oh, Sally, how could you?' said her mother.

'I didn't want to upset you.'

'And who are these friends he didn't like?' asked her father.

Sally told them about Myrtle, about the boat people, about her work with Myrtle, about the Calais camp. Sally was shocked by their reaction.

'The Calais camp!' shouted her father. You went with this woman to that camp! A dangerous place like that, full of desperate men. My, God, of course Jack would try to stop you. What a foolhardy venture; I never heard the like of it.'

It was a tearful Sally that left to catch her train. She left behind confused and shocked parents. They had left her in no doubt about what they thought of her behaviour. She had the return journey to nurse her injured feelings. The more she thought about her parents words, the angrier she became. It upset her to even admit it, but she thought Myrtle had been right when she said all Brexit voters were racist. Her father's voice rang in her ears; economic migrants, disturbed, desperate, brutalised, scarred. Ugly words!

She had been proud that her home city had voted to remain in the EU. She had kept quiet about her parents voting to leave. Her parents talked about the undemocratic nature of the EU, the need for a reformed immigration policy, a reclaiming of fishing waters. They talked about the same things that Jack and his father talked about.

Before the referendum was called, Sally hadn't had a view on the EU. She hadn't been aware of 'the rule from Berlin', which enraged her parents. She had no idea which, if any, EU laws had affected her life. She was aware that the UK was grouped together with other countries in a kind of club. She knew that France, Germany, Italy and Spain were in the club. She would have been guessing if asked to name the other twenty-three. Her red passport confirmed her as a member of the club; she hadn't thought much about its colour until it had been flagged up by Jack's father as a symbol of the country's subjugation by the EU.

Following Myrtle's crash course on the wonders of the club, Sally had voted to remain. All in the Peckham house had voted to remain. Julian, at odds with his family, all staunch Brexiteers, had voted remain. It seemed to Sally that all London had voted to remain. Sally got the impression that Julian didn't really care about the result, but Myrtle and Ert had been devastated. They had been confident of a remain result.

The day after the referendum, Sally had gone straight from work to Myrtle's place. It was a Friday and Julian was driving to Oxfordshire. She found Art in the kitchen. Spread across the table were newspaper maps and graphics showing the results of the previous day's vote; all were swathed in blue with small areas of red. London was very red! Row upon row of constituencies were listed, most with their little flash of blue. The blue leave columns were very long, the red remain columns, very short.

Art was a real mess; unshaven, shoulder-length hair escaping its leather tie. 'Jesus, Myrt, the whole country is fascist, fucking xenophobes.'

'Not the whole country,' said Myrtle.

'Fucking near enough. Look at the South East, Boston, seventy-five percent. Right across the country. Jesus, Bolsover, seventy point eight. Isn't that Denis Skinner's constituency, Myrt? How the hell has that happened?'

'I don't know, Art, but we can't start blaming poor Denis!'

**

Myrtle was Sally's best friend. She adored Myrtle, looked up to her, she was the older sister she would love to have had. Yet she knew that she was keeping more and more of her life with Julian hidden from her best friend. Although Myrtle didn't say too much, Sally knew that she had serious reservations about Julian. Partly for that reason and partly out of loyalty to Julian, she hadn't told Myrtle about the thing that was troubling her the most.

Sally was often woken by Julian's aggressive, angry shouts. The first time it happened, she had been terrified. Julian told her that his nightmares were driven by dreadful happenings in Afghanistan, by sights he was unable to forget. Sally's heart went out to him. But her sympathy was sorely tested when she woke to find Julian kneeling on top of her, his fingers digging into her arms as he pinned her to the bed, shouting and screaming into her face. The more Sally cried and begged him to stop, the tighter became the grip and the louder the shouting.

Sally's arms were badly bruised. 'I was very frightened, Julian. I know it's dreadful for you, but you really hurt me. Just look at my arms,' Sally pulled up the sleeve of her shirt to show the blackening bruises and the marks left by his fingers.

Julian, who had until that point been most apologetic, became suddenly angry. 'If you are so frightened, you had better move into the spare room, leave me to deal with my nightmares alone like my wife did. I must say that I didn't expect it of you, Sal.'

It was totally unreasonable behaviour on Julian's part; Sally knew that. But she couldn't bring herself to move into the spare room, to abandon him to his nightmares. She didn't sleep well. At the slightest movement from Julian, she was awake. When the kicking started, she was out of bed and into the bathroom. Behind a locked door, she would sit on the toilet seat, hands covering her ears, until the noise stopped. When fully awake, when the horrors of the Afghan desert had receded, he would knock quietly on the door.

'It's OK, Sal. I'm awake now. Come back to bed. You'll get cold in there.' He would put his arms around her, hug her, tuck her up in bed. 'I've frightened you, my darling. I'm a monster,' he would say, holding her to him and stroking her hair. Sometimes he cried and begged Sally not to leave him. 'What am I going to do, Sal?' he would sob.

Sally made soothing noises but didn't answer. She had learned that lesson. Once, she had suggested that he could get help. She had read an article in a magazine about Post Traumatic Stress Disorder. The article talked about trauma suffered during military service. He had flared up when she had made the suggestion.

'Do you really think me so stupid, Sal, that I don't know about such organisations. Those people can't help me. Nobody can remove those images from my mind.'

Chapter 11

Sir Richard Goffe

Jack decided to take up his parents' offer and move back home – just for the weekends! It was a compromise. He knew he should make a permanent move but couldn't bring himself to put himself under such close observation. He kept away from the Fulham house; he still went cold when he remembered how close he had come to coming face-to-face with Sal in her own bedroom. Despite Christian finding it a huge joke, he still worried that there were watchers on Edgar Street who would recognise the car or recognise him and call the police. He had visions of a squad car, sirens wailing, coming speeding down the street, boys in blue jumping out, dragging him from his car and putting him in handcuffs.

He spent weekends back in his old bedroom. On Mondays and Thursdays, he went straight from work to The Duck, where he met up with some of the old crowd. There were usually a couple of others at a loose end who joined him in a pub crawl that invariably ended with a curry in the Star of India. Tuesday and Wednesday evenings he spent in the flat.

When spending his evening in, he stopped off on his way home to pick up a ready meal and a few cans at the Tesco Extra. Christian was a regular, often overnight visitor. His present work was keeping him in London; there were people working in Westminster who were being watched. Who these people were or why they were being watched, Christian wasn't at liberty to say. Their meal heated in the microwave, the pair would settle for the evening on the lager and food-stained sofa and talk into the early hours, oblivious to the mess surrounding them.

Hoovering and dusting were operations that had departed with Sally over two years before. Jack did his washing on Wednesday evening, taking care to use the non-crease cycle. He retrieved his shirts and trousers from the dryer when just dry, smoothed them out and hung them up straight away. He was very proud of the process he had devised; he hadn't once had to use the iron. His bedding was rarely changed and the bathroom was filthy. When the kitchen worktops and sink could hold no more dirty pots and pans, he loaded the dishwasher; that usually kept him going for a few days.

He did make some effort to recycle. He believed in recycling. He worried a great deal about global warming. People who requested plastic bags in the supermarket made him very angry. He took care to keep his reusable bags in the car and carried them with him into the store. He had once had a blazing row with the store manager over their 'slavish dedication' to wrapping the most innocent piece of fruit in polluting crap.

Evenings alone saw him settled on the sofa in time for the 7 o'clock news. The news finished, he typed in 'latest Brexit news' on his laptop, had a good read through the headline reports and followed any interesting threads. He caught up on the latest statements from Michel Barnier, Donald Tusk, Junker et al. He was an online subscriber to various newspapers. He forced himself to read the liberal clap trap spewed out by the remain supporting publications; it made his blood boil, but it gave him an insight into that mindset. 'Know your enemy' - that's what his dad said. On his new SkyQ2TB box, he recorded all the political interviews of the week. He was sometimes up into the early hours catching up on the thoughts of those interviewed by Thornbury, Ridge, Neil and company. He had to stop himself from shouting at the TV since his neighbours on both sides had complained about the noise.

He had watched a mass of blue EU flags paraded across his screen as an anti-Brexit rally made its way through London. The 700,000 reportedly marching were headed up by young voters. At the front of the march was the Mayor of London, Sadiq Khan. A placard read, 'Brexit is Bananas'. A brief mention was made of the pro-Brexit rallies taking place in other cities around the country. Nigel Farage had led a Harrogate rally organised by Leave Means Leave. Nigel said that evidence suggested that a third of those who voted remain now wanted the government to get on with it and honour the democratic vote.

Well said, Nigel!

**

Bleary eyed Jack fumbled for his phone – 10:14am! His Saturday lie-in, the normal piece of his parent's home was disturbed by the sound of raised voices. He could hear his sister Julia's voice. What the hell was going on? He threw on his dressing gown and went downstairs. Julia's voice was coming from the kitchen. She seemed quite hysterical, drowning out his mother's slow, measured tones. He opened the dining room door; his father was sitting eating breakfast. At the table with him were Poppy and Sam, wide-eyed and silent.

'What's going on?'

'Left her, last night. Packed his bags and went. She's in a dreadful state!'

'Hell!'

'Yes, exactly!' Now Jack, Poppy, Sam and I are going out. We haven't yet decided where to go. We want to have a nice long walk while Mummy and Grandma have a good chat. We would be very happy to have your company, if you feel like joining us,' said Ron, casting a meaningful look in Jack's direction.

'Can we go to feed the ducks, Grandad?' asked Sam.

'Well, we all need to agree on where we are going. What about you Poppy, would you like to go to the park to feed the ducks?'

'Yes, but can we take some food for the parakeets too?' Poppy was absent-mindedly dangling a spoon over a bowl of cornflakes.

'I'll raid grandma's bird food box. But first, I want to see some breakfast eaten. I want at least three of those soldiers dipped into that egg and eaten, Sam. And, Poppy, start eating your cornflakes.'

With Poppy clutching a bag of birdseed, and Sam half a loaf of bread, they got the children into the car and drove to Windsor Great Park. They parked up at Virginia Water, the area of the park the children liked best. The upset of the morning, for the moment forgotten, the children ran ahead of Ron and Jack down to the shoreline, where they were soon surrounded by flapping, quacking Mandarins and Coots, their beaks to the ground, eager for their share of the bread pieces. The birdseed was carefully laid in trails on top of low walls and at the base of shrubs as the walk took them past the waterfall and on to the totem pole.

The totem pole was always the highlight of the visit to Virginia Water. Poppy and Sam were fascinated by the towering, colourful structure with its ogling faces and primitively carved creatures. Ron had told them all about the carvings and what they represented. They knew about the wisdom of the beaver and the dignity and strength of the whale.

'Tell us again about the curse, Grandad,' Poppy would say, gazing up at the 100 foot extravaganza. It was a ritual played out whenever they came to see the totem pole. It was, Ron thought, like the rereading of a favourite book. Ron had to repeat the story of the 600-year-old Western Red Cedar from which the pole has been carved. Of Chief Mungo Martin, who carved the totem pole as a present for the queen from the people of Canada in 1958.

'Was it for our queen, Grandad?' Sam would interrupt.

'Yes, Sam, our queen; Queen Elizabeth the Second.'

Ron would go on to tell how Chief Mungo became very angry and put a curse on the pole when he wasn't allowed to come to England to present it in person. At this point in the telling, both children would turn serious faces on Ron as though hearing the story for the first time and say, 'Ooh, did the curse hurt the Queen?' Ron would explain how a gentleman from Windsor had gone to Canada and sorted it all out, and how Chief Mungo had lifted the curse when he was allowed to come to England. Poppy and Sam loved looking at the online photographs of its ceremonial arrival and presentation to the queen.

A good trudge around the lake brought some colour to the children's faces and sharpened appetites for pizza and fries. Poppy surveyed her chocolate sundae for some seconds before putting down her spoon and fixing her eyes on her grandfather.

'Daddy has gone forever, hasn't he, Grandad? We will never see Daddy again.'

Jack looked at his father; he saw Ron's face crumble, tears springing to his eyes. 'What's this about, Pops? What makes you say that?' he asked, diverting the child's attention from his father.

'That's what Daddy said. He said, I'm out of here, Julia. I won't be back. I don't want to hear your voice again'.

'Daddy meant Mummy's shouting.' Jack reached across the table and took hold of Poppy's little hand; the knuckles were dimpled into soft puppy fat, the nails badly bitten. 'I have to tell you something, Pops, grown-ups don't always mean what they say. It's very bad because grown-ups should know better. It sounds like your mummy and daddy had a big row and probably said things they didn't mean.'

'I think Daddy did mean it, Uncle Jack. He hates Mummy's shouting. I don't think Daddy will ever come back.'

Jack felt a lump in his throat. There was an old-fashioned knowingness about Poppy, as though a wise, much older being existed in her child's body.

'I heard that it was very late when Daddy left. I'm surprised you weren't asleep,' said Ron.

'I was Grandad, but Mummy's shouting woke me; she was shouting very loudly. I came out of my room and looked down through the bannister railings. Sam was watching too. Daddy had a big suitcase, not the small one he takes when he goes away for his work.' Poppy leaned across the table towards Ron and said in a low, conspiratorial voice, 'We were spying, Grandad! Don't tell Mummy.'

A sudden, loud sob escaped Ben. 'I want my Daddy to come back,' he said, wiping away tears with the sleeve of his rugby shirt.

'Come and sit over here with me, old man. Bring that ice-cream with you. Let's see if we can make it disappear together,' said Ron.

They got back to find plans well under way for Margaret to accompany Julia and her grandchildren back to Weybridge.

Julia needs support, Ron. She's very distressed. She's finding it very hard to cope,' said Margaret.

'As are we all, my dear. I think it's time Julia heard a few home truths.'

'Oh, Ron! Please don't say anything; she's very upset.'

'No doubt. But Julia needs to understand that she isn't the only one who is upset. We are upset, no doubt her husband is upset. Her children are very upset,' said Ron, going in search of his daughter.

It was an awkward leave taking. Margaret covered her embarrassment by fussing over the children, Ron, by speaking very loudly. Julia, for once, silent, kept her eyes averted from her father. She looked dreadful. Her face, devoid of makeup, looked strangely naked. She was wearing jeans and a strange fake fur jacket with indigo spots and had shrunk into flat shoes. Ron made no pretence of approving his wife's actions.

'I would remind you, my dear, that you have your own commitments to attend to. Don't leave it too long before you return to us,' was his parting shot.

A bit high-handed, Jack thought, but he hadn't seen his father so angry and upset for a long time.

'Bloody difficult woman, your sister. Those poor children! Ron was still bristling with anger as they sat down to the casserole Margaret had left in the oven. Her fault, no doubt about it! You can't belittle a man in that way and not expect a reaction. OK, the fella's a mouse, but she married him. A damn good provider and no doubt if there's a divorce, she can expect a good financial settlement. Some question about the children, though. She thinks he'll want custody.'

'Really! Mind you, the kids seem very fond of him.'

'Are you surprised? Let's face it, their mother's a bloody tyrant!'

'Do you think there's any chance of it blowing over?'

'No. I think he means what he says. Didn't think he had it in him. I wonder where he's moved out to?'

'It's not much to go on, but a while ago I saw him with a woman. It was in the early hours; I was on my way home in a taxi. They were walking through Kensington.'

'Now that is interesting!'

Ron had poured a couple of double whiskies and they had settled in the sitting room to watch the news. Jon Snow was interviewing Richard Goffe. Jack had been tracking the MP for a while; a leading figure in a cabal of Conservative MPs whose stated aim was to stop any meaningful Brexit. Goffe was being grilled on a statement he had made outside his London home the previous day. The house formed a backdrop to the footage - a Georgian terrace, Belgravia or Mayfair, Jack thought. There he was, wealthy, upper-class; Eton, Charterhouse or some such establishment, no doubt, living a privileged life, attempting to subvert the will of the people.

Bastard! Must do a bit more digging on Richard, bloody Goffe.

'Strange bloke! Distant, you know. Never really got to know him. No idea what made him tick.'

Ron's words cut across Jack's thoughts. He looked at his father, who wasn't listening to Jon Snow; he was thinking of his shrewish daughter, his unfortunate grandchildren and the enigma that was Graham Fairbrother. Ron looked weary. Was it his imagination, or was his father's face showing lines? Ron was a good-looking man, tall, big framed. He wore his sixty-five years well. Only a sprinkling of grey ran through his dark hair. Jack feared that his sister's troubles were weighing heavily on his laid-back father.

**

Richard Goffe, KC, MBE, was, according to his online profile, a British, Conservative Party politician. Member of Parliament for Mickleford, Surrey, since 1999. Parents, Marcus Gideon Goffe, 5th Baron Sanfold and Pricilla Marjorie Oxbury, 1934 - 1969, granddaughter of Lord Martin Oxbury, elevated to the peerage in 1949 for his services to wartime industry. Sir Richard was born May 1960 at the family home, Buckshot Hall, Surrey, a fine eighteenth-century mansion designed by Sir John Soane. Sir Richard had a younger brother, Phillip and a half-sister Clementia, from his father's second marriage to Lady Pamela Lake in 1972. Succeeded to the title on the death of his father in 2011. Married the Rt. Hon. Jessica Spence in 1989. The couple have two children, Cynthia Monica, 1990, Henry George, 1993. Not known by his title in Parliament.

Entered Parliament at the start of Margaret Thatcher's

third term of office following a distinguished career at the bar. Held junior ministerial positions under John Major and shadow ministerial posts under William Hague, Michael Howard and Ian Duncan Smith. He had risen to prominence in David Cameron's coalition government but returned to the back benches in Theresa May's administration.

**

Jack had started to record the Parliament Channel. He spent hours trawling the footage. Goffe might be out of favour with the administration, but he knew how to make himself heard from the back benches. It seemed to Jack that Goffe was never off his feet. When called by the speaker, he stood up slowly, paused until satisfied that he was the focus of attention, gave the knot of his tie a tweak, looked about him with the air of a disappointed headmaster and berated those assembled for their confused thinking. Goffe fired broadsides at all who had the temerity to remind the house that 17.4 million people had voted to leave the European Union. Sitting around him were some dozen toadies who bleated like demented sheep at his outrageous pronouncements. The media adored him, followed him everywhere; assured of a steady flow of controversial statements. Footage of his parliamentary interventions was replayed on all news channels.

Jack thought that the tide was turning. The remainers were in the ascendancy. Most of the papers were in the remain camp. The Brexit supporting press was being drowned out. He spent his evenings reviewing footage, identifying the 'enemies of the people'. Jack was becoming bitterly resentful and angry. He wasn't alone; pro and anti-Brexit arguments raged in the office and in The Duck.

'No doubt about it, mate, they're getting the upper hand,' said Christian. He was sitting next to Jack on the stained sofa, balancing his microwaved M&S meal on his knee. They had just watched a knockabout in the Commons. 'They have both houses and the courts batting for them. We think it's bound to end in another referendum. It's what the EU wants and they always get their way!'

Jack didn't know who the 'we' were, but he did know that they knew things he didn't know. Christian's very secretive employers were very knowledgeable. It enraged Jack. The image of the pontificating Goffe standing in front of his huge, London pile, infuriated him.

Bloody traitors. Should be locked up - the whole bloody lot of them. Locked up and the keys thrown away!

**

Opening the front door, Jack heard the sound of rattling pots and the kitchen radio playing. His mother was home.

He put his head around the door. 'Hi Mum, when did you land?'

'At lunch time.' Margaret was peeling and chopping parsnips and carrots. 'I've got a meat pie in the oven; I'm sure you are both ready for something freshly cooked.'

'Smells good! How is Julia?'

'Dreadful! She isn't fit to be left on her own, but I couldn't have put up with it for another day.'

'Really, that bad. What's happening?'

'Oh, my goodness, where to start?' Margaret wiped her hands on a tea towel and sat down at the table.

Jack thought she looked tired. There were dark shadows below her eyes. The fine lines on her forehead and about her mouth seemed to have deepened. Grey was showing at the roots of her dark hair. It was unlike his mother to neglect her appearance.

'Nothing will convince her that she might in any degree be responsible for him leaving. Unless you agree with her every word, you are turned on and shouted down. She suspects him of all manner of things. There's no doubt about it, Graham can be odd, but my goodness, he's lived with her for a lot longer than I could. I spent the last week listening to her take on him. It was all I was allowed to do. She painted a picture of a man I didn't recognise. When he was in our company, he was quiet, inoffensive. Julia describes him as secretive, opinionated, silently contemptuous of those around him. 'Laughing up his sleeve at all of us,' was how she put it. I'm not sure I believe her. She would drive me to secrecy, and of course anyone who didn't agree with her would risk being considered opinionated.'

'Strange, "Laughing up his sleeve". Pretty much how Sal used to describe him!'

'She didn't like him then. That's interesting!'

'Yeh, well, I don't know, I found him OK. I would have liked to see him put her in her place. So, what does she think he's been up to?'

'She's been nosing into his emails and phone. The problem, as I see it, is that she had no idea what she was looking at; a lot of it was from colleagues, both men and women. She saw an email from a woman named Tia arranging a meeting at 'the cottage'. She thinks this is the woman he is involved with. Graham often took the children out at weekends - to the zoo, to see a film, on a boat trip down the Thames, down to the coast in the summer. Under Julia's relentless grilling, Sam revealed what Poppy calls 'Daddy's secret'. Poppy is very upset; she is very angry with Julia, who she says made Sam tell the secret.'

'What's the secret?'

'Well, all a bit odd! They were sometimes joined by someone called David. Sam says that David was very kind; he bought them sweets and ice cream. David had just finished university, so most probably early twenties.'

**

'A bit strange!'

There was no mention of Goffe's London house in the online entry. He wasn't listed in the phone directory; he had no social media trace. Enquiries at work drew a blank; nobody could identify the house location from the interview footage. He found Wikipedia entries for his brother, Phillip Goffe and his sister, Clementia; neither mentioned the London house.

Jack hit lucky when he stumbled on the report of a break-in at an address in Eaton Square. It was at the home of Lady Patricia Goffe. There had been quite a write up on the lady's pedigree. She was Sir Marcus Goffe's widow, his second wife, Richard Goffe's stepmother. Lady Patricia was from a prominent American banking family, formerly the widow of Lord Denborough, who had been killed in a car crash in Sicily.

The break-in had taken place in November 2016. Jewellery personal to Lady Patricia, together with family jewels, was stolen. The house had been her main home since the death of her husband. Living in the house with Lady Patricia were Richard Goffe, MP and his son George.

Bingo!

What Jack, in his more delusional moments, liked to think of as legitimate sleuthing, had for months been an integral part of his daily routine. Jack missed it. He quite fancied a trip to Eaton Square!

He made a quick exit from the office, grabbed a Classic Tuna from Subway and jumped on the tube to Victoria. From the station, he crossed Ebury Street, walked down Elizabeth Street, past Eaton Square Gardens and walked straight into a media pack gathered on the pavement. Nobody appeared to notice him as he edged his way in at the back. There was a television crew, their van bristling with aerials, parked a few metres down the street. Most gathered were on their mobiles, some had cameras slung about their necks, others carried the familiar, bulbous, press microphones. All looked bored. Jack recognised a few well-known faces from television.

The focus of attention was the third house from the end in a row of large, terraced houses on the north side of the square. The houses, five-storey, white stuccoed with pillared porticos, were unified by first-floor low balconies - stark in their uniformity!

On the opposite side of the road, a small group of onlookers were gathered. Jack walked over to join them. Behind them were the gardens, the private, most probably locked, domain of the square's residents. He had read somewhere that the Eaton Square gardens housed tennis courts. On a family day out, exploring the city, and there had been many such outings, his father had told them about the private gardens dotted about the capital. 'The lungs of the city,' he had called them, said there were some six hundred such gardens in the city. Jack remembered it because Julia had been yawning and looking bored. It was one of the few times he had seen his father lose his temper.

A shout of 'Here we go!' went up as a black Daimler approached. There was a flurry of activity as the big car pulled into the kerb. The pack jockeyed for position; cameras and phones flashed. A huge hubbub of shouted questions greeted Goffe as he stepped from the car. What looked like an aide jumped forward and together with the chauffeur, attempted to push back the crowd.

'Evening, ladies and gentlemen and what a lovely evening it is!' said the MP, beaming at his audience.

'Are you calling for a second referendum Mr. Goffe? What

about the 17.4 million who voted to leave? How will they feel about a second referendum?' shouted the guy from Sky.

'What questions would be on the ballot paper? Would remain be an option?' shouted a woman reporter.

'I can see no other option. The House will not support an agreement that leaves the country worse off. The British people now recognise the lies that were told by those advocating leave during the campaign. It was the narrowest of victories. Now that we better understand the full implications of the decision, we must take the matter back to the people,' said Goffe.

'David Cameron promised that even the difference of one vote would decide the matter; promised to implement the result,' was shouted from the crowd.

'How many referendums is it to be, Mr. Goffe? Is it to be the best of three?' asked the woman reporter.

'Thank you, ladies and gentlemen,' said Goffe, ignoring a further barrage of questions and heading towards the timely opening door.

'Didn't like the turn the questioning was taking,' said the woman standing next to Jack. 'Caused a right old rumpus in the Commons today. Got some strange ideas about democracy, that one!'

The square was clearing. Sky was piling back into their van, reporters jumping into cars and onlookers drifting away when Jack became aware of a girl who had come up the steps from the basement of the house. She had paused, her hand on a gate at the top of the steps. She had looked up and down the street before stepping out onto the pavement and setting off in the direction of Lyall Street. Jack wondered who she was; perhaps she worked for Goffe. Interesting! He set off after her. He kept his distance while taking care to keep her auburn, bobbed hair and green top in sight. He followed her along Upper Belgrave Street into Belgrave Square.

On the corner of the square was the most ornate, lavishly decorated frontage Jack had ever seen. The walls were pastel painted. The windows festooned in garlands of realistic, artificial flowers, the door framed by racemes of mauve wisteria and pink roses. On the pavement were painted metal café tables and chairs in the company of beehives and watering cans. Green and white striped awnings adorned the windows. Above the door, in black lettering, was the name 'Dilly Jones'. The girl went in; Jack gave it only a moment's thought before following her.

The interior was small, room for only a few tables. The girl was sitting down, ordering. Jack sat down at the next table and managed to catch her eye. She smiled, they were almost within touching distance.

'Wow! Everything looks amazing. I don't know what to have!' he said, looking from the menu to the dazzling selection of cakes laid out under the glass counter. What are you having?'

'I'm having a Sicilian Lemon Mini, a slice of Blood Orange and Lemon and a cappuccino.'

'Is that a recommendation?'

'Well, the Sicilian Lemon is one of my favourites, but I've tried them all, they're all yummy.'

'I'll have the same as the lady,' Jack told the waitress, who had drifted over to take his order.

'I take it you haven't been here before?' said the girl.

'First time! Great place! You seem to know it well?'

'I come a couple of times a week; walk over in my break. I love it, a bit zany. Takes you out of yourself.'

'Didn't I see you coming out of Richard Goffe's place in Eaton Square?'

'Oh, no, don't tell me, you're a reporter! I thought I'd got out unnoticed.'

'Don't worry, I'm not official press. I do a bit of freelance work, looking out for a good photo. Trying to make a few bob on the side. I take it you work for Richard Goffe?'

'For Lady Pamela, I'm her PA. It's a non-job, really. She doesn't need a PA. I write a couple of letters a week, usually to her family and usually pretty nasty. That's the height of it. The rest of my time is spent fetching and carrying and putting up with her spite and temper. She's an absolute cow! I'm looking for another position; when I get one, I'm off. But listen to me opening my mouth. I'll be quoted in some tabloid story if I'm not careful.'

'Not through me, you won't. I have zilch connections with the press, you don't need to worry about that. I'm after that shot that nobody else has got.' Taking advantage of the arrival of the cakes, he moved onto her table.

'Well, what do I care anyway. I won't be there long enough to get in hot water!'

She was called Kate and came from Sheffield. She had bright auburn hair, a very pretty face, with lovely, wide-spaced hazel eyes.

'What's Richard Goffe like?'

'Pretty full of himself. I don't have much to do with him, really.'

'Who else lives in the house?'

'It's his Lordship's house really, it's part of the estate, but Lady P has a right of lifetime residence. His Lordship has rooms in the house; he stays while Parliament is sitting. He's rarely here at weekends; goes down to the country. He has breakfast at the house but takes all his other meals at his club or at Westminster. George, that's his son, comes and goes; likes to be called Geo. Clementia, Lady P's daughter, stays occasionally. She's nice!'

'What does the son do?'

'Nothing that I know of! He disappears for weeks then turns up with a pile of dirty washing; he has Millie, that's the housekeeper, wrapped around his little finger. He thinks himself a real charmer.'

'I'm surprised that you use Goffe's title! He's known as Richard Goffe in the house.'

'Yeh, wants to be thought of as one of the people. Total phoney! It's His Lordship this and His Lordship that at home.'

'What about Goffe's wife?'

'She's called Jessica. She lives at Buckshot. She's decent; keeps her distance from Lady P. They don't get on. The old lady can't stand the idea of there being another Lady Sanfold.'

'There must be a big staff?'

'No, everyone is overworked. There's Millie Pugh, the housekeeper. Mary Jones is about to pack in; she calls herself a plain cook on plain cook's pay. She says if they want haute cuisine, they can employ a trained chef on trained chef's pay. There are two maids for the whole house and kitchen. Mrs. Darcy is termed Lady P's companion, but she's really her nurse. Baths her, dresses her, the lot. Dresses her several times a day. Her ladyship has her morning wear, afternoon wear and her dinner dresses. She dresses for dinner, even if it's only herself and Mrs Darcy dining. You would laugh if you could see her! Face painted like a china doll, hair dyed black, nails bright red, hands weighed down with rings. Then there's Pat, Lady P's chauffeur. Pat does all the running repairs. And there's me, of course.'

'Where does Pat live?'

'He has a flat above the coach house at the back. Pat's OK; he lets it all roll over his head, knows how to deal with them. Tom Bruce, that's his lordship's chauffeur, lives in the other flat. He's a strange one, doesn't mix with the rest of us. He spends a lot of time in Mickleford, drives his lordship up and down and sometimes stays there on business. We all wonder what the 'business' might be.'

'What about the place in Surrey? Do you go there much?'

'Me? No. I'm attached to Lady P. Nobody from the house has much to do with Mickleford.'

'I read that there was a break-in at the house a couple of years back.'

'It was before my time, but I've heard quite a lot of whisperings about that.'

'Really what sort of whisperings?'

'I shouldn't repeat it; it's just gossip, really, not much hard evidence.'

'Of what?'

Kate looked about her to check nobody could hear, then soundlessly mouthed 'insurance fraud.'

'God!'

'Yeh! There was a full investigation, but nobody was charged. Rumour has it that items of jewellery reported stolen have mysteriously found their way back into Lady P's jewellery case. Another version has it that it was George, that Lady P figured it out. I can believe that, because she's as sharp as a razor.'

'All sounds bloody risky!'

'For you and me, yeh, but this lot consider themselves fireproof. Friends in high places and all that. If it's a one-off photo you want, you should go down to Mickleford. Shooting parties and all sorts down there.'

**

'Tossers, the whole bloody lot of them. Half-brained inbreds! Get yourself down there, mate, see what you can find out about the arrogant bastard!' had been Christian's advice.

Chapter 12

Julian

The Eastaughffe Gallery had been the last place that Julian would have chosen to spend his evening. Caroline Parker, who headed up publicity, had been called to an impromptu meeting in Birmingham, dropping the gig in Julian's lap. The gallery was exhibiting the work of a young Eritrean asylum seeker who had been taken up by Redbridge Council. Several firms, including his own, had sponsored the exhibition. Sponsoring local charities and events had become an important aspect of promoting the caring face of business in the city; his own firm had an outreach department solely for this purpose.

Julian had straight away spotted the beautiful, blonde viewer. She was called Sally. He had spent the following week attempting to arrange a meeting. Sally had proved annoyingly resistant to his invitations - a reaction from a woman rarely experienced by Julian. He didn't quite know how it had happened, how he had drifted into such a serious relationship, how he had come to break all the rules, that had up to that point, had served him so well.

He had found her to be a good listener as well as a great talker. She was an open book. Before their first meeting had ended, she had told him her life story and the details of the breakup with her husband. On consideration, he thought he had found Sally 'comfortable'. She was a thoroughly nice person. She was touchingly appreciative of things that women in his own circle took for granted. Unlike such women, she didn't pry into his background. She didn't, on first meeting, attempt to work out just which branch of the Tennant family he belonged to, track his ancestry while boasting of their own unbroken blood line to the conqueror. Sally was 'out of the loop', knew nothing of the social snobbery that pervaded the society in which he normally mixed. She was a breath of fresh air! It had taken Julian several months of wining and dining to persuade her to move in with him.

It was no coincidence that they had met at an event in support of an asylum seeker. Julian had soon become aware of Sally's dedication to the cause of the underprivileged. Her left-wing activities had been a source of secret amusement. Her odd friends he viewed as eccentric, previously unencountered types – annoying but harmless. He couldn't imagine their interventions having any effect on Home Office decisions. Art and his kind could dig as many tunnels as they liked, spend their lives in tree houses, but wouldn't, Julian thought, halt the march of progress. It was shortly after meeting Sally that he heard about the planned trip to the Calais refugee camp. He hadn't, of course, voiced his horror that any sane person should voluntarily set foot in such a place; he had merely raised an eyebrow and advised her to take care.

The referendum had been a bit of a relationship tester. Julian hadn't given two hoots whether the country left or remained in the EU. His only thoughts had been of David Cameron's stupidity in calling it in the first place. His family were staunch Brexiteers, his London friends equally committed remainers. When in Oxfordshire, he paid lip service to the leave cause and when in London, to remaining. Sally, who, in Julian's opinion, had no understanding of the issues, parroted all the remain clichés that fell from her friend Myrtle's lips: leaving would be committing economic suicide, taking a leap into the dark, would threaten national security.

'We will be safer and so much better off if we stick together. I'm so worried; only a week to go and Art says the polls are tightening,' Sally had said, absent mindedly pushing her smoked mackerel salad about her plate.

They were dining at Hawksmoor. Julian had gone to some trouble to get a table. He had been irritated by Sally's lack of appreciation of her surroundings, her lack of interest in the food.

'How will we be safer, Sal? I thought we had a pretty strong security set up, close cooperation with the US. I think it's in the EU's interests to keep us sweet, don't you?'

Sally had flushed to the roots of her hair. Julian had regretted the words as soon as they were out of his mouth. He knew that Sally's knowledge of security matters would fit on the back of a postage stamp.

'Well, everyone seems very worried about it,' said Sally, flicking back her hair and turning her attention to her starter.

'Oh, come on, Sal, let's not talk about the referendum; let's have a night off from it. What do you think of this place? Really well done, I think!'.

Sally looked about her - at the dark wood panelling, the diner-style tables with leather-covered bench seating. 'It's lovely,' she said, looking up to the huge lantern dome set into the dark wood ceiling. 'Really lovely.'

He had let his irritation get the better of him, he had upset her and it wasn't her fault. He knew himself to be on a short fuse. Sally wasn't the only person getting under his skin.

It was a disappointment to Julian to discover, that despite her blonde hair, Sally lacked the ability of his more casual bedfellows to keep his nightmares at bay. Within a week of her moving in, he was back amid the desert carnage. He had woken, sweat drenched, to find Sally sitting rigid at the furthest edge of the bed, arms wrapped protectively about her chest, wide, terrified eyes fixed on him.

Sally had been sympathetic when he explained the cause of the nightmares. 'God! You poor thing. I'll go down and make you a hot drink.'

'Whisky, Sal, get me a whisky.'

Sally had put the whisky into strong tea. It had been a strange concoction, but it had worked. He had drifted off into a calm sleep, his head on Sally's shoulder, wearing the clean, dry pyjamas she had made him change into. But the nightmares continued; were if anything, more frequent. Sally had found her own way of dealing with them.

Julian had started to worry that Lucy had found out about Sally. Several times recently, she had suggested coming up to town during the week.

'We could go out to dinner or see a show, like we used to do. I could come up on an early train and spend the day catching up with Margo. I could meet you after work, get a cab back to Hampstead.'

It had been several years since Lucy and Julian had slept together. Lucy had set her conditions and stuck to them.

'Get psychological help,' she had told him. 'I'm not willing to risk accidental strangulation in the night. I have my children to think of.'

Lucy had good contacts in the city; he wondered what she might have heard. She knew of his cocaine habit; perhaps she was just worried about him. It could be as simple as that! She could have heard about a couple of less than flattering incidents at work; if his father knew, then his mother might know and could have told Lucy. That was the most likely explanation; a plan hatched between the three to keep him on the straight and narrow. Still, Julian was uneasy! Supposing Lucy decided to show up at the flat unannounced? It was unlikely; she had never shown the least interest in the flat. Her London base was with Margot. Nevertheless, there was some risk. It was what gave him the idea of buying the house in Fulham.

He had taken care to cover his tracks, bypassed the firm's solicitors and covered up any evidence of the purchase. He had locked up the flat in Tavistock Place and moved with Sally into Edgar Street. The flat could be opened up if any member of the family showed signs of wanting to visit. He had arranged for contract cleaners to come in a couple of times a year, had set the heating on low for the winter. Any emergency would be dealt with by the management group, who had keys to all the flats. He told Sally that the flat had been rented.

He had given Sally carte blanche to decorate and furnish the house. Her impeccable taste had surprised Julian. Like many of his class, he had imagined a discerning eye to be exclusive to the privileged and wealthy. Sally had shown Julian an internet image of an impressive, contemporary extension to a house similar to Edgar Street. He had thought it a good investment idea and thought it would please Sally! He had plans drawn up and applied to Hammersmith and Fulham Planning Department for permission to build a similar extension.

Engrossed in the planning of the extension, he had neglected to secure the house. This neglect had been commented on by the police, who when called out, had made plain their opinion that unimpeded entry into the house through an old, rotten window wasn't the wisest security measure. They pointed to the private nature of the back gardens; trees and shrubs blocking a view of the house from neighbouring properties. They advised him to install an alarm system sooner rather than later. A guy came out to take fingerprints from around the smashed window frame and the door leading from the old toilet into the hall. He had heard nothing further from them; he wasn't surprised.

Sally had come home mid-afternoon and discovered the break-in. She had taken time off work to go through paperwork with Myrtle. Fortunately, Sally had been late. Myrtle had been waiting outside the house, so they had gone in together. Sally had been very upset, found the idea of someone in her bedroom touching her possessions very hard to deal with.

'I think it was Jack,' she told Julian later that evening.

'Jack, your husband, Jack! What do you mean?'

'I think it was Jack who broke in.'

'What?'

'I'm almost sure that it was him, Julian.'

'Sal, I can't believe what you're saying. What's put such a barmy idea into your head?'

'It's not barmy. When I came into the house, I got a really strong sense of his presence. He's been in our bedroom, I'm sure he has. He's taken my nightdress, Julian; it's really spooked me.'

'Jesus, Sal, you can't say things like that! You have absolutely no justification for saying such a thing - no justification whatsoever.'

'I know I haven't any proof, but I'm sure it was him. I haven't said anything before, but I think he's watching me.'

'Watching you?'

'Kind of stalking - secretive, sly! A couple of things he's said in messages have made me think he watches me.'

'What's he said?'

'Well, he talked about picturing me in a jacket that he couldn't have seen me in. I bought it long after we split up.'

'For God's sake, Sal, that means nothing. He may have seen you somewhere; you both work in the same city. You can't say he broke in here, you can't make those kind of accusations. Crazy way of thinking; bordering on paranoia, Sal.'

There were aspects of Sally's behaviour that he found very irritating. Unless served in a restaurant, she called meals eaten in the evening 'tea'. In Julian's experience, 'tea' was a light meal served by his grandmother in mid-afternoon or a drink brewed in a pot or cup. Despite Julian's assertion that 'lounges' belonged in airports and couches in doctors consulting rooms, Sally persisted with the terms. Niggling irritations! But it was the matter of the cleaning agency that really rankled.

The agency had cleaned and organised the Artley House flat. Julian had presumed that the arrangement would continue in the Fulham house. Sally hadn't liked the idea but had agreed to give it a trial. She had found fault from the beginning. She was spooked by strangers touching her belongings. She disliked the way the bed was made, their organisation of the bathroom and kitchen. She hated what she called their constant rearranging of her personal things.

Julian had reluctantly ended the contract and left the cleaning and organisation of the house to Sally, who, driven by what Julian thought of as some strange working-class urge, wished to turn herself into a house maid - a most inefficient maid, as it turned out. He had become accustomed to returning to an ordered house: floors hoovered, surfaces dusted, bedrooms, bathrooms and kitchen pristine. On Sally's watch, the kitchen was messy, only obvious surfaces were dusted, the bed was left unmade, bathrooms were grubby and washing was piled on utility room worktops. Sally declared herself very happy with the arrangement, no longer feeling that she was living in a hotel!

17th June 2017, had been Julian and Sally's 'first anniversary'. It was unfortunate that the 17th had fallen on a Saturday and even more unfortunate, that it was the Saturday that Julian's family were celebrating his father's 70th birthday. Julian had explained to Sally the importance of the occasion to his family, offered a weekend shopping trip to New York to compensate, but she wasn't to be placated. For once, the easy-going Sally dug her heels in. Julian was shocked at the outpouring of pent-up frustration. She questioned the reason for his weekends in Oxfordshire, the exact state of his relationship with his wife.

'Surely, Julian, you can't stay together indefinitely for the sake of the children. I can't think it the best way forward for yourself, your wife or the children. You led me to believe that your marriage was over. Have you discussed a divorce?'

'Of course we have, Sal; it's just waiting for the time to be right.'

'Right for whom?'

'The children, for the stability of the children, really! Benedict is going through a bit of a bad patch; started bedwetting again. It's difficult, you know!'

'Yes, no doubt!'

Julian had thought it a bit rich from Sally, given the status of her own marriage, which remained unsettled. Sometimes she would spend the best part of the evening dealing with a ringing or bleeping phone. She would pick up the phone, bring up and delete the message, or shut off the call. The calls, all from her husband, seemed to come in irregular bursts, sometimes for several days. Julian found it incredibly annoying - an intrusion into their privacy.

'Sal, don't you think it's time you put a stop to all this?' he said.'

'How can I do that?'

'Tell him that the relationship is over. It seems to me that he hasn't yet got that message.'

'Unless I used very cruel words, he wouldn't stop and I can't bring myself to be so cruel. He will give up eventually.'

Julian saw red. 'For God's sake, Sal, get a grip. How long am I supposed to put up with that noise, it's bloody trying. At least put the damned thing on silent.'

**

Julian had left Sally in a huffy mood. She had hardly spoken to him over breakfast. She was still sulking about him going down to the country on their anniversary weekend. He had stopped off at his parent's house on his way home on Friday evening. He had found his mother standing in the middle of a huge marquee that had been put up on the top lawn. A wooden floor was being laid and oceans of yellow fabric was being draped over the interior canvas by people on tall ladders. Above their heads, great swathes of the same yellow fabric had been draped from the sides to meet in the centre of the roof in an elaborate rose design.

'What do you think, darling?' said Daphne, taking his arm. 'Isn't it amazing what can be done with a tent! It's exactly what the Addingtons had for Eleanor's wedding.'

Daphne and Lucy were putting the final touches to the preparations for the birthday celebration. Daphne had started months before. She had hired the company that had designed and decorated Cosima and Benedict's rooms to redecorate several bedrooms and had a new kitchen installed. Ted thought it 'an inordinate, unnecessary fuss for an old codger.' A catering company from Oxford had been hired; Daphne had spent hours deciding on the menu for the dinner.

He got home to find the house deserted; a note told him that Lucy was last-minute shopping in Swindon, was going straight from there to Daphne's, that herself and the children would be late and not to wait up. The following morning, he came down to breakfast to find the kitchen taken over by a production line, manned by his mother and Lucy, for the making of floral table decorations.

He scrambled eggs, made toast and coffee and went to the dining room. The children were running about the house, almost bouncing from the walls with excitement. It was all too much for Julian; he took himself off for a long walk and lunch at the Dragon.

It was late afternoon when he returned home. He was greeted

by Cosima, who was twirling about the hall in her new party dress. The dress was an elaborate affair in blue velvet and satin with shoulder straps - far too old for her, he thought!

'Are you wearing makeup, Cosima?' he asked, peering closely at his daughter's face.

'Just a little, Daddy. Mummy said I could, just for this occasion.'

'Where is Mummy?'

'Upstairs, getting ready.'

Julian paused on the landing outside Lucy's closed door. He put his hand on the knob, hesitated for a moment before opening the door. Lucy was sitting at her dressing table, her back towards him. He watched her reflection in the mirror as she drew a hairbrush in long strokes through her dark hair. Julian was transfixed. Seeing him through the mirror, she turned.

'Are you all right, Julian? Time is pressing on; you need to change,' she said, getting to her feet and facing him as he crossed the room towards her.

He put out a hand and ran his fingers down the satiny curtain of dark hair. 'What's happened to us, Luce? We used to be so happy. Can't we go back to being happy together again? I love you, Lucy. I love you so much, my darling!'

Lucy looked into his eyes and caught a glimpse of the man she had loved, the man who had been missing for so long. It brought tears to her eyes.

'Oh, Julian, if only that were possible. But if we are to be happy again you need to become the person you once were. You need help; more so now than you have ever needed it. You are destroying yourself, destroying any hope we have of happiness as a family. You know what you need to do.'

Julian slid his hand to Lucy's waist and pulled her towards him, 'Only for you, my darling, only for you would I do such a thing,' he whispered, before turning from her and walking across the room. As he reached the door, he turned, 'Don't ever mention such a thing to Dad.'

Lucy had gone on ahead with the children. Daphne had booked a children's entertainer called Torcall Twist, who was to kick off the celebrations for the children with a magic show. The magician's assistant, a multi-talented lady named Tiggy Twist, was to be available after the show to paint faces.

'For the younger ones, Daddy. Ben will probably have his face painted,' Cosima told him, making it quite plain that she was far too old and sophisticated for such an activity.

Julian had geed himself up with a fix before setting off. It had got him through the dinner and the speeches and a couple of circuits of the dance floor before he had gone up to his parent's en-suite for a top-up. He had managed to somehow get himself through the evening. It was gone midnight, many of the guests, particularly those with children had left. Julian had found a quiet corner where he sat nursing a lager. He sat with his elbows on the table, a wodge of paper tissues held to his running nose. His head ached, his throat felt like sandpaper, he could barely swallow.

Near the stage, where the band was packing up, a couple of tables had been pushed together to accommodate a noisy group of twenty odds. A cheer went up from the group as a glass crashed to the floor. It felt to Julian as though the splintered glass had been driven straight into his brain. It had been some time since he had attended a similar event, he was shocked by his inability to cope with the noise, with the people.

He looked over to the table where his seventy-year-old father sat with his friends. Ted, despite his protestations of unnecessary fuss, was having a great time. The dinner and formalities over, he had gathered with contemporaries from the firm and a number of his old comrades from his regiment. It had been later noted that they had been first in the queue at the omelette station when the 'survivors' breakfast was served at 4. a.m.

His father was still a good-looking man; tall, his classical, aquiline features still firm, his blonde, grey streaked hair swept back from a high forehead. Julian was very like his father, but the likeness, Julian considered to be skin deep; he would never be the man his father was. He wondered just what his father thought about him at present. He had felt the need to confront Julian about incidents at the office; he had been sympathetic, hinted that he might still be suffering from his time in Afghanistan. What he couldn't bear was for his father to uncover his weakness - his inability to leave behind the images that blighted his life. That he couldn't live with!

Lucy was standing at the entrance to the marquee, talking to a couple of departing guests. She had returned from taking the children home. A sitter had been arranged, the idea being that Lucy and Julian would make a night of it, stay until breakfast was served. That wasn't going to happen! As soon as he could slip away unnoticed, he was going to leave. A great, black cloud of depression had enveloped him. The evening had been too much for him. His day-to-day life - his working day, his home life with Sally - followed a predictable pattern that he dealt with by means of a growing number of recreational and prescription drugs. He knew himself to be barely coping, sliding into an abyss from which he was unable to extricate himself.

On Monday evening, Sally had asked pointed questions about the birthday celebration. Her tone was suggestive of a degree of rancour that she should have to ask, the implication being that she should have been there with him. It came as a shock to Julian. He had viewed his London life and his home life as distinct entities. He had never imagined that the two might converge. He hadn't thought the thing through; he wondered how he could have been so blinkered!

A letter, addressed to Sally, had been delivered to Myrtle's address. It came from a firm of city solicitors acting on behalf of her husband. They were asking her to contact them regarding mortgage payments on a flat held in joint names. Her husband wanted to sell the flat, which, without Sally's contribution, had become a financial burden he could no longer meet. Attached to the letter was a statement of mortgage payments made since Sally's departure and an account of the money owed by Sally as a joint owner of the property.

Julian knew he should have seen it all coming down the line – the unresolved issue of the flat she co-owned with her husband, Sal's refusal to speak to the guy, her hopes of a permanent relationship, marriage, no doubt! He had to admit that he hadn't been completely up front with Sally. What a bloody hole he had dug for himself! Sally needed a home and Julian wasn't at all sure that he wanted the permanent responsibility of providing one. Sally had been all over the place since receiving the letter. She was shocked at being confronted with a debt of over £17,000.

'You know, Sal, it would be a pity to let the flat go. It's in an up-and-coming area, bound to increase in value. You should think of buying Jack out.'

'How could I afford to do that? Anyway, why would I need the flat?'

'It would be a nice little investment for you!'

'That's way beyond me. The £100,000 deposit was given to us by Jack's parents. I'd have to pay that back, plus the payments I so stupidly forgot about. I'd have to take out a mortgage.'

'You wouldn't have to pay back the £100,000, the flat is in joint names. You are entitled to half of that when the flat is sold.'

'Oh, Julian, that doesn't seem right. Jack's parents are lovely people, I couldn't do something like that to them.'

'OK, well, how much did you pay for the flat?'

'£350,000.'

'Tell you what you could do: first, pay up the outstanding mortgage payments, then offer to repay the deposit. He will know that you are entitled to half of it and will probably be so glad to get his parents' money back that he won't think about a revaluation. It's bound to have risen in value; depends on the increase being greater than 50K. It needs a clever solicitor's letter! What do you think?'

'Oh, I don't know Julian. How could I afford to pay that kind of mortgage? Who would lend me that kind of money?'

'Of course, you could afford it. The rental money would pay the mortgage, and I can call in a favour and get you the loan. No problem!'

'I don't know. I've got to find the money to repay the outstanding payments first.'

'Don't worry, Sal, I'll get you a loan at a rock bottom rate. Think about it!'

Sally did think about it; she could think of little else. She wasn't convinced by Julian's argument. Besides, she wasn't at all sure that she wanted to buy the flat. She had never considered such a move, didn't see herself in the role of a landlord.

He let the matter lie for a week before returning to the conversation. 'Remember us discussing the possibility of you buying the flat? I was in a meeting last week with a guy from our real estate department. I asked him to get me a valuation on your flat; concocted a reason for my interest. He came back to me today - the flat's valued at well over 500 K.'

'What! My God.'

'Yep! Told you to think twice before selling.' Julian had been busy during the week phoning estate agents.

Chapter 13

Jack

Just under 50 miles from Richmond to Mickleford. The route planner directed him to take the M25 and join the A22 at junction 6. An hour there, an hour back and an hour or so for a recce and he could be back in The Duck before closing.

An hour and four minutes later, he was driving into Mickleford. Houses, white painted or of mellow brick, a hotchpotch of ages and styles, sprawled about the edges of a rectangular green. There was a post office, tea rooms, a florist and what appeared to be a thriving book shop. At the far end of the green, opposite an impressive war memorial - a life size figure of a First World War soldier, leaning on his rifle, head bowed, looking down on the stone plinth on which were recorded the names of his dead comrades - was The Black Swan. The old coaching house was set back from the road, a long, low building of Reigate stone.

The whole village looked deserted, not a person in sight. He had looked out for signs for Buckshot Hall on his way into the village; looked for a signpost, estate gates, or walls, continued for a mile or so beyond the village, but had seen nothing. The Swan car park was accessed through an old arched coachway. Given the quietness of the village, he was surprised to find the yard to the rear practically full. He left the car sandwiched between a white van and a wall and went in through a narrow passageway that led directly to the lounge bar. Pushing open the door, he was met by a wall of noise; the place was heaving.

He found himself in a big room, low-ceilinged, the walls a combination of exposed stonework and greyed, oak panelling. A mahogany bar, almost the full length of the room, faced him. Benches and wheel-back chairs surrounded the tables that hugged the walls. To one end, occupying a couple of tables, was a young, lively group, to the other, a gathering of brogue-wearing, tweedy types: gentleman farmers Jack thought.

Weaving his way through a standing crush, he made for the bar, caught the eye of a bar tender and ordered a lager. Holding tight to his drink, he edged his way to the end of the room and stood with his back against a glass partition. The partition divided the bar from the hotel reception area, where a man was standing in front of a highly polished desk in conversation with the receptionist. Both had their eyes fixed expectantly on a copier about to deliver paperwork. To the right of the desk, a wide, uncarpeted oak staircase gave access to the upper floors.

Jack liked the place, obviously privately run; none of the repetitive, mock features of the chains. From the wall facing the bar, a narrow passageway disappeared into the depths of the old building. The passageway appeared to give access to smaller rooms; most likely, he thought, the private drinking and dining rooms used by the coach travellers of the eighteenth and nineteenth centuries. He liked the functionality of the place, flagged floors, the seating sturdy, the fireplace on the far wall of the bar huge and fire blackened. The walls were hung with old black and white photographs. They showed May Day celebrations, hound packs, the hunt gathered on the village green and groups of locals standing about the inn.

'Not seen you here before! God, got to get the weight off my feet for a few minutes. It's been manic tonight!' said a girl bartender, seating herself on a stool next to Jack. 'Are you staying here?'

'No, just passing. On my way to London. Stopped for a break. Nice place, never been here before.'

'Yeh, it's not bad.'

'Is it always this busy?'

'Not on a Monday night. But we've had an engagement celebration, and there was an afternoon conference. It's usually weekends when we get busy. Recently, we've had an influx of reporters arriving on a Friday evening. Some of them hang about all weekend. They all head up to the hall - well, to the main gates - to catch his lordship when he arrives back from London. Proper interested in him they are!'

'I'm in that line myself. One of the reasons I decided to stop here. I drove about a bit, but couldn't see any sign of Buckshot Hall.'

'Well, the hall is in Little Mickleford; that's why you missed it.'

'Ah, I didn't realise that.'

'Yeh, you have to turn off before you come into the village. It isn't signposted; they all miss it and complain.'

'I'm freelance; photography! I'll probably make my way back and join the Friday influx.'

'If you want a room, book in early,' advised his informant as she reluctantly got to her feet and re-joined her hard-pressed colleagues.

Jack finished his drink and went, via the glass doors, into the reception area and up to the desk.

'Friday night?' mused the receptionist, 'Weekends are very busy at present; a lot of press interest in Lord Goffe. I'd book well in advance if I were you.'

He got a printout of the hotel rates; he might book in some time! Why not? It was a nice place, he liked it. It would be interesting to see Goffe on his home turf, interesting to get a good look at Buckshot Hall. On the drive home, Jack tuned into the car radio.

**

Theresa May had summoned the Cabinet to Chequers. The media were reporting that taxis had been put on standby by No.10 to return resigning ministers to London; May having told them that dissenters would be replaced by a talented new generation and be quickly forgotten.

The resignations began the following day. David Davis led the charge; his letter of resignation was an eye opener. Boris Johnson followed him out of office. The details of May's deal were out. Jack couldn't believe what he was hearing and reading. The media were calling it a 'Soft Brexit'. May's so called 'red lines' not breached but consigned to the bin. The upside was the criticism it had met with from all sides. It wasn't soft enough for the remainers, seen as no Brexit at all by Brexiteers. A bad deal by most.

Two years it had taken the woman to come up with her lousy deal. Jack was furious!

**

The letter had arrived midweek. Jack had picked up the long envelope that had caught his eye before putting his toe to the remaining mail and flyers, shunting them to join the already heaped up pile behind the door. Apart from junk mail, the pile was mostly made up of bills, demands and final demands for payment of utility bills, store accounts and credit cards. He had managed to pay the mortgage, but all else had slid into the red. He had given up trying to manage the matter, taking from one to pay another, or concentrating on the most threatening communications. He now just toed them aside.

The flat had to be sold; he knew that! He thought the letter most probably a response from Sal's solicitor. He had gone straight from work to The Duck, drunk a lot and was ready for bed; too tired to deal with solicitor's letters. He turned the envelope over; the back stamp confirmed its source. It felt heavy- he tore it open.

There were several sheets; at first glance, a long and complicated reply, not what he had expected. He went into the kitchen, sat at the table and scanned through the letter. It couldn't be saying what he thought it was saying! He got up, switched on the kettle and put a couple of heaped spoons of coffee in a mug. He opened the fridge, swore when he found he was out of milk, sat down again with his black coffee and forced himself to concentrate.

Andrew, Wood and Khan explained their client's willingness to buy him out of his home. That's what all the fancy language amounted to. He was furious. He pushed the coffee aside and opened a can of lager from the fridge. He re-read the offending sections. The property being in joint names, their client accepted her responsibility regarding mortgage repayments from March 2016, a total of twenty-eight months to date, a figure calculated on a separate sheet at £17,340. Their client wished to make reparation for the oversight by either paying the debt immediately or making payment at the final settlement. That was it in a nutshell - what it had taken two and a half pages of legal speak to explain.

Their client was mindful of the sum of £100,000 given by her estranged husband's parents and paid as a deposit on the property in question. Their client, despite being entitled in law to half of the above-stated sum on the disposal of the property, felt uneasy in profiting from what was given in good faith as a wedding gift. Their client proposed that on transfer of the property to her name, Ms. Sally Willett will pay Mr. John G. Willett, a sum not exceeding £100,000 plus a sum to the value of fifty percent of the reduction, if any, of the debt to the Chetham Building Society.

Jack's fury had turned to rage. Who the hell did Sal think she was kidding? No way could she afford to buy the flat, Jack couldn't get his head around the thing. She was well set up with lover-boy; why should she be interested in the flat? All thought of going to bed forgotten, he took another can from the fridge, opened the double doors and stepped out onto the balcony. Jack often sat out on the balcony. When sitting watching TV, he liked to keep the patio doors open. He liked to let the noise of the outside world into the flat; it made him feel less alone, less isolated. He stood leaning against the railing, looking down on the car park.

The flat was on the second floor of a complex of twelve. It was a late 1990s build in grey brick with dark blue facias and windows and a grey tiled roof; it was a decent-looking block. The management company did a good job maintaining the place. The balcony looked down onto a small car park and gardens and beyond to the road. He watched a car drive in; a woman got out, saw Jack, and waved up. It was Debbie from number two. Most people in the flats knew each other; all in all, it wasn't a bad place to live. Jack suddenly remembered the estate agents blurb that had talked of 'A Juliet Balcony' and remembered how Sal and himself had laughed at the pretentious jargon.

He took one of the fold-up chairs from against the wall and sat with his feet on the railings. The cool night air had brought his anger down a few notches. He applied a cooler head to Sal's proposal. It looked like Tennant was financing her; he couldn't imagine why! Perhaps he was going to buy her a property portfolio. Seemed a strange thing for someone with Sal's views to go for. But, hey, who could tell, people were full of surprises. But why would they be talking figures? The settlement would surely depend on the valuation!

Jack hadn't really thought through the details of a sale; he just wanted the mounting debt off his back. He knew that Sal would be entitled to half of any profit that they might make; he hadn't thought about the deposit, but he could see that the same applied. It made his blood boil that she was entitled to walk away with £50,000 of his parent's money.

He jumped up, went into the kitchen, got another lager and picked up the letter. Yeh, he thought that was what it said - a figure not in excess of £100,000. As his mother would say, 'the penny dropped!' She was making a big deal of paying back the deposit, but there was no mention of a valuation. What it amounted to was that she was taking over the mortgage and foregoing £50,000. What the hell was the place valued at to make it worth her while. That would be easy to find out. It was far too devious a plan for Sal to have dreamed up. It was Tennant's doing. He walked about the flat; he couldn't settle. He picked up the car keys and went out. *Bastard. Robbing bastard.*

It had been months since he had been near Fulham. It was 4 a.m., a July morning; daylight was already breaking when he drove into Edgar Street. He crawled slowly past the house. It seemed to have had a bit of a face lift, been repainted, the door was a very glossy black. Turning right at the end of the street, he took an immediate sharp right and looped around into Florence Street. His old parking space was occupied. Cars were lined up bumper to bumper along the entire street. Jack wondered how they manoeuvred in and out of the tight spaces. He had driven over on impulse - the sort of behaviour that had almost landed him in deep trouble before. He couldn't risk being seen, couldn't risk going down the back entry, putting a couple of bricks through the windows, setting fire to the place. Christian was always warning him against hot-headed reactions.

He drove slowly past the entry. Two large skips were parked at the back of the house. The extension looked to be underway! Driving back into the street, he spotted a parking space a few doors down from the house. He turned around at the end of the street, drove back and parked up facing the house. It was 4:35 a.m. his nerves were in shreds.

He was jolted awake by the sound of the car behind him starting up. He sat forward, gripped by panic. *Jesus! He had fallen asleep in full view of the street.* The dashboard clock showed 7:00 a.m. He had slept for two and a half hours. He looked nervously about him. A couple more cars were driven away. A guy emerged from a door across the street and walked off in the direction of the station. He was cold and stiff; he wanted to get out and stretch his legs but couldn't risk it. He was shocked at how close he was to the house. He should leave, go home, have a shower, grab some breakfast and go to work. That's what a rational person would do. But then he wasn't rational, not when it came to Sal; he knew that. A rational person wouldn't be sitting in his car on a street where he didn't belong in the hope of seeing a woman who didn't want him in her life.

He pulled up his coat collar, pulled down the front and side visors, tried to disappear into his coat and fixed his attention on the newly painted, black door. More people were leaving for work, parents were shepherding children into cars, curtains were being pulled back; the street was suddenly alive.

At 7:20, the black door opened, and Sal stepped out. As she came down the path, a little girl ran from the neighbouring house. The child stopped at the gate and turned, waiting for her mother, who was speaking to Sal. Jack's attention was riveted on his wife as she turned from her neighbour, waved to the little girl and went on her way. She looked as though she didn't have a care in the world. Jack's anger flared. He wanted to run after her, grab hold of her, shout into her face, tell her what a selfish little bitch she was, make her understand that she wasn't the good and caring person she imagined herself to be, that under the tutelage of her lover she had turned into a sly little crook, a confidence trickster. He wanted to wipe the self-satisfied look from her face.

He watched her walk away, dressed for work in a black trouser suit, a tan bag slung from her shoulder, blonde hair swaying about her shoulders as she strode confidently forward. The raw emotion, the hurt he had felt when she had left him had over the months turned to anger, to bitter resentment. He no longer loved Sal; he no longer wanted her back, but he wanted revenge for the hurt she had caused him.

Sal was barely out of sight when a black Merc came slowly down the street. It stopped in front of the house, engine running, blocking the road. The black door opened, Julian Tennant came out, walked quickly down the path and got into the passenger seat of the car. Jack caught a glimpse of the chauffeur and Tennant's blonde head as the car pulled away and drove past. Not for the first time, Jack's mind turned to violence. He was late getting into work but congratulated himself for resisting the temptation to pull a sickie.

In his lunch break, he called the estate agents who, a couple of months previously, had sold a ground-floor flat in his block. Jack thought them certain to be able to give him an up-to-date valuation.

'Yes, a very popular development. There was a lot of interest in the last property we sold in the block; a bit of a bidding war developed. In the end, it went for considerably more than the asking price. Depending on fixtures and fittings, we would value a first-floor, two-bed apartment between £570 and £590,' explained Zoe of Combe-Baily.

'She's an avaricious little cow,' Christian was walking about the kitchen, reading the letter from Andrew Wood and Khan. 'Jesus, does she think you bloody stupid? You're right, mate, Tennant's behind this. Typical of his type; think themselves so bloody clever. Audacious Mate, audacious,' he said, stopping, and fixing his eyes on the oak knife block. Reaching out, he pulled out a medium-sized knife, turned to Jack and pulled it across his throat, saying, 'Handy, mate, just the right size.'

**

The following Saturday, Jack kept an appointment with his solicitor.

'The one thing I would say, is that the lady hasn't been well advised.'

Clive was young, stylish and slick. Jack liked him. Clive had read the letter from Sal's solicitor; it had taken him less than three minutes.

'What's proposed isn't illegal, but it's unethical. It's surprising that a solicitor has put his name to this. I don't know the firm, but that doesn't signify, there are a lot of solicitors in London, a lot of comings and goings. *He's calling them 'fly by nights', Jack thought.* 'Still, we have it in writing that your estranged wife admits responsibility for her debt. Having admitted liability, I think it unlikely that she will backtrack; it could prejudice her rights regarding the property. My advice would be to accept the back payment and her commitment to meet future repayments. Make no comment on the derisory offer. From what you tell me, it's financial considerations that are forcing you to sell. This development may be to your advantage, enabling you to settle your debts and stay in your home. A nice little sum will be coming your way. 17K should sort you out nicely.'

It was agreed that Jack would follow Clive's advice and that his decision be communicated to Andrew Wood and Khan.

Bloody excellent! Let the greedy little cow deal with that.

**

Jack was in for the night. He popped the ready-made M&S chicken dinner in the microwave and set the timer. Opening the cupboard to take out a plate, he stared, uncomprehendingly, into the empty space. Where the hell were all the plates and the mugs? He swung round, gripped by a kind of mild panic. The microwave hummed, the green illuminated numbers were on countdown, soon the bleeps would start. He needed a bloody plate! He looked helplessly around the kitchen and with a sudden clarity of vision, saw the mess around him. The plates were still there; they were stacked together with mugs, glasses and cutlery on the draining board and adjacent worktop; all smothered with dried and congealed food. They were in the company of pans, empty lager and coke cans and ready-meal containers. A small saucepan caught his eye, its original contents covered in something grey and nasty. Fuck! How the hell had he allowed this to happen? He found a lone fork in the cutlery drawer, carried it with the chicken dinner into the dining area and set the non-stable container down on the dining table.

Sitting down, he felt quite odd; he couldn't remember sitting at the table since Sal had left. Struggling to cut the chicken pieces without a knife, his eyes travelled about the room. He saw carrier bags piled against the outer wall; what was in them, he wondered? He couldn't even remember putting them there! With the bags were shoes and a couple of pairs of worn-out, muddy trainers. It appeared as though a veil had been lifted from before his eyes. He stood up and began walking about the room. The sofa was filthy. It was surrounded by more dirty plates and empty cans The carpet was black-stained. Everything was dusty. He went into the bedroom. *'Jesus!'* Dirty clothes littered the floor. The wardrobe door stood open, revealing almost empty rails; the floor being the preferred repository for its contents. He tried to remember the last time he had changed the bed linen. He didn't look too closely at the ensuite after noticing the brown-stained toilet pan.

He sat on the edge of the bed, kicked dirty socks and underpants from under his feet and reflected on the mess Sal had made of his life. ' *Bitch!*. Something glittery on the floor beside the chest of drawers caught his eye. On closer inspection, he identified what remained of the broken glass from a smashed wedding photograph. A sudden thought brought him up short: someone might come! Sal herself might come. His mother might take it into her head to visit; she was always saying how worried she was that he wasn't taking proper care of himself. He was going to have to clean up the mess straight away! He rang home to tell his parents that he wouldn't be home that weekend. He made up a story about helping Simon fix a leak in his bathroom. The clean-up was going to take time; he could see that!

He took a can from the fridge, turned on the TV, put it on mute and flicked open his laptop. Richard Goffe had been speaking in the house. Still spouting his traitorous crap. He must make that weekend trip to Mickleford that he had promised himself - have a scout around Goffe's domain. But not until he had cleaned the flat and restored some order. He couldn't believe the state that Sal had left him in.

The following evening, he came straight home from work and drove into Richmond centre. He headed for the cut-price store. He tried to remember the cleaning products Sal had bought. Black bags were the first thing to come to mind; there was a lot of rubbish to be cleared. He walked around, looking at the bottles, packets and aerosols on the shelves. He piled surface cleaners, toilet cleaners, polish and disinfectant into his basket. Then he thought about cloths; he added two rolls of dishcloths, a pack of dusters and pan scourers. A yellow plastic bottle caught his eye; 'Magic Carpet and Fabric Cleaner'. Could he clean the carpet? Could he clean the sofa? He put the bottle in the basket. Light bulbs! He definitely needed light bulbs; the bulb in his bedside lamp had been gone for ages. Queuing up at the till, he noticed a sign advertising carpet cleaners for hire.

'What are the carpet cleaners like? How do they work?' he asked the woman behind the desk.

'Have you never used one? If you hang on a couple of minutes, I'll show you. There's one in the back.'

The cleaner looked like an upright vacuum cleaner. It had a see-through container that held water and cleaning fluid. You plugged it in and rolled it over your carpets.

'Doesn't it soak the carpets?' Jack asked.

'No, it sucks a lot of the water back out. I don't know, you men! I thought you were the mechanically minded ones,' said the woman, laughing.

Jack was impressed. He couldn't have the demo cleaner; that was booked, but he could have one on Saturday morning.

£30 for the weekend, plus £8 for the fluid. Bargain!

He couldn't settle at work, found it very hard to concentrate, imagined his mother paying a surprise visit. He could see her at that very moment getting ready to catch a train to Richmond, a nourishing casserole in a Tupperware container in her shopping bag. On the stroke of 5:00, he had rushed out, grabbed a sandwich on his way into the station, and was back in the flat by 6:00 to get straight into the cleaning.

He stacked the dishwasher and started collecting rubbish. Cans alone filled three large black bags; they were in the kitchen, around and under the sofa, in the bedroom. The plastic carrier bags thrown against the wall contained cans, a couple of unwashed shirts that had gone missing, five pairs of socks, newspaper, food cartons, the wedding photograph without glass and the wedding album left by Sal together with her card and wrapping paper. The album and card he put into the wastepaper bag; no way was he going to look at those photographs; he was finished with all that! He didn't care a damn for Sal, but it wasn't the end of it; no way was it the end of the matter.

The plastic bag was just about to follow the rest of Sal's parting gifts into the black bag when he heard a tinkle of metal. At the bottom of the bag were Sal's wedding and engagement rings. He tipped them onto the coffee table, sat down on the sofa, and looked at the shiny gold circles, one set with quite a decent-sized diamond. It had cost £968. He remembered the day they had bought it - the evening they had sat in together over a candle-lit dinner - when he had put it on her finger. What the hell was he supposed to do with it? Another problem left by Sal! He wrapped the rings in a wad of paper and flushed them down the toilet.

He worked into the early hours. By the time he went to bed, he had collected the rubbish; all correctly bagged to take down to the recycling bins. He had cleared the backlog in the kitchen, put crockery, cutlery and glasses in their proper places and collected up the dirty washing. The place was dirty, but it looked a lot better. Jack was encouraged.

On his way home on Friday, he picked up the carpet cleaner. He dragged the hoover from the hall cupboard. The woman in the store had told him to get all the grit and dust from the carpets before cleaning them. Carpets hoovered, he got out the surface spray and cleaned the coffee table. He was amazed at the effect! He was on a roll, dusting, spraying, polishing. Jack moved like a whirlwind through the flat. The bathroom proved quite a challenge, but he persisted. He was finding the process quite satisfying. The cleaning products did what they promised to do; he was very pleased.

By mid-afternoon on Saturday, he had finished cleaning the carpets. It was hard to tell as they were still damp, but they looked promising. The fabric and carpet cleaners proved less effective on the sofa. He could see that it looked much cleaner, but there were stains that wouldn't shift. It didn't help that the sofa was cream and the stains well established. It was fortunate that the carpets were a darker colour, more of a toffee. He remembered the debate with Sal before they were bought. She had wanted a much paler shade. Good thing he hadn't given in to that fancy!

He made beans on toast for his lunch. He marvelled at the ease of the operation: plates at the ready, knives, forks and spoons in their own slots in the drawer, worktops unencumbered and shining. He stacked the used plate, pan and cutlery in the dishwasher and wiped the cooker and worktop. He walked about the flat admiring his work; the place was transformed.

Pity about the sofa! He could see that the stains were quite noticeable. He remembered the blanket-type thing that used to be thrown over it. What had happened to it? He couldn't remember! Had Sal taken it? He could buy another one; it would hide the stains. A throw, that's what Sal had called it. Or maybe he would buy a new sofa? Why not? He had 17K coming his way. Yeh, that's what he'd do; why should he have to put up with a shitty mess while she sat on her velvet throne?

He returned the carpet cleaner and drove to the out-of-town shopping centre. There were two stores selling sofas; he had a good look around both. He was really very pleased with himself; he felt better than he had felt for a long time. He felt in control, he was thinking straight. He had a strategy for choosing the sofa. It should be a darkish colour that wouldn't mark easily. It was to have a supportive back and seat. He wasn't going to pay a fortune, but neither was he going for anything too cheap; he believed that you got what you paid for. He was open-minded as to style.

He narrowed down his options to three sofas. After walking several times between the two stores, trying for comfort and deliberating on colour, he chose a retro, three-seater in a deep lime green linen with splayed 60s legs, costing £875. He put it on a credit card. During the clean-up, he realised why so much stuff lived on the floor; there was nowhere else to put things. His darling wife had stripped the living area bare! She had taken the oak sideboard, the chest of drawers that had stood next to the balcony door, two side tables and the bookshelves. What the hell had the bitch done with it all? They weren't in the house in Fulham! Maybe she'd given them to Myrtle, or perhaps they were still in the storage facility in Tottenham.

Spiteful!

While looking at the sofas, other furniture had caught his eye. He particularly liked a sideboard in deep navy with light oak, inset handles and trim, and legs similar to those of the sofa. There was a matching chest of drawers. Why not? Why should he struggle for storage? He bought the sideboard, the chest of drawers, plain oak bookshelves and an oak sofa table. The £2,030 he split between his cards.

On his way home, he parked up and went to the shop on the high street that sold cushions. He showed the photos of the sofa and furniture to the girl in the shop. Between them, they chose cushions of a 60s design in a wavy pattern in navy, mustard and lime green. A throw, similar to the one that used to cover the sofa, was draped across some shelves. He bought one in cherry red. He would move the cream sofa into the spare room to replace the one Sal had taken and cover it with the red throw. He bought two copper-coloured throws to protect the new sofa. He was amazed by his decisiveness and invention.

Chapter 14

Lucinda

Cosima was in her pyjamas. She was standing in the kitchen doorway, hair tousled, half asleep. 'Daddy's crying again; I can hear him and it's making me very sad. I can't go to sleep.'

Lucy looked at her daughter, nine years old, striving to be grown up but still attached to her rabbit slippers. Not yet out of prep school and used to hearing her father crying in his bedroom while her mother sat at the kitchen table with a bottle of wine.

'Go back to bed, Cos, I'll go and see Daddy.'

Halfway up the stairs, Lucy could hear the noise. She flung open the bedroom door. Julian was sitting on the edge of the bed, his head in his hands, making pathetic whimpering sounds.

'For God's sake, Julian, pull yourself together. Stop the noise. You are upsetting the children. Are you listening to what I'm saying?' said Lucy, her voice rising.

'I'm sorry, Luce, sorry if I've upset the children, but I feel so bloody awful.'

'You feel so awful because your brain is scrambled by the crap you snort up your nose. You might as well stop the damn awful noise and go to sleep because you won't get any sympathy from me.'

Lucy was beginning to think the unthinkable; she was going to have to involve his parents. She hesitated, no longer out of loyalty to Julian but out of consideration for Daphne and Ted. They were so proud of their hero son, learning the true state of his mental and physical health would come as a dreadful blow.

It had been past midnight when he had arrived home - drunk on alcohol and drugs, hardly able to stand, his speech slurred. He had driven in that state from London. Lucy couldn't believe that he hadn't been stopped by the police; he must have been all over the road. She had managed to support him up the stairs, left him, fully clothed, collapsed on his bed.

The following morning, the children were up and dressed early, bouncing with excitement. Julian was supposed to be taking them to the Saturday matinee showing of Nutty by Nature in Swindon, an outing postponed from the previous Saturday when he had fobbed them off with a tale of having to call some very important people. Julian had surfaced at 11:00, still in a shambolic state. Lucy noticed that his hands were shaking; she had never seen that before. He sat at the table, nursing a mug of black coffee, stealing furtive glances at Lucy, trying to judge her mood.

The children bounded in making a racket, she saw him flinch at the noise.

'Daddy, Daddy!' piped Benedict 'When are we going? Can we go early and have lunch at McDonald's? Please, can we?'

Julian, eyes glazed, stared uncomprehendingly at the child. Lucy knew he had forgotten. Knew that he didn't have a clue what Benedict was talking about, hadn't a clue where he was supposed to be taking them.

'Can we, Daddy. Can we?' said Cosima, practicing her pirouettes around the table.

'Cosima, go and get your things together. Daddy doesn't feel very well today, I'm taking you to the cinema. If you are quick, we will have time to go to McDonalds.'

Benedict was a nuisance in the car, bouncing in his seat and making noises.

'Stop it, Ben, you're annoying me,' said Cosima. She was looking very serious.

'Penny for your thoughts, Cos,' said Lucy, looking at her daughter through the driving mirror.

'I'm thinking about Daddy!'

'Are you, my sweet. What are you thinking?'

'I'm wondering what's wrong with Daddy? He looks so very sad!'

'Oh, darling, you mustn't worry about Daddy, he's just a little bit under the weather today.'

'But he is so often very sad! Is it because Daddy is very sick, Mummy? Is Daddy going to die?'

'You're stupid, Cos. Don't say that, don't say Daddy's going to die!' said Benedict, pummelling his sister with his fists.

'Stop it, stop it Ben, or we will have to go back home. Daddy isn't going to die.'

Lucy was trying to stay upbeat, but she felt very angry and stressed. At the last minute she had to cancel a lunch with friends; the last thing she felt like doing was sitting through a children's film.

They got back in the evening to find Julian showered, dressed and in the best of moods. Lucy knew exactly what that meant. While driving home, she had listened to endless nut shop chatter with impersonations of Surly, Andie and Mr Feng, all very loud and animated. The last thing she needed was Julian whipping them up to a higher level of excitement.

'What's for dinner, Mummy, is it nutty nuts?' said Julian.

'No, cheese quiche, green salad and potato salad. Go and wash your hands, you two,' said Lucy, rushing about, setting the table and taking the pre-prepared food from the fridge.

'Holy macadamia, no nuts!' said Julian.

'Holy macadamia,' parroted Benedict. 'Holy macadamia, we want nuts, we want nuts, we want nuts --!'

'Stop it, Ben!' said Lucy, banging down a bowl of potato salad on the table. 'Sit down and stop that noise, it's very annoying.'

'Well, looks like Mummy is keeping all the nuts to herself. What are we to make of that? Perhaps mummy has eaten all the nuts!' said Julian

Cosima, who was delighted to have found her father in such a good mood, stood in front of Lucy, looked quizzically into her face and said in an imitation Andie voice, 'Oh, Mummy, have you been very greedy? Have you?'

Julian's upbeat mood had lasted until the cocaine hit had worn off. After dinner, when the children had gone upstairs, he turned on the TV in the study, collapsed into an armchair with a bottle of wine by his side, and fell asleep.

Daphne was doing Sunday lunch, the weather was promising and a garden buffet was planned. Lucy was searching the freezer for a pineapple gateau, her contribution to the lunch, when Julian appeared at the utility room doorway.

'Do you know, Luce, I think I'll go up early. I'm a bit tired; it's been a busy week.'

Lucy lifted her head from the freezer, 'OK, Julian, good night.'

The animated Julian had gone, the haggard shell of a man was back. Lucy found the gateau and closed the freezer. She stood holding the frozen package with anxiety-filled eyes fixed on the spot where her husband had stood. The charade, so innocent and well-meaning at its inception, had turned deadly. The bizarre life of pretence, of lies, of self-deception was their joint creation, but it was to be left to her to kill the monster they had created. She had to act for them both, Julian was no longer capable.

Julian was in a spiral of decline, falling deeper into depression. Lucy recognised that what had started as the recreational use of cocaine had turned into a serious addiction. She wondered what other substances, apart from cocaine, he was relying on. She didn't really have much of an idea about Julian's weekday life. There was his work and he talked about a couple of guys he met up with in the local pub who he sometimes went to football matches with, but it didn't seem to amount to much of a social life. She had suggested coming up to town so they could have an occasional night out together; hit some of the new restaurants. But he hadn't liked the idea; had engineered her suggestion into an argument.

'And where would you stay if you came up?'

'Well, with Margot. I thought we could have a shopping day together and I could meet up with you in the evening.'

'And return to Margot's for the night, I presume. Well I think I can manage without the charitable scraps from your table, Lucy. I thought for a moment that you proposed coming to share my bed.'

'You know why I won't be doing that, Julian. You promised me that you would at least look at what those organisations could offer and that we would then talk it through. What happened to that promise?'

'Broken, Lucy. Another broken promise. I'm living up to your very low expectations of me.'

'That's not fair, Julian. Not fair at all.'

'Oh, I think it is. But you're right, absolutely right. I'm a damn waste of space. A disaster!'

**

The Sunday was glorious. Wicker chairs and garden cushions were brought from the summer house and set out on the middle lawn under the old horse chestnut. Lucy had helped Daphne and Pat carry the food down the garden. Pat, described by Daphne as 'an absolute marvel', lived in the village and 'did' for Daphne. They had what Daphne called a 'flexible arrangement, with give and take on both sides'. Pat spent so much time 'doing' at Daphne's that Lucy wondered how she found time for her own home.

Julian had got himself together. He was always careful to put on a good show when in the company of his parents. It was wearing thin with Lucy. She was tired of carrying the burden of her husband's instability alone. The smoked salmon, roast beef and savoury rice disposed of Daphne had removed the cling film from the puddings and Lucy was busy dishing out strawberries and ice cream to the children when Ted dropped the bombshell - not altogether innocently, Lucy later thought.

'Been dipping your toe into the London property market, I hear?' said Ted, addressing Julian.

Julian stared at his father; the colour drained from his face. All conversation had stopped, all eyes were turned on Julian, Ted's revelation was news to them all.

'Who told you that?' Julian spat out the words, his hands gripping the sides of the wicker chair, his knuckles white, his eyes blazing.

'Do you know, I can't quite remember. I seem to think it was a remark I picked up on in my club. I didn't attach much importance to it. Excuse me if I have spoken out of turn.' Ted sat unruffled, as cool as a cucumber.

'Shall I tell you where you heard it? It was from your buddy Hubert Monk or from one of the other old buffers who like to stick their noses into other people's business. My business seems to be of particular interest to them. Back off, Dad, bloody well back off.' Julian jumped from his chair and walked off across the lawn.

'Oh, my goodness, what was all that about. Julian's very upset. You have really upset him, Ted. I'll go and see if he's OK.'

'Stay where you are, Daffers, please. Don't go running after him; I'd much rather you didn't.'

'What on earth was that about? Has Julian been buying in London, Dad?' asked Julian's sister Clara.

'I'm not quite sure, Clara. As I said, it was just a passing remark. I may have misunderstood. Has Julian said anything to you, Lucy about buying a house?'

'No, of course not. I would have told you about something like that!'

'Very strange! I don't usually get things so wrong. I'm still in the dark; I didn't detect an answer amid the abuse of my friends.'

Julian was gone when Lucy got home. The children were tired. They had both fallen asleep almost as soon as they were in bed. Lucy came downstairs; the house felt chilly after the warmth of the day. She felt very cold. She put a match to the kitchen fire and watched the flames leap through the heaped logs. She took a woollen throw from the back of the chair and put it around her shoulders. The chill seemed to have got into her bones. She was shocked to find that her teeth were chattering! It wasn't just cold; Lucy knew that she was afraid, fearful of what the future held.

She couldn't believe that Julian had been buying London property, but the day's events had convinced her that there were things going on that she didn't know about. She was sure that Ted suspected something, perhaps even knew something. She didn't believe Ted's line that it was a chance, overheard remark. It was out of character for Ted to be repeating overheard conversations and he had shown no surprise at Julian's reaction. Something had prompted Ted's behaviour.

What she did know was that Julian was in a bad way. She had done her best; researched organisations, given him addresses, emails, emergency help lines. She had pleaded, she had cried; all to no avail. He had begged her to keep it from his family; she had respected his wishes. It hadn't been the right thing to do; she recognised that now. She knew that her silence had helped his descent into depression and drug abuse. Julian was no longer rational. He was blind to, or perhaps careless of, the effect his behaviour was having on the children and herself.

The following morning, Clara rang. 'What was that all about yesterday with Dad and Julian?'

Clara was Julian's sister, but she was also Lucy's best friend. The dam burst. The tears came.

'Oh, Luc, what's wrong?'

'Julian isn't well, Clara. No, what am I saying, he's in a bad way, a very bad way! I can't keep it to myself any longer, Clara. I don't know what to do!'

'I'm coming over, Luc. It's going to be tomorrow morning now; I'll have to make arrangements for the children. I'll stay over tomorrow night. I'm not totally surprised; I haven't thought Julian himself for some time. I'll be with you mid-morning.'

Lucy told Clara everything. Once she began, the words tumbled out. The disappointment, the hurt, the fear.

'Oh, Luc, you shouldn't have kept this to yourself. All this time and you haven't said a word.'

'Margo knows, she's the only one I've confided in.'

'Why didn't you tell me?'

'He was so insistent, Clara, so determined to keep his problems from his family. He made me promise. He thought it would pass, that when he regained his strength, got involved in the business, the nightmares and depression would go away. I really have tried, Clara, I really have!'

'I'm quite sure you have. But Julian shouldn't have asked you to shoulder this alone. Bloody selfish of him.'

'It's a sham marriage, Clara; I haven't slept with Julian for years. The violence that accompanies the nightmares is terrifying. He nearly killed me, very nearly strangling me. As I flailed about on the edge of consciousness, I managed to get hold of the bedside lamp and bring it down on his head; the blow stunned him and saved me. You hear of people who were accidentally killed in their sleep. It very nearly happened to me! I was shocked, terrified! It had a profound effect on me.

Julian saw dreadful things in Afghanistan, it's a terrible thing to have happened to him; it wasn't his fault. But he returned a changed person. He was a person I didn't recognise. He knew what he had done to me; he knew how frightened I was; he knew what he was capable of, yet it was all about Julian, about hiding his frailties from the world. I didn't like the person he had become and over time I stopped loving him. It's all supposed to be for the children, but I don't believe that's true anymore. But your parents! It would break their hearts to know the truth; they are so proud of him.'

Clara was speechless, eyes fixed on Lucy.

'It's been a dreadful weekend. He was very late home on Friday night. He could hardly stand; high on coke, alcohol and god knows what else. And then there was yesterday!'

'When did the coke taking start?'

'Oh, I don't know, three years ago? I thought nothing of it at first. I thought it was just occasional, social use. Let's face it, Clara, most people working in the city seem to be using. It was about a year ago when I realised it was out of control. But it's his relationship with the children that I find heart-breaking. He can't cope with them unless he's as high as a kite. One minute he's the life and soul of the party, the next they are listening to him crying in his bedroom. There have been so many excuses made to them when Julian has been incapable of keeping a promise. They have been told so many times that he isn't feeling well that Cosima thinks her daddy is dying. He has been unable to bond with Benedict. I don't know if he loves the children, but he certainly doesn't like them. Isn't that the most awful thing to say! But it's true, Clara.'

Clara got up, stood behind Lucy's chair, put her arms around her shoulders and hugged her tightly.

'You poor, poor darling. You should have told me, Luc. I can't believe that you have kept this from me! But something has to be done and straight away. We need to think this through, but let's go and have lunch out, then we'll pick the children up from school. We can take them to the ice-cream parlour or to McDonalds. Then we'll go to the emporium. I'll get Cosima those fairy lights she wants and something for Ben. What might he like?'

'Crazy balloons. But you spoil them, Clara.'

'And what else should I do with my niece and nephew?'

The children, stuffed with mayo chicken burgers, were in bed. Cosima twinkled to sleep by the fairy lights hung about her mirror and Benjamin happy beneath the 'Crazy Rainbow Balloon Bunch' sailing above him. Lucy and Clara sat down together by the fire and made their plans. Their thoughts, words and emotions witnessed and committed to memory by the stout old walls of the house.

Chapter 15

Die Drachentoter

A rucksack slung from one shoulder and a black canvas bag from the other, Jack set off for The Black Swan. He hoped his baggage looked the part. He had seen media photographers with very similar bags. Mickleford wasn't the type of place that people visited without a purpose; he hoped to morph into the media pack.

5:30 on a Friday evening hadn't been the best time to hit the M25. A journey previously made in an hour had taken him the best part of two. On arrival, he found part of The Swan car park cordoned off for reserved parking. What remained was solidly parked. He had to park some way down the main street. Heavily burdened, he made a great show of battling his way through the front door and struggling up to the reception desk, where he dumped his book-filled bags on the floor. The place was very quiet. A few locals stood around the bar. An elderly couple sat at the far end beside the log fire. To his right, he had a view into the restaurant. It looked to be very quiet.

Checked in, he was handed a key on a tag and directed by the receptionist to room eight on the first floor. No card locks, he noted; still operating on the old system! Jack approved; in his opinion, traditional, old places like The Black Swan should have proper locks and keys.

'Can I get a meal here tonight?' Jack asked.

'Yes, sir, certainly, but I should warn you that within twenty minutes there won't be a seat to be had when your colleagues return from Little Mickleford. I would get into the dining room as soon as you can.'

He humped his rucksack and bag across the floor and into the lift. The guy had taken him for media; so far, so good.

The room was much better than he had expected for sixty-five quid a night. There were nice repro fittings, an excellent ensuite - big shower cubicle, nice fluffy towels. The bed felt comfortable and the pillows were good. Jack had a thing about hotel pillows, which in his experience were either rock hard, lumpy or ridiculously soft. He had been known to kick up quite a fuss about hotel pillows. But what he really hated were the ubiquitous little cushions and useless padded quilts piled on the bed. When removed, both of these annoyances had to be stuffed into corners from where they had the dangerous habit of creeping out during the night to trip you on the way to the bathroom. Room eight was quilt and cushion free and had enough pillows to facilitate reading in bed.

The window looked onto the village street. He had pulled back the blind just in time to see a convoy of vehicles, among them two media vans, ladders on roofs and sprouting aerials, heading into the car park. He took the receptionist's advice and hurried to the restaurant, where he was shown to a two-person table. It had been good advice; within ten minutes, the place had been filled to capacity.

Seated at the table next to his own were a silent, preoccupied group, heads buried in phones or tablets. It was interesting that even in silent mode, body language and eye movement gave the clue to the dynamics within the group. In charge was a guy in his fifties, grey hair, overweight, large horn-rimmed glasses. Next to him, and obviously an important player, was a middle-aged, blonde woman.

'I'm done,' said the woman, switching off her phone. 'You OK with that Fred?'

Yeh, that about does it,' said the guy in glasses, snapping closed a laptop. I'm bloody starving. Let's eat.' A raised arm brought a waiter to his side.

Jack ordered a mixed grill and took out his phone. He wondered what a person sitting alone in a crowded restaurant did before the advent of mobile phones. Awkward! You couldn't sit staring into space; that would be ridiculous, and you couldn't risk appearing to be looking at other people. Bury your head in a newspaper, perhaps!

'Mind if I join you?', the voice broke across Jack's thoughts. The guy standing beside the table was a vision of round paleness - round face, round middle, round glasses, tousled flaxen hair.

'No, help yourself.'

'Just spotted you over here on your own. I left it a bit late, thought I wouldn't get in! Not part of this scrum then?'

'No. Freelance, photography! It's not my day job.'

'Right! Like myself. Gossip's my bag. Amazing the choice tit-bits you pick up hanging around this lot. They don't deal in the mundane nitty gritty. Happy to pass the dirt on, though, when it suits their agenda. Take Little Maddy over there; she has her nose in the air and her ears flapping in low places. Put a gem my way last week; nice little earner if it checks out! Something she wouldn't dirty her hands with, but was quite happy for it to fall into my grubby little paws.'

Little Maddy, real name Madeline Murry, was the blonde woman at the next table. She looked a real toughie; long, narrow face, bony nose, sharp, jutting chin, small, close-set eyes. He could hear her voice, high and reedy, as she leaned across the table in conversation with a young guy with a mass of green-sprayed dreads.

Jack's dinner companion was called Ralph Braxton. He was a mine of information. He seemed to spend most of his time following in the wake of the national media pack. It was the third weekend he had trailed them to Mickleford.

'Making a lot of noise, old Goffe. Very interested in him, this lot. Arrogant bastard; loves the sound of his own voice. I get the impression that they don't like him, which is unusual; usually give the remainers an easy ride, but not him. Always trying to trip him up, wrong foot him.'

'What do you think that's about?'

'Don't know! Maybe he just gets under their skin. Gets under my skin, but then I'm not a bloody remainer.'

Brexiteer credentials established, the pair finished up their meal and grabbed seats in the bar. Ralph seemed well informed about the comings and goings at the hall. He confirmed much of what Kate, Lady Patricia's PA, had told him. Jack sat and listened; he kept what Kate had told him about the jewel theft to himself.

'Have you been up to the hall?' Ralph asked.'

'No, not yet.'

'Goffe operates Schengen style borders. Next to the entrance gates on the main road, there are old estate walls, but that's about it. The area about the house is a maze of narrow roads and lanes; impossible to distinguish public from estate roads. First time I was down here; I took a turn down a narrow lane and ended up driving into the back of the stable block. The bar staff are all locals; know what goes on at the hall. I'm told that until recently, there were two Gurkha security guards. They were employed by Lady Goffe, Lady Jessica, that is, Goffe's wife. There's no sign of them now; speculation is that he got rid of them. He's an awkward old sod by all accounts. Lady Jessica is well liked, involves herself in the village. "No airs and graces" as they put it. Influential in raising the money to rebuild the village hall. If I were you, I'd have a good drive around the back lanes; some give a view of the house. You never know who or what you might get with a long lens.'

It was getting on for midnight when Jack and Ralph finished up their drinks and went to their rooms. Less than fifteen minutes later, Jack was confused to see his new friend on the street. Before getting into bed, he had pulled back the blind to let in some light; he didn't like sleeping in total darkness. He had seen a man appear from the coach entrance, bobby hat pulled down over his ears, his coat collar turned up. He had stood in the shelter of the old archway, looked up and down the street, before stepping out and walking away from the village. There was no mistaking his round figure.

What's he up to? Damn odd! A chilly night for a midnight stroll.

Jack slept well. He showered, dressed and was down to breakfast before 8:30. There was no sign of the media; that they had been up and about early, evidenced by the yet to be cleared tables. Ralph Braxton had either followed them or was catching up on his sleep after his midnight walk.

Old, silver-plated serving dishes were set out on a long, Victorian sideboard; below their domed tops were to be found the essentials for a full English breakfast. Bread rolls, croissants, fruit and cereals were there for those who preferred something lighter, as was assistance in the making of fresh toast, coffee and tea. All as it should be, Jack thought as he helped himself to nice crispy bacon, evenly cooked sausages, scrambled eggs and fried tomatoes.

He took his plate to the opposite side of the room, where old, time-worn benches were set against panelled walls and bulbous legged oak tables were paired with an eclectic mix of fiddle backs. His cutlery, coffee and toast followed him to the table on a tray, carried by a helpful waiter. The elderly couple he had seen in the bar the previous evening and a group of six American tourists were having breakfast.

At dinner, the previous evening, the restaurant had been so packed that Jack hadn't fully appreciated the quirky features of the room. Heavy, blackened oak beams sloped downward from the inner to the outer wall. Between the two long windows that looked out onto the street ran a section of Elizabethan timber and plaster wall, strangely at odds with the much later oak panelling to the interior. The beamed roof stopped short of the outer wall to be replaced by glass panels, which rose to one side to become an octagonal glass dome. Jack thought that the glass roofed area could have been a passageway in the old inn. What he couldn't make any sense of was a floor-level window set into the wall to the right of the fireplace. The place was an architectural historian's dream!

Among the old photographs that decorated the walls was one that Jack found particularly interesting. It showed the present-day car park as it had been in the mid eighteen-hundreds. Wagons, horses and men in leggings and long cotton frock coats occupied the cobbled yard. The lower walls were hung with iron hay stalls and supported huge stone water troughs. Doors no longer in existence opened onto a cobbled yard. What was now an 'L' shaped structure had at that time been three-sided; a wing had either fallen down or been demolished. Wooden stairways climbed to a gallery that ran at first floor level around the yard. Washing hung from the wooden railings. Two women stood at an upper door, looking straight into the camera. A man in a bowler hat and dark suit, pipe in hand, leant against the railings and looked down unto the yard - a manager, perhaps?

After breakfast, taking Ralph's advice, he set out for Buckshot Hall and an exploration of the surrounding roads and lanes. Following directions, he took the road signposted Chomley Green. Half a mile brought him to the left turn for Little Mickleford. It was a fairly narrow road with treacherous, tyre-wrecking gullies at its edges. It was shooting country, dense hedges on both sides of the road, deep undergrowth. A cock pheasant, its feathers iridescent, dashed out from the hedge and ran across the road, narrowly avoiding the wheels of the car. It occurred to Jack that the road must run parallel to that running through Mickleford village; Buckshot Hall couldn't be more than half a mile distant from The Swan as the crow flew. Interesting!

Almost immediately, within five hundred metres of the turn, he caught sight of the media pack. They were parked in a pull-in that faced high, ornate, cast iron gates. There were no more than ten of them - nothing like the numbers of the previous evening. It looked as though Sky and the bigger players had got their story and left. He stopped on the road, engine running. He couldn't see the hall; beyond the gates, the driveway swung sharply to the left and became obscured by heavy tree growth. He drove on. After a few hundred metres, the stone estate walls petered out to be replaced by hedgerows, thickets and fern-covered scrubland.

At a distance, he saw an oncoming Range Rover, saw it slow and make a left turn onto an unsigned road. Jack decided to follow; the road might afford a sight of the hall. The turn took him onto a narrow lane, little more than a car's width, further narrowed by hedges of hawthorn and elder that threw out encroaching branches.

After a couple of tight bends, the lane opened out. Speeding up, he caught sight of the car ahead as it slowed to negotiate a further series of bends. Closing in, he saw the number plate. Jack couldn't believe what he was seeing; it was Graham Fairbrother's number plate. He leaned forward across the steering wheel, stared at the black letters and numbers. Hell! This was unexpected! What was Graham Fairbrother's Range Rover doing down a country lane in Little Mickleford? Instinctively, he hung back, allowing the car to move on. As the roof of a building came into sight, the car slowed and made a left turn. He crawled past the driveway; the car was parked up, the door thrown open, someone was getting out. A few metres down the road, he pulled in and parked against the hedge, got out of the car, and moved cautiously back towards the house. There were no walls, no gates, nothing but the hedges edging the garden. The density of the shrubbery provided perfect cover. He was able to get right up to the boundary, was able to look through the foliage at Graham Fairbrother, taking a travel bag from the boot of the car, walking to the door, putting a key in the lock, and going into the house. Jack was completely stumped! He couldn't think of a single reason why his brother-in-law should be staying in a house in Little Mickleford.

He spent a couple of hours driving through the warren of narrow roads and lanes that Ralph had talked about. He didn't end up at the back of the stables, but did hit upon an accommodating pull-in that overlooked a shallow valley and gave an unimpeded view of Buckshot Hall. It was a large Georgian country house, built in red brick with a low, deep parapeted grey slate roof. A wide flight of steps rose from a gravelled forecourt to an entrance set flush at the centre of the building, the door capped by a huge, raised eyebrow pediment.

Some place.

Graham's Range Rover was still parked up on the forecourt when he passed the house on his way back to The Swan.

**

'How much property does Lord Sanfold own in these parts?'

Jack had ordered a coffee; he was sitting at the bar chatting to the girl he had spoken to on his first visit.

'Around Mickleford, not a lot, but in Little Mickleford, most of the property is on estate land. They haven't sold anything off that I know of.'

'I drove around a bit today. There's a turning a bit past the main gates of the hall. I passed quite a big house on that road.'

'That will be his sister's place.'

'His sister?'

'His half-sister really. His father married twice; his first wife died quite young. She is his lordship's stepmother's daughter. She's called Clementia.'

'Does she live there?'

'Sometimes. I've heard that she spends a lot of time in New York, or did. She has quite a big job; don't ask me what she does. She's an 'honourable', I think! She's rented the house out in the past. I don't know if she still does that.'

'Interesting, How the other half live, eh.'

'Yeh, exactly. But she seems OK. My mother has met her through the WI. She was with Lady Jessica. Those two seem to hit it off well. Her own mother, the old lady who lives in London, is a tyrant by all accounts. My mother thought Clementia was very nice, kind of ordinary, if you know what I mean.'

Jack decided to take a walk up the village street to see if the book shop was open. They would probably have a local map; it would give him a better idea of the area around the hall. He was in luck. The shop was just about to close, the owner had on his jacket and was switching off the lights as Jack pushed open the door.

'That was good timing! A couple of minutes later and you would have found the door locked and my good self - ensconced in The Swan. What can I do for you?' The voice was upper-class, the appearance eccentric, scatty!

He was well over six feet tall, middle aged, with straw-like, greyish-blonde hair sticking out from underneath a tweed cap. He wore a mustard jacket, faded pink trousers and a dark green shirt with a red paisley cravat.

Ah, yes, a map of our fair lands is something I can provide,' was the answer to Jack's request. 'Let me see! Now I can give you a county map, a map showing the north of the county or a much larger scale map of the immediate area showing our own dear little villages in some detail,' said the verbose person, taking three maps from a plastic rack and spreading them fan like on the counter.

'The map of the villages looks good.'

'Good in looks and enlightening in content. An excellent choice, excellent! Are you touring or here to interview the lord of the manor?'

'A good photo of his lordship that nobody else has got; that's what I'm after.'

'Good luck with that, my boy. He has plenty to say for himself; he certainly has! Doesn't represent our views; I hope you people understand that. Damn disgrace! No mandate from his voters for his pronouncements, none at all; Brexiteers to a man in these parts. Old Sir Marcus will be turning in his grave, indeed, he will. Listened to local people, respected their views, old Sir Marcus.'

The map was put into a brown paper bag, sealed with a sticker showing a sketch of the shop and handed to Jack with the exhortation to 'bring his lordship to book'. Leaving the shop, Jack looked up at the name above the door; 'Porchy's Tomes and Trivia'. He wondered if Porchy was a real name or a nickname; he thought it most likely the latter.

He returned to The Swan, went to his room, propped up the pillows and settled to do some searching. He hadn't been wrong! His newly acquired map, together with Google Earth, showed the distance between The Swan and Buckshot Hall to be less than three quarters of a mile. Between the two lay an area of forest, a biggish farm with barns and outbuildings and two fields. The farm bordered the B road, opposite the main gates of the hall. It could easily be walked. He estimated that the hall was set back about a quarter of a mile from the road. He was certain that the hall had been Ralph Braxton's late-night destination.

He Googled Clementia Goffe. She was forty-four, had held various posts at The UN Office of Legal Affairs in New York. Her home was in Little Mickleford, Surrey, close to the family residence, Buckshot Hall. There was no mention of her marital status, but she had a son, David, aged twenty-three. There was a photograph of a serious-looking woman with glasses and dark, curly hair.

He dozed off and dreamed of Sal. He was at Simon's wedding, walking along the hotel corridor, being dragged into the bedroom. The dark-haired bridesmaid had morphed into a dishevelled Sal. She tore at his clothes with red, talon-like nails and sucked at his mouth with lipstick-smeared, swollen lips. As she pushed him towards the bed, he raised his arm and struck her a blow that sent her sprawling backwards towards the stone hearth of The Swan bar. She lay with her head wedged against the iron grate, her blue, dead eyes staring.

He woke with a start; something was rattling against the window; the room was dark. He glanced at his watch; it was 5:20, he must have slept for a good two hours. Disorientated, it took him a while to realise that a storm was raging. He looked out of the window onto a black sky and a water-washed, windswept street. He didn't feel at all good; his mood matched the dark gloom of the room. He had a shower, got changed and went down to dinner. He found Ralph Braxton waiting for him.

'I waited to order; I thought you'd be down. Have you seen the news? EU membership extended to 22nd May; 12th April if she can't get her deal through. Fucking shambles! Bloody Civil Service in charge; she's like putty in their hands.! Parliamentary amendments coming thick and fast. Amendments carried, amendments defeated, amendments allowed, not allowed. Make your head spin! So wrapped up in their own importance, in the brilliance of their own intellect, in the rightness of their own opinions, that they can't see what figures of ridicule they've become in the eyes of the public.'

'Yeh. It's crazy. It's as though some collective mania has taken hold of the place. I don't think they care what the people think. I don't think they care what their own voters think. I don't think they are aware that there's a world outside Westminster. The Goffe brigade will be happy!'

'Anything from them?'

'Who?'

'The Goffe brigade.'

After a quick look about him, Ralph leaned conspiratorially across the table. 'It's a bloody charade, Jack, with Goffe as the main player. It's all designed to confuse and mislead. It's not some boy's brigade; it's a traitorous amalgam of some of the most powerful in the country. I shouldn't be telling you this, I'm trusting you to keep your mouth shut. Goffe is a key player in a group that call themselves Die Drachentoter. It's German for 'dragon slayer'. They have a logo showing the tip of a spear on a blue background. It's all linked to Saint George and the slaying of the dragon. The implication being that the British people have conjured up an evil comparable to a fire breathing dragon.'

'What!'

'Yeh, unbelievable. You might ask why they have given themselves a German title. God knows! Maybe it was suggested by one of the EU officials or civil servants who attend the meetings to be given the heads-up on internal discussions within the civil service and UK cabinet.'

'Come on! That's crazy! Sounds like something from a 1930s spy novel!'

'I tell you. my friend, crazy as it sounds, it's true. While Goffe and his cohort in the house shout about a second referendum and the disastrous result of a no-deal Brexit, the big players get on with the real business of having Article 50 withdrawn and tying us even more securely to the EU. They're a tight-knit, powerful group.

They've been working undercover since December 2016, after the Supreme Court judgement in the Miller case, when the court ruled that parliamentary authorization would be needed to invoke Article 50. That was their breakthrough.

It's the 'Deep State' at work. Bloody frightening! It's all a sham, a piece of elaborate theatre played out for the deception of the nation. The game is to let parliament believe itself in control. Most MPs are easily controlled and manipulated. These people are arch manipulators; they float lots of diversionary ideas for the representatives of the people to latch on to; concepts sufficiently nebulous to be developed into a myriad of conflicting ideas and opinions; the resulting chaos, leading to an impotent - what the media like to call a 'log jammed parliament'. They've been very successful so far.'

'Who are they?'

'High-ranking civil servants, ex. ministers of state, judges. It's controlled from within the establishment; by the dark, enigmatic figures who operate in the shadows, see themselves as the nation's guardians. They don't think leaving the EU is in the national interest. They're not overly sold on democracy!'

'How the hell can a thing like that be going on without it being flagged up by the media? It doesn't seem credible!'

'That's how they get away with it! Any mention of a thing so insidious would be written off as wild conspiracy theory! Last year, there was a row over a leaked document forecasting huge Brexit damage to the economy. The European Research Group said that all the figures had been fiddled, but the damage was done. Few believed in such insider skulduggery. There are those in the media who want to expose them, but they need proof. Madelaine Murry has a contact in the Department of International Trade who has given her amazing info on the group, members' list, meeting places and times, even copies of the minutes of meetings.

'It's mad!'

'Yeh, hard to get your head around! But here's the thing. They have to take care when and where they meet. Meeting in London is out of the question, so it's down to places like Buckshot Hall where they can creep in and out undetected. You can imagine that there are a number in their ranks with similar places. They had a meeting up there last weekend. I was up there and saw them arrive.'

'Hell!'

'Yeh, I walked onto the estate through a gap in the wall not far from the main gate, walked right up to the house and around to the stable block. The place is dark, the only lights are around the front of the house. The stable block is unlit and there is dense shrubbery around the cobbled yard and along the pathway joining the complex to the main house. The stables are built with a short dog leg that accommodates cottages. There looks to be one groom who lives in the end cottage; the other cottages are empty. I was worried about dogs. There was no sign of any but I had to make sure so I drove down the Wednesday before, parked up in the rear yard and left the car door open in case I had to make a run for it. I took a metal bar with me. It was pretty scary; I was expecting hounds to come tearing around the side of the building. There were no dogs; there's no security.

I knew Goffe and Bruce were in London, so I had a good scout about. I was able to walk right up to the hall itself and around the building. The groom in the end cottage watches TV with the sound right up. I doubt he would hear a bomb go off at the other end of the yard.

They started to arrive around midnight. They drove in along the road that I told you about; parked up in the stable yard, most were driving themselves. A guy with a torch, looked like Goffe's PA, was running backwards and forwards, guiding them up to the house. I reported back to Maddy. Buckshot is our best chance of getting some incriminating stuff. If I had been a competent photographer, I could have got endless footage - great stuff for the Brexit-supporting press. You could do it! What do you think?'

'Me?'

'Why not?'

'What's wrong with their own photographers?'

'Come on, you know how it works! They won't risk their job and reputation on that kind of work. It's trespass for one thing! It's got to be a freelance job. There's good money in it!'

'Seems risky!'

'There's zero risk. The shrubs give perfect cover. We can get footage of the number plates, of them getting out of the cars. We need to pin them to the location: wide views of the hall and close-ups of the door with individuals going in. The footage would be dynamite.'

'When are they likely to have another meeting at Buckshot?'

'Could be a month, could be next week. There doesn't appear to be any pattern to their choice of venue. Maddy will get the heads up. What do you think? Are you in?'

**

It was like scrabbling for a solid footing on quicksand. Ralph's revelations had swept away the points of reference through which Jack had made sense of his world. It had driven from his mind the curious question of what Graham Fairbrother was doing in Mickleford, living in a house owned by Clementia Goffe. Was it a coincidence that she had a son named David, that a young man named David had accompanied Graham on outings with the kids? Intriguing, but of little consequence to Jack, as he left Mickleford with tales of betrayal and treachery in mind.

Chapter 16

Jack

Jack was buzzing, he had a mission. He would await news from Ralph Braxton, but in the meanwhile, he needed to get his hands on a camera - a pretty sophisticated camera at that. He knew nothing about cameras, nothing about photography. Apart from a basic digital job and the camera on his phone, the only cameras with which he was familiar were the site cameras used at work. His search of the internet had left him more confused than informed, so he had gone to Camera World. They were very helpful. They prided themselves on the expertise of their sales staff; many themselves were expert photographers. After explaining his requirements, he was presented with an array of cameras with eye-watering price tags, most topping 2K.

'More than you had budgeted for?' said the assistant, registering Jack's discomfiture.

After a gradual scaling down of performance and cost, he had come away with a reconditioned Canon that he was assured would do all he required for under five hundred. The camera had come with instructions. – the fat, detailed handbook was a challenge in itself. Jack had spent hours getting his head around the camera's many and varied functions. It was a steep learning curve. After evenings of trial and error he took the camera with him to his parents. He intended to put his new knowledge to the test in the garden; trial the head spinning suggestions on apertures, shutter speed and the many technicalities of night-time photography. He needed to get it all nailed down. He couldn't afford any slip-ups at the hall. Keeping a steady hand, that was the thing. The suggested tripod wasn't going to be an option.

**

There was little that Jack didn't know about Sally's life. He knew all about her comings and goings and where she would be at a given time. He had spent months building his dossier.

His solicitor had tracked down Myrtle's address; it was amazing how easy that had been for Clive. But it made him very angry to think back on that affair. It had been three months after Clive had written to Andrew, Wood and Khan that he got the money from Sal. She had tried to wheedle her way out of it, trying to force him to sell his home; it had made Jack's blood boil.

He was very proud of his home, his tasteful furniture and furnishings. When he thought back to the state Sal had left him in - the dirt and the squalor that he had dealt with - he was infuriated. Christian said that he had turned into a fussy old woman; Jack didn't agree. He was maintaining the standards he had grown up with.

Christian didn't really understand; he hadn't been brought up in a well-ordered house, as Jack had. His mum had gone out to work, and his gran hadn't been overly particular. He had to keep an eye on Christian - make sure that he took his plate into the kitchen and put it in the dishwasher, kept the throws in place over the arms and seat of the sofa and didn't spill lager on the carpet.

It was curiosity that had compelled him to take a look at Myrtle's place. It had been a surprise when Sal turned up. He was even more surprised when she turned up every Friday evening to stay for the weekend. What the hell was going on? Where was lover boy? Something appeared to be amiss!

He followed the pair to food banks, where they spent a great deal of their time. They usually headed back to Myrtle's at around 6 p.m. Sometimes, they were in for the night; other times, they went out with Art and other undesirables to the local pub. He wondered what they were drinking in there; he couldn't imagine The White Horse being big on vegan fizz. It was amazing the number of scruffy, hippy weirdos that went in and out of Myrtle's place. They had been to a couple of Afro-Caribbean gigs on Queens Road and they were fond of the vegan restaurants off Rye Lane. Occasionally, they got in the van and headed off to places like Barking and Dagenham or Redbridge, places Jack was to discover, where a lot of asylum seekers were housed.

One night, he followed them to Redbridge. He had parked, out of sight of their van, in the car park of a high rise and watched Sal and Myrtle disappear into the building. They were in there for two hours, came out and drove straight back. While sitting in the car, he was harassed by a group of boys who squeezed their faces against the windscreen and ran away across the bonnet of the car, making howling noises. He didn't follow them out of Peckham again; he couldn't see the point.

**

He had finally caught up with Mark Aitkin in The Duck. He had been popping in on his way home for a couple of weeks, hoping Mark would be in. He thought that Mark's wife, Clare, might still be in touch with Sal. It took some careful manoeuvring, but he finally contrived to steer the conversation to Sal.

He took a punt. 'It's a pity it's not working out for her. I wish her well; I really do. It didn't work out for us and I must admit it hit me hard. But I'm over it now and I'd like to see her happy.'

'Yeh, sad! Clare says it's going nowhere. It's been a good couple of years and he's still not committing. Goes home every weekend, supposedly to keep up some pretence of a relationship for the sake of his two kids. Needless to say, Sal's not happy!'

'I didn't realise it was every weekend! Poor Sal!'

'Without fail, apparently!'

Job done. Well played!

If Clare Aitkin was right, Sal's romance was in deep trouble. He had to find out what was going on. But he had to be careful. He drove over to Fulham on his way to his parents the following Friday evening. There was no sign of life in number 34. The house was in darkness. He thought it worthwhile hanging about for a while and rang home to say he'd be late. He found a parking space a few streets away; he couldn't chance parking anywhere near the house.

He turned on his laptop and settled down to catch up on political events. Another disaster! The dark forces were in the ascendancy!

**

May's deal had been voted down for the third time - 286 to 344 against. He had to hand it to the woman; she wasn't easily knocked off course. The bloody Irish backstop! Dominic Raab was saying it was worse than staying in the EU. A number of top Tories were calling for her resignation. Boris called it 'a paint and plaster pseudo-Brexit'.

The EU was, as usual, dictating terms! An extension until 31st October was to be allowed, but only if EU elections were held! May saying the latest lost parliamentary vote was a 'matter of profound regret' that 'an alternative way forward must be found'. There were to be 'indicative votes' the following Monday. Indicative of what? Of the mindset of the muddle-headed crew that sat on the green benches - the traitorous mob that shuffled their way in and out of the parliamentary lobbies, attempting to overturn the vote of the

British people! Almost three years since the country voted to leave and EU elections were looming.
It was all going the way of The Drachentoter!

**

The days were lengthening; it was 9:00 before he felt it safe to leave the car and walk to Edgar Street. People were home, settled in for the night, the streets were quiet with cars parked bumper to bumper. Light filtered through drawn blinds and curtains beneath the yellow glare of street lights. Jack walked with his collar pulled up and his head down. There was a vacant space where a dark blue BMW usually parked. It confirmed what he had suspected - the beamer belonged to Tennant. It was unimportant, useless knowledge that Jack nevertheless enjoyed having. It also meant that Tennant was most probably out.

Reaching the end of the street, he turned into the entry. It was pitch black, there wasn't much of a moon and the backs of the houses were, as usual, devoid of light. He switched on his torch; kept it trained on the ground. The back of the house had changed beyond all recognition. Even partly obscured by darkness, the extension was overpowering and out of place. He couldn't believe that there hadn't been objections from the neighbours; he couldn't believe they had been given planning permission!

It was a huge, double-storey, sharp-angled box. The absence of light gave it the look of sheet metal. It was beyond ugly; it belonged on an industrial estate, not on a residential street. He imagined that it was some kind of privacy glass - no such privacy for the overlooked neighbours! He estimated that the glass walls extended some five metres into the garden.

He would have liked to take a closer look, but had no intention of emerging from the shadows to be picked up on security cameras that may or may not have been installed. He had no wish to draw attention to himself. He could hear Christian's voice; 'Anger can be a positive or negative force. It's just another emotion that has to be controlled. Controlled anger is a weapon at your disposal. You can't let anger control you; that's a pathway to disaster. Get a grip, mate.'

Jack had heeded the advice. He had learned to drive out ideas of petty revenge; driving a sharpened screwdriver into tyres would feel pretty good; sending anonymous threatening emails was tempting but stupid. 'The police always look for the person who might hold a grudge. You'll be top of the list, mate. Keep your powder dry. Anonymous street crime, robbery gone wrong, that's the game!' He knew Christian was right; Christian knew a thing or two. He had been sorely tempted to sabotage Myrtle's garishly embellished tin lizzie that she parked in the unlit area at the back of the flat, an easy target, but he had resisted.

**

Myrtle's flat was over an Indian dress shop on Peckham High Street. It was next door to a fruit and veg shop run by a big, loud West Indian bloke called Dexter, who seemed to be permanently open. Boxes of yams, sweet potatoes, oca and squash tumbled onto the pavement. Great bunches of green bananas hung from hooks and enamel jugs sprouted green herbs. Dexter tipped his produce into capacious bags held open by large ladies or expertly twirled soft fruit into paper bags; Jack liked that; Dexter didn't deal in plastic bags. The problem was that he seemed to know everyone. He greeted all passersby and waved to those on the opposite pavement. Jack couldn't afford to bring himself to Dexter's attention.

The back of the flat was a different matter. A turn off the high street led to the back of the buildings and a large communal parking area. The land at the back dropped away steeply, adding a further two stories to the buildings. Open tread, iron stairways provided the upper-floor occupants with access to ground level. Old hedges and patched up walls bordered the yards. Coloured recycling and commercial-size grey bins stood outside back gates. A mattress and two 60s Formica topped bedside cabinets had been dumped against a wall. At the foot of one stairway, a garden table and chairs sat incongruously amid overgrown, leggy privets and long grass. The area couldn't have been more dissimilar to the bustling vibrancy of the high street. The silent, unpeopled space had an eerie, almost sinister feel. Jack availed of its dark corners to park his car, but didn't spend time there; it held no interest for him.

He sometimes delayed going back to his parent's place until Saturday afternoon so that he could spend the morning in Peckham. He had been in a café some way down the street, had just finished a breakfast of two sausage muffins when he saw Sal and Myrtle come out of the flat. He paid the bill and looked cautiously along the street before stepping from the cover of the doorway and following. The place was busy with Saturday morning shoppers. It made following easier. Sal, her hair scraped back into a low ponytail, was unremarkable in jeans and a black puffer jacket, but the same couldn't be said of Myrtle! She was wearing an ankle-length, knitted coat in a multi-coloured zigzag pattern with a purple beret crammed down on her head.

Myrtle had her arm through Sal's and was doing all the talking, occasionally peering into Sal's face. Sal kept her head down; he could see that she was upset. When a Chinese woman stopped to speak, Sal pulled away and stood looking into a shop window, her face averted. They continued down the high street. The place was a melting pot. The air was redolent with diverse ethnic cooking smells. Foodstuffs from every corner of the globe lined the pavements. Soul music belted out through shop doorways; the world's languages assailed his ears. He felt himself to be in some ill-defined alien space, a stranger in his own country.

Myrtle and Sal had disappeared into a purple painted place that wrapped itself around a corner. Black lettering on a puce sign promised 'A Taste of the East' and boosted fine foods and handicrafts. The place had the look of an eastern bazaar. In the windows were cubby hole compartments housing jars, tins and packets, all of exotic origin. Shelves were draped with fabrics and piled with shisha pipes and musical instruments. 'I Love Peckham' T-shirts in yellow with a black heart motif hung beside oriental wall hangings. Viewed from the opposite side of the street, the interior appeared to be a similar mishmash of piled-up, eclectic goods.

From the opposite pavement, he could see into the shop where the two women had sat down at a table and were having an order taken. As soon as the waiter had walked away, Myrtle put her arm around Sal's shoulder. Sal had a wodge of tissues in her hand and was dabbing her eyes. What he would have given to listen in on that conversation.

After half an hour, they came out and headed back in the direction of the flat. Crossing the street, they went into a pawn shop. He couldn't begin to imagine what they might be doing in there! They were in the shop for only a couple of minutes before coming out and heading back across the street and into a TLC charity shop. He had heard of the charity; they were all about talking and listening; 'an emotional wellbeing charity'. Right up Myrtle's street! Their next stop was at an African food market, where they had a long conversation with a woman in a bright, African-print dress and turban. Criss-crossing between the pavements, he followed the pair up the street. They shopped in a foreign mini market, from where they emerged carrying plastic bags.

The unbranded bags looked like the cheap, flimsy things still dished out by unprincipled shopkeepers. Bloody typical of people like Myrtle and Sal, so busy overburdening the health service and cluttering up schools with the world's needy that they had no time to consider the far more pressing needs of the world itself. Their final stop was at a shop advertising eggless cakes. He wondered what eggless, vegan cakes were like. Probably as tasteless as the tofu feast that Sal had cooked up when Myrtle and Art had come to Sunday lunch! Sal looked dreadful! Pale and drawn!

He drove to his parents' house feeling quite buoyed up by the events of the morning. Sal was very upset indeed. It must be to do with lover boy's absence; the relationship was definitely falling apart.

Served her right, the treacherous little cow!

**

Julia had started to call 30 Court Road home. She would say things, like, 'Poppy has violin after school, so we'll be a bit late home'. At weekends, Margaret and Ron had a full house. Julia occupied her old bedroom while Poppy and Sam slept on bunk beds in the spare room. Ron and Jack had spent a weekend clearing the room for the children. In latter years, it had been used as a storage room. Margaret had peered into bags deposited in the room years before.

'Oh, Ron, I do wish we had labelled stuff. What were we thinking of?'

'We always imagine that we'll remember what we are putting away and where we are putting it. It always seems quite straightforward at the time. Of course, we weren't expecting to have to move it all so soon; we didn't expect our daughter returning with two children!'

'Oh, Ron, don't say that. It sounds as though we don't want them!'

Ron made no answer. He picked up one of the boxes designated for the loft and passed it up to Jack, who stood at the top of the ladder. Boxes and bags sorted by Margaret were dispatched to the loft or the garage. After three trips to a charity shop, the room was finally emptied.

Margaret and Ron were very worried about Julia and even more worried about the children. Ron had laid down what he called 'some ground rules' before Julia had been allowed to take up residence. There was to be an undertaking from Julia that she must fit into their lifestyle, respect their wishes, refrain from criticism of her mother's cooking, furnishings and housekeeping and under no circumstances criticise Graham in the hearing of the children. Surprisingly, Julia was restrained, quiet, not the bombastic woman they had become used to dealing with. She seemed to Jack to be overly anxious to please her parents. She helped Margaret with the cooking, she sat amongst her mother's 'clutter' without comment and made no criticism of her father's politics. His mother said Julia needed their support and was making a big effort to fit in.

'It's so unlike her; it's unnerving!' Jack had said.

'She's had a dreadful shock, dear. She's still coming to terms with it all.'

That was the belief in Court Road until the day Ron and Jack took the children to the Zoo. They had been up to the education centre and collected the quizzes and colouring sheets, been to see the lovebirds, had a good look at the gorillas, been in the reptile house and spent time with the tigers. Poppy and Sam were familiar with the zoo and knew exactly what they wanted to see. The 'Dragons' Lair' was their favourite. They liked to keep the Komodo Dragon until last.

'I wish Ganas would come closer; I want to see his razor-sharp teeth,' said Sam with his nose to the glass.

'We saw him killing a water buffalo, Uncle Jack,' announced

Poppy. 'Not this dragon, of course; a dragon on television. It was horrible! First of all, he bit the buffalo and because he has poisonous saliva, the buffalo couldn't move or defend himself. Then he kept nipping at its legs, waiting for it to die. Ooh, it was so gross.'

'Slash, slash, a big gash,' Sam was spinning around, waving an imaginary knife above his head. 'A big gash in Daddy's head.'

'Shut up, Poppy shouted, 'It wasn't Daddy's head.'

'I'm making a rhyme, silly.'

'It doesn't rhyme, stupid. Shut up.'

'What's this about, Poppy?' said Ron.

'Mummy with a big knife, slash, slash.,' Sam had recommenced his spinning.

'Shut up, shut up!' Poppy ran at her brother, pummelling him with her fists.

Jack grabbed hold of Poppy and pulled her away. Ron brought Sam to a standstill, took his hand and began marching up the path towards the café. Having unceremoniously dumped two glasses of orange juice on the table, Ron sat down and faced Poppy.

'Now, Poppy, you are going to tell me what this is all about.'

Poppy, head down, tears pouring down her face, didn't respond.

'Come along, Poppy, this won't do.'

'I can't tell you, Granddad, we haven't got to talk about it.'

'Poppy, you and Sam seem to have a lot of secrets. You are keeping secrets for Mummy and for Daddy. When I was your age, it would have made me very unhappy to have to keep secrets from my family. Who told you not to talk about this?'

'Mummy said we mustn't talk about it because if people found out, we would be taken into care. It means we wouldn't see you anymore, Grandad,' Poppy fixed tragic eyes on Ron.

'I think you should tell us, Pops. One thing I do know is that

Grandma and Granddad would never allow you to be taken into care,' said Jack.

'It's about things Mummy has done - things she has done to Daddy.'

'What sort of things, Pops?'

'Mummy did a lot of things that really upset Daddy. She was always hitting him; Daddy used to grab her arms and hold her until she stopped kicking and shouting.' Once started, Poppy was on a roll, the stored up secrets poured out. 'She broke Daddy's things; she broke his computer and smashed up his mobile phone. She took a lot of Daddy's clothes and burned them in the garden. She built a big fire and threw his things on it. That was quite a long time ago; I was very young at the time and didn't realise what a bad thing Mummy was doing. I just remember the great big flames that leapt up into the air and thinking it was very exciting. Now I can see how very upsetting it was for Daddy. I would hate it if my clothes got burned.'

'What did your Daddy do, Pops?'

'Well, I don't remember it all, but I do remember him saying that the clothes could be quickly replaced but that the lawn would take some time to recover. You see, there was a big black patch where Mummy's fire had been.'

'Why did she do those things, Pops? Had Daddy done something to upset her or hurt her?'

'No, Uncle Jack, Daddy didn't hurt Mummy. She just didn't love him. She loves us, but she hates Daddy.'

Ron, his face ashen, said, 'Tell us about the knife, Poppy.'

'That was very upsetting. It wasn't long before Daddy left us that it happened. Mummy was very angry; I don't really know why; I think it was to do with emails. Mummy picked up a knife and before he could stop her, she put a big cut in Daddy's arm. It was while we were having dinner. Daddy was wearing a shirt with short sleeves, so we could see the cut. Sam was screaming; that's why he talks about slashing and gashes. He dreams about it sometimes and wakes up crying. When that happens, he comes into my bed. Daddy's arm was horrible, there was a lot of blood on Daddy and on the table. Mummy ran away and locked herself in a bedroom.

Uncle Les came and took Daddy to the hospital. Daddy told me to take Sam upstairs and wait for Aunty Patty, who was coming to look after us. He said we weren't to worry, that he would be OK and he would come in and see us when he came back.'

All colour had drained from Ron's face; he was speechless. Sam, who had sat silently anxious while Poppy spoke, moved himself closer to his sister and took hold of her hand. Both sat with tragic eyes fixed on Ron.

'Are you angry with us, Grandad?' Poppy asked.

'Angry with you, Poppy? I should think not! I'm very angry with the adults who have upset you and made you keep secrets. You have done the right thing telling us. You needn't speak to Mummy about it; I will speak to Mummy.'

The children were very quiet as they made their way from the zoo, but once in the car, Poppy perked up.

'There was a very famous Komodo Dragon called Slasher; have you heard about him, Grandad?'

'No, Poppy, I can't say that I have!'

'Have you, Uncle Jack?'

'No. I haven't.'

'He was an American. Well, American by birth but ethnically Indonesian, because the Island of Komodo, where his species come from, is Indonesian.'

Jack's ears pricked up; it looked like they were in for a lesson in zoology. He found Poppy very amusing when she embarked on one of her informative talks.

'He wasn't really born; he was hatched. Most reptiles come

from eggs, except a very few lizards and snakes that give birth to live young. Slasher was hatched in the Smithsonian National Zoo in October 1992. He was transferred to Zoo Atlanta when he was nine months old. David saw him there in 2006, when David was 10 and Slasher was 13; he showed us photos and a video of Slasher on his phone.'

'When was this, Poppy?' Ron was suddenly interested.

'When we were at the zoo, Granddad. Daddy and David had taken us to the zoo. It was while we were looking at Ganas.'

'Snap! He can snap your leg in two,' said Sam.

'Yes, Sam, Komodos can, but Slasher didn't do that; he was well behaved. In fact, he was very intelligent and learned to do a lot of clever things. He was just happy, basking in the sun. But he's dead now; he died in 2013, when Sam was one and I was four. He was euthanised because of age-related conditions. Poor Slasher! But he seems to have been happy and twenty is a good age for a Komodo Dragon.'

'Was David on holiday in America when he saw Slasher?' Ron asked.

'Well, kind of, Granddad, He was on holiday in Georgia; that's where Zoo Atlanta is, but he lived in America with his mummy, so he wasn't on holiday in America.'

'So David is American?'

'He's American and English, Granddad. He belongs to both. His Mummy and Daddy are English, but he was born in America. He lived with his Mummy in New York, in an apartment - that's a big flat. When he looked out of the windows, he could see a beautiful park where he went for walks with his nanny. His nanny was called Terry. David's mummy had a very important job, so Terry looked after David when she was at work. David promised that one day he would take Sam and me to visit the apartment and take us for walks in the park. I don't know if that will happen now!'

said a wistful Poppy.

'Well, well, so that's what it's all about,' said Ron, as the children ran ahead of them into the house. 'No wonder she's worried about Graham taking the children! He may well have a very good case. He has at least one witness to an assault in his brother. One thing is clear: he loves those children and I doubt he will leave them with Julia. I'm surprised he hasn't already applied for some type of order. My God, he could have had her charged with GBH - well ABH at the least.'

'What will you do, Dad?'

'Speak to your mother. I think she will agree that the matter needs to be brought out into the open. We will have to speak to Julia. I feel inclined to contact Graham; we need to know what his intentions are. I could contact him through his firm! We have had our heads in the sand. We have worried about her abusive behaviour, but never for a moment dreamt of anything of this order.'

Jack was shaken by Poppy's revelations. Poppy and Sam were very close. It was understandable that they clung to each other for comfort. But Jack thought it was more than that; Poppy and Sam loved one another. It had never been that way with Julia and himself. He remembered a self-obsessed, jealous little girl. He could still feel her bony elbows digging into his ribs in the back of the car; her sharp-featured face, peering into his, anticipating the enjoyment of seeing the tears come to his eyes.

She was a dark haired, thin child, pale, with brown, threatening eyes. She reminded Jack of the witches in his story books. He had once called her a witch and been told off by his mother. Jack knew very little about children, but he did know of the propensity of siblings to disagree, to tend towards petty jealousies. It had been something more with Julia; she had been a small tyrant, a wielder of pain and fear. As she got older, her thinness padded out, her features became less severe; she was considered an attractive young woman. But Jack saw, hidden behind the pretty veneer, the sadistic tormentor of their childhood. He wasn't surprised when she started to abuse her husband. What had surprised him, was Graham's acceptance of her abuse.

Poppy's unhappy tale left Jack with a feeling of deep unease. A sense of déjà vu. What would Ron make of his own actions? He thought things were looking pretty black for Julia. It didn't look like a marriage that could be patched up, looked to him like Julia was back to stay, at least in the short term. Hell, she was turning their lives upside down, the selfish bitch. His parents were going to need his support. He had to get his act together.

Chapter 17

Julian

Julian stopped just long enough to repack his weekend bag before jumping into the car and heading for London. He was shaking with anger. He gripped the steering wheel, put his foot down on the accelerator, tore along, flung the car around bends, his mind racing in pace with the car. He had been sure that he had covered his tracks with the Fulham house. How the hell had his father got wind of it?

When out and about with Sally, Julian took care to avoid places where he thought it likely he would be recognised. He kept away from Mayfair and St. James' where the older directors hung out in their clubs. He avoided restaurants he knew to be frequented by the younger cohort. But most of the younger group were family men who commuted and fortunately spent little time in the city. What he hadn't taken into account were the junior staff, who were also out and about. Although most were unknown to him, he wasn't unknown to them. They gossiped amongst themselves and their gossip had a way of percolating upwards. His relationship with Sally was common knowledge in the upper echelons of the firm. His disparagement of Hubert Monk was unfair. There was much that Monk could have reported to his old friend, but he confined himself to matters affecting the office.

Ted's information had come from a different source: from an old army friend who had called at Julian's flat to leave some updated information for a military charity. He had left with his information undelivered, having been told by the concierge that Mr. Tennant was no longer in residence. Pressed, the concierge had told him that the flat had been 'mothballed', that he had heard that Mr. Tennant had bought another property elsewhere in the city. Ted, put on the spot, when asked where Julian had moved to, had been acutely embarrassed to have to admit to knowing nothing of the matter.

Julian drove to his flat. He couldn't face Sally. He needed to be on his own to come to terms with the conflicting emotions that were tearing him apart. His carefully constructed life was collapsing about him. Much of his anger was self-directed. He had started to think that the purchase of the Fulham house had been a mistake. It had been a reaction to what he thought of as insufferable interference into his life - a foolish belief that he could sustain a parallel life with Sally.

He hadn't thought it through. He hadn't anticipated that Sally would expect their relationship to evolve and move on to a more formal footing. He had become accustomed to women who didn't make demands - women who came and went without asking personal questions, without trying to delve into the details of his family life. He had thought of Sally as a more permanent iteration of these women. Looking back to the start of their relationship, he could see that 'the new life together', the 'new beginning' they had spoken of, had meant something different to Sally than it had to him. He had overegged it; he could see that now. He had been bowled over by Sally, determined to draw her more closely into his life.

What did his father know? Would Lucy find out? He was gripped by panic; his shirt was wet with sweat. He had a dreadful headache. He went into the kitchen and took the tin box from the drawer, took an envelope from his inside pocket and sat down at the table.

Showered and changed, he headed for The Bell and Whistle. Brad might be in; he hadn't seen much of him recently. He messaged Sally to say he was delayed and wouldn't be back until Tuesday evening. He needed a good long weekend in his own company, away from Sally and his family.

**

He had arrived at the Fulham house on Tuesday evening to find Sally in quite a state. She had received a letter from her husband's solicitor; it wasn't what she had been expecting.

'He wants me to pay the mortgage arrears but doesn't want to sell the flat,' said the tearful Sally.

'OK, Sal, calm down. I'm sure it says nothing of the sort!'

'It does!' wailed Sally.

'Make me a coffee while I read it.'

The letter didn't comment on the sale of the flat; it was an acceptance of Sally's offer to pay over 17K in mortgage arrears. Julian was surprised that they hadn't jumped at the offer to repay the 100K. Looked as though Andrew Wood and Khan had made a hash of it. They were solicitors recommended to him by Brad. They were willing to operate on the fringes of legality. He had used them for the conveyancing of the Fulham house.

'It doesn't say anything about the sale, Sal. This is just about the repayment. Don't worry about it, I'll speak to the solicitors.'

It hadn't turned out well. Morton Green had stood their ground on behalf of their client. Letters had flown backwards and forwards. Morton Green drew attention to Sally's perilous position regarding her financial interest in the flat should she fail to meet her commitments. Sally had taken out a loan to pay off the 17K. Julian had got her a good rate of interest. She had found it all very upsetting. He got the feeling that she blamed him for the failure of the plan. It was a blow to Julian. He had hoped to make her independent, to give her a home other than his.

He was spending less time with Sally, often just two nights a week. He left on Thursday morning, usually returning on Tuesday evening. He cited Benedict as his reason for spending more time in Oxfordshire: Benedict was showing signs of insecurity, he needed a male role model, he was worried about Benedict. But he no longer drove to Oxfordshire on Friday evening; he arrived Saturday midday and left on Sunday afternoon. His extended weekends he spent in the London flat. Andy had moved on, but Brad was still about and a lively, like-minded crowd frequented The Bell and Whistle. His pre-Sally lifestyle was in full swing.

Julian hadn't spoken to his father in weeks - not since the incident in the garden. Ted had made no effort to contact him, to resolve the matter. This had surprised Julian. The following weekend, he apologised to Lucy for his outburst. She had received the apology with less than good grace. She had asked him what Ted had meant by his remark. Julian had called it unfounded tittle-tattle, indulged in by the old cronies in the office. Lucy had said it was all so unlike Ted, she wondered what had possessed him to repeat 'tittle-tattle'. His shortened weekends at home, he put down to pressure of work. Lucy made no comment, but he could see that she doubted the explanation.

Julian returned home with a heavy heart. He went because he needed to see Lucy, but Lucy had changed. She no longer pressed him to get help. She made sure his bed was made, provided meals, kept up a pretence with the children, but he knew she no longer cared what he did. It was breaking his heart. Often, he returned to an empty house; Lucy out shopping or taking the children to one of their many activities. Benedict no longer asked him to take him to rugby - accepting that Daddy was far too busy to spare the time. Lucy had put a stop to him driving the children; he didn't blame her; he knew himself to be unfit to be behind the wheel.

He normally found a plate of sandwiches in the fridge, a bowl of soup for heating in the microwave and a note explaining his family's whereabouts. He would change into cords, put on walking boots and jacket and set off on a long walk. He enjoyed the exercise; he didn't get enough cooped up in London.

He walked in all weathers. His path wound around hawthorn and blackthorn-hedged fields. He had become attuned to seasonal changes, aware of the microcosm of life that lived amid the tight, thorny branches of the hedges, had learned to identify the birds that built their nests in the twiggy mass. It was balm to his turbulent mind, his anguished soul. He trudged through the seasons, his boots sinking in winter mud, crunching on frost-covered ground, or bouncing on the dry, mossy grasses of summer.

Where the hedges ran out, a broad stream meandered its way through the meadows. It was the stream that ran through his own garden, grown fat and deep on its way to meet up with others of its kind. Julian knew nothing of its destination; he wasn't interested. He was content to sit on its grassy bank and watch its progress over a bed of rocks made smooth by years of gentle washing. He sat still, waiting for the soft plopping sound made by the water vole as it took to the water. He liked to watch the creature as it swam along the bank, its nose raised above the surface of the water. At the top of the bank, in what looked like an old rabbit burrow, a female stoat had made her home. Julian had once seen her emerge with a string of young in her wake.

A defined pathway ran for a distance beside the stream before becoming blocked by heavy, overgrown willows that laid their branches along the banks and dipped their heads into the water. It formed the edge of an area of old native woodland. If he felt sociable, Julian would turn into the woods, the property of family friends Diane and Phil Wheeler.

The Wheelers kept Oxford sandy and black pigs. The pigs had freedom to roam and it wasn't unknown for a big, ginger, black spotted body to come hurtling out of the undergrowth towards him, stopping just short of knocking him from his feet. Phil had taught him to stand his ground and lean his full weight against the boisterous creature, who would snort with delight and trot along after him.

Diane and Phil had inherited the pigs. They had been farmed by Diane's father. Having no intention of continuing what they termed 'a barbaric occupation', they had turned their 1000 acres over to arable farming. But the pigs had remained; they had freedom to roam thirty acres of woodland and had access to a number of adjoining fields. They had wooden shelters dotted about their territory and a 'pig man', named Jim, to care for them. Jim rode about on a small tractor, towing bales of fresh bedding and removing trailer loads of muck-filled straw. Through an expensive process of neutering and spaying, Phil kept his pig family under control and they in turn controlled and managed his woodland. The pigs were well cared for pets.

The woods led Julian to the rear of a white stuccoed Georgian farmhouse, its well-laid-out formal gardens protected by picket fencing.

'Well, me old china, wondered if I'd see you today?' 'It was Phil's usual greeting.

He had retired, age forty, having worked on the London currency market from the age of eighteen. Although himself a Home Counties boy, Phil had adopted the slang speech of the Cockneys that had worked alongside him. His mistakes were 'Cadbury's flakes', when going out, he put on his 'turtle doves' and 'ones and twos' - his gloves and shoes. Phil had a wide, East End vocabulary. He was short, dark-haired with dancing brown eyes - a jolly bloke who could talk for England.

Diane came from an old Oxfordshire family, spoke with the type of upper-class accent that would today bar her from the BBC and was a good six inches taller than her husband. She had been an only child, had inherited the estate on the death of her parents.

They found Diane in the boot room, a large stone-floored appendage to the back of the house. The high-ceilinged space was brightened by half-moon windows set high in the walls. The room was home to saddles, tack, gardening equipment, cricket bats and croquet sets. The walls were lined with deep shelves for boots, shoes and anything else that fitted there. Lying in the middle of it all, in a large, straw-lined dog basket, was a big piglet, fast asleep.

Seated at a long pine table, nursing a steaming mug of freshly ground coffee, Julian looked around the bright, well-ordered kitchen. An end wall was dominated by a big navy-blue Aga, set into the space once occupied by the old range and surrounded by the original blue and white tiles. On both sides were ceiling high old cupboards painted cream to match the handmade units occupying the two side walls. On the inner wall was a huge stone fireplace, its blackened back standing testament to centuries of comforting warming.

It was a cheerful room - an homage to their beloved pigs. Mugs bearing sandy and black images hung from hooks and old oil paintings of strangely elongated, long-dead pig ancestors occupied the walls. All manner of memorabilia of an Oxford piggy kind, unearthed by Diane in the process of her dedicated searching of junk shops and country house sales, occupied open shelves.

A ceiling-high Welsh dresser displayed a one hundred and fifty-five-piece Victorian dinner service that Diane had found in boxes, shoved under a table at a local auction. There were plates of different sizes, dishes, gravy boats and vegetable tureens, all pig decorated. There were gingery Tamworth's, Gloucestershire old spots, black pigs and pink pigs and their own Oxford sandy and blacks. Nobody, other than Diane, had been interested in the lot, which had sold for its reserve price of thirty pounds. It was, according to Diane, a unique record of the development of the

British pig, a snapshot in time of a stage in development of a number of breeds.

Diane and Phil were dedicated to their pigs; the pigs were their family. By choice, they had no children. They hadn't wanted children in their lives. Phil had upset a number of the more sensitive of his acquaintance, by offering his sympathies for their misfortune, their misfortune being their children.

'I say nothing about your own pair, Julian. I do hope they turn out to be the exception to the rule. But dear me, poor old Cecil Wakelin! You know Cecil? Yes, of course you do! Barrel load of barney rubble with his eldest. Eighteen and ruling the house. I should cocoa; not in my house he wouldn't!'

Diane took freshly baked scones from the oven, put out a dish of strawberry jam and a bowl of cream and poured tea from a pot sporting a very handsome ginger pig with black spots. Julian spent a pleasant hour catching up on local gossip.

Julian left the companiable warmth of Diane and Phil's kitchen and headed home to a distant Lucy and demanding children. Walking along, head down, hands in his pockets, he contemplated the accord and order of the home he had just left. Lucy kept an ordered house, but there was no accord between Lucy and himself. There was little accord between Sally and himself, and Sally kept a very disordered house. He realised that to him they had become houses - Lucy's house and Sally's house. In neither did he feel he had a home. His flat was a place of refuge from the two women in his life, where he led what he knew to be a disreputable lifestyle. Diane and Phil had a home; he didn't.

He was becoming increasingly irritated by Sally's slovenly housekeeping. It was more than irritation; he found it distressing. He liked order; he had always liked order; the army existed on order. He had re-engaged the contractors to clean and order the flat; the flat might not be a home, but it had clean bathrooms and kitchen, his clothes were cared for and his shirts hung perfectly laundered in the wardrobe. It was with a heavy heart that he returned to Sally's grubby mess.

Julian had a germ of an idea. He had been brought up in the countryside, played in fields and woods, been a scout and a venture scout. When he left the army, he had drifted into the family firm; it had seen the logical thing to do, in truth the only thing he could do. He didn't enjoy his work in the city, when honest with himself, he had to admit that he was disinterested and hence, wasn't very good at the job. He suspected that he was disliked; he wasn't surprised, as he himself disliked a number of the people he worked with and dislike inevitably led to dislike. He had begun to think that his city life and work destructive to his mental wellbeing.

He was never happier than when sitting in Diane and Phil's kitchen. He had an idea of buying a working farm, of employing an experienced farm manager so that he himself could learn the ropes, perhaps get some appropriate qualifications. He had spoken to Phil about it, but to nobody else. He had been considering broaching the subject with his father before the bust up. He would have to draw on his stake in the company. He had thought his father would be sympathetic if disappointed; there had always been a working Tennant in the firm since his great-great-grandfather's time.

Phil had alerted him to a possible property: a five-hundred-acre arable farm near Lechlade. The owner, recently widowed, was considering selling. He had an only child, a daughter, who was pursuing her own career and had no interest in farming. He wondered what Lucy would think of the idea.

Returning in time for dinner, he would find Lucy busy in the kitchen. It wasn't unusual to find shopping bags and boxes littering the floor, new trainers or shoes, or items of clothing draped across the end of the table where Lucy was preparing food. Benedict, having abandoned the mess, would be found stretched out on the floor in the family room playing with his games consul, while loud music from Cosima's room disturbed the peace. Comment on the mess, a suggestion that the children might tidy up and remove their newly acquired items from the kitchen, would be met by a black look from Lucy and an exasperated explanation that they had just come in.

Only when ready to set the table for dinner would Lucy appear to notice the chaos. She would pick up and tidy away packaging, put the discarded items of clothing to one side and send Benedict upstairs to get Cosima, who was unable to hear Lucy calling due to her loud music. Julian thought them undisciplined and spoiled. He thought Lucy a pushover.

One particularly distressing incident occurred on just such an occasion. Cosima had bounced downstairs, showing off white, ankle trainers, bought that afternoon. As soon as they sat down to dinner, Julian noticed her fingernails; they were black.

'What's happened to your nails, Cosima?' Julian stared in horror at the ugly colour on his daughter's juvenile nails. One of his 'one-nighters', named Chloe, had sported long nails of the same colour. On her, it had been seductive; on his daughter, it was shocking.

'I've put nail polish on, Daddy,' said Cosima, holding out her right hand for admiration.

'Why on earth have you done that? It looks downright ugly!'

'That's not a nice thing to say, Daddy. It isn't ugly! All my friends wear nail polish.'

'I don't care if every ten-year-old in the country is wearing black nail polish; it doesn't suit you. As I say, it looks very ugly.'

'Mummy!' wailed Cosima.

'For goodness sake, Julian, you're upsetting her. Is it so serious? It's nail polish, for goodness sake!'

'No doubt you approve. But I object to my child daubing a particularly repulsive colour onto her nails in imitation of a girl twice her age.'

'Oh, Mummy, he's being horrible, really horrible. I hate him,' Cosima shouted as she jumped up and ran from the room.

'Yeet, gotchoo Dad. Fatty, fatty fingers, ughhh,' sang Benedict, delighted at his father's criticism of his sister.

'Stop that, Ben, don't you dare. Eat your dinner. We don't need to hear from you,' said an exasperated Lucy.

Julian had no idea what his son was talking about, 'No idea what all that means, Ben.'

'It's ridiculous rapper talk or some such. He's supporting your criticism of his sister.'

'Yeet, Dad!'

'Leave the table. Go to your room at once,' said Lucy in an unusually raised voice.

Benedict, having stomped from the room, Lucy turned her wrath on Julian. 'Well done! If this is to be the result of your flying visits, I suggest that you stay away. I allowed Cosima to use the nail varnish. How dare you undermine me in that way.'

'Am I to have no say in what my children are allowed to do? She's far too young to be wearing nail varnish. I bet the school don't allow it!'

'Of course they don't. They don't allow jeans, trainers or jewellery. There's a whole list of things the school doesn't allow. In school they have a uniform and conform to a code of rules. Their weekends are their own time - a time to experiment, to develop their own style. It's a good balance.'

'I can't agree. Cosima's a child; she needs guidance. She will be having her ears pierced next!'

'Well, as you mention it, I should tell you that it's under discussion. I'm inclined to make it her birthday present.'

'I don't understand it, Lucy. I think it's a dereliction of duty!'

'Do you really, Julian!' Lucy was at boiling point. 'Well let me tell you that your opinion carries little weight with me. You have no interest in the children; you are becoming more and more distant from them. I bring them up. Your only input is criticism. You have no idea about ten-year-old girls or their needs. You do nothing for the children; you haven't done for years. Don't you dare come here criticising us.'

Lucy was on her feet, plates were crashing, uneaten food was being vigorously scraped away. His own hardly touched meal was whipped from in front of him and scraped into the bin. The dishwasher noisily stacked; Lucy turned her attention to cleaning down surfaces. The energy applied to wiping down the table forced Julian to jump up to avoid the flying cloth and the food debris being flicked his way. Lucy stormed from the kitchen and ran up the stairs. He heard a door bang. Gone to comfort her daughter, Julian presumed.

Julian sat staring at the open kitchen door. Lucy had made matters very plain. The words had been cutting, - 'don't come here criticising us'. Lucy, Cosima and Benedict were the bonded 'us', he was the outsider. He packed his bag, left a note on the hall table and left. He could see no point in staying.

He drove straight to Fulham. He meant to take advantage of Sally's absence. Sally spent her weekends with Myrtle. Julian didn't blame her; there was no reason why she should spend them alone and she and Myrtle always found plenty to do. But he did think that she might spend a little time cleaning and organising the house. She had, after all, taken full responsibility in the matter. He hadn't wanted Sally to turn herself into a cleaner cum housekeeper. Neither his mother nor his wife attempted to manage their home without help. It was a foreign idea to him. But Sally was no housekeeper; she reigned over chaos.

Behind the door was an accumulation of mail. It looked as though Sally hadn't been home since he had left the previous Wednesday morning. The house was stuffy; it needed a good airing. He walked through the kitchen into the utility room, where he found an overflowing basket of dirty washing and the washer still switched on; it's red light flashing. Opening the door, he found the cycle finished and a drum full of wet washing. He tipped the dirty washing onto the worktop, used the basket to unload the washer and transferred it to the dryer. He reloaded the washer, added detergent, turned it on and went into the kitchen.

The pan with the remains of the scrambled eggs they had eaten on Wednesday morning was still on the cooker top. A loaf of bread, half out of its packet, was strewn across the worktop beside a knife smeared with butter. The breakfast plates, cups and cutlery were still on the table with an uncovered bowl of marmalade and the butter dish. Julian just didn't know how anybody could leave such a mess unattended.

He could imagine Sally rushing back, when she knew he was returning, to quickly clear up. He put the butter and marmalade into the fridge, stacked and turned on the dishwasher and wiped down the table and tops. Cloth in hand, a vision of Lucy angrily wielding a similar cloth only hours before came to his mind. What a bloody mess he had made of his life!

He went upstairs, picked up a case from the spare room and took it into their bedroom. He laid it open on the bed and began filling it with underwear and pullovers. He took shirts from his wardrobe and put them folded into the case. He was damned if he was going to go short of clean clothes, be dependent on Sally's dilatory efforts. He found suit covers and selected suits that he thought would be of more use to him in the flat than in the house.

The bedroom was a mess. Sally's stuff was strewn all over the place. The ensuite was grubby; it wasn't exactly dirty, but it wasn't properly cleaned. Julian was used to a shine to his sinks and taps, to fluffy, nicely arranged towels. The taps and shower fittings were dull with a buildup of soap scum and the towels draped across the bath were damp and not at all fluffy.

He took the case and suits and put them in the boot of the car, together with selected washed and dried items from the utility room. He would have to tell Sally that he needed the stuff in Oxfordshire. He was beyond caring whether she believed him or not. It was quite pleasant to have the house to himself. He found Carl's latest number on his London phone and gave him a call. Carl was always changing his number; Julian had to take particular care not to mix the numbers up. He sent out for a meal and settled himself in for the night.

Julian returned to the flat after work on Monday evening. He had been about to go out to meet up with Brad. He was dressed for a night on the town, as high as a kite, when an unexpected visitor arrived. It was his brother-in-law, Freddy Northcott. Freddy had come straight to the point. He was there on behalf of Lucy and Clara. Lucy was very worried by the alarming note Julian had left for her on Saturday evening. Freddie understood that there had been something of a row and that Julian had left without a word to Lucy. Something similar had happened some weeks previously, when Julian had driven off without a word after a confrontation with his father. Lucy had finally confided in Clara and not a moment too soon, in Freddy's opinion.

'Has Clara spoken to my father? What does my father know?' Beads of sweat had broken out on Julian's forehead. He looked at Freddy through terror-filled eyes. Freddy was shocked. He hadn't expected a good reception, but he hadn't expected his words to cause such dread.

'No, she hasn't. It's what Lucy is trying to avoid; has been avoiding for far too long. You can't subject your family to any more of this.'

Julian was chalk white, his hands shaking, a pulse above his right eye throbbing.

'This won't do, old man. You need support. You know you have Lucy's support and you have Clara's and mine. But you need professional help. Let's get it sorted, Julian!'

'No. I've said no to Lucy and I won't change my mind.'

'Well then, things will end badly. Lucy doesn't deserve this. Think about it, Julian. Think about how your actions are affecting your family.'

Freddie had talked on, but Julian hadn't listened. Lucy breaking confidence had come as a huge shock. After Freddy had left, he had taken diazepam and tried to pour whisky into a tumbler; his hands had shaken so violently that the bottle had tipped over, spilling the contents across the table.

Chapter 18

Lucinda

Lucy had seen him leave from her bedroom window. The relief she had felt had turned to panic when she read the alarming note left on the hall table. She had phoned Clara. Freddy had answered the phone.

Freddy Northcott had been in the same regiment as Julian. The Tennants and the Northcotts had a long association with the Oxfordshire. It was through the regiment that Clara had met her husband. Freddy had also served in Afghanistan. She knew herself to be one of the lucky ones; Freddy had returned unscathed. Before Lucy confided in her, she had imagined that Lucy too had been lucky. Clara knew too many military wives whose husbands had been killed or returned without body parts or worse.

Clara had known something was wrong as soon as Freddy picked up the phone the previous Saturday evening. He had mouthed, 'Lucy!' Freddy had been told that there had been a row about Cosima's nail polish and that Julian had driven off, leaving an alarming note. Freddy had driven up to town, but Julian hadn't been at the flat. It wasn't until Monday evening that he found him at home.

'So where did he spend Saturday night and Sunday?' Clara had asked.

'In answer to that question, I got a blank stare. He's in a bad way; high on something.'

'Coke, I told you!'

'More than coke, I would say. It was shocking to see him in that state. But he's bloody determined, Clara. He doesn't believe in shrinks, and unless he changes his mind, he's done for!'

'Lucy has spent several years trying to change his mind. Maybe we should tell Dad.'

'Good God, no, he wouldn't cope with that. He's terrified of Ted finding out. In any case, Ted isn't equipped to help; he would tell him to pull himself together and act like a man; wouldn't be at all helpful. Julian's problem is that he thinks as his father thinks. He sees it as a shameful weakness that he can't cure himself. He's not on his own, I've seen it before; guys determined to battle their demons alone, refusing help, self-destructing. But Ted's heard something, that's for sure. Julian's got some bolthole that he's disappearing into.'

**

Lucy was going to spend a couple of nights with Margot Hadleigh. Daphne was looking after the children. Lucy felt guilty; she was being less than honest with Daphne, who took it for granted that she was going to spend time with Julian. The children were excited; they liked staying over with Daphne and Ted, who spoiled them and gave them the sugary treats banned at home. Daphne said that the spoiling of grandchildren was one of the primary functions of grandparents. The six-month-old tabbies, Trevor and Tammy, were also going to Daphne's. They were to have their own accommodation in the conservatory.

After dinner, Lucy dropped off the children and kittens and returned to a strangely empty and silent house. She couldn't remember a time when she had been alone there without the children. Standing in the hall, she felt a strange sense of being transported back in time. She crossed to the kitchen and looked in through the open door. Cosima was there, she was sitting at the old table they had brought with them from Oxford. She was wearing a grey, cord pinafore and a pink top. Her chubby legs were in navy tights and her feet in navy and white striped pumps. She was just out of her highchair; Lucy could see the giraffe printed cushion beneath her that had been used to help her reach the table.

As though becoming aware of a presence, Cosima turned her head and looked towards the door. Excited, she clambered down and held up her arms to be picked up. Lucy had made an instinctive, involuntary move forward before being checked by the figure that appeared beside her in the doorway, arms outstretched towards the child. It was Julian. He was wearing a close-fitting, navy frock coat, tight-fitting trousers, and peaked cap, the dress uniform of his regiment. He was tanned, just returned from Afghanistan. He flung off his cap, lifted Cosima up in the air and spun her around. She listened to her daughter's baby giggling and shouts of 'Daddy, Daddy' as the scene faded.

Lucy found that she had been holding her breath. She could have reached out and touched them. She was stunned. She went into the drawing room and poured a whisky, her hand shaking. She became suddenly gripped by panic, by a fear for Cosima's safety. She picked up her phone and called Daphne.

'They're fine, darling. Forget these two and have a nice break. I promise to look after them.'

Whisky in hand, she walked about the house; along the uneven passageways, their boards warped and scarred with age. She ran her hands over the old bumpy walls with their patches of bare plaster and old greying wood. Julian had wanted to level the passageway floors, bring plasterers to smooth out the bumpy walls. But Lucy had stopped the rude assault on the venerable old place. Lucy thought that the house was speaking to her, but she was unsure of the message. It had been the old Julian she had seen in the kitchen; the man who hadn't returned from Afghanistan. Had her mind really managed to conjure such a vivid vision - a vision of the outcome she had so longed for - the outcome she had spent too long waiting for. She thought not; she wasn't given to visions. A cold shiver ran down her spine.

She slept fitfully and was up early. She drove to Shipton, parked the car in the long stay car park and caught the 7:23 train to London. Margo had been pressing with her invitation. Lucy thought she knew why. Margo had things to tell her that she didn't think would be best communicated by phone. She had put Margo to work some weeks previously. She thought Ted had heard something but was probably as much in the dark about what Julian was up to as she herself was. Lucy was tired of intrigue, of lies, of excuses. She wanted to know the truth. She had suspected for some time that there were other women; she suspected a string of affairs. She doubted a serious, meaningful relationship, for the good reason that she knew Julian loved her. It was his misfortune that she no longer loved him. She loved a man lost in Afghanistan.

Lucy needed her sleep; she never felt good after a bad night. She sat in a window seat, watching the tinted Cotswold countryside roll by her eyes heavy with tiredness. The spectacular reds and golds of autumn had claimed the landscape. Autumn was Lucy's favourite season. 'The dazzling spectacle of nature governed by a primeval knowledge secreted within the heart of the great forests,' was how Miss Fitzgerald had spoken of autumn.

Eyelids drooping, she saw Miss Fitzgerald leading a group of third formers down a woodland path. The girls in their maroon uniform skirts and blazers and 'outdoor shoes', Miss Fitzgerald in her Harris tweed, serviceable suit and brown brogues. Miss Fitzgerald was elderly, small and thin; her grey hair scraped back in a tight bun. She was a lady of her time, very correct, with perfect diction. Her 'nature walks' were a weekend optional activity that took place on the first Saturday of the month. Despite being the least 'cool' teacher in the school, her walks were always well attended and quite a long line accompanied the straight-backed figure through the woods. Slouching wasn't tolerated in Miss Fitzgerald's presence. Walking with hands in pockets was a grievous offence, as was linking arms - a lazy, over familiar habit.

She taught 'her girls' to observe, to look for the small things that went unnoticed. To look up at the giants of the woods - the oaks with their tortured branches that could live for a thousand years and had formed the planks of Nelson's battle fleet. The wide, low-branched limes, the stocky beeches and the silver trunk birches - they learned to identify them all. In spring, they admired the blossom whitening the bare branches of the blackthorn and the yellow primroses crouching on grassy banks. In autumn, they searched for and learned the names of fungi, both edible and noxious. It was through Miss Fitzgerald that Lucy acquired her love of the natural world.

Drifting in and out of sleep, she saw snapshots of stubbled, harvested fields, farmhouses nestled in the shelter of shallow valleys, villages of mellow Cotswold stone and the old, circular tree groves on their hilly mounds, reminders of the old magic. She was woken by the jolting and rocking of the train as it crossed points and slowed for signals before pulling into Paddington.

Margo was waiting at the far side of the barrier, waving wildly in case Lucy might not see her; there was little chance of missing Margo! In their manner of dress, Margo and Lucy couldn't have been more dissimilar. Lucy liked to be comfortable in jeans, her concession to the seasons being the replacement of trainers with winter boots and t-shirts with woolly jumpers and jackets. It was with reluctance, and for 'occasions' only, that Lucy 'dressed up'. For this trip, she was wearing a smart black jacket and had packed a couple of outfits suitable for dining out and a theatre visit. It was the antithesis of Margo's flamboyant style. Lucy smiled at the sight of her friend, dressed more appropriately for the catwalk than the concourse of a busy London station. She was wearing a double breasted, mid-calf, military-style coat in emerald, green, much embellished with navy leather buttons and faux lynx, collar, a slouch hat in sea green silk and high, black patent leather boots. Margo was a city girl; she liked a lot of bustle and buzz in her life. She was a networker; had her finger on the pulse. Little went on that escaped Margo.

It took twenty-five minutes in the back of a black cab to get from Paddington to Hampstead. Lucy hated the congestion, the fumes, the mass of humanity. London wasn't for her, but what a crazy place it was! Within only metres of the choked arteries was the tranquillity of Margo's garden. Seated on the stylish deck, an outdoor extension of the dining room, shaded by a massive cream canopy, the air was breathable, the traffic noise barely an audible hum.

Over coffee, Margot updated Lucy on the progress of her twin, twelve-year-old sons, in their first year at boarding school. Lucy talked about Cosima and Benedict. Small talk! Both putting off the moment. Finally, Lucy took the matter in hand.

'Just tell me. Margo. Please don't spare me the details. It can't be worse than I suspect.'

'Not worse, Luce, but not what you're expecting. I was very surprised. The talk in the office had been that Julian was no longer living at Tavistock Place. He had been spotted with a woman and it was thought that he was living in her place. Don't ask me how they knew that he had moved out of the flat; it's amazing how these things become known. The office stuff was gossip and Paul wasn't much use. Paul isn't interested in gossiping; his head's in an entirely different place and of course he spends so much time abroad that things do pass him by. I couldn't afford to ask too many questions, so I hired a private investigator.'

'Really!'

'Yes, I hope I did the right thing! They tracked him for two weeks. Easy work for them. So, what's he up to? Well, from October 2016 to July 2018, the flat was unoccupied, but since then Julian has used it on and off, and for the last four months has been spending quite a lot of time there. I tell you, Luce, if you want to keep your business to yourself, don't live in a place with a guy sitting behind a desk, watching your every move! Information on Julian's comings and goings all came courtesy of the concierge. They paid him!

He now has a fairly regular routine. He arrives at around 6:30 p.m. on Thursday or Friday, usually Thursday. He goes out at around 8:00 to The Bell and Whistle pub, where he meets up with a group of friends described as 'city types'. The extended weekend follows a regular pattern of pub and club crawls with the same group. He arrives back anytime between 2:00 am and 6:00 am, the earlier time if accompanied by a 'young lady'. Sorry, Luce, this must be painful to hear.'

'I've suspected affairs for a long time. To be perfectly candid, Margot, I'm well beyond caring.'

'Well, darling, I don't think we're talking affairs, more casual pickups. Anyway, on Saturday afternoon, he drives home. Sunday afternoon, he's back in the flat, back down to the pub and the same routine. The interesting thing is his mid-week location, a house in Fulham, where he lives with a woman named Sally Willett.'

'That does surprise me! Who is she?'

'She's thirty-two, separated from her husband; she left him. They have a two-bed, mortgaged flat in Richmond, where the husband still lives. She's a high-end window dresser employed by Bianchi Partners in Clapham. She's been living with Julian since June 2016, first in his flat and later in the house in Fulham.'

'So the house doesn't belong to her?'

'No, and here's the twist in the tale: it belongs to you.'

'To me!'

'You are the sole owner of a house in Fulham with a recently completed contemporary extension; value, two and a half million.'

'Oh, God, Margo, what's he done!'

'I don't know. It's a personal acquisition. Paul has checked; nothing is known about it in the company accounts department and whoever did the conveyancing, it wasn't the company solicitors. But that's not surprising, as forgery is involved.'

'My signature!'

'A number of times, I would imagine.'

'Why on earth would he do such a thing?'

'I've had a good think about that one and have drawn a blank. It can't be for investment or tax purposes, because surely he would have done that openly through the firm's financial department.'

'How devious, Margot; I can't believe it.'

'It seems that Sally Willett isn't happy. She was led to believe his marriage was over when she first met him. Now she finds he's spending more and more time 'at home', and tells her that he needs to devote more time to his son, who's going through a difficult stage and needs a father about.'

'How despicable! To think he would use Benedict as an excuse. It's all been about Julian's ego; I should have seen it years ago. He's become a narcissist, Margot, plain and simple. But tell me, how do we know so much about Sally Willet?'

'I know, that surprised me. It's quite frightening, really. They seem to get a lot of information by striking up conversations in pubs and the like. It's amazing what people will reveal over a glass of wine about people they consider friends; disclosures made with absolutely no malicious intent.'

'God!'

'Yes, they have given us quite a long print-out.'

'I need to reimburse you, Margot. You must give me the bill.'

'I'll do nothing of the sort. Sally Willet seems a nice person. Now that Julian is on his 'extended family visits', she spends her weekends with her friend in Peckham. They run food banks together and help asylum seekers.'

'Oh, Margot!'

**

'That's it, number 34,' said Margot, slowing down, pulling into the kerb. It was a pretty common place terrace that the women sat looking at.

'What are they - three, four beds, a couple of rooms downstairs? Over two million, it's amazing,' said Lucy.

'Very popular area! And yours, my dear, is very desirable. I wonder if we can get a look at this astronomically priced extension. Let's have a walk and see if we can get around the back.'

Finding an entry that ran along the back of the row, they picked their way along the uneven surface. It wasn't difficult to spot the back of number 34.

'What do you think of that?' Lucy asked

'I think it's damn ugly.'

'So do I. I wonder what the neighbours have to say about it. I certainly wouldn't want it next to me.'

'I suppose they've got away with it because it's all glass!'

'As a ground-floor extension, it wouldn't have been too bad - a kind of conservatory! But what's the point of a big glass box tagged on to your first floor?' said Lucy, shielding her eyes against the glare of the glass, 'Is it furnished? It's quite hard to see.'

'It doesn't look like it, but I think it's a semi opaque glass, difficult to tell.'

'To think that this monstrosity has been built in my name.

Apart from all the other deception, I find that quite unforgivable.'

'I'm so sorry, Luce. I hear what you're saying about being beyond caring, but this must be very upsetting.'

'I will always mourn the man that Julian used to be. But don't worry, Margo, I'm not upset; I'm just very angry. He's been using this woman, deceiving her - building castles in the air; in this case, tangible, ugly ones made of glass. I really don't think he can be in his right mind. This ends it, Margo. I won't be a party to his lies and deceit.'

'What will you do?'

'What I should have done five years ago, when I lost the battle to make him see sense. I don't want to see him again and I won't if I can avoid it.'

**

There was a letter to be written and a story to be told that she had hoped never to have to tell. Lucy looked out into the gathering darkness of the October evening as it flashed by the window and dreaded the journey's end.

Chapter 19

Sally

Sally rushed into the station and onto the platform. She had been in luck; a train had just pulled in. She took to her seat, hot and out of breath. She had rushed along Camden High Street into Camden Station. Julian had messaged her mid-afternoon; he was on his way home. It had been ages since he had returned on a Monday evening. She needed to get home before him and do a quick tidy-up. Sally usually caught the bus, but even allowing for the change onto the District line she would save a good twenty minutes. She got off at Fulham Broadway and rushed along Fulham Road. It was 6:15; if she was lucky, she might have half an hour before he got back.

**

The state of cleanliness and tidiness of the house was becoming a big issue between them. Sally knew herself to be untidy. Left to herself, she was quite happy for a considerable amount of mess to build up before having a good old clean up. Then there was the matter of her cleaning, which wasn't up to Julian's standards. It wasn't good enough that the sinks and showers were clean and disinfected; she believed in the liberal use of disinfectant sprays, taps and shower fittings should be buffed up to a shine, shower enclosures smear and drip-free and toilets always left cover down.

It was becoming such an issue that Sally sometimes regretted having made such a stand against the contract cleaners, but she had hated the clinical order they imposed. To be fair to Julian, he didn't expect her to do the cleaning or the laundry. Unlike Jack, he was quite willing to put his clothes in the washer and iron a shirt. He could cook as well as Sally herself.

But Sally had come to realise that an untidy house wasn't Julian's only problem. As she rushed from room to room, picking up from the floor, quickly clearing the kitchen tops and firing pots into the dishwasher, she knew exactly what to expect when he arrived. While giving her a quick peck on the cheek, his eyes would glide surreptitiously about the room, taking in its state of order. He would go upstairs to 'freshen up' and come back down a changed man, in high good humour. Myrtle had been right; Myrtle was usually right.

The stash had been an accidental discovery. Sally kept her toiletries in the main bathroom, where there was a big cabinet; she needed a lot of shelf space! Julian used the ensuite cabinet. She had had a splitting headache, had run out of paracetamol and had gone in search of Julian's supply. A black toilet bag in which Julian kept medication for his nose bleeds had fallen from the shelf. The bag had been open and the contents had scattered on the floor. Sally picked up a scratched bank card, two tightly rolled ten-pound notes, a bag of white powder, a pack of nasal plugs and a saline spray. She had no doubt that the powder was cocaine. The powder itself was odourless, but the bag smelled of burnt plastic. She had read that cocaine residue could smell like that.

She replaced the contents and put the bag back in the cabinet. Sally didn't mention her discovery to Julian; she avoided criticism, having discovered his antipathy to challenges to his behaviour or decisions. It did confirm Myrtle's explanation of Julian's wildly varying moods.

Sally was now spending more time with Myrtle than she was with Julian, who was spending the greater part of the week at home. Sally didn't believe him when he talked about his son,

Benedict, going through a difficult stage. When Julian's weekends in Oxfordshire had continued after they had moved together to the Fulham house, Sally had asked questions. Julian resented questions, so Sally had stopped asking. Julian had been shocked when Sally suggested they separate. He couldn't understand what had put such an idea into her head. When yet another violent night-time episode would have played itself out, sitting propped up in bed, shaking violently, he would pull Sally into his arms and cry. He would beg her not to leave him – 'Never leave me my beautiful darling!'

Since discovering the true contents of Julian's 'nose bag', and Myrtle's insistence that he would be on 'all sorts of other stuff', Sally was noticing what she should have previously been alive to - the amazing amount of heavy prescription drugs Julian kept around the house. She was also becoming more aware of what she thought of as his 'twitchiness'. Loud music, the TV volume turned too high, the barely audible tapping of her laptop keys frayed his nerves. The previous November, the fireworks set off in their neighbour's back garden had drained him of colour and set the pulse above his right eye into a wild throbbing.

Once, when she had been off work with a bad cold, she had seen two women standing in the back entry. She had watched them from an upstairs window. One was blonde, very stylish in a calf length, bright green coat and matching hat. The other was dark-haired and more casually dressed in jeans and a dark jacket. They were looking up at the house, talking, pointing, shielding their eyes to get a better look. Sally was intrigued. Her first thought was that they were neighbours, critical of the extension. A number of those living nearby had objected to the plans. A very strongly worded objection had been submitted to the planning authority by their next-door neighbour.

But the women were unknown to her; she didn't think they belonged on the street. They were in the entry for a good thirty minutes. Although unable to hear their conversation, their body language told her that they weren't impressed. It was Julian's reaction when told of the incident that made Sally suspicious.

'Two women! In the back entry! What were they doing?' he had asked, looking up sharply.

'Looking at the back of the house.'

'What do you mean looking at the back of the house? What exactly were they doing?'

'Just that, looking up at the house. I think it was the extension that was interesting them. I don't think they liked it, there was a lot of discussion and pointing.'

'What did they look like?'

'Just two women. I didn't recognise them, so I don't think they lived locally. Quite strange, I thought.'

'But what did they look like? Young, old, blonde, dark haired?' Julian was sitting in an armchair beside the fireplace. He had turned as white as the wall behind him. He snapped shut his laptop, 'What did they look like, Sal?'

Sally had never seen him so alarmed. 'One was blonde and quite overdressed and one was in jeans with dark, shoulder length hair.'

Julian stared at Sally.

'What's wrong, Julian?'

'Nothing, nothing at all. It must have something to do with the objectors!' He opened his laptop and stared at the screen.

Julian had never used the word love with Sally. She was wonderful, amazing, his rock. Sally didn't think he loved her; he liked the way she looked and needed her in some strange way that she didn't quite understand. But when being honest with herself, she had to admit to never having loved him. In the beginning, she had imagined herself in love, but in retrospect, thought it had been nothing more than physical attraction and the head-turning, dizzying lifestyle he had introduced her to.

Although she knew it was unfair to put all the blame on Julian, she did feel very let down over the episode of the flat in Richmond. She hadn't been in favour of the plan from the beginning but had gone along with it. Julian had somehow persuaded her, much against her better judgement, that she should buy Jack out. It had ended in an acrimonious exchange of solicitors letters, in which his solicitor had all but accused her of attempting to defraud her husband of his property rights.

In the same week that Sally had taken out a loan to make a payment to Jack of seventeen thousand pounds, Julian had made a bank transfer of 50k to the builder of the extension. Julian had used his contacts to get her a good rate of interest, but left her feeling that he had put himself out on her behalf. It had left Sally questioning the nature of their relationship. She thought it was quite mean of Julian. She didn't understand Julian's attitude towards money. When she had first moved into the flat in Tavistock Place, before the 'new beginning', she had raised the question of sharing food and other costs. Julian had been horrified!

'I can't believe that you have thought of such a thing! Please don't mention it again, Sal.'

Most of their food came in a Waitrose van and was paid for by Julian, as were all other costs and bills. On her birthday, their 'anniversary' and at Christmas, Julian gave her an expensive piece of jewellery and flowers - huge bouquets always made up of the most expensive blooms, peonies, gardenias, hydrangeas and the like. Sally picked the brains of those around her for ideas for affordable presents for the man who had everything.

A semblance of order restored; Sally picked up her phone. Periodical bleeps had alerted her to left messages. They were all from her mother. She turned off her phone. She had told her parents that she was living in a rented flat in Peckham and given

Myrtle's address. She hadn't told them about Julian. Her parents were becoming quite a problem. They were way behind the curve; still hopeful, after three years of separation, of a reconciliation between herself and Jack. There were constant questions about Jack. Had she seen him? Had they spoken? Was he still in their flat? Never-ending questions about Jack and always the tacit criticism of her behaviour. Twice, she had put her mother off when she wanted to visit and was running out of excuses.

'Another mess of your own making, Sal. Putting your head in the sand doesn't work. Come clean with them; it's your only option, my darling!' Myrtle had told her.

'They are very critical, Myrtle. In their opinion, it's all my fault.'

'Leave them with their thoughts, but make it clear that there is no chance of a reconciliation. Why you lied about being in a flat, I don't know; it's causing all this trouble with your mother wanting to visit.'

'I'm going to say that I've left the flat.'

'And living where? Are you going to tell them about Julian?'

'No, I couldn't cope with all the questions they would ask. They would want to meet him!'

'Would that be such a bad idea?'

'Yes, I think it would.'

'You don't want them to know because you don't have much confidence in the relationship, Sal. For goodness sake, face facts, he isn't going to leave his wife. Dump him, my darling. And while you're about it, divorce that controlling husband of yours. Why you are allowing that to drag on, I can't imagine! You have a home here with me; you know that. But there I go, telling you what to do.'

Sally thought a rapprochement between Julian and his wife the most likely reason for him spending so much time in Oxfordshire. The previous week, she had come home to find that he had been back during the weekend and taken some of his clothes. He had done some washing, used the dishwasher and cleaned up the dining room and kitchen. When asked what was going on, he made the excuse of having to go straight to work from Oxfordshire.

'I can't keep turning up in the same suit and shirt, Sal.'

She was confused. Julian's words contradicted his behaviour. Julian's crying tugged at her heart strings. She didn't know what to make of it all. Myrtle was urging her to leave him, but it wasn't that easy. Julian still spoke of the house as their home; everything in the house had been chosen by her. It was at her suggestion that he had gone ahead with extending the property. What Sally felt was a sense of responsibility towards the life they had built together. But respect and affection had turned to pity and distrust.

It was with a light heart that Sally left work on Thursday evenings and jumped on a bus to Peckham. In Myrtle's, she could relax. She could slip off her shoes and kick them to one side. Leave magazines on the sofa. Sit about the table after dinner and chat without feeling the pressure to jump up and clear the table. There was so much to do and talk about that the days flew by. When busily employed with Myrtle, Sally wondered just what she did with her time when with Julian. She didn't talk to Julian about the things she did, the places she went to, or the people she met because Julian wasn't interested.

Together with Myrtle, she had been to Dagenham to visit Jamila and her family. It had been difficult, but Myrtle had managed to keep up some patchy contact with Jamila during the family's torturous journey through Europe and into the UK. Jamila considered herself fortunate to have a brother-in-law living in America who had paid for their journey from Ijmuiden in the Netherlands to the UK. It had been a risky, frightening journey in the back of a lorry carrying car parts.

'It was not a cold lorry, a freezing lorry, I think it is called. I was very desperate, but I would not have put my children on a cold lorry.'

Jamila was living in a two-bedroom, semi-detached house with her younger sister, Abida, who had already been in the UK as a student. Myrtle had arranged for Jamila to get advice from an immigration lawyer before she attended the screening unit in Croydon and her asylum interview. It had taken a year for the decision to come through, but asylum had been granted and Jamila was attempting to build a new life in a foreign land. Ahsan was in year two at school and baby Rima was now five and in the reception class.

Myrtle was battling with the company contracted by the council, which managed Jamila's house. There were damp patches in the living room and black mould in the kitchen and bathroom. Myrtle said the house was a disgrace and the money paid to Jamila paltry. But Jamila was far more grateful. She was thankful that her children were safe from Bashar Al Assad's bombs and were receiving an education, grateful for a roof over her head and money to buy food.

'My good, English lady friends are very kind to worry for me, but I am happy. If I knew that my dear Karim was alive, that would make me very, very happy.' Jamila's husband, Karim, had joined the Free Syrian Army. She hadn't heard anything from him for three years. She feared he was dead but prayed he was alive.

They sat in Jamila's colourfully decorated sitting room, eating home-baked semolina and fig cake and drinking sweet hibiscus tea. Rima sat on Sally's knee, looked up into the face of 'the beautiful English lady' and played with the stone that Sally wore about her neck.

The obsidian, which the child played with, was jet black, highly polished and hung from a long silver chain. It was a birthday present from Myrtle. On Sally's wrist was a bracelet of lapis lazuli and beneath her pillow were stones of amethyst and jasper. The obsidian, Myrtle believed, would help Sally find her true self. The lapis lazuli would provide spiritual guidance, the amethyst would relieve fear and anxiety, and the jasper absorb negative energy. Sally believed in the power of the stones. She had tried to persuade Julian to wear a morganite stone around his neck.

'It carries the energy of divine love and compassion, Julian. It's well known to be beneficial to those needing to come to terms with past pain and trauma. If you embrace the stone's power, you can transform the pain into wisdom and compassion.'

'If only Sal! I don't have your confidence in a bit of pink rock.'

Myrtle had evolved her own earth religion. It was a bit of a mishmash of Animism and Druidism with a heavy dash of Wicca. In Myrtle's bedroom was an altar to Abnoba, the Celtic goddess of trees and rivers. On the altar was an eclectic gathering of objects: candles, crystals, incense, pots of herbs, a willow branch wand – all laid out on a cloth decorated with a pentacle within a circle. Myrtle liked to evoke the power of the goddess on Sally's behalf. Sage, rosemary and lavender were set alight in a brass bowl that Myrtle called a chalice. They sat together, cross-legged on the floor, within a circle marked out with salt - a sacred place separating them from the 'mundane' world. They reflected on the blessings of the seasons and called on the goddess to join them. Sally wasn't totally convinced of the actuality of Abnoba, but enjoyed listening to Myrtles' incantations and the smell of the burning herbs.

**

Dashing in, Sally had picked up the mail. Always first back after the long weekend, she would sort through the letters and leave Julian's on the hall table. Most of his letters were official with a printed address, but he did receive the odd personal letter. Sally had noticed the hand addressed letter but thought nothing of it. Julian would usually pick up the letters, flick through them and put them back on the table to be opened later.

That evening, she had put her head around the kitchen door to say hello and had seen him standing in the hall, a letter in his hand. Julian's good looks were vulnerable to tiredness, to adversity. The face he turned on Sally was drawn, emaciated, his eyes unseeing, terror-stricken. Sally rushed forward as he staggered and gripped the banister rail.

'Julian, what's wrong?' She put out a steadying arm, thinking he was about to fall. She didn't think he was even aware of her presence, as he reached for his car keys and stumbled out through the door, the hand addressed letter unopened in his hand. Sally watched him drive off. He wasn't fit to drive! She got into a panic. She didn't know what to do, so she called Myrtle.

'What can you do, Sal? You have no idea where he might be going or who he might be going to. You don't know his family; he has made quite sure of that. There is absolutely nothing you can do. You say he hadn't opened the letter; it was obviously writing he was very familiar with then. Interesting! Calm down, Sal. Leave him to it, the secretive bastard.'

**

Sally was still in her dressing gown, sitting at the breakfast table. Myrtle had just gone upstairs to get dressed. They had a busy day ahead of them doing chilled food pickups from local supermarkets. Art put his head around the door.

'A visitor for you, Sal. I've put her in the front room. Looks official. I'd get dressed!'

'A woman?'

'Yeh, definitely a woman, Get dressed, she's waiting.'

She had been standing, looking out of the window. She turned as Sally came into the room and came towards her, hand outstretched. Sally recognised her straight away; she was one of the women she had seen standing in the entry at the back of the house.

'My name is Lucinda Tennant; I'm Julian's wife. I know my being here will be a bit of a shock, but please don't be alarmed. I haven't come to remonstrate, or to tell you to leave my husband alone, or any such nonsense, but there are things that need bringing into the open.'

She was about Sally's own height. She had shoulder-length brown hair with a heavy fringe and wide-set brown eyes. She was plainly dressed, without make-up. She had a nice voice, cultured, but without the upper-class edge of Julian's accent. She was nothing like the woman who had lived in Sally's imagination.

'Shall we sit?' said Lucy.

'Oh, sorry, yes, of course.'

'You are no doubt wondering how I know about you and Julian. You were a purely accidental discovery made by a private investigator. To make sense of this, I think I should start at the beginning, the beginning for our purpose being Julian's return from Afghanistan. Shall I do that?'

'Yes, please do.'

Sally listened as Lucy recounted the painful details of the collapse of her marriage and her distressing decision to end all contact with her husband.

'We are both victims of Julian's deceit and lies. He has used my affection for his parents to silence me, to make me complicit in his macho charade. I've been very stupid! He has been lying to you, telling you that he is at home with me and his children, while he pursues his destructive life in town. I suspect that he has led you to believe that he intended to end our marriage; that was never the case. It has been a poor excuse for a relationship, but he had no intention of walking away, of allowing his fragility of mind to become known to his father.'

'So there was never any question of a divorce?' Sally was stunned by what Lucy was telling her.

'I'm sorry, Sally, this is very painful for you to hear, but divorce was never on Julian's agenda. Things came to a head quite recently when he drove away after an argument, leaving me a note threatening his own life. My brother-in-law was dispatched to find him. He didn't turn up at the flat for two days and refused to tell Freddy where he had been. I turned to my friend Margo to see what she could find out. It was Margo who hired the private investigator. It has come as a shock to me, to discover that I am the owner of a house in Fulham. Quite shockingly, my signature has been forged on conveyancing documents.'

'The house that I live in?'

'Yes, the house that you live in.'

Sally was stunned. She tried to take in Lucy's words to force back the tears that had sprung to her eyes.

'I'm sorry, it's a shock. I've known for some time that he would never marry me. Recently, I have come to think that he doesn't really like me. I suggested that we split up, but he cried and begged me to stay. I felt sorry for him, the nightmares are truly terrible for him.'

'Ah, yes, the nightmares!'

'I don't love him. If I am being honest with myself, I don't think I ever did. He isn't an easy person to love. It isn't that I'm broken-hearted, but I feel so used. He always referred to the house as our home. He left the decorating and furnishing to me, wanted me to feel ownership and all the time the house belonged to you. How nasty is that! I've been like a little girl with a dolls house, arranging the expensive furniture and believing it was all mine; believing in the fairy tale story invented for the dolls who lived in it. If you have been stupid, I've been doubly stupid.'

Lucy moved to the sofa and took hold of Sally's hand. 'We've both been used and deceived. I knew that Julian was in a bad place and should have taken action much sooner. I've been very irresponsible, Sally. But I never for one moment imagined him capable of such duplicity. Julian has become a very selfish man.'

Chapter 20

Jack

Poppy and Sam's presence had quite an impact on his parent's home. Margaret's well-ordered sitting room wore something of a dishevelled look. The cushions, no longer well plumped up on chairs and sofas, lay on the floor, used for lounging and propping TV-watching elbows. Tablets, phones and digital gaming equipment kept company with china figurines on tabletops, their chargers dangling from wall plugs. Shoes and school bags were deposited on the floor under the hallstand. Except for the news, to which he tenaciously clung, Ron had lost control of the TV and Margaret's ban on drinks and the eating of biscuits, cake and sweets in the sitting room was a battle long lost. As Jack came through the front door, he was greeted by Poppy, who was dashing through the hall carrying a can of lemonade.

Ron was in his usual armchair, book in hand. Sam was sprawled out on the floor in front of the television, watching alien type creatures doing their thing. Poppy had taken up a perching position on the arm of the sofa, head in a girlie comic, can of lemonade in hand.

'I thought Grandma had banned drinks in the living room, Pops?'

'In glasses, Uncle Jack. Cans are fine; they don't spill.'

Jack found his mother in the kitchen, taking a batch of chocolate muffins from the oven.

'Where's Julia?'

Margaret pointed to the ceiling, and said, low voiced, 'She

heard you come in, she's gone upstairs to see to her face.'

Jack found the change in Julia's behaviour disturbing. He was all the time on edge, awaiting the return of the harridan of old. She had lost weight. Naturally thin, she was now skeletal. Her face was drawn and pinched; stripped of padding, the pointed, bony features of his childhood tormentor had returned. She had practically moved in with her parents. She was there from Friday evening until Monday morning and had now started to return on Wednesday evening, driving the children to school from Richmond the following morning.

'She doesn't look good, Mum!'

'No, dear, she doesn't.'

'Any news of Graham?'

Margaret looked nervously towards the door and lowered her voice. 'Your father's spoken to him. She doesn't know, so don't mention it.'

'How did he get hold of him?'

'He rang the London office and spoke to his secretary. She passed on the message and Graham rang on Tuesday evening. They are meeting for lunch on Thursday. Ron got the impression that he was relieved that contact had been made. He was very anxious for news of the children.'

'Are you OK, Mum? It's turning your life and Dad's upside down!'

'We're not letting that bother us, dear. It's good for the children to be here. I'd prefer that they were here permanently; she really isn't able to cope with them on her own.'

'She's very quiet!'

'Yes, it's hard to know what's going on in her mind. She's withdrawn into herself since we got to know what was going on between them. She admits to being spiteful and destroying his things, but tries to play down the incident with the knife, saying she hadn't really meant to hurt him.'

Jack wasn't surprised about the destruction of Graham's belongings. Julia had always cared about things; things were very important to her. She would be unable to imagine a more effective means of punishment than loss of, or damage to, one's personal things. The young Julia had adopted something of a lopsided approach to belongings. Julia's belongings were exclusively hers, unlike other people's belongings that Julia was entitled to use and make free with.

Jack had once borrowed Julia's goggles for his school swimming lesson. They were still in his bag when, after school, he had been sitting at the kitchen table doing his homework. Julia had descended on him like a vengeful fury, demanding the return of her property. Her punishing nails had put a nasty scratch on his cheek. He was left staring at a clump of pulled-out hair lying on his maths textbook. He was nine and hadn't yet learned to meet violence with violence. Julia lost a week's pocket money for the attack, increased to a month for refusing to admit she had been in the wrong.

**

The week was to end in high drama! Ralph Braxton had messaged; Madeline Murry had received word. There was to be a meeting of the self-appointed 'dragon slayers' the following Saturday at the hall. Jack had arranged to spend Thursday and Friday evenings at home in lieu of the weekend he would be spending in Mickleford, or, as his parents had been told, helping Simon with some decorating.

As he had turned onto the drive on Thursday evening, he had been surprised to see Graham Fairbrother's Range Rover parked up. The garage doors were open and there were step ladders in the bay window. It looked as though someone was taking down the curtains. The curtains hung askew across the windows, the broken poles hanging from the walls. A side table, unable to stand on its broken legs,

He let himself into a strangely quiet house. He put his head around the sitting room door and saw a scene of destruction. On the hearth were what remained of the Ladro figurines. Some of their broken parts grouped together, awaiting some miracle of restoration, others, beyond salvation, occupied a dustpan. Paintings, some with broken frames but all with smashed glass, had been taken down from the walls and were stacked beside glass-filled boxes. The carpet and chairs were covered in feathers.

'You have to be careful, Uncle Jack, because there's still pieces of glass about.' Poppy had crept up beside him.

'God, Pops, what's happened?'

'Mummy did it. She went crazy. "She's deranged", that's what Granddad says.'

'You're mother did this? Why?'

'She found out that Grandad had met Daddy and she didn't like what they had been talking about. Poor Mummy, she really lost it. But Daddy's here now, so it's OK.'

'Where is everyone?'

'Grandma's upstairs having a rest. It's been very upsetting for Grandma. Daddy and Grandad are out in the shed finding tools to take down the broken curtain rails; they don't want to pull the plaster off the walls.'

'Where is Mummy?'

'Well, that's the thing, Uncle Jack, we're not really sure, but she's probably gone home. She wanted to take us, but Grandma and Granddad wouldn't let her. It wouldn't have done, you see, because Mummy wasn't fit; she wasn't in her right mind. Granddad phoned Daddy and he came straight away. "Not in your right mind," Poppy repeated the words - slowly and deliberately - that's what people say about you when you go crazy like Mummy did' and turning frightened eyes on Jack, 'Grandma's very worried about Mummy!'

Over lunch, Graham had opened up to Ron; told him everything. Told him how his early hopes of a happy marriage had gradually faded because of Julia's jealousy. The relationship had been in a downward spiral for some time. Graham had always had to travel for his work. He was often away from home for several days. Julia was convinced that he was having affairs; that the business trips were a cover for time spent with the endless stream of women she had identified as his mistresses. He had lost one excellent secretary because of the abusive calls she had received from Julia.

He had kept close to his son, David, who was now a young man of twenty-three. He had maintained contact with David's mother, who, for some years, had worked in New York, where David grew up. She had returned to work in the UK and during the past two years, as his marriage fell apart, as Julia made his life hell, he had again grown close to Tia. The old spark had been rekindled. They had realised just how much they had in common, how easy and happy they were in each other's company.

Tia was Clementia Goffe; she was the half-sister of Richard Goffe MP, the present Lord Sanfold. During the week, Graham was living in a rented flat in Woking and at weekends with Tia and with David, when their son could join them at Tia's home in Mickleford.

But Graham was very worried about his younger children. Apologetically, he explained to Julia's father his belief that his daughter was unbalanced and spoke of his concern for the welfare of his children. He didn't want to separate Julia from her children; it was the last thing he wanted to do, but he was plagued by doubts and worry for their safety. Julia had never shown the least sign of wishing to harm the children, but desperate people often did desperate things. He intended to apply for custody.

An idea had been suggested to him, an idea to which he was giving serious thought. The idea of assigning a guardian to the children - a type of authoritative, nanny-type figure who would be constantly with them. Under such circumstances, he would be willing to allow the children to live with Julia. But, said Graham, Julia was unlikely to admit to any fault in her own behaviour, or agree to such an arrangement. He didn't know what to do! He was reluctant to serve her with divorce papers, fearing her reaction. He had found out that she was spending time with himself and Margaret and had taken some comfort from that. It was agreed that Ron would speak to Julia, try to make her aware of the seriousness of the situation, prepare her for what was to come.

Ron's talk with his daughter had been disastrous. His well-chosen, kind, understanding words were met with a level of anger and violence that stunned her parents. She had screamed abuse, accused them of colluding with Graham, plotting against her.

'How dare you meet him without my permission,' she had screeched as she made a dive towards the curtains. Grabbing handfuls of blue velvet, she tugged and pulled and jumping from the ground, using her full weight, managed to pull one of the drapes to the floor. Encouraged by her success, all the while shouting, 'How dare you, you bloody creep,' she set about the remaining curtains. The stout poles, made to carry the considerable weight of heavy, interlined velvet, had given way under her determined attack. Ron, recovering from the initial shock, had tried to restrain her by grabbing her arms and attempting to pin them behind her back. But possessed by a surge of superhuman strength, she had broken free, delivered a heavy blow to his face, fled from the room and returned moments later carrying a heavy wooden meat tenderiser.

Wielding the mallet like object, she swung it across the table where Margaret's Ladro figurines sat. Headless and limbless shepherds, shepherdesses, angels and dancers had flown through the air and crashed to the floor, followed by their finely painted extremities. The meat tenderiser had been applied to the wall paintings with devastating effect. Side tables had been picked up, kicked and flung to the ground. Abandoning the tenderiser, she turned her attention to the destruction of the cushions. Ron had given up any attempt at intervention and Margaret, showing amazing calmness, had taken Poppy and Sam into the garden, where she had sat on a bench, hugging the sobbing children.

Amidst the scene of destruction, sitting on a feather strewn floor, Julia sat silently for some time before getting up and announcing her intention of returning home. Ron and Margaret's refusal to allow her to take the children had brought forth threats of violent retribution. She had finally left; all attempts to stop her having failed. Ron had phoned Graham. He had been uncertain about his legal right to stop her from taking the children. He had expected her back at any moment, accompanied by the police. Graham had come right away.

'I'm afraid that Mummy has made a bit of a mess in your room, Uncle Jack,' said Poppy.

Jack had found Sam sitting on his bedroom floor, surrounded by Lego. He was trying to sort jumbled pieces and return them to their proper boxes. The Black Knight, together with other mounted characters, lay amidst turrets, drawbridges and pennants. Julia had wreaked vengeance on the sets that had lived on his shelves for over twenty years.

Jack hardly recognised the man, who, in a pair of worn cords and bobbled pullover, stood at the top of the step ladders, carefully removing the curtain pole fixings. Graham Fairbrother appeared to have turned into a regular, uninhibited person. Freed of Julia's critical, sharp-tongued presence, he was a different man. He was completely at ease as he chatted with Ron, who held the ladders. Ron had a black eye and a nasty scratch across his forehead.

'I'll get rid of that glass when we've got these down, Ron. I'll put the boxes in the boot and take them to the dump. If Margaret came with me, we could stop off and get replacement poles. Be good to get these curtains back up. We'll have a good look at the paintings. I think they need more TLC than we can give them. I'll find a good restorer,' said a loquacious Graham.

Bloody women, bloody Julia. Bloody Sal! Destructive bitches. Praying mantis, sapping the life from the men they latched onto.

Julia had made Graham Fairbrother's life miserable. And for what? For trying to be a decent husband, for working hard to give the spoilt bitch everything she asked for. It was the same game that Sal had played. He would have given his life for Sal, given her every penny he possessed. He had given her a comfortable home, holidays, her own money to buy what she wanted. But as soon as a guy had come along who could give her a better address, a bigger house, the expensive furniture featured in the stupid magazines that she had drooled over, take her to extortionately priced restaurants, she had been off. They were both stupid, empty-headed little cows. It had all gone pear-shaped for Sal and Graham would have the last laugh on Julia. Graham had found a woman who would appreciate him, a woman in a different class than his scragbag of a sister.

Well done, Graham Fairbrother. Good on ya mate!

Jack knew exactly what Julian Tennant was up to. Finding Sal weekending with Myrtle, he had been curious to find out where Tennant was. He had followed him from the Porteus offices to the flat in Bloomsbury, where he had originally lived with Sally. Jack had been surprised about that; he had presumed that the flat had been sold when they had moved to Fulham. Nice little bolt hole!

He had spent a few evenings watching the flat and a couple of weekend evenings following him around London nightspots.

Tennant hung out with a group of yahoos with loud voices and sloaney nicknames. One obnoxious toff with a particularly high-pitched squeaking voice was called 'Stiffy'. It was one endless pub and strip club crawl. One Saturday night, Tennant picked up a blonde in a pub near China Town Gate and headed back to the flat.

Following people around London at night wasn't the easiest occupation - jumping in and out of taxis, in and out of bars, the endless hanging about behind pillars and in corners. He couldn't take the risk of Tennant recognising him. There was always the possibility that he would have seen photographs. They were expensive trips that Jack didn't intend to continue. In any case, he was satisfied that he had got the hang of what Julian Tennant was up to.

But something needed to be done about the arrogant wife stealer. He knew that Christian thought him feeble. He knew that had Sal been Christian's wife, the matter would have been dealt with long ago. Christian was decisive; he didn't vacillate, he had total belief in his own mantra, 'You have to be strong, mate. You are either strong or weak, there isn't anything in between. Don't let anyone tell you otherwise.' But Jack lacked Christian's single-minded devotion to his own self-preservation and defence.

So what do you think of that then, mate?' Christian had asked.

'Fucking arse!'

'Tell you what, I'd be wanting to do something about the posh git - sooner rather than later. Jesus, Jack, he turns your wife's head, wrecks your marriage, then gets fed up with her and dumps her.'

'He hasn't dumped her. He ambles back to Fulham mid-week. No idea what she knows or where she thinks he is. Probably still swallowing a pile of lies, the air-headed bitch. He's taking her for one hell of a ride.'

'So?'

'Soon, mate, soon.'

He remembered the first time that Christian had called him a 'wobbler'. He remembered the playground fight, the excited crowd circling, the girls screaming, the blood, the boy on the ground curled into a foetal position, arms wrapped around his head in a desperate attempt at defence, He pictured Christian's foot, pulled back, heavy-booted, ready to strike through the fragile defence. None dared interfere; all were frightened of Christian. He could still feel the rush of blood to his head, remembered the quieting of the excited crowd as he pushed forward and blocked the boot, stood sentinel while the cowering form rose from the ground and fled. He had been sixteen; it was his first rejection of Christian's extreme brand of retribution.

He had run all the way home, ignored his mother's alarm as he pushed past her and dashed upstairs to his room. Throwing himself face down on the bed, he had buried his face in the pillow, overwhelmed by a conflict of emotions and Christian's sneering words. Christian would despise him. His mother and father would approve, but their council had offered no protection against the bullies who had made the life of a twelve-year-old boy intolerable. 'Using your fists will solve nothing,' his father had counselled. 'Make friends with the nicer boys, Jack; that way you won't be on your own. Try to stay part of a group. Don't be hanging around on your own,' had been his mother's advice. Well-meaning twaddle, Jack thought.

He had gone into the bathroom, locked the door, thrown off his clothes, and turned the shower to cold. The shock of the freezing flow had made him gasp and stopped his breath. He had stood still, allowing the numbing deluge to turn his body to ice. It had pounded his face, turned his hair to an icy cap covering his neck and forehead. The pain that had engulfed his body had numbed his mind. He had stood becalmed beneath the torrent.

His mother's knocking - her loud voiced, 'Are you OK Jack? What are you doing?' had broken across his cold-induced trance. Wrapping his frozen body in a towel, he felt a strange warming emanating from his chest and stomach. Mini daggers were striking at his legs and arms. He had looked at his chalk white face in the mirror, at his staring, startled eyes.

For some time, a new idea had been occupying Jack's mind. He felt certain that Tennant knew of his presence, knew he was being followed, was taunting him. The woman he had picked up in Covent Garden was very like Sal: tall, long blonde hair. He had watched as they had come out of the pub together and climbed into the waiting taxi. He had seen the way Tennant had stood at the open door of the cab, looking up and down the street; seen his searching gaze light on the dark doorway in which Jack was sheltering; seen the sneering smile he directed at his watcher. The message he was sending was clear: women like Sal were ten a penny, nothing special, there for him to pick up and drop at will. He needed to stop Tennant's arrogant game.

'It needs to be something you can cope with, mate, non-contact, that's the thing! No good giving you a knife, you'll definitely bottle that. Poison would be perfect, but you don't have the opportunity. I'm thinking a nasty accident on the tube, an unfortunate stumble under a train. All you need there is good timing and a bit of nerve,' that was Christian's advice.

He was right; Christian usually got it right! Jack was wary of Tennant's ability to defend himself. He was ex-army, drilled in the arts of offence and defence. He pictured Tennant as he had so often seen him, standing impatiently at the edge of a crowded platform. A dash along the edge, a bit of momentum to give power to the nudge were all that would be needed. Job done!

Jack's conversations with Christian fired his imagination, bolstered his determination to punish Tennant. He longed to find a way to get back at the man who had stolen his wife, taken his beautiful Sal. Sal was his; how could he let the bastard get away with it? With Christian asleep on the sofa in the spare room, Jack would take himself to bed and cry himself to sleep. He took care to make no sound, lest Christian might hear and discover his weakness.

For three years, Sal had tormented him, refused to let him move on, clung to him, leach-like. The long days of following and watching had wearied him. He had come to hate it all, to despise himself for bowing to her tyranny. Where was it to end? What was to become of the all-consuming hatred that was destroying him? In his rational moments, he was filled with loathing for the person he had become. He felt ashamed to sit in front of his parents and hide from them their newly formed, belligerent, deceitful son.

He had spoken very little about the breakup of his marriage. They thought he was doing OK, had put it behind him. That's what they would have expected him to do; that's what they would have considered the correct and courageous thing to do. And there lay Jack's dilemma! He knew they would be shocked by his actions. It would be a weak man, in their opinion, who couldn't face up to his loss. But something had been taken from him; something important, something highly valued, something at the very core of his life. Jack couldn't move on, couldn't see it as weakness.

**

It was Friday evening, he was on his way home to Windsor, to the scene of Julia's rampage. He was walking to Waterloo after delivering drawings to a client in Leicester Square. He almost bumped into them as he crossed the road at the junction of Exeter Street and Wellington Street. They were heading in the opposite direction. For a second, he thought it was Sal with Tennant; she was the requisite tall blonde. He turned in the middle of the road and stared after them. Tennant was the last person he had been expecting to see!

He felt the sweat break out on his forehead. He watched Tennant put an arm across the woman's back to guide her through the crowd on the far pavement. He barely hesitated before turning and following them. The woman was chatting, smiling up at Tennant. It reminded Jack of a scene he had once witnessed from a bus, when he had seen him walking with Sal. Was this some other man's wife? One thing was for sure; he needed stopping.

He put up a hand to wipe away the sweat that was running into his eyes. His face felt red hot; he felt as though his whole body was on fire. Pulses beat in his neck and head. He followed them along Bow Street and Floral Street and on into Covent Garden station. He fed his ticket into the machine and pushed his way through the barrier, all the while keeping the blonde heads within sight.

Chapter 21

Buckshot Hall

He was sitting on the top deck of the bus; it was the 65. He knew it was the 65 because he remembered getting on. It was about all he could remember! He felt damp and sticky, his mouth tasted like shit. He had a raging thirst. He looked down on the rush hour crowds thronging the pavement. Why was he taking this tortuous route; it would take forever? Was there a problem with the trains? Why was he on his way home when he should be going to Windsor? He couldn't remember. He couldn't bloody well remember!

He gripped the back of the seat in front of him. He leaned forward and rested his head on his hands. He felt the now-familiar panic rise in his chest. The stopping and starting of the bus in the heavy traffic was making him feel sick. He felt cold; a clammy coldness, his wet shirt clung to his chest.

Snatches of memory were returning; above him was a vaulted ceiling. He was in a tunnel-like space, the passageway of a tube station! He was standing with his hands against the wall, being violently sick. He had seen Tennant with a woman. He had followed them into a tube station; the memory was flooding back; focused, vivid and silent.

He was backing away through a tight crowd, eyes fixed on leaping figures, their arms outstretched, their hands grasping. He saw a blonde woman, her hand out flung, her fingers red-tipped. He saw them as a snapshot, motion suspended, the gasps and shouts from their wide, contorted mouths muffled in a dense, soundless blanket. He went unnoticed, an anonymous face in the startled crowd as heads turned and attention focused on the tumbling blonde-haired man, on his terrified eyes. He looked with horror at the contorted face, the shock of blonde hair fanned out halo-like about his head; it was the face of the golden Christ in his grandmother's painting; it was Christian's face. He pushed to the back of the crowd, a crowd populated by tall blonde men and women.

He was shivering violently. He clamped his feet to the floor of the bus to stop the involuntary drumming of his heels against the hard surface. He made his hands into fists and pushed them against his mouth to stop the loud noise his teeth were beginning to make. What the hell had happened? He remembered seeing Tennant, remembered feeling a dreadful, all-consuming anger. He had followed him down Bow Street and into Covent Garden station. Had he pushed Tennant under a train? Had he really lived out that fantasy?

It was 7:45 when he drove into Mickleford. He had gone home, showered and changed, collected his bags and driven straight down. He wasn't booked into The Swan until the following evening, but he had to do something. He wasn't in a fit state to go anywhere near his parents. He had to get his head straight, make sense of the jumbled images from the tube station, get his nerves under control.

He found the village unusually lively. Quite a few people were out and about. Driving along the main street, he saw that a crowd was gathered outside a well-lit building some way up from The Swan. Posters had been pasted onto the walls of the single-storey, unprepossessing, flat-faced meeting place; Jack thought it most likely the village hall. He became aware of fliers tied to lampposts and around trees. He pulled in further down the street and read what had been posted: 'CALLED TO ACCOUNT'. A meeting was taking place at 8:00 that evening. Richard Goffe was being required to explain his calls for a second referendum to his Brexiteer constituents.

Jack drove to The Swan, parked up, managed to book in for an extra night, dropped his bags in his room and headed for the meeting. He couldn't miss an opportunity to see Goffe face the music. He edged in at the back of the hall. The place was full; people standing four deep behind the seated area. At the front of the hall was a makeshift platform, behind which a lone woman sat, arranging papers.

The drive down had gone some way towards calming his nerves. Wits sharpened; he looked around him. It was as he was entering the building that the possibility of bumping into his brother-in-law had occurred to him. He edged into a corner and stood behind a couple of big blokes from where he had a good view of the room. There was no sign of Graham Fairbrother.

A quieting of the crowd, followed by a low booing, greeted the arrival of the MP. Marching purposefully to the front, Goffe raised a hand in greeting and smiled widely at the booers. The boos might as well have been loud applause. Quite a number accompanied him. The group, having seated themselves behind the table, Goffe introduced his entourage. To his left was his election agent, Marvin Quick. Next came Quick's secretary, a young, leggy brunette named Janie Wood. To the MPs right sat his own secretary, Mark Jones and to his left a big guy, introduced as Tom. Introductions made, Goffe was about to launch into a speech when a tall figure on the front row jumped to his feet, held up a restraining hand and stepped up onto the platform. It was the bookshop owner, who Jack was to learn, was a village councillor named Michael Porcherne.

'If I could stop you there, Richard, this meeting is under the auspices of the Village Council. The meeting will be opened and chaired by our Chairperson, Evelyn Banks. We would be grateful if you would adhere to the planned agenda. I must say that we weren't expecting such a large coterie accompanying our parliamentary representative; it leaves Evelyn cutting quite a lone figure, indeed it does! Under the circumstances, I'm sure you won't object if we give her a little support. No, of course you won't, why would you!'

It was the signal for half of those occupying the front row to stand and carrying their chairs join Michael Porcherne and their chairperson at the far side of the table. It was quite a crush, with a lot of jostling for position. Marvin Quick was trying to move his chair back in order to rid himself of the too-close company of Michael Porcherne on his shoulder. The bookshop owner looked studiously towards the audience, ignoring the frantic pushing and shoving. Quick was a short, thick-set guy, puffy-faced, with suspiciously dark hair plastered to his head. He wore a light navy suit with a white collared navy and white striped shirt. A flashy-looking watch could be seen below his shirt cuff and looped over the knot of his tie - something very heavy and gold. He looked the very image of what Jack's grandparents would have called 'a spiv'.

Richard Goffe was attempting to look unphased. Mark Jones had placed a restraining hand on the arm of the guy introduced as Tom; Jack recognised him as the chauffeur, Tom Bruce. Bruce wore a deep scowl and looked quite willing to get up and, single handedly, clear the invaders from the platform. A heavily bearded individual had pushed in between Evelyn Banks and Bruce, shielding the chairperson from the latter's angry stare.

Some order established, Goffe got again to his feet, 'Well, perhaps I could make a start on what I have come to talk to you about ......'

'I'm sorry, Richard,' said Michael Porcherne. 'We don't wish to be rude, but we have heard all we wish to hear of your thoughts, we don't intend to give you another platform to espouse your antidemocratic ideas. What we want are answers. The chair has a list of questioners, who will each in turn ask their question. It's all been very nicely and fairly organised. Do please bear with us.'

'If you would do me the courtesy of bearing with me, Michael. This is all very irregular. I have come here to speak to my constituents. Please allow me to continue,' said Goffe.

'Sit down and behave yourself', was shouted from the audience. Tom Bruce, red with rage, was being held down in his seat. Goffe was getting no help from his agent, who answered his silent plea for direction with a shrug of the shoulders.

'Call the first questioner, Chair,' shouted Michael Porcherne.

The questions came thick and fast, with the temperature of the room rising with every unsatisfactory answer. What the answers amounted to was Goffe's arrogantly stated opinion that they were failing to appreciate his superior knowledge and their own ignorance in all matters relating to the EU, which had resulted in their disastrous, uninformed vote to leave. He saw it as his responsibility to try to save the country from such a catastrophe. It pained him that his own constituents had contributed to the peril the country now faced. He felt shamed by it; found it difficult to hold up his head in parliament. He felt compelled to right the shame that they had brought upon the noble seat, which had been represented for so long by members of his family.

'He thinks he's back in the 1830s. He thinks it's a rotten borough!' shouted one of the farming types standing in front of Jack.

'He'll be trying to buy our votes with pints at The Swan next!' shouted the guy with him. This latter was applauded by heavy foot stamping and uproarious laughter.

'Get him off, Michael. Call an emergency meeting of the party. Get him de-selected. He's a bloody disgrace!' was shouted from the floor.

'Let's have a real, democratic people's vote!' shouted a woman on the front row who had risen to face the room. 'Let's have it now. Hands up all those who have no confidence in their MP.'

Every hand in the room shot up. 'Carried!' shouted the woman, 'No need for a count on this occasion. Get him out, Michael!'

While Michael Porcherne, obviously big in the local Conservative Party, stood to acknowledge the request, a very shaken Richard Goffe was leading his party from the room. The boos and cat calls were deafening. At the door, a fracas had broken out between Tom Bruce and locals who objected to being sharp elbowed out of the way.

On his walk back to The Swan, Jack found himself accompanied by half of those who had been at the meeting. All piled into the inn where a substantial buffet had been laid on. The village was making a night of it! He ordered a lager and being assured that the buffet was open to all, joined the queue. The food was laid on by the Village Council; a tradition, he was told, after important meetings at the village hall. He realised just how hungry he was; he hadn't eaten since having an early lunch. What a stroke of luck that he had arrived when he had. He wouldn't have missed seeing that pasting of Goffe for love or money.

They certainly knew how to lay on a spread in Mickleford. There were whole poached salmon, thick sliced beef, chicken breasts, pork pies, salads, chutneys and oceans of sandwiches. He piled up his plate and found a quiet corner to eat and watch the crowd. All the talk was of the meeting and of Richard Goffe. He caught snatches of conversation; 'arrogant, that's his problem' -- 'thinks it's a serfdom' - 'should have been drowned at birth. If old Sir Marcus had known what a filthy little rat he had in the cradle, he probably would have done just that.' Jack, considering this last comment, wondered just what was known locally of Goffe's activities. He went back for seconds before going to the bar for another lager.

He was recognised by Michael Porcherne, who hailed him as 'our young photographer friend.' It transpired that Porcherne was the chairman of the local Conservative Party Association. His informant behind the bar had more interesting information to impart. The appointment of Marvin Quick as agent had caused bad feelings in the local association. Quick, a Londoner with no links to the village had replaced a local man who had acted as agent from the time Goffe had been elected. Quick had appeared out of nowhere after Goffe had dismissed his agent, citing what was considered by all to be trumped-up accusations of incompetence. Tom Bruce was considered a thug with a questionable past. His continued employment by Goffe was the source of much speculation and rumour.

'Old Sir Marcus was a different kettle of fish. Very popular was Sir Marcus. He cared about the people, always took local opinion into account. This one got in on his father's coattails, but he couldn't give a toss about the people who elected him. It's been a tradition in these parts that someone from that family represents them in parliament. People didn't think about it much, just voted that way. It won't happen again, that's for sure! Anyway, it looks like they are about to kick him out. Good riddance, I say.'

It was gone 8:00 when he woke the following morning. He hadn't expected to sleep well; he hadn't really expected to sleep at all! Once alone in his room, memories of the tube station flooded back. He had fallen asleep to images of a screaming blonde woman, a hand flung out towards a falling man. He had slept for over seven hours - a peaceful, uninterrupted sleep. If he had been dreaming, he had no memory of it! His phone lay on top of the cover, where it had slipped from his hand.

Before falling asleep, he had scoured the news for reports of serious incidents on the underground but had drawn a blank.

Propped up on his pillows, he picked up the phone and made the same search - nothing!

Were the vivid memories imagined? The run along the edge of the platform, the push, the yielding body, the surprised turn of the head. It was how he had visualised it when he had talked with Christian. One thing was for sure: if there had been an incident at Covent Garden tube station, nobody was interested. Perhaps death on the system was so common that it was no longer reported.

His phone had been on mute; he had missed a number of worried messages and calls from his mother. God, he had forgotten to phone them. They had expected him home for dinner and he hadn't shown. What a stupid arse he was! He rang home and told them he was at Simon's. He apologised and made up a story about having a few too many with Simon and forgetting to ring them.

A mirror hung on the wall facing the foot of the bed. Reflected, he saw a pale, dark haired man, bleary-eyed, unshaven, sitting in a bed that wasn't his own. An open bag sat on a chair; underpants draped from its handle. There was a blue and white striped wash bag on top of the chest of drawers beneath the mirror. A coat hung on the back of the door.

The panic, when it came, overwhelmed his mind and body in seconds. Sometimes it came when he was just falling asleep; it was often there in his waking moments. It welled up as a black blanket of fear and confusion. It came now as he met the dark eyes in the mirror. He took deep breaths, pushed the darkness down.

He listened to conflicting voices; one was Christian's voice, the other that of his father. His father's voice was strong, his arguments sound. He belonged to a generation that valued integrity and honesty. A generation of men and women who loved their country and valued tradition. His boss, Arthur Curlow, was one such man. It was he who stood between Gordon House and destruction. There were many who would enjoy seeing a wrecking ball applied to that ornate brickwork.

The man his parents believed in attempted to convince himself of the hallucinatory nature of the more alarming events of recent months. He had a problem remembering, in particular remembering his actions when very angry. That was what it all amounted to. The break-in into Tennant's house had been an imagined event after an episode of lost memory and heightened anxiety. His stalking of Sal and his following of Tennant could be narrowed down to a few isolated incidents. It was possible that the alarming memories from the tube station had been brought on by his anger at seeing Tennant with yet another woman.

That was the voice of the man who was happy in his old home, secure in his childhood bedroom, happy with his parents, with Poppy and Sam. Happy until the stab of pain seared his chest - the pain that came when he remembered that Sal should be there with him, the pain that turned him into the man he concealed from his parents, the man that Sal had created. It was Sal who sent him running back to his other life - to Christian! He had no alternative; how could he allow such treachery to go unpunished? He loved his father, respected his father, but his father didn't understand today's world of takers and users.

He looked in disgust as tears streamed down the face of the self-pitying man reflected in the mirror, a man longing for the security of his father's home, for his childhood room! How pathetic he was! He hadn't planned it like this! He had meant to come to Mickleford with a clear head. It was Tennant's fault, all his doing, appearing out of nowhere, taunting him with another blonde! He drew his eyes from the mirror, jumped out of bed and headed for the shower. If only he could remember – memory - that was his problem. If only he could throw a light into those black voids from where so much of his torment and dark imaginings emanated, into those lost hours that were becoming more and more frequent. But he had to pull himself together; there were things to be done. There was another rich, arrogant man to be dealt with.

Chapter 22

Slaying a Dragon

Sliding back the hinged covers of the domed serving dishes, Jack helped himself to a fried breakfast and ordered toast and tea. He forced himself to focus on the architectural idiosyncrasies of the room in order to keep at bay the distressing, confused images from the previous day.

He imagined the room as it would have been two hundred years before - the rush-strewn floor, the bustling servants, the pewter plates piled with meats, the tankards of ale. It looked to have been the central room, the hub of the inn, the space most likely frequented by the stagecoach drivers, the grooms, the guards and all those obliged to travel squashed together in and on top of the great, lumbering conveyances, while those arriving in their private carriages enjoyed the privacy of the small rooms at the back of the bar. Buildings fascinated Jack. In sixth form, he had given serious consideration to a degree in architecture, but the seven years of study had put him off.

While enjoying his fry, he looked up the electoral history of Mickleford. A long line of Goffe men had represented the constituency since 1823, all elected with huge, solid majorities. Jack could quite see how Richard Goffe had come to believe that the seat was his own private fiefdom. He finished his breakfast and went out to the car park. He didn't expect Ralph Braxton until late afternoon and thought he would use the time to get more practice using the camera.

He photographed what remained of, or gave clues to, the old coach yard: the filled-in sections of stonework at first floor level where the old doors had opened off the raised walkway, what remained of the walkway supports, the cast iron hoist posts still in position, water troughs, now converted to planters. He stopped on his way out through the old coach entrance to photograph unusual mason marks he had spotted in the stonework. Driving along the village street, he decided to pull in and grab something to take with him for lunch.

On his way back from the mini market, balancing a sandwich, crisps and several cans of coke - having refused the offer of a plastic bag - a new display in Tomes and Trivia caught his eye. Arranged in front of a backdrop map of the village and around artfully positioned blow-ups of its front and back covers were books entitled 'The Old Black Swan at Mickleford'. A write-up introduced the author as Valerie Pugh, a local historian and promised a meticulously researched, rollicking tale of the fascinating events in the history of the four-hundred-year-old inn. It had an attractive cream cover with a fine line drawing of the inn in green. The inn sign, prominently positioned in the drawing, showed a sad-looking swan, its head semi-buried in its wings, lying in a bed of rushes. He took the sandwich and drinks to the car and returned to the book shop.

There was no one in attendance, but voices could be heard coming from the back of the shop. One voice was recognisable as that of the shop owner, Michael Porcherne, the other was that of a woman. They were making no effort to keep their voices down. Jack's ears pricked up when he heard Richard Goffe's name mentioned.

'It makes things very difficult for Jess and me, naturally, it does. We really hope, Michael, that this unpleasantness with Richard won't come between the two of us and the village. We have so many good friends here.'

'Don't worry one jot on that score, my dear; none of us will think any differently of you or Jess. We will, of course, hope to remain on friendly terms with Richard.'

'A vain hope, I'm afraid. I'm told that he's very angry. Richard isn't used to being challenged. My God, Michael, I'd love to have seen it.'

'Quite a spectacle! But sad, my dear. Sad that it's come to this. But people have had enough; just won't put up with Richard's arrogance and dictatorial behaviour any longer.'

'And rightly so! Of course, we don't fare any better, as you well know. How Jess puts up with him, I don't know! If he's no longer required to be in London during the week, if he decides to stay at the hall, I don't know what she will do.'

'It would be some company, I suppose! Did she get the alarm system sorted out?'

'Company she can well do without, I can tell you! But yes, the system has been installed. Only a part system, covering her own apartments. It's linked to the police which gives her some sense of security. I don't know how she would cope without Marina Payne. More of a companion than housekeeper, really. When the two Payne boys are home from university they keep a good eye on the place; they cover a lot of ground on their bikes. Jess pays them; helps them out financially. Richard knows nothing about it, of course. The boys have to keep well out of Bruce's way at weekends.'

'Damn hard place to secure, open to so many public roads. Not a good place for a woman on her own and nothing like the staff of Sir Marcus' day. What did happen with the Gurkhas, Tia?'

Tia? Was the woman Clementia Goffe, Goffe's sister, Graham's new partner? Jack's ears really pricked up.

'Gave them three months' pay and told them to leave by the

end of the week, said they were too officious, acting without orders.'

'Were they?'

'Not a bit of it, they were doing what Jess had hired them to do, setting up patrols and introducing normal security measures. They were very good at their job. It hadn't been easy to get them. She was furious!'

'Very odd behaviour! What do you think was behind that?'

'Jess thought it was because they were putting Tom Bruce's nose out of joint. Richard never likes upsetting him. Doesn't care who else he upsets, incredibly dependent on the horrible man. But if there's anything in the other matter, Gurkhas would be the last people he would want around the place. They all descend on her, sometimes at a few hours' notice. Poor Jess! She would be gone if she had anywhere reasonable to go. My mother is the only one who can get the better of him, but then she's quite a madam herself. But I mustn't keep you, Michael. I'll take the books and be on my way.'

They came into the shop through a door behind the counter.

'Val has signed both copies and added a personal message,' said Michael Porcherne, handing over a cream paper carrier bag bearing the shop logo.

'That's very kind. I'm looking forward to reading it. I think it will do really well. The promotional display is very eye catching!'

She was an unremarkable looking woman. Medium height, slim, unruly, dark curly hair pulled back and anchored by combs, angular features, no makeup, jeans and black linen jacket.

'Oh! Our young photographer,' said Michael Porcherne. Seeing Jack as he stepped out from behind a card display. He looked quite taken aback, wondering no doubt how much of the conversation had been overheard.

'The book on The Swan looks interesting! I'd like to buy a

copy. It says the author lives locally!'

'Val! Yes, you may have noticed her place. The low, thatched cottage just before the turning for Chomley Green. Garden's always beautiful. If she isn't writing, Val is pruning or planting.'

'Really! I'm a bit confused with the title, though; I thought it was The Black Swan, not The Old Black Swan?'

'Ah, now, that is interesting! Surprised us all. One of the hitherto unknown facts that Val has unearthed. You will notice the inn sign on the cover; it's taken from an original photograph, dated 1887. The next photograph, showing the sign clearly, is dated 1921. Sometime in the intervening years, the poor old decrepit fellow was replaced by a younger, altogether more lively version of himself and the 'old' was dropped from the name. Lord only knows why, my friend. Val can find no reference to the change. Perhaps it was after the first war - an effort to show a more upbeat image to counter the death toll. 'Out with the old and in with the new,' so to speak.'

Jack paid his £9.99 and was handed his book in a smaller version of the carrier bag in which Clementia Goffe had carried away her books. He had a good look at Valerie Pugh's house before turning off to Chomley Green. It was a nice-looking old place, with a garden that spoke of hours of loving attention.

He parked in the pull-in before the gates of Buckshot Hall, crossed to the opposite side of the road and photographed the imposing, locked gates to Goffe's poorly secured estate. His was the only car there, which surprised him; perhaps news of last evening's events were yet to reach London. He wondered about 'the other matter' which Clementia Goffe had spoken of and those that 'descended on Jess at a few hours' notice.' What, he wondered, was known or suspected about Richard Goffe's nefarious activities.

Driving on would take him into Graham Fairbrother territory. He turned the car and drove back in the direction from where he had come. He drove back to the Mickleford junction and turned left towards Chomley Green. He had driven for a good mile, was about to turn around; the road was tunnel-like, treed to the edges, offering no views, when he saw a dirt parking area and a Woodland Trust sign. He pulled in. The sign showed a map of a woodland walk of 1.3 kilometres. Might be interesting! Leaving the car to be recognised at the side of the road was a problem! Graham being around was a complication he could have done without. He moved to the end of the pull-in and parked side on under some low-lying branches and set off along the pathway.

He was surprised to discover that woods so close to the hall were under the auspices of the Woodland Trust. He wondered what that was about. It was lovely old woodland, deciduous, traditional English trees! He found himself on a steeply sloping path. To his left was a deep ravine, its banks clothed in gnarled, exposed roots and perilously leaning trees. A shallow stream trickled at its base. The ground to his right banked up to road level and was covered in heavily pruned-back laburnum. He recognised the distinctive, dark core of the wood; he had seen a laburnum pruned in his parents' garden.

After some three hundred metres, the pathway led onto a wooden bridge, that spanned the ravine. Beyond the bridge the land flattened, the pathway winding through ecologically managed woodland. Self-seeded saplings were thinned, the wood stacked in piles; left to home wildlife and maintain the biodiversity of the woods. A woodcarver had been at work turning the trunks of felled or fallen trees into animal and bird carvings. He had just come upon a huge owl, some six feet tall. He had passed a squirrel and a badger. He got good shots of the sculptures. The camera was performing well.

He tried to work out the direction of the path. He thought he was walking in a westerly direction, quite a distance from the hall, but he couldn't be sure. The wood was dense and disorientating, but a sudden shaft of light signalled a break in the greenery through which glimpses of stonework could be seen. Making his way to the tree edge, he saw that it was a long, low building. The woodland had encroached on what must once have been a yard; some of the old flags and cobble stones, raised and displaced by tree roots, were still visible. He picked his way, with some difficulty, along the side of the building; thick briars had invaded the space and clumps of ivy, with stems like small trees, covered the ground and climbed, in places, to roof height.

He found it to be a group of old, derelict cottages. The back walls were windowless. To the front were gaping holes and rotting timber where once window frames and doors had filled the gaps. The rampant ivy had grown through the apertures and tumbled in clumps from the walls and stone fireplaces. In the end cottage, a strange montage occupied the centre of the floor. It was where ivy had wrapped itself about an abandoned wooden table and chairs, its stems rivalling in girth the table legs, about which it wrapped itself in hungry coils. Great cannon balls of cobbles, raised from their foundations by invading tree roots, occupied a front yard. Beyond, just visible through spindly, self-seeded sycamores, was what looked to be open ground.

Pushing through the thorny, tangled undergrowth beneath the sparse copse, he found himself at the top of a deep, grassy bank. He was amazed! His sense of direction was usually good, but he had been way out on this occasion. From his high perch, he was looking down onto the Buckshot estate. The house, the stable block, the main drive, the tangle of minor roads that ran about and onto the estate and a number of estate houses were laid out, map-like, before him.

He thought he could identify Clementia Goffe's house lying to the west. Branching off the main drive was another substantial house and on a loop that ran from the back of the stables to the main driveway was a thatched house, again of some size. He wondered which of the houses was occupied by Marina Payne, the housekeeper come companion and her two security providing sons? He could see the road that ran right up to the stables - the road that Ralph had stumbled onto. Ralph hadn't mentioned the houses! Jack hoped he knew what he was about.

The stables lay at the back of the east wing. To the west was a domed, glass orangery. At the back of the house, steps ran through a series of terraces, to formally laid-out gardens with pathways converging on a stone fountain.

He paid particular attention to the area around the stable block. It was fronted by the cobbled yard from where they hoped to get their first shots. He could see the dense, bordering shrubbery that ran in a heavy swathe towards the house. He imagined the cars driving in, pictured the best spot amongst the shrubs from where to photo the number plates. He was confident that he could get clear night-time images without using the flash. The camera had amazing capability, but they were going to have to move about a lot. He thought it a risky venture that they were about to undertake.

For a moment, he felt like returning the car and driving home. Ralph was confident, but then how much of the set-up was he really aware of? He didn't like what he had seen of Tom Bruce. Bloody, scary character! But as the doubts surfaced, he could feel the anger rising, could hear Christian's voice: 'What's this, mate, what's this feeble minded thinking? The guys a traitorous bastard; he needs stopping.' Too damn right - Christian was always right. He would be there tonight with Ralph; they would get the images that Maddy Murry needed.

He was hungry and needed a drink. His food and cans were in the car. He fired off quite a few shots and was standing up to leave when, from around the side of the house, two dogs raced into the garden. Jack got quite a shock. A woman followed, calling to them. It wasn't until they were running about her feet that he saw their size. They were King Charles spaniels, not the guard dogs feared by Ralph and himself. Perhaps the woman with them was Jessica Goffe, or perhaps it was Marina Payne? He felt sorry for Jessica Goffe and wished her well. The dogs were cute!

**

Over dinner, they looked at the photos Jack had taken in the afternoon.

'It's handy to know exactly where the houses are. I must have passed pretty close to that thatched property and had no idea that it was there,' said Ralph.

'Could be the Payne home. You sure those boys are not around the place? They cycle about.'

'From what you overheard in the bookshop, I'd say there are a few people asking questions about Goffe's late night gatherings, but my bet would be that those boys will keep well away. I don't think they will be anxious to cross Bruce.'

'Yeh, that's probably right!'

'Maddy wants us to look out for two representatives of the EU Secretariat General who she's been told will be there: Mathys Meier, a German from the Department of Economic and Financial Affairs and Simon Bakker, a Belgian working in Eurostat, their statistics department. She's posted photos of both,' said Ralph, handing Jack his phone.

Meier was a tall, thin guy with grey, receding hair and wearing heavy, dark-rimmed glasses. Bakker looked to be fortyish, close-cropped brown hair, heavy features.

'There will be a handful of present and former MPs, including two ex-ministers, easily recognisable. Others will be from the judiciary, we are unlikely to recognise them; we need to get clear, identifying shots.'

They left The Swan at 10:45. Allowing themselves thirty minutes to get to the hall, they hoped to be in position at the stable yard by 11:15, in time to photo any early arrivals.

They crossed an area of open ground behind The Swan before coming to dense tree cover, not the native woodland of Jack's earlier walk but a commercial plantation of firs. Ralph turned on his torch and trained it on the ground to guide them across the spongy carpet of fallen needles. The trees were tightly packed, their rough, branchless trunks forming orderly rows. It was an oppressive, silent place, the crunch of their feet on the soft ground echoed eerily into the night. Clearing the cops, they crossed a farm track and climbed a gate into open fields. A further ten-minute walk, along hedges and across styles, brought them onto the dirt pull-in fronting the hall. Crossing the road they entered the estate through a gap in the wall.

'So far, so good. It's taken us twenty-five minutes.

Straight ahead from here. When we clear these trees, the building comes into view and we'll know where we're heading,' Ralph explained.

There wasn't a sound to be heard. The night was dense and black. It was the quiet, the total darkness of the countryside, unknown to the city dweller; Jack found it unnerving. They walked through thickets of laurel and rhododendron, through an undergrowth of tangled roots and snagging brambles. They made their way across pathways and scrubby, unkempt patches of land towards the shrubbery that bordered the stable yard. From the cover of the shrubs, they looked out onto the 'L' of the stable block. The silence was broken by the sound of a television at top volume.

'The guy in the end cottage must be half deaf!' said Ralph.

'Maybe he can't stand the silence. It would get to me. I don't know how easy this is going to be, Ralph. It would be OK standing in one place, but I'm going to have to move along the shrub edge to get shots of them parking up and going into the house.' Jack had begun moving through the dense growth. 'We're going to have to stamp some of this stuff down and push these stragglers to one side. We need to break off and clear any dead wood, anything that's going to make a noise. Bloody good job we came early.'

As the first headlights lit up the yard, a guy with a torch came from the direction of the house and approached the incoming car. The occupant was a small, fat guy in his forties in a long, dark overcoat. Jack had got a shot of the number plates and several of him getting out of the car before moving into position in front of the door. He had pre-set the camera and was able to shift from photo to video mode. The sound of the video kicking in sounded very loud. The shrubs were quite close up to the front of the house, Jack froze, but nothing had been heard.

Two of Goffe's cronies from Parliament, Grace Duxton and Adel MacAllen, were the next to arrive, followed by a guy they didn't recognise. Simon Bakker and Jack Sargent, an ex-Minister of the Crown, arrived together. After Sargent and Bakker came two more unidentified men. It was going well. The last to arrive was Mathys Meier.

Meier was much older than he appeared in the photograph. With the help of the torch carrier, he struggled out of the car and stood unsteadily while a metal walking aid was fished from the back seat. With an impatient wave of his arm, the stick was pushed aside. An alternative stick, brought from the car boot, was grudgingly accepted and having beaten away the proffered arm of his helper, he set off across the uneven surface, briefcase in hand, the metal stick, beating a loud tattoo against the cobblestones. He looked like your archetypal, crotchety old man.

Jack photographed his arrival before getting into position at the front of the house. He listened to the rattle of the stick and the whining, complaining voice as the old man made his slow way along the path between the stables and the house. While waiting, he had time to replay some of the footage; it was good, detailed. Looking over his shoulder, Ralph gave a thumbs up. Jack was feeling a growing sense of excitement, a kind of euphoria that he knew he had to control. It was then that the front door opened and Richard Goffe came out.

Walking to the bottom of the steps, he stood looking towards the stable yard. It was the first they had seen of Goffe. Meier, it seemed, warranted a special welcome from his host.

'Hello Mathys! How are you?' said Goffe, moving forward to meet his visitor.

'How am I? You can see how I am! Being in your infernal country makes me feel very bad. Such ignorance! So depressing.'

'Arrogant, old bastard!' said Ralph.

Meier stopped dead, held his head to one side and turned to face the bushes. Ralph's remark had been made in a barely audible under-tone, but the old man had heard something.

'Do you know that there is someone concealed in your trees, Richard?'

'Shit, time to go! What's with this old fart? What's he got, super-engineered German hearing aids? Come on!' hissed Ralph, attempting to pull Jack away.

The resulting noise and movement alerted Goffe, who moved towards the bushes, shouting, 'What's going on? Who's there? Come on, show yourself!'

Jack looked at the angry, arrogant, contorted face and didn't move.

'Jesus, come on.'

'Come out of there. Skulking in bushes. Cowardly behaviour.

Show yourself,' shouted Goffe.

Jack was no longer at Buckshot Hall; he was behind the toilet block at Harriman Hal Comprehensive, leaning against the wall, smoking. He was listening to the voice of the Deputy Headteacher, Mr. Denys, 'Come on, have the courage to face the music. You can skulk about in there as long as you like; I'm quite happy to wait all day.' Mr. Denys was a hated figure. Jack had wanted to come out from behind the block and smash his self-satisfied face.

Tossing the camera into the undergrowth, Jack pushed through the bushes and stood for a moment, contemplating the amalgamous face of the man confronting him. He saw the anger drain away, saw the fear in the eyes as he advanced to land the first blow into the soft belly. Raining blows to the head and body, he moved in on the staggering figure. He didn't hear Meier's high-pitched cry of alarm; he didn't hear Ralph's shouted voice, telling him to turn and run. He heard the encouraging playground shouts - the girl's half-fearful, half-excited screams. As the body fell to the ground, he felt again the old sense of elation, of triumph at gaining the advantage, of winning the right to wreak vengeance. His boot struck into soft flesh, into bone; this enemy wouldn't be spared. He felt the scull bones crumble, heard the crack of the neck as the head spun, felt the blow to his own head and had a momentary memory of a descending blackness.

Chapter 23

Sally and Lucinda

Lucy was sitting in a quiet corner at the far side of the room; she was sitting upright, absolutely still, her eyes cast down, hands folded on her lap, deep in her own thoughts. Sally felt a great wave of sympathy. In one sense, she hardly knew Lucy, yet she understood well the cost of the practiced smile that greeted her as she reached the table and the eyes that mocked the effort.

'This is nice! I haven't been here before!' was Lucy's greeting.

It was a small place in a side street next to St. Paul's in Covent Garden. Sally had chosen it because it was quiet, comfortable and the coffee good. Lucy had asked for the meeting. She wanted to talk, 'to tie up some loose ends'. Sally was shocked at her changed appearance; she was thinner, her face drawn, the skin beneath her eyes taut and dark, some fine grey hairs streaked the heavy fringe.

**

It had been two months since Julian's death. It had been Sally and Myrtle who had found him. Sally had moved out of the Fulham house after Lucy's visit. She didn't tell Julian she was leaving; she didn't leave a letter, not even a note. She couldn't see the point of voicing the hurt and anger that she felt towards him. She didn't think of it as leaving him because Julian was no longer really there. For months, he had come and gone. Sometimes she had thought him unaware of her presence; she knew he no longer cared whether she stayed or left.

The following week, Myrtle drove her over to the house to pick up some small pieces of furniture. She had messaged Julian to tell him what she was doing and got the reply, 'Sure, Sal, no problem. Take what you want.' The reply had annoyed her; she wanted nothing that wasn't her own.

Sally had picked up the mail from behind the door, checked there was nothing for her, put the letters on the hall table, remarked that the place was stuffy, that Julian mustn't have been back for a few days, left Myrtle carrying a box out to the van and gone upstairs. They had been in a hurry, hoping to get back to Peckham before the rush hour. Sally had thrown open the door of the master bedroom and had been halfway across the floor before she had seen him.

Thinking about it afterwards, she couldn't remember when she had first realised that he was dead. The initial shock was of seeing him so unexpectedly. She remembered thinking that he was asleep, wondering why he should be sleeping in mid-afternoon, of going over to the bed and crying out as her fingers encountered the cold skin of his face.

He was in a semi-sitting position, propped against the pillows. His eyes were half closed, his head turned to one side. A dribble of sick trailed from the left side of his mouth into the blonde stubble of his jaw. His lips were drawn back, giving the impression of a very slight, ironical smile. His left hand lay semi-curled on top of the bed cover, his right hand gripping a tumbler from which a yellowish liquid had spilled out and stained the sheet. There were tablet bottles and packets on the bedside cabinet, sitting in spilled white powder. Tablets had spilled onto the bedcover and floor. An empty whisky bottle lay beside the bed, with a half empty bottle on the cabinet. Looking down at the still face, the waxen pallor, the dull, lifeless hair, Sally wondered how she could have imagined him asleep.

She had got to the head of the stairs before her legs had failed; it was there that Myrtle had found her, sitting on the top step, head down on her knees. She had felt very faint, sick. Once over the shock of the discovery, Myrtle had blown her top.

'What a selfish, uncaring bastard! He knew you would be the one to find him. He knew that you were coming today, didn't he?'

'For God's sake, Myrtle, he's dead!'

'Of course he's bloody dead! It's what he wanted, he made sure of it. Looks like he took enough pills and dope to kill the street. Selfish bugger!'

'He was very unhappy, Myrtle!'

'Unhappy! Poor little rich boy. My heart bleeds for him. It didn't stop him from making other people very unhappy, did it?'

'Oh, Myrtle, it's horrible. I've never seen anyone dead before! It's weird; life gone, just like that!'

'Life and death, my love, both weird from what I can see!'

Propped on the mantelpiece was a sealed letter addressed to Lucy. Both women had stood looking at the white envelope, the name written in black ink, in a small, neat, upright script.

'Take it, Sal. Put it in your bag.'

'Why?'

'It will confirm it as a suicide. It's a bloody, awful thing for a family to have to live with. It's another example of the man's self-absorption. She's been decent to you, Sal. Post it to her; let her decide what to do with it.'

'What if the police ask if we've touched anything?'

'Well, we haven't, have we? We've touched nothing in the bedroom. If they ask if he left a note, which is most unlikely, give it to them.'

The police had arrived within twenty minutes of being called, but it was 6:30 by the time the black van had arrived to remove the body. The afternoon had seen a succession of people in white, protective clothing, their feet wrapped in baggy overshoes, going up and down the stairs. There was a scene of crime officers; foul play had to be ruled out. A forensic pathologist came and went. They made no noise, working in a strange, concentrated silence, broken only by the crackle of a radio or the banging of a car door.

Sally and Myrtle kept to the kitchen, drinking copious amounts of coffee. Both had been questioned regarding their connection to 'the dead man' and their reason for being in the house. Sally hadn't got through it all without shedding tears.

'Should we warn Lucy? She's going to get a dreadful shock!'

'It wouldn't help, Sal. It's going to be terrible for her, whoever she hears it from. I'd leave it to the police; they are practiced in that kind of thing. Ring her tomorrow and tell her about the letter.'

**

'It's good of you to come, Sally.'

'How are you, Lucy? How are the children?'

'Oh, up and down! Ben is behaving badly at school and indulging in silly, attention-seeking behaviour. But at least it's a reaction. Cosima's relationship with her father was always more complex. She was old enough to have memories of Julian before his last tour. Happy memories! She has spent the last eight years trying to understand the man who returned and searching for the man she had lost. We were both searching but I was able to articulate my loss and Cosima wasn't. I don't know what the long-term effects will be. I sometimes find her sitting in a quiet corner, lost in thought.

I remember well the first time I took the children to the hospital to see Julian after his return. Cosima was very excited. I can see her now, strapped in her car seat, talking about her daddy. It was quite a drive to Birmingham and she was getting fed up, telling me that Daddy wouldn't like it if we were late. When she saw Julian, she hid behind me and looked at him with suspicious eyes. Cosima was always a very sensitive, knowing child.'

'One day, quite soon in Cosima's case, I would have had to tell them that their father had taken his own life. But they will be spared that, at least. I shall be eternally grateful to you for that, Sally. My God, what a selfish, uncaring man Julian had become! It was a maudlin, self-flagellating epistle that he left for me. You got a mention: 'Tell Sal, I'm sorry'. Imagine that!'

'And Julian's parents?'

'Not at all good. His father, Ted, is doing what he always does, putting on a brave face, but I know that it's slowly killing him. Daphne is far from coming to terms with her loss. She has blamed me for keeping so much from them. Although they don't say so, they both blame me for his death.'

'How unfair!'

'Is it? I'm not so sure. However noble my reasons, I didn't do the right thing. I allowed Julian to manipulate me like some rag-headed puppet. What Julian experienced in Afghanistan was brutal, an outrage to the sensibilities. I tried to help him, Sally. I tried very hard. But the army had pinned a medal on his chest and called him a hero and in Julian's book, brave men didn't go whinging to counsellors. He had to get over it, keep a stiff upper lip like his father did! Ted was as much Julian's problem as were his nightmares! To be honest, Sally, it's being estranged from Daphne's that hurts most. The ridiculous thing is that I did it to protect them from the knowledge of what Julian had become.'

'Will she come around?'

'I hope so. Clara, that's Julian's sister, is doing her best. Clara and Freddy are the only ones who know about the letter. They told me to burn it and forget that it had ever been written.'

'What about the house? Will you continue to live there?'

Lucy leaned across the table, her eyes suddenly brightening,

'Oh, I will never leave the house. The house is my great comfort and support! My refuge! I love the house. But enough about me. Tell me how things are with you. Where is Jack Willett at present?'

'Securely locked away at Rampton. Undergoing psychiatric assessment to determine if he is sane enough to stand trial.'

'How bizarre! I mean, you were with him for quite some time. I'm presuming that he wasn't showing signs of mental illness then?'

'No, he was just very controlling, opinionated! He had old-fashioned ideas about male and female roles. He was determined to convert me to his way of thinking in just about everything. He was big into politics. He came from a conservative background; my family was staunchly Labour. In the end, I just gave up and let him talk. It wasn't until I met Myrtle that I realised what a manipulative, stultifying relationship I was in.

But it turns out that Jack has quite a back history of mental illness. The problems first surfaced in his early teens. A series of assessments suggested borderline personality disorder - nothing very definite, all tentative. There's a reluctance to pin labels on twelve-year-olds. After a serious assault on a teacher when he was sixteen, persecutory delusional disorder was diagnosis and Jack was shipped off to complete his secondary education in a residential special school.'

'You knew nothing about that?'

'No, when he talked about school, it was the local comprehensive he spoke of. It was while he was under assessment in the residential school that the associative identity disorder came to light. Unusually, for this disorder, Jack had only one alternative identity, a person he named Christian. It was Christian who resorted to violence; it was Christian who assaulted the teacher. Strangely, it was Jack who killed Richard Goffe; Christian is to be allowed no part in that action. Jack speaks so convincingly of Christian that the police were absolutely convinced that he was the escaped accomplice.

He was in therapy throughout his time in university but appeared to have 'turned the corner' - his father's words - when he went to work for Carter and Curlow. He loved the job and had been off medication and out of therapy for some time before he met me.'

'Sally, are you telling me that nobody in his family thought to tell you of his past history?'

'Were they obliged to, Lucy?' Did they have any duty of care towards me? I don't know!'

'Damn right they did, Sally. The man had been seriously mentally ill. When did you find this out?'

'Well, the first inkling I got of his history of mental illness was when I read about it in the papers. But I went to see his parents a couple of weeks ago and they told me the whole story.'

'A difficult visit!'

'Yes, it was difficult to know what to do, but in the end, I decided I should pay them a visit. I found a much-changed house. Ron opened the door to me and told me that Margaret wouldn't be long; she was collecting the children from school. That surprised me, as the children had been at school in Weybridge, where the family lived. But they were no longer living in Weybridge; they were no longer a family. I could have cried at the welcome I got from Poppy. She threw herself into my arms, saying, "Sally, where have you been? I've wanted to see you for so long." I felt dreadful. God! How children are punished by adult actions!'

'What had happened?'

Graham had walked out. I wasn't surprised to hear that the marriage had broken down. Julia had a very sharp tongue, and often goaded him in front of other people. But despite that, I liked Julia, I understood her frustration with a man who wouldn't stand up and defend himself. I didn't like Graham. To me, he came across as sly and smug. How wrong I was! The man was living a nightmare. It was an abusive relationship; she was the abuser. She was obsessively jealous, violent, and unpredictable. He had hesitated to end the marriage, fearing the reaction it would bring. She's quite obviously unbalanced. He is applying for custody of the children.'

'So the children are living with their grandparents?'

'Yes, Graham appears to spend a lot of time there with them. Julia, prevented by her parents and Graham, whilst displaying extreme deranged behaviour, from taking the children, decided to cut loose. She's gone to Italy to teach English. Ron says that she knows she hasn't a cat in hell's chance of getting custody, there being witnesses to her abusive and violent behaviour.'

'How sad! Sad for him, for her and dreadful for the children. But it begs the question as to whether there's a history of mental instability in the family.'

'I agree, but his parents are the most normal, level-headed couple you are likely to meet!'

'Really!'

'Ron talks about Jack being bullied in school. He thinks that was where the problem started. Graham arrived while I was there. I couldn't believe that I was speaking to the same person. Friendly, eloquent, even! So good with the children! And they adore their father. He is giving Margaret and Ron the support they so desperately need. He gave me his number. He told me to keep in touch: 'There could be sticky times ahead, Sal. We are all going to be touched by Jack's actions. If you need help, call me,' - those were his words. I thought it was very kind of him! He has managed to clear away the press that was camped outside Ron and Margaret's. He got all manner of injunctions slapped on them. Handy having someone with legal clout! But, Lucy, here's the most extraordinary thing: Graham intends to remarry and you would not believe it, but the woman he is marrying is Richard Goffe's sister.'

'What!'

'Yes! Isn't it the strangest thing?'

'Unbelievable!'

'Clementia Goffe lives on the family estate in Mickleford. Ron says that Jack suspected that Graham was seeing another woman. He wonders if he had been following Graham; if it was that that drew him to Mickleford in the first place. He was there on a number of occasions, always staying at The Black Swan. But the police, who seem to have a good idea of what he's been doing during the last three years, say the connection is immaterial to their enquiries. His computer and laptop have been a mine of information. They have evidence that he had been tracking Richard Goffe for some time.

Lady Pamela Goffe's PA has identified him as a man who had mingled with the press pack outside Goff's London home in Eaton Square and followed her to a nearby coffee shop. He told her he was a freelance photographer and tried to pump her for information on the family. That was in 2017. There was endless footage of Goffe on his phone and laptop: speeches in the house, press interviews and uploaded photos he had taken in Mickleford and around Buckshot Hall. Jack had become obsessed with Goffe and a group of Remain MPs who were vocal against leaving the EU. They think that he was on another stalking mission when the assault took place.'

'My God, how frightening! Who would be a public figure today?'

'Absolutely terrifying! But, Lucy, the whole thing looks to be very dark. The official version of events is that on the night of the attack, Goffe had arranged a meeting with a couple of close political allies. They had come, they said, to discuss the decision of the local association to deselect Goffe as their MP. A member of the party, Adele MacAllen, when arriving at the hall, is said to have spotted Jack taking photographs from some bushes opposite the front door. Challenged by Goffe, Jack had come out onto the forecourt and launched the fatal attack. In her statement to the police, Mrs. MacAllen described it as a frenzied, violent attack. She talks of the hatred etched on the face of his attacker, of the threats, including death threats, received by those like Goffe, who opposed Brexit, who fight to keep the country in 'the family of European nations'. I could quote her word for word, Lucy because she is speaking of the man I spent four years of my life with. It sends a shiver down my spine.

It's almost certain that Jack had an accomplice who hasn't been found. The police interviewed a man named Ralph Braxton, who had been seen in Jack's company in The Swan. But Braxton was known to the rest of the press as a genuine freelance journalist and could prove that he had left The Swan before 11 p.m. and been in London at the time the attack took place. The camera Jack was using hasn't been found.'

Sally lowered her voice and leaned across the table. But here's the thing: Ron thinks that Jack may have got involved in something very dangerous. Photographs, claimed to have been taken on the night of Goffe's death, appeared in a German, ultra-right publication under the headline 'The Death of a Dragon Slayer'. The article claimed that Goffe was at the centre of a covert movement to subvert the Brexit process. The dated photographs show a succession of people arriving at Buckshot Hall. Clearly seen entering through the main door are two high-ranking EU civil servants, their UK counterparts, retired members of the UK judiciary and parliamentarians, past and present. Buckshot Hall, it was claimed, was one of a number of venues in the UK where the group regularly met.

When the police arrived at Buckshot Hall, the only visitors

present were Adele MacAllen, another woman Conservative MP, Goffe's private secretary and his chauffeur. The appearance of the photographs has thrown the case wide open and cast considerable doubt on the evidence given by those interviewed at the hall on the night. Ron senses that there is pressure on the police to bury the matter, write the photographs off as fakes and close the case.'

'I bet there is, Sally! The establishment won't want to admit to such subversive activities, so close to the centre of power! How very interesting!'

'Jack, who Ron says is 'very unwell and confused', says he went to the hall with Christian to get photographic evidence of those attending the covert meeting that was taking place there that night. He names the members of the group who were present - the same people who appear in the German publication! He describes Goffe as a traitor who had to be stopped. Ron is worried for his safety!'

'His insanity will probably save him, Sally. They will declare him unfit to stand trial, so nothing will come out in open court. It's a strange position that Graham Fairbrother finds himself in; the woman he intends to marry being Goffe's sister.'

'Well, it seems that Clementia Goffe had little time for her half-brother. Although shocked by the manner of the man's death, it appears that few tears will be shed either by his family or his constituents for Richard Goffe. He's known to have been a very arrogant, opinionated man. Under the terms of their father's will, Clementia was left a house that is situated close to the hall. Richard Goffe challenged the bequest, arguing that the property was part of an entailed estate over which his father had no right of gift. It emerged that the house didn't form part of the estate but was the personal property of her father. The High Court ruled in Clementia's favour, and her brother ended up paying the costs.'

'Say if you would rather not tell me, but was Jack violent towards you?'

Sally hesitated before saying, 'He didn't hit me. I think he was clever about that, knew how far he could go, but there was pushing and shaking. In the months before I left, I saw a growing pent-up anger. I thought he was on the edge of real violence.'

Sally paused before continuing.

'Do you know, Lucy, you are the first person to hear that confession. I haven't even told Myrtle. I feel so ashamed to have allowed myself to be treated in that way. Why did I put up with that?'

'Oh, Sally, in retrospect, it all looks so straightforward! Why didn't we do this or that? Why did we allow things to happen as they did? But it's very hard to break the influence exerted by a dominant, determined and manipulative personality. I should know! You had the courage to get out. Some women never escape. Some women die. God, it doesn't bear thinking about!'

'No, it doesn't. It's amazing what comes to light once a person gets flagged up to the police. They have CCTV footage of his car parked up and driving about Tavistock Place when I was living there. For months at a time and for hours on end, he was parked up on or close to Edgar Street. Just sitting in the car, watching the house! Isn't that the creepiest thing? He shows up on London street cameras, following Julian and myself. Not too long after we moved into Edgar Street, the house was broken into; it was during the day when we were out. They got in through an old window at the back.

I was convinced that it was Jack; I got this weird feeling of his presence in the house. As well as jewellery and small valuable items - things that might be taken in any robbery - my nightdress was missing. I just knew it was him. Julian said it was a ridiculous idea and told me not to mention it again. Now, the police say it was almost certainly him; his car can be seen on a house camera, parked in the next street during the afternoon of the break-in.

There's an entry running at the back of the house. It was from there that he got into the garden and in through the window. The police think that he probably hung about quite a bit in the entry. It's terrifying to think of it! He could have got in at night when we were asleep. We could have been murdered as we slept!'

'I know the entry. I walked along it to view the back of the house.'

'I saw you there, Lucy. I was at home that day. You were with a tall woman who was very smartly dressed.'

'Did you, Sally? We didn't think there would be anybody at home at that time of day. That was Margo, that I have told you about! So he was stalking you! That's so frightening!'

'Lucy, I think I've been very, very lucky. I've been the angry focus of a very sick man, a man capable of extreme violence. There's something else, something quite dreadful. It was Graham who told me; Ron didn't talk about it. I'm not surprised; I don't suppose he can bring himself to think about it. Jack tried to push Julian under a train!'

Lucy's hand flew to her mouth. 'My God!'

'It was the day before the attack on Richard Goffe. It was at Covent Garden station. Julian was with one of the company secretaries. They had been at a conference in the afternoon and were on their way to meet up with other colleagues in the city. Julian had very nearly ended up under a train. It had been the super quick reactions of another passenger who had saved him; managed to grab him and pull him clear. Julian had brushed it off as an accident, didn't want to take any action, but the woman who was with him, Laura, Laura something or other, was having none of it and insisted on involving the transport police and a report being filed. She was adamant that he had been pushed, said she had seen exactly what had happened. She had been shown CCTV footage of the crowd on the platform but was unable to identify the man as she hadn't had a clear sight of his face and it had all happened so fast.'

'Laura Dixon. It will have been Laura that was with Julian!'

'Yes, that was her name. It was later, when the police were tracking Jack's movements, that the report cropped up and they reviewed the camera footage. He can be seen rushing along the edge of the platform and pushing Julian. He is clearly identifiable as he backs away into the crowd.'

'Oh, Sally. How shocking!'

'Yes. My leaving him appears to have set it all off. It was a coincidence that I met Julian just as I had decided to leave Jack, but of course, he thought otherwise and developed and nurtured a deep hatred of Julian.'

'It would have been the same whenever you left him and whoever replaced him in your life! Have you moved in permanently with Myrtle?'

'Yes. We are going to get a place together. Myrtle's relationship with Art has run its course. It's mutual; it was always a very casual thing! Myrtle doesn't believe in serious relationships with men. "Believe little of what they say, never be surprised by what they do, and keep relationships short and sweet or long and casual," that's Myrtle's advice.'

'I like the sound of your Myrtle! She seems to know her own mind.'

'She's been my saviour, Lucy! She's always looking out for me. We are waiting to see what will happen with Jack. If the case goes to trial, Myrtle thinks it would be better for me to be out of the country. The press are bound to track me down if I'm here. She wants us both to arrange leave from work and go to Italy. Myrtle wants to visit a centre in Naples called Je so'pazzo. The centre is in a former criminal asylum; the name translates as 'I'm so crazy'! It was occupied on behalf of the people in 2015. It's organised by

The People's Solidarity Network, but other local groups are involved. They do really good work, providing shelter for the homeless and supporting migrants. If there's a trial, we will probably stay in Naples for a while; if not, we will go for a holiday.'

'An unusual holiday, Sally!'

'It's what we like to do!'

'Yes, just so! But, on a lighter note, tell me, what are your plans for Christmas? Not many more 'shopping days' to go! I can't see Christmas 2019 being the happiest for either of us!'

'No. I will spend a couple of nights in Newcastle with my parents. I intend to spend Christmas Eve at Jack's parents. Poppy wants me to come and that poor little girl needs support. Myrtle and I will be very busy with our usual commitments. How about you, Lucy. What will you be doing?'

'Well, Clara and I have had a good think about it and decided that it's best if they come to us and we spend the few days in our house. Running away to Clara and Freddy's isn't the answer. We have to get used to special times without Julian. It will help the children to have their cousins with them. We are hoping that Daphne and Ted will join us, at least for Christmas dinner. The strange thing is that I'm surrounded by people who are grieving. They are grieving for their father, son or brother. I'm affected only by their grief; my own grieving ended a long time ago. I have a photo next to my bed of Julian and me with Cosima as a baby. That's how I want to remember him - the real Julian, the man I loved.

But Sally, I want to talk to you about the Fulham house. As it is in my name, I must deal with it. Margo's husband, Paul, who is a director in the company, has eventually unravelled the web of deception thrown up by Julian to cover his tracks. The money, it turns out, was taken from a trust fund set up for the children's education. My signature was forged, together with those of other trustees. Although a criminal offence, I don't imagine that Julian meant to defraud the children; probably saw it more as a temporary loan.

The house must, of course, be sold and I have had an offer a little above the asking price, which leaves me with a small profit. Reclaiming the money for the children is quite obviously the right thing to do, but profiting by such an ill-fated venture is quite different. There will be about twenty thousand profit after expenses. I want you to take it and place it where it will do some good, bring a little happiness.

'Oh, Lucy, that's a lot of money!'

'Enough, perhaps, to do a little good. It's what the man that I married would have liked.'

Thank you for reading my book. Reviews help other readers to find my work (and keep me writing), so please consider leaving an honest review of the book on Amazon.